F Jones
Jones, Douglas C.
This savage race
Henry Holt and Company,
c1993.

THIS
SAVAGE
RACE

OTHER BOOKS BY DOUGLAS C. JONES

THIS
SAVAGE
RACE

DOUGLAS C. JONES

HENRY HOLT AND COMPANY

NEW YORK

Henry Holt and Company, Inc.
Publishers since 1866
115 West 18th Street
New York, New York 10011

Henry Holt® is a registered
trademark of Henry Holt and Company, Inc.

Library of Congress Cataloging-in-Publication Data
Jones, Douglas C. (Douglas Clyde).
This savage race/Douglas C. Jones.—1st ed.
p.   cm.
I. Title.
PS3560.0478T48   1993
813'.54—dc20   92-36881
CIP

ISBN 0-8050-2243-0

First Edition—1993

Map design by Jeffrey L. Ward

Printed in the United States of America
All first editions are printed on acid-free paper. ∞

1 3 5 7 9 10 8 6 4 2

Fic.

AUTHOR'S NOTE

In recent years, it has become fashionable in some quarters to make judgments of our antecedents on the basis of moral indignation, accusing great-grandparents, as it were, of being abusive to the twentieth-century high opinion we hold of ourselves and therefore bruising tender sensibilities.

This book is in honor of those who went before us, no matter the barbarian manner of their living in which sometimes they saw it necessary to survive by rather savage means, unaware that what they did would someday be used against them by a progeny who chose to ignore their circumstances. Had they known of the standards by which they were to be measured in an age of microchips, laser beams, instant communications, television evangelists, and sanctimonious causes, one might suspect, considering their individualistic natures, that they would have done everything exactly as they did. Let us hope so.

The title of this book I owe to Judge Morris S. Arnold, whose research has made him as familiar with Arkansas when it was French and Spanish as anyone around, and whose book *Unequal Laws unto a Savage Race* proves it.

Thank you, Buzz!

Douglas C. Jones
Fayetteville, Arkansas

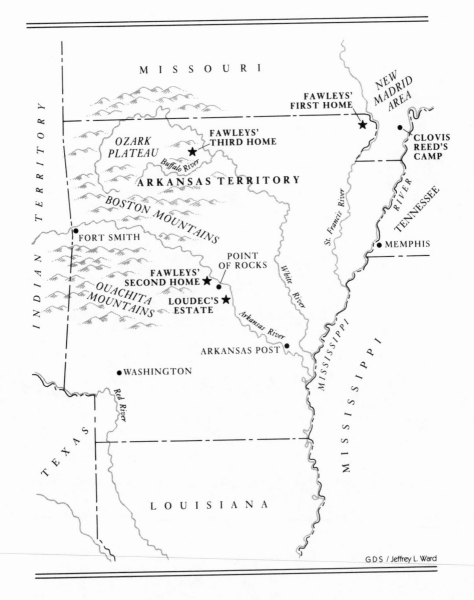

MISSOURI

OZARK
PLATEAU

ARKANSAS TERRITORY

BOSTON MOUNTAINS

FORT SMITH

OUACHITA
MOUNTAINS

FAWLEYS'
FIRST HOME

NEW
MADRID
AREA

CLOVIS
REED'S
CAMP

FAWLEYS'
THIRD HOME

Buffalo River

St. Francis River

RIVER

TENNESSEE

MEMPHIS

POINT
OF ROCKS

FAWLEYS'
SECOND HOME

LOUDEC'S
ESTATE

White River

Arkansas River

INDIAN TERRITORY

ARKANSAS POST

WASHINGTON

Red River

TEXAS

MISSISSIPPI

MISSISSIPPI

LOUISIANA

GDS / Jeffrey L. Ward

PROLOGUE

There were giants in the earth then.

—Genesis 6:4

Maybe Boone Fawley would have become a productive citizen of Mr. Tom Jefferson's republic—without ever understanding it—if his wife Molly had killed one of those Osage warriors on the Fawley trek into the wilderness. Maybe that would have changed everything. It most certainly would have shortened Boone Fawley's life. But Molly missed, it being prior to the time you would expect that she became expert in the use of firearms.

And had Boone Fawley's young son not seen dismembered corpses along the great Mississippi, perhaps there would have been a different ending. As there most surely would have been had the world not opened to swallow all of Boone Fawley's earthly goods in a thunder of fire and water.

Or maybe it was because a beautiful girl, not yet woman, danced too well. Or maybe it was Eli Whitney who was responsible for the final bloody passion, or even Napoleon or Stephen Austin. Or a large cottonmouth moccasin snake. The only thing certain is that the serpent was not the one from Genesis and you would suppose it never had any contact with Eli Whitney or Napoleon or Stephen Austin.

Well, perhaps it all came together a long time after it started, as most things do, with a glorious, terrible flash of power from God or whatever it is that controls static electricity along the Arkansas River and can etch words on stones that Moses is supposed to have carried down from Sinai.

Or maybe it was just the normal rhythm of things, which everybody then took for granted and everybody now doesn't believe.

I f you stood today under the gleaming arch in the city of St. Louis, symbolic, they say, of the Gateway to the West, you would have no notion that a family named Fawley had a part in the riotous era of advancing civilization and unimagined vast spaces so varied in their composition and quality that even the nation's first true geopolitician, Thomas Jefferson, could not conceive the possibilities. And Thomas Jefferson was a man very expert at conceiving possibilities.

But they did.

You will not find the Fawley name on brass plaques or granite monoliths or etched chrome steel tablets buried in capsules for future anthropologists to discover. The name is not in history books or pamphlets or carved on tree trunks, as Daniel Boone's was supposed to have been; nor in their lifetimes were their descriptions pasted to barn doors alerting the populace to suspected criminals. Although maybe they should have been so posted on a few occasions.

But they had a part in it. Unbeknownst to themselves. Innocent of any involvement except survival. But a part, nonetheless, of events they could no more escape than they could stop trying to survive. Simply because they were there.

Not totally there, from start to finish. But along the way. As you might catch a ride on a railroad train at your station, knowing it has been going across the countryside for some time before you flag it, then riding to a point where you dismount, through choice or death, and knowing then it will continue on its way.

Of course, the Fawley people did not think of it in this way because it was the kind of thinking they had developed little use for, and besides, they didn't know what a railroad train was, nor did anybody else at that time.

But not knowing didn't make them any the less a part of it, you see? They were, without knowing it, the bottom rung. The gritty, ill-fed, hookworm, unlettered, workaday, pray-we-don't-get-cholera common folk. The kind who have never really made much splash in the business of recognition but who were, you see, critical to it all, because for anything to have happened, somebody had to be there. Not just the mayors and the sheriffs and the presidents and the counts and the barons and the princes and the kings and the Daniel Boones, all of whom you and your children have heard so much about in school—if you and your children were listening—but all those Fawleys, too.

It all started in the thirteenth century when the Turks were in control of a lot of terrain along the Mediterranean rim, and when King Louis IX of France led a crusade into North Africa with the avowed purpose of thrashing a few infidels. He was himself rather soundly thrashed and captured besides. After paying a handsome ransom and returning to France, he licked his wounds and collected money for another attack against the Saracens, this time in Tunis, where both disease and the Turks vanquished not only his troops but himself as well. Louis's body was brought back to Paris and buried in Notre Dame cathedral on the island of the Seine. He was eventually declared a saint of the Church by the people who declare such things.

You would expect that something in the New World, so variously and vigorously explored and exploited at a later date by the French, would be named after the only king of France ever canonized. And such was the case. A town on the Mississippi River.

But a long time before the naming—in fact a long time before there was a town to name—there was an exploration out of Canada by a French official named Jolliet who was accompanied, as all French officials were in that time and place, by a Jesuit. This particular Jesuit was named Marquette. They passed the town site twice, once going south, once going back home to the north. Then René-Robert Sieur de La Salle, nine years later, came along the river from the opposite direction and, being a soldier and understanding the value of a water highway like the Mississippi and its drainage system, claimed the whole business for France.

La Salle called it Louisiana after the then-reigning monarch, King Louis, this one number fifteen. At the mouth of the river, a city began to grow, and still does, and it was named New Orleans after one of the provinces of metropolitan France. It was early apparent that the fur trade would be a valuable asset, and the French began looking for a suitable inland site for a post to deal with Indians who would trade furs for metal goods and woven cloth and grain alcohol cut with water and called whiskey. In 1735 they established such a post, north of where the Ohio River empties into the Mississippi, and called it St. Genevieve. But it just wasn't right. So twenty-nine years later they moved upriver to the mouth of the Missouri and tried again.

Auguste Chouteau found a nice rise of ground and staked out a stockade. That was the beginning of St. Louis.

What Auguste Chouteau had done was a lot more than stake out a town. What he'd done was establish the eastern terminus of the continent's greatest and longest highway to the Far West—the Missouri River, whose tributaries included the Kaw-Smoky Hill, the Platte, and the Yellowstone. One of the tributaries of the Yellowstone was the Sweetwater, whose source was only a few miles from what would become known as South Pass, the only place in that country where wagons could cross the Continental Divide.

St. Louis was to become the fur trade capital of the world and pelts from the shining mountains bailed on her riverfront. And fortunes would be made and lost there, depending on the population of beaver along the mountain streams of the Absaroka, Wind River, and the Bitterroot. And men would assemble there in old age to tell the stories of the Crows and Flatheads and Shoshones and Blackfeet. And Christian men—and a few women, too—would depart from there on their fruitless mission of saving aboriginal souls, fruitless because there was not enough time for such an enterprise, which had taken many centuries around the shores of the Mediterranean Sea. That virgin trappers' country where the aboriginals lived would be gone in little more than six decades, and old St. Louis with it, to be replaced by a new St. Louis with changed purpose, new directions, fresh ambitions, machine-age visions.

And in those first decades, in a place huffing and puffing along its furious and sometimes barbaric track, Noah Fawley got on and rode to his own final destination. Amazingly, all of that before Thomas Jefferson bought the place (along with the biggest damned hinterland anybody had ever heard of), named it Capital City of the district of Louisiana, and from it sent Lewis and Clark out to the end of the Missouri River highway. And beyond.

Well, after Old Man Fawley died, his son Boone and Boone's family struck out from the city, encouraged by tales of private ownership and real estate in a land flowing with milk and honey. Never mind the brutal day-to-day struggle for survival.

But the big difference between Boone Fawley and most other folk hungry for freedom and land was that he did not go west into shortgrass plains and rock mountains but south into hardwood jungles. There were no jaguars or constricting reptiles there, but things much worse. And before it was finished, Boone Fawley figured he'd found every one of them.

And indeed, he had.

ONE

THE WILDERNESS

I have been a stranger in a strange land.

—Exodus 2:22

I

On the first day of his trek into the wilderness toward a new life, Boone Fawley figured he'd made a monstrous miscalculation. For the rest of his life, he never once revised that opinion, though you'd expect there were a considerable number of days left to him for contemplation as he was only twenty-nine years old. Now, sitting on a fallen shagbark hickory tree on a small lift of ground near the first timberland campfire of his family, and looking back along the route they'd traveled, it seemed damned astonishing and unfair that he could still see the place they'd started from more than twelve laborious hours earlier.

Most of the light had gone from the sky, but Boone Fawley could still make out the pencil marks of slate gray smoke rising in the windless June twilight, rising from various chimneys toward the darkening dome where a few stars were crystal cold pinpoints in contrast to the tiny warm daubs of orange below marking the location of whale-oil lamps burning in the windows of the city. Well, actually, the town. In 1808, it was of considerable size, but not a city yet. Maybe a place of two thousand souls, if you counted the transient tame Indians, river pirates, keelboat men, fur trappers, land speculators, slave merchants, and their slaves. Not to mention the temporary residents from the city of Washington, seat of the federal government, who were unhappily stuck with the task of working out some plan for dividing the vast Louisiana Territory into manageable parts.

Boone heard one of his boys coming up behind from the campsite, stumbling through the short growth of sassafras scrub, and figured it was likely Questor, the eight-year-old, but he didn't turn to look. The movement stopped, close behind his back. For a long time, there was only the racket of crickets and tree frogs and God only knew what all, making the timber around them pulse with a strange, nocturnal life unfamiliar yet in no way menacing.

"Them lights yonder is St. Louis, ain't they, Pa?" Questor asked.

Boone was silent. He took out his clay pipe and began to fill it with rough-cut tobacco from a small pouch, all of this coming from one of the large pockets in his leather smock. Suddenly, directly above them, there was a tiny, shrieking sound, metallic and sharp, and then gone as quickly as it had come. Boone knew it was a flight of bats off on their evening hunt and thought, Well, at least there's something out here in the woods that knows what it's doing. We sure'n hell don't.

"Must be some caves around here," Questor said. "Bats live in caves, don't they, Pa?"

"Sometimes." He stripped a sliver of dry bark from the log and, taking a flint-and-steel fire starter from the same pocket, ignited it, lit his pipe, and puffed.

"Pa?" Questor said. "Pa. Mama says it's mite near time to bed down."

"Well, why don't you go on and bed down, then?"

After Questor had gone, Boone Fawley sat smoking. Soon he heard bats again, and he thought about how simple everything was for these little darkness predators. You sleep all day, then you go out and kill something and eat it, then you go back to the cave or tree or whatever and hang upside down and sleep all day again.

He'd have enjoyed getting his hands on the man who had suggested they take a two-wheeled cart. A contrary vehicle at best and almost impossible when you tried to get it pulled along what passed as a river road by a mule and a horse who had never worked in harness together. It hadn't helped that Boone didn't know much about harness rigging and nothing at all about how to convince the two stubborn animals what they were supposed to do once he got them hitched to the cart. In fact, by the end of the day, his boy John, the ten-year-old, was doing all the driving, for he'd taken to the whole routine quickly. Which didn't help Boone's disposition much because it confirmed what he'd suspected for a couple of years now. That his boys, both of them, were a lot smarter than he was.

They'd had to stop a total of five times to reload the cart to keep various things from falling off. The furniture and trunks of shoes and clothing and the grub and pots and tools and powder and lead and a twig crate of chickens. Once, one of their two pigs had broken her tie rope and run off toward the Mississippi River, squealing with the joy of freedom. After almost an hour, Chorine, Boone's old-maid sister—well, she was twenty-seven—came back carrying the pig and for the rest of the day complained about all the beggar's-lice burrs she'd collected on the hem of her ankle-length rough woolen skirt.

As soon as they stopped, everyone except the boys exhausted, and unhitched the horse and mule, the mule bolted into the timber, heading in the general direction of Mexico. It took John almost an hour to run him down and bring him back and then devise rope ties for the mule's forelegs, and the horse's, too, saying this was a hobble he'd heard about God only knew where, but anyway, it worked.

Molly, Boone's wife, had come by the idea that the bigger the campfire the better, so she soon had a roaring blaze that threatened to incinerate the cart, and would have except for the frantic pushing and shoving of all in the party until the cart was safely out of range of leaping flames. The fire was too hot for anyone to get close enough to cook anything over it, so they fed on corn dodgers and brown beans that had been prepared the day before when they had a decent stove in a decent house in St. Louis.

Actually, there was only a fistful of beans for each of them. They had been carried all day in a covered pot, which had turned over at least twice, spilling beans all over the floor planking of the cart. Some of the beans lodged in the .50-caliber muzzle of the rifle Boone's daddy had used in the Revolution, which upset Molly more than losing the beans. She made a frantic effort to clean the weapon and after that carried it in her hand all day. Since leaving the last shack on the southern edge of St. Louis, Molly had seemed obsessed with the idea that a drunken red savage was ready to leap out from every bush and scalp her after doing other hideous things to her person.

"Why fret about it?" Boone Fawley asked. "When this red savage jumps out, you can shoot him with a bean!"

"Stop makin' jest of her," Chorine shouted.

"For Christ's sweet sake, listen to the crosspatch!"

Sitting on his log and thinking about it, Boone Fawley had the only grin of the day. Not only had Molly cleaned the beans out of the rifle muzzle and carried it the rest of the day, a rifle as long as she was tall, but also the powder horn around her neck on a leather thong and the bullet and flint pouch, too, on another leather thong, and all the while, the damned rifle wasn't even loaded, much less primed.

Except for the money, nothing had gone right. The money was a collection of Spanish gold coins in many and varied sizes. Spanish gold was about the only hard money in circulation along the entire Mississippi. This horde had been collected over many years by Boone Fawley's daddy, who used fair means or foul to add to the legacy that Boone would enjoy because the old man didn't spend much of it. Now, thanks to Boone's foresight, it was in a heavy leather pouch and safely nailed to the inside of the cart's headboard. When Molly had asked what if they tried to ford a deep river and the cart sank, Boone told her he didn't have any plans for crossing a deep river except on a barge ferry maybe, and besides, the cart was made of wood and would float, and if it didn't, the boys could dive for the money. They'd learned to swim like muskrats along the St. Louis riverfront where drunks and fumble-fingered pilgrims would sometimes drop things into the water. For retrieving these items, John and Questor earned any number of pennies, most of which were in that same heavy leather bag with the Spanish gold.

Two coins were not in the pouch nailed to the cart. Since his daddy died, Boone Fawley had carried the two largest coins in an otter-skin sack suspended from a brass chain around his neck. As a good luck charm, maybe, like people wore amulets of garlic to ward off typhus or cholera or some such thing. They were large coins, probably worth about twenty dollars American, and they had been issued during the reign of King Philip V of Spain, whose likeness was on the coin and who had been the grandson of King Louis XIV of France and whose coming to the throne had touched off the War of the Spanish Succession. Boone Fawley had no notion of the load of history he carried around his neck, but his ignorance didn't reduce the value of the gold.

Now, as he sat and puffed, even the silver trace of the Mississippi gone, he kept on thinking of St. Louis. There he had learned to speak French because it was mostly the only tongue anyone spoke. And without any hint of formal schooling. There, too, he'd watched the beginning of the fur trade, dugouts and then keelboats with Frenchmen and a few curious aboriginals bringing in the first of beaver and marten and buffalo pelts.

And he'd heard, like everyone else, the stories of unknown marvels in the hinterland. Some of which had actually been seen, but a lot that had not, except by white men who did not write travel brochures. And much of it, being unknown, could be described in fantastic ways indisputable to those who had not seen it. Like the story that much of the soil of Louisiana was so rich that it was dangerous to plant it unless one had the ability to leap back quick after the seed had been inserted; else one stood the chance of personal injury from the sprout bursting forth. Or on the other hand, that all of that vast area was a kind of desert where nothing would grow and inhabitable only by bands of goat-herding nomads, like the Bedouins of the Sahara.

Boone Fawley, like so many of his kind in that time, was going from a life he knew well to something he knew not at all. Just for the pride, the dignity, the security of having and holding something to himself alone, and to his progeny. A quilt-piece slice of the earth's surface into which he might push a seed, any kind of seed he chose, and wait to see what would grow.

Just how this was all supposed to work, Boone Fawley didn't know. But he would find whatever it was that he was supposed to find. With that firm conviction in mind, Boone knocked out his pipe against the shagbark hickory log and rose and went down to the camp toward the woolen blanket where he knew that despite all the day's wrangling, he would find warm and soft delight with a woman who, brimstone and spit in daylight, became melting butter in the dark.

B oone Fawley carried a large weight of the past on his shoulders. He got it from his father, Noah. The old man enjoyed telling stories, especially as he got on in years, when yesterday's memory was vague as smoke but things long gone came with crystal clarity. He told mostly about himself, and that necessarily meant he told a lot about many things. Like most oral historians, Old Noah was not too concerned with dates. His idea of chronology was to put a story in context by beginning with a landmark he expected everybody else to identify.

"It was the year," he'd say, "when that blind Frenchman came down the river from Mackinac with a Fox squaw who led him around all the riverfront taverns so's he could sang songs mostly about petticoats and bloomers. Which I expect is the kind of songs most Frenchmen like to sang. An' the boatmen an' the hunters an' the whores would give him an' his squaw brandy an' some hard-boiled eggs to eat, an' she'd peck on this heathern tamborine with feathers hanging on it while the blind Frenchman sang, an' I'll testify she was a surely comely wench, too."

The old man had told all those stories so many times, they were etched in Boone Fawley's memory. Boone had always been reluctant to say much about those yarns, their source being a man he was sure Molly would not approve of. And besides, Boone always felt a rather proprietary responsibility for them, as though they belonged to his daddy and nobody else had any right to nose about in them.

Of all Boone Fawley's family who left St. Louis that spring of 1808, only Chorine had ever set eyes on the old man. Boone resented her a little for that, having to share with her at least the image of Old Noah's face if not his tales because Chorine had never heard any of them. Maybe to Boone, the old man's words were the only thing he had for a religion.

When Old Noah's voice came in memory it was about Shawnee Indians; or about Henri Larous telling of Creole culture in New Orleans; or the backsliding Methodist preacher Owen Prather who came across the river from Illinois one summer with a lot of wild tales about how he'd converted the Cherokees in Georgia. But nothing about anybody named Fawley being foolish enough to wander off to a place where oak trees were so thick the sun in summer never touched the ground because of their foliage and so big two men couldn't reach around the trunks, sprouting from acorns, those trees, at about the time Mary, Queen of Scots, had her head chopped off. Absolutely nothing about hacking out a living in such a place with the closest neighbor five miles away.

2

Noah Fawley was set on his great adventure by an English
criminal sessions magistrate in Portsmouth during the reign of
His Majesty King George III. It was the first time Noah Fawley had
ever been in the city of Portsmouth, having arrived there purely by
chance in his flight from a London master to whom he was a
cobbler's apprentice.

At issue was the theft of a pig. As luck would have it, the owner
of said pig had apprehended Noah Fawley before the young cobbler's apprentice could sell it for coin, trade it for gin, or kill and
eat it, so there was no problem of restitution for stolen property.
Only restitution to the Crown for the affront to peace and dignity.

On the King's Bench—well, actually, he was little more than a
simple justice of the peace—was the jurist Berthram Farnsworth, a
corpulent man who wore a powdered wig in keeping with his social
and economic station, which was established and maintained by the
rather large rake-offs he made from his official duties. It was to be
Noah Fawley's first direct experience with a person whose personal
well-being was in direct proportion to talents in manipulation of
political position. In short, Noah Fawley was beginning to learn
what the world was all about.

By good chance, or at least so he thought, Berthram Farnsworth had received from friends in Boston the intelligence that shoemaking was becoming a profitable enterprise in New England and therefore it might be of mutual advantage to send immigrants who had some talent in that direction, particularly if they were lowborn and destitute and therefore in the position of having to work for almost nothing, thereby, of course, establishing a good trade for themselves at some point in the future.

It also happened that Judge Farnsworth held a few shares in a certain Portsmouth shipping venture and on the very day Noah Fawley appeared before him, a vessel of this charter was due to sail for the colony of Massachusetts. Therefore Noah Fawley found himself escorted to shipboard by a constable and turned over to the mercies of the ship's master, who was also allowed custodial care of a parchment to be delivered in Boston to certain parties who would take Noah Fawley in hand as indentured for seven years in the trade of leather and shoe lasts. Noah was to serve on board the vessel in passage as a common deckhand, all pay then and later, until service of indenture was complete, dispatched to the Portsmouth court of Berthram Farnsworth in payment for that affront to the king's peace and dignity which he'd talked about at great length, along with serious quotations from Genesis about stealing things, before sending Noah Fawley on his way.

All of this left a decidedly bad taste in Noah Fawley's mouth regarding pigs and royal magistrates and Portsmouth, which was nothing compared to what he began to think of ship's masters and sailors and ropes and tar and holystone, even before the vessel on which he was consigned had passed the Isle of Wight and set her sails into the Channel and thence into the Atlantic. The only thing that prevented Noah Fawley from thinking throughout the voyage of harshly blistered hands, scabbed knees, and lashed back was his monumental seasickness.

One would expect that a youth of Noah Fawley's low station set in opposition to the power of the colonial state and the connivers of eighteenth-century finance would be impotent. But if one so thought, one would be ignoring the instinctive initiative of a weasel in a wire cage. Indeed, the document indenturing Noah Fawley to some associate of Justice Berthram Farnsworth arrived in Boston. But Noah Fawley didn't.

For on sight of dry land as the ship entered the Charles River estuary, Noah Fawley made his covert departure, by that time having through humble obedience convinced the master that he would never rebel against anything and therefore needn't be watched by armed sailors or chained to a mast. And so into the tidewater and swimming with the strong dog-paddle strokes he had learned in His Majesty's river Thames, he made the south shore. Lucky for Noah Fawley the ship had arrived after dark. And there, on that south shore, before his clothes were even dry, he appropriated a chicken from a colonist's coop, only partly tearing off the feathers before eating it raw, and set out south.

Come daylight, he soon discovered a number of delightful things. Like the fact that housewives in this New World hung their washed clothes on lines, and that sometimes men coming into their homes from the barnyard left shit-smeared shoes on the doorstep to avoid tracking on floors inside. Hence, after the theft of only two more chickens, Noah Fawley found himself clad in completely new apparel, some of which even had buttons. Something unknown to his class in London.

He set out in the direction of Philadelphia. At least, he supposed it was the right direction, for although he had heard of the greatest city in the American colonies, he had no idea where it really lay and numerous road signs did little good because he couldn't read. It didn't matter. He traveled at leisure, already feeling some heady wine of freedom. Certainly he had never seen so much land sparsely populated. Along the way, he ate pilfered raw chicken and some goose eggs, also raw, and then found that for shoveling out stalls and once a privy, housewives would provide various fish and green fodder and heavy bread. He was both eagerly energetic and handsomely friendly. Although none of it fit exactly, his newly acquired apparel was decent, from the wide-brimmed floppy hat to the knee britches and paste-buckle shoes.

Nights he spent in wooded areas, except when it rained, and then he slept in barn lofts or roofed pig sties—after which he was careful to clean his clothes by finding some clear brook and immersing himself, fully clad, in the cool water. He quickly became accustomed to being stopped at various crossroads by bands of somewhat drunk and rowdy men, well armed, who demanded to know his politics. On the first such encounter, Noah Fawley quickly perceived that these people were surely not representatives of the

Crown. Hoping that his response would not result in tar and feathers or maybe a rope and the nearest tree, he simply said that he thought all royal magistrates were sons of bitches. Which was a true statement.

This was the best possible thing Noah Fawley could have said to these roving members of some local Sons of Liberty mob, so he was welcomed, his back was slapped, lewd stories were told, and he was introduced to his first taste of rum, the local beverage of choice. Then he was sent on his way to Philadelphia, whose whereabouts those who stopped him knew no better than he, but pretended they did, and they waved Noah Fawley along the road with admonitions to avoid any Tory he might run across and lobsterback British soldiers as well.

Noah Fawley was smart enough to hide most of what he really thought, for example, that he much preferred gin to this murky, thick rum so many Americans apparently enjoyed. Or, for example, that despite his hatred of judges, he felt a somewhat warm and personal attachment to King George, that kindly, fat old man who had to contend with a palace full of rowdy and worthless offspring and a queen whom Noah Fawley had heard couldn't speak English too well, not to mention a snooty bunch in Parliament much in the mode of Magistrate Berthram Farnsworth. These contacts with colonials also gave him some strange kind of perverse pride in being an Englishman, albeit a rather disreputable-looking one, a condition he expected to change as soon as he had figured out a way to steal a razor.

He tried to avoid large settlements, knowing there was a possibility of royal judges lurking in such places. And by whatever fates order such things, he managed to miss New York and Philadelphia and Baltimore, too, ending finally at a small hamlet on the border between Virginia and Pennsylvania not far from Hagerstown. With cold weather coming on, Noah Fawley decided to stop there and forget Philadelphia, not realizing he had passed by the City of Brotherly Love some five weeks before.

It was not a difficult place for a young man of energy to find work and lodging, if he wasn't too particular about the lodging. So he passed his first winter in America as a harness maker's assistant and began to make friends with young men of his age who seemed interested in talking only about the virgin land beyond the mountains to the west. Actually, there was plenty of talk about the Continental Congress now meeting and the troubles between the various colonies and the mother country and the patriot riots that broke out here and there, but Noah Fawley ignored all such talk because he figured none of it concerned him. What did catch his interest was the Richard Henderson Transylvania Company, an organization directed toward colonizing the country beyond the Appalachian Mountains. Or better put, an endeavor in land speculation. To participate in such a venture appealed to Noah Fawley primarily because roustabouts serving with the company on future explorations would be provided with good wilderness clothing and a Pennsylvania rifle. To this point in his life, Noah Fawley had never held a firearm in his hands.

So the following spring, March of 1775 it was, Noah Fawley found himself part of a group of rather hard and lusty men whom Henderson, encouraged by the Continental Congress, sent to establish a trail into Kentucky. The leader of this party was a man named Boone, a man with a heritage of English and Welsh blood and a distaste for courtrooms as pronounced as was Noah Fawley's. What Boone and Noah and the others did was build the Wilderness Road through a gap in the mountains. Calling it a road was perhaps stretching the point a mite because at the start it was a rough, stump-interrupted deer path. But it would surely become a road someday and celebrated by those who traveled it with many songs about the good old Cumberland Gap and Daniel Boone. Noah Fawley was never mentioned in any of the songs, at least not in any that were fit to be sung in mixed company.

Kentucky wasn't a colony or any other kind of organized territory, and even who owned it was much in question. Maybe Pennsylvania or maybe Virginia. In fact Kentucky wasn't even a place then. It was an *idea*. It meant freedom and it meant the Great Unknown There for the Taking. As time went down, Kentucky moved steadily across the continent, down the Ohio River, across the Mississippi to the wooded hills and the prairie and the High Plains, and finally into the Rocky Mountains. Of course, as it moved west, the name changed. The idea stayed the same for about a century. When immigrants on the Oregon Trail said "Willamette Valley," it meant the same thing as "Kentucky" to Daniel Boone's trailblazers. A good place to go looking for a home, but a place nobody knew a hell of a lot about.

"At the far distant end of the Wilderness Road," said Old Noah, "we built a town and called it Boonesborough. Daniel brought his family there. I expected it was a nice place to keep out of all that war trouble they had back east in the colonies, so I stayed, too."

All colonial settlements had a militia, and Boonesborough was no exception. On its rolls could be found the names D. Boone and N. Fawley. They drilled once a week, these citizen-soldiers, and the drills consisted of two things. Answering muster call and getting drunk. The beverage was not one of choice but of necessity due to their isolation. Rum from east of the mountains was hard to come by so, as with all frontier settlements, there was an enterprising soul who set up a still. Corn mash was the basic ingredient, and the final product was a clear liquid that Noah Fawley thought looked like his favorite London gin but after his first sip he knew it wasn't like any gin he'd ever tasted. Then after a while, they began to store the stuff in oak or hickory barrels that had been charred inside and let it age, and what they got was an amber-colored liquid unlike anything else they'd ever known. Someday it would be called Kentucky straight bourbon whiskey.

Upon later recall, such things as militia muster, his new rifle, or else the quality of local whiskey always took up all of Noah Fawley's attention. Boone Fawley could not remember a single instance of his father speaking of what had to have been the glorious beauty of the Ohio Valley in the eighteenth century. The sights and sounds, the smells and tastes of it pristine and pure. Green summer billows of hardwood foliage, streams running clear, the pattern of wilderness interrupted only casually here and there with a faint trail or cleared patch in the timber where Indian corn was planted. That endless rolling landscape that had been there through a passage of time so endless it was impossible to imagine.

None of that seemed to catch Noah Fawley's attention. It was as though he were sitting on a rock smoking a clay pipe and the very earth itself created before him without his even noticing it.

But if Noah Fawley gave little thought to this new world, he had attached himself to somebody who did. Daniel Boone was not one to suffer town life for long at one stretch and so spent a great deal of time out in the woods exploring and making maps. Usually, Noah Fawley accompanied him. They saw a lot of ground no white man had ever seen before. Now and then they killed a black bear or a big cat, which they called a painter but which was really a cougar.

"Mr. Boone," said Noah, which is how he always alluded to his mentor, "could reload a rifle quick'n anybody I ever saw. He could do it all fast as most men could do it with a musket. He learned me how, too, but I never done it quick, like him. When I tried to do it fast, Mr. Boone said I got too damned much powder in the pan. By Gawd, I did singe an eyebrow now and again!"

On one of their excursions, they encountered a large hunting party of Shawnees, a group of aboriginals who held definite pro-Loyalist sentiments mainly on account of all the fine things the British gave them, like guns and whiskey, with plenty more of the same if they scalped every patriot they happened to run across. On this occasion, there was no outbreak of hostilities, and the Shawnees asked them to come back to their village for a little visit. Of course, Daniel Boone and Noah Fawley both knew they were going not as guests but as prisoners. Walking to the Shawnee camp, Noah Fawley had a lot of time to think on what was likely in store, because he had heard about some of the exquisite tortures at which the Shawnees were expert.

"Mr. Boone told me," said Noah Fawley, "that them Shawnees didn't do as much of that kind of thing as maybe the Mohawks or some of them Canadian heathern, but it don't take much of that kind of treatment to be more'n enough."

However, Daniel Boone had a winning way, it seemed, and so the Shawnees adopted him into their tribe and he became brother to a couple of powerful medicine men and spent a few nights lying in a Shawnee lodge with a nice Shawnee woman. This last wasn't the kind of thing that would show up in many schoolbooks after Daniel Boone became a national hero in the age of Noah Fawley's grandchildren, but when he told this detail, it was not meant to be salacious. It was the natural kind of thing you'd expect, so Noah Fawley passed it along as just a regular part of the tale.

Maybe because he didn't want anybody to think he was boastful Noah Fawley neglected to mention that he himself had spent more nights in carnal bliss and with a wider variety of Shawnee women than did Boone. But probably only for the reason that Boone made such a splendid impression that he was allowed to depart when he chose and Noah Fawley was not. So Noah Fawley remained in the Shawnee town while Daniel Boone hurried back to Boonesborough and started preparing the militia and everybody else for an attack, for from what he'd heard, he suspected that some British redcoat officers were on the way to lead the Shawnees in an attack on the whites in the area. Which meant Boonesborough.

Sure enough, about twenty British soldiers came to the Shawnee town, and perhaps Noah Fawley found it expedient to explain at that time his great love and respect for King George III, that being a safer course of action than trying to escape and get back to Boonesborough. It was an episode that Noah Fawley always skipped over rather quickly. But for whatever reason, soon the Shawnees and the British officers and Noah Fawley were laying siege to the town, taking potshots at the rough log buildings where the militia and Daniel Boone were hiding and taking potshots at them. The British officers wanted the Indian braves to assault the walls and gouge the patriots with hatchets and war clubs; the Shawnees explained that they had plenty of courage but that they were not stupid, so after a bit more ineffectual potshotting, the British officers departed in disgust and the Shawnees went home.

Noah Fawley retreated farther than the Shawnees did. There was considerable confusion in the village what with arguments over whether it was a victory or not and at the same time a noisy ceremony going forward in honor of the only Shawnee casualty of the affair, whose body had been carried back to the village for proper dispatch of the spirit to the land beyond the sun. It was an ideal time to slip away, which Noah Fawley did, being sure that he had with him adequate powder and ball and a parfleche of dried venison. And a half-gallon jug of clear whiskey the British had brought.

He made his way downriver along the Ohio for a number of miles, having a wonderful time as long as the whiskey lasted. He found, to his surprise, any number of migrant people on barges with whom he could float without much danger from hostile tribes. The Ohio Valley had been a bad place for white colonists since the time of Queen Anne's War back at the beginning of the century and going right down through King George's War and the clash Europeans called the Seven Years' War—the French and Indian War in North America—the only difference now being that it was the

British stirring up the redskins with guns and whiskey, whereas before it had always been the French.

A few of these people were going to the Father of Waters, which sounded fine to Noah Fawley, and after a little less than a month, he was on the Mississippi paddling north with two hunters in a dugout canoe, coming to rest at the small, shanty, muddy trading post of St. Louis. Noah Fawley had no notion of who laid claim to this portion of the earth's surface but soon discovered in conversation with the few men he found who spoke English that he was in Spanish territory. It was confusing because mostly everybody spoke French, even though Noah Fawley was assured that the flag flying from the stockade fort was the standard of King Charles III of Spain. That was fine, too, because at least he was far removed from the thing now being called the American Revolution and also from people like Magistrate Berthram Farnsworth.

So Noah Fawley fit right in, being by now almost as tough as all the other people in St. Louis and besides that having some talent in leatherwork, of which there was plenty.

Unlike Boone Fawley, a lot of people around St. Louis were fairly well educated and tried to keep informed of what went on back east because what went on eventually affected business along the Mississippi. So some of these, unlike Boone Fawley, on hearing Old Noah's recitation of the Boonesborough battle, asked which one was being described seeing as how there had been at least two fights there during the Revolution plus a skirmish and an ambush besides. And Noah Fawley always responded rather hotly that you couldn't expect a man to keep track of every damned battle of the war, for God's sake, and all he'd ever told about was what he'd seen with his two eyes and what he knew about his ownself!

It didn't cut into the old man's credibility, especially with his son. The fabric of it seemed to be a tight weave. It was well-known that Daniel Boone had indeed spent considerable time visiting—or captive of—the Shawnees, and there were those who said he was entirely too friendly with these bloody allies of the British—meaning all those adoptive warrior or medicine men brothers and the fair Indian maiden in the wigwam—and maybe this Daniel Boone ought to be tried for treason and hanged. Such talk stopped only when

Boone proved over time that he was as willing as anybody else to shoot Tories, lobsterbacks, and his brothers the Shawnees.

Nobody was ever unkind enough to suggest that maybe Noah Fawley should mount the traitors' scaffold. They figured he was just an alien passing through on his way to a colony of the Spaniards west of the Mississippi, and was even an alien there, too, along with a lot of other people, a sort of nonperson refugee. But whose son, when the son appeared, would indeed be a subject of King Charles III, being born in Spanish territory.

"That's when," Old Noah said, with his wink at Boone, "you'll get into the story."

3

No matter how far he thought he'd distanced himself from the Revolution, Noah Fawley could not seem to avoid it. Not even in Spanish territory. For Spain was involved in the Revolution. When the East Coast colonies of King George III started a fight for their independence, the Spaniards saw it as a wonderful opportunity to take a good whack at the British. The French had recognized the same opportunity earlier, and you'd suspect that King Charles III of Spain figured better late than never. So he pitched in alongside the French. Not so much to assure a new autonomous country in America, but to drive the English *out* of America.

Noah Fawley didn't understand that this was how you got a lot of allies in a war. They join you not because they like you but because they dislike your enemy. This was the kind of thing Noah Fawley never bothered his head with, so it came as a shock to him—and just as he was settling into a nice job with the Chouteaus as a leatherwork man—when a metal claxon started clanging and representatives of the military governor or commandant or whatever he was called ran about yelling for everybody to man the stockade and blockhouse because the town was about to be attacked. This call to arms was meant particularly for men like Noah Fawley who had weapons like the Pennsylvania rifle he had brought to St. Louis from his venture with the Henderson land company in Kentucky.

So, grumbling to himself, Noah Fawley took his position in the wooden and sandstone fortification that his present employer, Old Auguste Chouteau, had staked out when all this area belonged to the French. He was hardly in position at a firing port when he saw the enemy, a rather impressively large bunch of naked savages and a few British redcoats, at the edge of the woods just to the north of the settlement. Only these Britishers were wearing forest-colored uniforms, so must properly be called greencoats. Immediately alongside Noah Fawley were two trappers and a few of their own Indians, whom Noah Fawley had been informed were Osages. Their heads were shaved except for long roaches at top and back. They were squealing and shouting, waving hatchets, daubing black paint on their faces, and making obscene gestures toward the British Indians at the wood line.

The battle seemed to fall quickly into a set pattern. The British warriors would whoop and jump and run toward the stockade, shooting muskets straight up in the air, the defenders would loose a volley, the British Indians would turn and run back into the woods, everybody would pause to reload, and the whole exercise would begin once more. It did not seem at all incongruous to Noah Fawley that the last time he fired his rifle he was shooting at the enemies of King George and now he was shooting at the English king's friends. What seemed of much greater importance and interest was the argument that his two trapper friends were having between shots as to just who these aboriginals they were trying to kill might be.

Sauk and Fox, said one. Hell no. Miami. Or maybe Menominee. It was likely they were until recently allies of the French, and now here they were with the greencoat English, so therefore all were dirty turncoats. True. But, said the first again, they are Sauk and Fox because look how excited our own Indians are and that means those in the trees must be the enemies of our Indians.

"Hell," said the second. "It don't signify. Our red sticks is Osage and *everybody's* their enemy!"

Whoever they were, they made a bad job of capturing St. Louis.

Soon they had faded away completely, and, taking their few dead and wounded with them, they went with the British greencoats back to Iowa or Wisconsin or wherever it was they'd started.

With the cessation of hostilities, brandy and Indian-trade clear whiskey were provided by Noah Fawley's employer, Mr. Chouteau, and the militia and the trappers and the Osages and Noah Fawley settled themselves in the stone blockhouse and proceeded to get drunk in celebration of their great victory. Noah Fawley had no earthly idea what any of this had been about, but he didn't care so long as the brandy and clear whiskey held out.

During the course of the celebration, Noah Fawley's face became smeared with Indian paint as each of the Osages insisted on embracing him closely, jabbering and shouting incoherent words which Noah Fawley took to mean that they loved him dearly. Later, one of the largest of the Osages—and they were all big men—sat in one corner sobbing, great tears streaming down his face. Then he began a soulful chant which one of the trappers said told the story. Just the past spring, this Osage had been out on the shortgrass buffalo plains for the annual hunt, and there a band of Kiowas had taken his favorite woman captive. Although there were plenty of other women, it was a great tragedy because at the time of her capture she had been wearing a solid ivory Spanish hair comb the Osage had given her, a comb he himself had from the hand of his father, who got it from a Frenchman in trade for two Caddo slaves the Frenchman planned on taking to the Sugar Islands to work in the plantations.

"Where is the Sugar Islands at?" asked Noah Fawley.

"God knows."

With nightfall, Noah Fawley staggered to the shed behind one of Mr. Chouteau's riverfront warehouses where he had taken up his abode and, lying on his mattress of hides, thought of all the wonderful things he was hearing about this New World.

In years ahead, Noah Fawley would return to that stone blockhouse. Because it was the most substantial building in the settlement, it would become the courthouse and jail on the corner of the future Walnut and 4th streets. Noah Fawley would spend a few evenings there at the invitation of the governor's constables, locked in a barred room and left to sleep it off after a drunken spree that had become disruptive of the public peace. And you may properly suppose that in early St. Louis, this meant very disruptive indeed!

There is every reason to believe that Noah Fawley knew when the American Revolution was over. So he would no longer be forced to take those potshots at one side or the other, as circumstance dictated. There is equal reason to think that, like most of his common-folk kind, he hadn't the slightest notion how it would affect the rest of his life or that of his family. Once he had a family.

But this was not an ignorance exclusive to Noah Fawley's class. The power elite in the Louisiana Territory, including St. Louis, had no idea how the conclusion of that war would change the face of things. There may have been jubilation among the Spaniards that a powerful Great Britain had been replaced on the east bank of the Mississippi with a weak, probably short-lived republic. Such thinking was somewhat premature. As it turned out, nothing could have been more devastating to Spain or anybody else who got in the way.

Of course, the British were still very much in North America. In Canada and along the north bank of the Ohio. They were there in the form of Indians led by greencoats, with a musket in one hand and a jug of whiskey in the other.

Much more serious was a quickly obvious tendency of many citizens of the United States, who naturally called themselves Americans, to ignore boundary lines proclaimed by secretaries of state and foreign ministers, by presidents and kings. Because it seemed these rowdy folk went where they damn well pleased. And it began to please a great many of them to look for new homes along the Ohio Valley. From early indications the Mississippi River would pose no obstacle, so when they got there, they'd cross over and keep right on looking. On Spanish soil.

As a few farsighted Spanish officials in the New World suggested, it was not yet time to be concerned with the United States government. The thing to be concerned about, they said, was the Americans. For these people went wherever the notion struck them to go. Noah Fawley could understand that. What he couldn't understand was why it irritated the Spaniards so much, hence getting him thrown in jail on many occasions for no other reason than that he spoke English. Like the Americans did. Hell, he told them, I'm not an American!

Well, said the Spaniards, you Americans do it ass-backwards. An explorer with priests is supposed to come and plant the flag and then traders come and finally the people. But you, they said, come first and your flag finds it necessary to follow you. But, explained Noah Fawley, I am not one of these damned Americans. And then attempted to bloody the nose of the closest Spanish soldier, which convinced everybody that he was indeed an American because that's exactly how they all reacted to civil authority.

Noah Fawley was convinced Spaniards were very sensitive people. Their officials most sensitive of all. And he was right.

Just when things looked so good. Getting Louisiana from the French after the Seven Years' War—because the defeated French didn't want Louisiana to fall into the hands of the British—meant they, the Spaniards, had finally bypassed what had for nearly two hundred years been the great barrier to their northern expansion out of Mexico. A barrier called Comanches. And now, here they were, in the upper midcontinent, and the pesky Americans were just across the river, or at least soon to be.

In St. Louis, it would be almost a decade before the first American family settled. But already there were men like Noah Fawley wandering about whose primary language was English, and they had come to make a profit on furs. To get in at the start of what everybody expected to be a fine business.

The Spanish trade was an exact pattern of what they'd taken over from the French. Posts were established and the tribesmen brought in their pelts. The closest big, powerful tribe was the Osage, whose domain covered the dense woodlands south and west of St. Louis all the way to the tallgrass prairie and including most of the vast Ozark Plateau. A Spaniard had come up from New Orleans to monopolize this market, and he was given a license to trade with the Osages, a plum of patronage. The Chouteaus ignored it and kept trading with their friends, the Osages. They traded with British goods, and British guns and powder were a lot better than French guns and powder, which the Spaniards dealt in, and the Indians knew it.

"It was always crazy," Noah Fawley often said to his oldest son.

"So many folks thanks these red-stick niggers was dumb children. They was good businessmen. They was lookin' for the side was likely to win. They was lookin' for the best deal. Chouteau give it to 'em."

So even though he might try to take a small bite out of the Osage trade close at home, Manuel Lisa, the first big Spanish trader, knew better and so started some of those early ventures up the Missouri to the High Plains and mountain Indians.

"Why hell," Noah Fawley said, "Ole Lisa maybe had hisself two wives, one here, other in New Orleans, and maybe he was a squinch-eye Spaniard, but he warn't no dumbbell. You don't knock heads with Mr. Chouteau around here!"

Yes, it was Mr. Chouteau to Noah Fawley. And St. Louis and the river south to New Orleans were French, yes sir. Despite the flag of Charles III flying over the old stockade. Why, even most of the Osage men who came into town could speak French!

Well, no matter. All were inward-looking, Spanish and French alike. Availability of furs was important, nothing else. Noah Fawley knew that, so even along the rather cosmopolitan riverfront he seldom thought of outside things, like the Constitutional Convention being called in Philadelphia, or the continuing European troubles between England and France, Spain nervously looking on, or the turmoil in Paris that was a foretaste of the French Revolution.

Noah Fawley had arrived in time to be a part of this early, fumbling start toward a business that would become the focus of the world fur market. And a vicious, cutthroat business it became, with swindles, robberies, treacheries, and murders, not to mention trapping outfits inciting various Indian tribes against competitors. And the beauty of it was that Noah Fawley could view it from afar, through hearsay, beyond the danger of mayhem and dismemberment and bloodshed. In St. Louis, as he was, safe from all the plundering brutality.

Well, relatively safe. Although there were moments of the expected frontier-town perils you would expect him to fall heir to, and sometimes he mentioned these.

"They was this breed they called Maroc who got hisself tattooed acrost the arms when he was winterin' with the Otoes," Noah Fawley said. "He was a liver-colored son of a bitch, likely nine-tenths African nigger. One day he made a high fuss about the way I was gradin' these marten pelts for Mr. Chouteau and he taken it unkind when I said he was a club-head fool, and he come at me with this here Spanish clasp knife with a ten-inch blade so I brained him with this arn bailing hook. It laid open his head but he never died. All the commandant's constable said about it was that iffen I killed somebody someday with that arn bailing hook, I would likely hang.

"So I found this Yankee said he'd fought with George Rogers Clark at Vincennes and who'd come back from a cast with Manuel Lisa's trappin' outfit and drank up all his wages and was sellin' his truck for whatever he could get to drank that up, too, so I bought this pistol from him and it was made in Lancaster, Pennsylvania, and was a surely comely pistol, about a .58 caliber. I carried that pistol around in full view for a while on the riverfront to dishearten anybody else who taken a notion to pull a Spanish clasp knife, but it got to be such a nuisance carryin' it around, I quit. After that, anybody taking exception to the way I done my work for Mr. Chouteau, I merely laid in with fists and teeth."

Noah Fawley's aptitude in hide work stood him well. With the growing trade in such things, he advanced quickly. He was a cheerful worker and he worked hard. He did not become vicious or loud or morose when he was drunk. Well, not too often. Working in the fur warehouses he learned what all men have learned who work on waterfront jobs where there is access to large quantities of valuable but portable materials. That modest pilferage is generally overlooked as a hazard of the business. And so he laid aside for himself, over time, furs enough to translate into considerable Spanish gold coin.

No one would have suspected from looking at Noah Fawley that he was a man of means. From start to finish, he was a scruffy, hairy, bad-smelling, rotten-toothed river rat. He did nothing for the local economy by putting his coin into circulation and maybe had no idea even why he was collecting them except that now and again he enjoyed taking them out and admiring their oily glitter.

But he did his part in populating the frontier.

The girl was large and no girl at all, really, but a full-bosomed woman. Yet "girl" was what Noah Fawley called her from first blush to deathbed. When he first saw her, she was serving pewter steins of beer and six-ounce glasses of brandy and keeping fresh sawdust on the floor of a tavern one street away from the waterfront. She was indentured. She had a soiled and crumpled contract paper to prove it, and she carried it with her in a pocket of her stained half-apron. She could not read it, but was happy to take it out and let anybody else do so if they expressed a desire. The paper identified her only as the female Otis, as English as anyone could possibly get, but certainly no kin to the famous James Otis of revolutionary Boston fame.

She made no claim to be so related, possibly because she had never heard of James Otis of Boston nor of Boston, either. Or if she had, had forgotten. The person to whom she was indentured was the owner of the tavern, one Henri Larous, who said that she was a good worker but crazy as a drunk duck.

"Ole Henri was a fine man," said Noah Fawley. "He taken me in friendship right off, and he talked English good and he talked French even better because that's what he was, and he helped me learn a few of the words, enough to get me by anyway, in the frog language. And in all the years I knew Henri, I never seen him eat a single frog. He may have eat a crawdad now and sometimes, but never a frog."

Otis had been indentured out of Southampton to a British ship owner and captain for the usual term of seven years, her having at the time been nine years old, and the document revealing this dated April 1756. Which meant that she had served her indenture a long time ago. And all without any Christian name provided. If she'd ever had one, she'd forgotten that along with everything else, so those who came in contact with her called her Otis or whatever came to mind.

Otis had only a foggy recollection of how she'd come to be working in a Frenchman's saloon in St. Louis. What Noah Fawley knew of her, he got from Henri Larous. Apparently her sea-captain master had been doing business in New Orleans, perhaps connected with some of the pirates who hung about the islands near the mouth of the Mississippi. Or maybe he was one of those British sea dogs who had formed the habit of trade in the Crescent City as a holdover from the old days when the English held license from Spain to import African slaves for labor in the West Indies sugar plantations. No one cared to guess why a ship's master would take a nine-year-old girl for long sea voyages. Or maybe they did.

But whatever went before, Henri Larous bought the girl's paper, and her with it, of course, in New Orleans and brought her upriver along with certain commodities in a string of bateau boats. The Frenchman would not divulge what he had paid for her, but he was willing to sell her for the equivalent of seven dollars American, which Noah Fawley paid.

There was more to it than that. By this time, Noah Fawley had taken up residence in a two-room storehouse, no longer used, in the alley behind Henri Larous's tavern. There, in frequent wee-hour encounters, Noah Fawley taught Otis the things he'd learned among the Shawnee maidens of the Ohio Valley, and she undoubtedly taught him a few things, too, maybe learned from that sea captain. In any case, Henri Larous was aware of these amours and had no objection until it became obvious from the increasing tightness of his barmaid's clothes that she had entered an advanced stage of reproduction.

Henri Larous confronted Noah Fawley with his responsibility in the affair, pointing out that the woman's usefulness to him would henceforth be on a diminishing scale and that Noah should assume his role as Papa, with proper recompense, of course. Noah Fawley agreed, and it was an amicable transaction all around. In fact, Henri Larous began to consider himself somewhat of a father-in-law to Noah Fawley and to prove it gave Otis a wedding present of a linen waist shirt, a velvet bodice that laced up the front—or would, once the swelling had gone down—and a pair of Mandan moccasins with colorful quill beads on the toes that he had taken in trade for a half gallon of grain alcohol from a British army deserter who had spent some time hiding with the Missouri Indians.

However, Henri Larous was still a businessman. Now that Noah Fawley was starting a family in the tavern storeroom, Larous decided a rent should be paid, agreeing that four dollars a quarter would be fair. There were no windows in the place, but two good doors, leather hinged. The floor was packed dirt, the walls were sound, and the roof leaked only a little when it rained hard with the wind from the northwest.

Soon, there were adequate furnishings, including a brass bed and straw mattress. And a good cookstove. These were items that the new bridegroom quickly assembled from various places—most especially from riverfront warehouses with faulty door locks and no night watchmen. Henri Larous supplied a number of broken chairs from his tavern taproom, which Noah Fawley repaired as good as new.

Noah Fawley did not beat Otis or deal with her in any way that either of them considered to be mistreatment. Within time, he came to have considerable affection for her, as a man does for a favorite sheepdog. It was a position she accepted with good cheer and faithfulness because it was a lot better than anything else she'd ever had from a man. She was carefree. Noah Fawley quickly saw that she had no interest in his bag of Spanish gold coins, even when he took them from beneath the bed to fondle them in the lamplight. A good sign, he figured. In time, they developed little secret jokes known only to themselves, a sure sign of a solid marriage, and there was a lot of laughter, especially in bed.

Said Noah Fawley, "The day that damned Portsmouth judge sent me packin' off to Boston, I never reckoned to find any contentment like I done with that girl. Why, we'd get to carryin' on at night and even the skitters and bedbugs never caused us a commotion."

Boone Fawley was born later in the same year that the British and their Indians tried to take St. Louis. That was 1780. Henri Larous knew what was happening in the storehouse behind his tavern, but he had no part in it. Except reporting to his patrons the progress of the birthing. As they would do with all their children, Noah Fawley and Otis handled the whole thing themselves.

"I seen calves born, and lambs, back in Boonesborough," said Noah Fawley. "I helped sometimes, too. They ain't much difference in birthin' a man child. 'Cept you can't run your hand up in there. That girl come down with the babe slick as a constable's whistle. I never done nothin' much about it. Only watched."

With the announcement that the baby had arrived, healthy and squealing like a Quapaw warrior, about an hour after sunset it was, Henri Larous did a remarkable thing. He passed out a free gill of brandy to all his shouting customers. Then Noah Fawley came in and bought everybody another. By midnight, it was a damned fine party. Then Otis herself appeared, grinning, holding the baby in her arms, and everybody had a good look, including the Delaware squaw that one of the trappers had recently acquired somewhere in the Illinois Territory.

Otis didn't stay long, but she looked as though she'd been doing little more than chopping a batch of kindling except that she walked very carefully. After she returned to her bed, Noah Fawley remained for another three hours, and everybody got noisy. One of the commandant's constables came by to see who had started the riot and stayed and before it was finished at dawn was as drunk as everybody else, including the Delaware squaw and two Spanish soldiers who'd come by to rescue him. And about noon, Mr. Chouteau, old Auguste, sent along a big box of horehound candy for the new mama.

Henri Larous designated himself godfather of the new Fawley. In less than a month, when a Jesuit priest arrived for the beneficence of all St. Louis, it was Henri Larous who hurried Noah Fawley and Otis and the new child before him to put the stamp of holiness on the union and to baptize the child. It was, perhaps, the child's one and only contact with organized religion throughout his life. They named him Boone, of course, in honor of the man who had led Noah Fawley through Cumberland Gap.

This French godfather would contribute substantial things to Boone, particularly in the way of advice. As when he said, *"Mon cher,* you ever go to deep woods, you wear deerskin *blouson,* big, big, lots of pockets, *comprends,* these fringes, long fringes on *la manche,* no decoration either but so in deep woods you need some string, lots of times need string in deep woods, you just cut him off the sleeve. *Apercevois?"*

After Boone, Otis began to produce children at more or less set intervals of fourteen months, as regularly as geese flew to Canada. In grand total, there were four boys and four girls. The three oldest boys and the oldest girl were the only ones who survived infancy.

One of the girls was stillborn, but nobody knew why the others died. They just did, and each time Noah Fawley would go into Henri Larous's tavern, sit in the corner, get drunk, and cry for a couple of days. Then everything would be back to normal again. People said Noah just used it as an excuse to get drunk.

Both the younger boys he apprenticed out to riverfront business-men when they were six years old. And that done, the two boys never again showed their faces in the Fawley house in the tavern alley. Now and again Boone saw them in the warehouse area, but that didn't last long. They went to New Orleans or up the Ohio someplace with those mercantile men to whom they'd been appren-ticed. And Old Noah didn't seem to care one way or the other.

The sole surviving girl, Chorine, second born after Boone, was hired out as a kitchen maid to one of the well-to-do families who had a house in the elms west of the town, where Boone heard she helped a black slave woman, which likely meant the girl spent her time scrubbing floors, scouring out pots, or drawing up water from the well. Chorine was seven when she left the tavern alley home.

With Boone, it was different. Old Noah had him on the river-front learning about hides and furs almost by the time he could walk, or so it seemed in Boone's memory. The boy was a fast pupil. And he was sometimes impertinent, too. Once when Mr. Auguste Chou-teau was nosing around in the warehouse where he was working, Boone, about ten then and bold as brass, asked Mr. Chouteau if he had any more of that horehound candy he'd sent around on the day of Boone's birth. For an instant, everybody was horrified, but then Auguste Chouteau roared with laughter and not long after that had one of his best-traveled straw bosses taking Boone aside each after-noon to teach him to read and write. In English. Old Auguste Chouteau was no fool. He knew the language that was approaching rapidly from across the river.

Old Noah began to change. He bought a house on the western edge of the settlement near the big stone houses where the rich merchants and governor-commandant had sandstone homes. This one wasn't sandstone, but it had windows and metal hinges on the doors and four rooms and a good well in the backyard. It was the kind of backyard where you could sit on a summer evening and watch the purple shadows growing in the trees that marched like brown bark soldiers away from the rear edge of Otis's garden, stretching toward the upper regions of the Ozark Plateau. You could just imagine the Osage hunters in there stalking deer or turkey, all the way south to the Arkansas River, three hundred miles of virgin hardwood, so close you could sit on Noah Fawley's back step and spit on the near edge of it.

Old Noah got a little extravagant, too. He took some of those Spanish coins to a Jew who had started selling things from a little clapboard shop on Walnut Street and bought a gold, stem-wind watch. It was maybe the first time Noah Fawley ever bothered telling time by anything except the sun. At night, under the yellow shine of an oil lamp, he'd wind that watch and listen to it ticking and snap the face cover shut, snap it open again, listen some more. It was like a prayer before sleep. Well, for a couple of days. Then the watch went into the money sack along with the rest of the Spanish coin and stayed there to run down and lie silent until Boone took it out later and wound it again.

That was about the time the backsliding Methodist preacher Owen Prather came over from Illinois. He had a King James Version of the Bible with him and when he realized saving souls was not his line, he sold the Bible to Noah Fawley, who swore to Otis that he'd now learn to read. He didn't, of course, but by then Boone could sound out most of the words so sometimes in the evening he'd sit under the feeble glow of that oil lamp and read aloud to his mother and father. Mostly from the Psalms and a little now and then from Revelations. Noah Fawley and Otis liked the reading.

"That girl," said Noah Fawley, "she was puffed up with pride, her son readin' like that. Why hell, it was a surely handsome miracle to her, like as if young Boone taken into his head to walk right acrost the river to Illinois, and done it, that kind of a miracle."

Of course, none of them, including Boone, could make heads or tails out of Revelations.

Boone Fawley reckoned that his daddy was soaking up a lot of credit entries on his ledger, listening to the Word from the Book, which is how the old man put it. To cancel out all the debit entries of the past, Boone reckoned, and wondered if maybe someday he'd be doing the same thing. Making a last desperate effort to find salvation.

On the third day of 1797, maybe Otis Fawley discovered if the Word had done any good. She died during the night with little more than a choking sound, and beside her Noah Fawley didn't even know it had happened until he tried to wake her the next morning. You'd expect that after years of having drunk the water from the tavern alley well nothing like typhoid or pretty near anything else could have dented her constitution. So maybe her time had just run out.

Noah Fawley went into the same drinking and crying spell he'd once displayed when a baby died, and Boone had to go get him out of Henri Larous's place, limp and wet, for the funeral. As soon as he dried out, tears and booze both, Noah Fawley began to realize how much Otis had meant to him on a day-to-day basis, and so he started a frantic search for another wife. Well, maybe on a night-to-night basis, because in Noah Fawley's search among very slender pickings he contracted a savage case of syphilis. Nobody knew anything was wrong until he started having fainting spells right in the middle of one of Mr. Chouteau's warehouses. After passing it off as summer vapors or bad pork or too many baths—hell, he'd had two in the course of four months—Boone finally convinced the old man to call in the only medical man in town. Maybe in the whole territory.

This was a real doctor, all right. He'd claimed all along to have studied under Dr. Benjamin Rush, of Philadelphia, a signer of the Declaration of Independence and who would shortly advise Meriwether Lewis on how to avoid sickness among his men on the long expedition that Thomas Jefferson, now vice president, was already thinking about. Whether Dr. Rush covered syphilis during his instructions will never be known, but at least the St. Louis medical man knew as much about it as anybody, and so began administering the only known cure. Arsenic.

Perhaps the good doctor's administration of the deadly metal was too enthusiastic, or perhaps the offending spirochete did the dirty work, or maybe, like Otis, it was just Noah Fawley's time. For whatever reason, Noah Fawley died.

He clung to life long enough to extract certain promises from his son. Boone agreed to find a good English girl like his mother had been and marry her. He promised to join an Anglican church as soon as one got to St. Louis. And he would avoid Frenchwomen, who could be identified, Noah Fawley said, because they all smelled of garlic. The last words Boone heard his daddy say were, "And for Christ's sweet sake, no matter how surely comely they may be, stay the hell away from riverfront whores!"

Boone Fawley was eighteen.

4

Boone Fawley owed more to Auguste Chouteau than his ability to read English. What he owed Auguste Chouteau was Molly and John and Questor. And even Chorine, because without Molly, Chorine would have faded completely out of Boone Fawley's life just as his brothers had done. And maybe owed him, too, a capacity for self-respect that his own daddy and Henri Larous were incapable of giving.

And that was another thing that made Boone Fawley reproach himself for deciding to strike out into the wild, unclaimed country. Auguste Chouteau knew he, Boone Fawley, could represent the company because he already had done so.

It came about after Old Noah died. Soon after. Just by coincidence. Or maybe by fate, whatever that is. Boone Fawley, anxious to make good his word to a dying daddy, let it be known he was going up the Ohio River in search of a wife. One, he hoped, who was of English lineage, out of respect for his daddy's admiration for old George III, still king of England and by now blind and crazy as one of Henri Larous's drunk ducks. And by the way, Henri Larous knew about how crazy drunk ducks were because he always had a few in his tavern waddling around that he allowed to sip—or whatever it is ducks do—from saucers of French brandy. Hell,

Henri Larous's ducks got better booze, it was said, than any of the Indians who traded with Chouteau's people!

At the same time, old Auguste Chouteau was thinking about the Ohio, too. Because in 1792, Kentucky—no longer a name just the vision of wilderness—became a state of the Union, as did Tennessee four years later. So now there were products up the Ohio River, not confined to Pennsylvania. Closer to St. Louis. Woven cloth, axes, pots, firearms. None of it fancy. All of it durable. And Auguste Chouteau was aware that bringing goods downriver along the Ohio, then upstream a short ways along the Mississippi to St. Louis was one hell of a lot cheaper than poling, paddling, sailing boats all the way north from New Orleans against the flow.

He was also aware, or maybe naturally forewarned because he was French, that soon the national boundaries between Pittsburgh and St. Louis would disappear, hence making smuggling—which he was very good at—unnecessary.

So the two purposes were wed and, carrying papers identifying him as a representative of M. Auguste Chouteau of St. Louis, Boone Fawley found himself on the way to Louisville in a large cypress dugout with four Chouteau rivermen, none of whom spoke English too well. Boone was dressed in new knee britches, a woolen waistcoat, and a wide-brim felt hat, and armed—against river pirates, of course—with his daddy's Lancaster pistol. And privately, some Spanish gold coins and the stem-wind watch, now loudly ticking as it had been doing from the first hour after Boone Fawley returned from planting his father.

The Chouteau transactions were accomplished with a contract certified before a Kentucky justice of the peace, the kind of man they would someday call Colonel. To the effect that in the following year a certain number of specified merchants would dispatch a specific number of keelboats, loaded with various named merchandise, to one A. Chouteau, to be received at the landing of his choice on the Mississippi River between thirty-seven and thirty-nine degrees north latitude. One-third value paid on faith, the remainder on delivery. All in gold. Chouteau gold, not Old Noah's.

The bridal search was even more spectacular. There was no Anglican—or, as the Americans called it, Episcopal—church in Louisville. But there was a solid Methodist one and, being that John Wesley had started as an Anglican divine, Boone Fawley figured that was close enough to qualify under his promise to Old Noah.

In two weeks Boone Fawley was going back downriver with a bride who his daddy would've said was a comely wench. Dark hair that came almost to her waist when loosed, as Boone Fawley would discover only when she loosed it, and only she would decide when to loose it. And a solid mouth and jaw and strong back. And a pair of darting gray eyes within black lashes. She was almost as big as Boone Fawley himself, and he standing seventy inches crown of head to floor.

You'd say it was a contract as quickly made as the one for Chouteau's merchandise. For in that time and place the bickering over the price of a length of calico could last longer than a courtship.

Her name was Molly Winter, before he changed it to Fawley, and her father was a respected blacksmith. Hence his eldest daughter would be moving up the social ladder if joined with a merchant like Boone Fawley who carried all those Chouteau papers in his purse. And those four Chouteau rivermen clucking around him wherever he went like a small flock of French hens. Oh hell yes, they'd heard of Auguste Chouteau! And any man who carried the credentials to make certification before notary public for Chouteau was held in the kind of high esteem reserved usually for such as John Rogers Clark, who was the patron saint of Louisville, having founded it.

The illusion of grandeur was not damaged by Boone Fawley's new clothes or the stem-wind watch or the Lancaster pistol or his handsome good humor, all except the new clothes attributable to his dear old dead river-rat father. And it was so nice that among these sweet Methodists he could speak English, quote a few lines now and then from Revelations, and converse eloquently in French as he instructed his retinue of rivermen, who throughout all the socializing among the Methodists, like good Frenchmen, were capable of some dignity and appearance of sobriety, even though they were drunk as lords the whole time on Kentucky bourbon whiskey. Not bought on Chouteau's gold, but rather Old Noah's. Well, now the gold of Boone Fawley. Who here, now, in Kentucky, and on his gold and Chouteau's and the acceptance of good people willing to provide his woman, knew he could do anything. He was ready to challenge anything, yet not really knowing it. Not yet.

So, having been sighted and approved of by father and Methodist congregation alike, and wed there, in the chapel, with good

Welsh hymns sung afterward, Molly and Noah Fawley went down-river with waving and the cypress dugout outlined in white and orange crepe paper. At least until the first bend of the river, when the Frenchmen tore it all off, and one even took a taste of it. The bride now and for the days to St. Louis remained demure and at arm's length from all, including Boone Fawley, except there was some secret promise in the eyes, which from the start seemed to be less starry from tears of parting family than glowing with some anticipation of furious combat. Boone Fawley, looking at her as the river slid past underneath, suspected hot blood here.

He was right. After the first night in the house that Old Noah had bought and was now Boone Fawley's and his wife's alone, he wondered what the hell it was that John Wesley had said to make a nice lady during sunshine such a liquid wanton after dark.

When Boone Fawley delivered the contracts to Mr. Chouteau, the old Frenchman wanted to talk about commerce along the Ohio. Boone Fawley, who did not know or care much about commerce along the Ohio or anywhere else, told his boss what he'd heard. That merchants and farmers and politicians from Pittsburgh to Cairo were very upset because the Spaniards were always closing the Mississippi to American shipping. Now even Boone Fawley could figure out that floating merchandise downriver to New Orleans, where the Spaniards owned both banks of the river, was less expen-sive than freighting it over the mountains to Atlantic seaboard cities, Daniel Boone's and Noah Fawley's Wilderness Road through Cum-berland Gap notwithstanding. So what it meant was that the Span-ish squeeze cost Americans in the Ohio Valley a great deal of profit. Which was making a lot of people very angry, indeed.

Mr. Chouteau remarked that all this meant there were some very large changes in the wind, one way or the other. Boone Fawley failed to perceive how prophetic this statement was and so returned to fur grading and raising a family with the totally mistaken impres-sion that such things were problems only for people like Mr. Chou-teau or the president of the United States, who was, at the time, John Adams, so Boone Fawley had heard.

Boone Fawley had never suspected the furious determination of his wife once she'd made up her mind to something. They had

been back in St. Louis a year and John just born when Molly
discovered by a chance remark her husband made at the supper table
that he had a sister, now a girl of seventeen, working at scullery to
some frog-eating French fur trader in the west end of the town.
Molly commenced to raise such a stink of sulfuric-scented hell with
him that Boone finally went to fetch his sister so Molly could meet
her, expecting that would be the end of it.

It wasn't the end of it. It was the start.

Once Chorine walked into Molly's kitchen and the two women
saw one another—they were very nearly contemporaries—Chorine
never left again. In fact Boone had to go back to the house where
Chorine had been working since Old Noah had put her there, to
retrieve her pitifully few belongings.

All the positive things Chorine added to the household were
canceled out by one item of baggage she brought with her. And his
name was Clovis Reed.

Clovis Reed was an Ulsterman and had drifted into the area after
the Revolution. He was one of those people called Scotch-Irish but,
like all the rest of them, had not a drop of Irish in him. Typical of
this tough lot, he was rawboned, straight haired, and big, and not
afraid of the devil himself and certainly not of any of the New
World's aboriginals. And he was almost old enough to be Chorine's
daddy. Which meant he was almost old enough to be Boone's
daddy, too. And although along the riverfront he had a reputation
that made most men, unless they were out-of-their-mind drunk,
avoid any trouble with him, when he came near Chorine, he was
transformed into a bowing, scraping, doe-eyed, mumbling, stumble-
footed adolescent who followed her about on his huge moccasined
feet, or maybe just with his huge hound-dog eyes like a suckling
shoat follows its mama sow. That was Boone Fawley's analogy.

And Chorine treated Clovis Reed like dog dirt. So Boone's
concern wasn't that Clovis Reed would dishonor his maiden sister
because she never allowed him to come close enough to touch her
with a hoe handle, much less a shorter and more personal member,
always looking at Clovis Reed with a contemptuous turn to her lip
and ordering him around as though he were a black African slave
boy. Clovis Reed acted as though it was the ordinary turn of nature
that a woman could do such a thing and acquiesced to it. A man able
to break a big oak sapling with his two bare hands, and a man whom

Boone Fawley, not himself any sort of coward, would never think of confronting, yet this same man on the string of a woman no more than half his weight and age as though he was a kitten in her sewing basket. That was Molly's analogy.

Often Boone Fawley and Molly discussed it after dark, if "discussed" is the right word. When they were lying spent and quiet under the comforter after the usual acrobatics which occurred generally every night except for those that came about once each month when Molly said she was cultivating. All Boone had to say was "he" or "him" without any proper name attached, and Molly knew exactly who Boone meant.

"I wish he'd stop moonin' around here," Boone Fawley said. "I can't even go to the privy without maybe he's squattin' in the path, grinnin' at me and whittlin' a stick!"

"You're a mean man, Boone Fawley," Molly said. "Want to take away your sister's courtin' years, you do."

"Years is right," Boone said. "For Christ's sweet sake, why don't he marry her? It ain't natural, just draggin' around and not horny for the wedding bed."

Always before it was over, Boone Fawley would get in his best lick.

"Damned Lisa man!"

It was true, and Clovis Reed never hesitated to talk about it. He'd come to St. Louis and pitched into the fur trade, gone up the Missouri with some others, got as far as the Mandan villages in Dakota country. And there discovered that the Rees that year had closed the Missouri to whites because of some slight. And closed it, too, for other Indians farther north and west so they couldn't canoe their hides downstream to the traders. And there he was, stuck for the winter with the Mandans and the only thing he brought back to St. Louis in the spring was the skimpy crop of furs the Mandans could provide. A few prairie fox and some buffalo robes and some almost useless wolf pelts. So after he'd come back and sold his sad collection, there wasn't enough to pay what he owed for the supplies and trade goods he bought to start with, and he found himself in the same position of most independent trappers, then and thereafter. Deep in debt. Way over his head in debt.

Most of the independents went out again. And again. And again. And the debt never got any smaller. Clovis Reed didn't go out again.

He became a riverman, working mostly for pennies with the mercantiler he'd become obligated to, and that man was Manuel Lisa.

"That goddamned Spaniard sure-as-daylight son of a bitch," Boone Fawley said, meaning Manuel Lisa, who was the most ambitious competitor the Chouteaus had, and of course, Boone Fawley was a Chouteau man.

"You talk dirt when you on the riverfront," Molly said, turning away from him in the bed and yanking at the quilt around them. "But not under my covers."

You would think that anybody living in that time would have known and appreciated Napoleon. But the average, high-quality fur grader in St. Louis, no different from his contemporaries, knew little more than that some small Italian artilleryman had become dictator of France. Even if they knew that much. When Auguste Chouteau spoke of the French situation, which he often did to Boone Fawley, he hardly knew more than his meanest boatman.

Of course, when Chouteau spoke, Boone Fawley nodded and said, "Yes sir, yes sir. I see." But really didn't and seldom even bothered to mention such talk to Molly when he came home at night.

Well, what was happening would certainly touch them all. It had started with that Spanish closing of the Mississippi to American trade, which upset a lot of people, one being Thomas Jefferson. And he was not a good man to upset, particularly after he became president of the United States two years after Boone Fawley's first child, John, was born in St. Louis.

An intensive effort was made from the new capital in Washington City to buy a bit of land at the mouth of Father of All Waters to secure passage of Ohio Valley goods into the Gulf of Mexico and hence onward to the markets of the world. The Spaniards in Madrid, holding all the trump cards, were naturally not interested.

Then Napoleon—who had risen to power on the crest of chaos created by the French Revolution—suggested to Charles III of Spain that Louisiana should now be returned to France. Charles was in no position to refuse.

Not very many people knew about this deal, for it was not made immediately public, but Jefferson knew and became really upset.

Because it meant that France was back on the North American continent with a vengeance. Sure enough, Napoleon began to plan for reconquest. In order to control the mouth of the Mississippi, and hence Louisiana, the first thing he had to do was obtain a solid foothold in the Caribbean—because the British navy was about, you see, and if there was one enemy Napoleon could always count on to be his enemy, it was Britain.

So Napoleon sent an army of about twenty thousand soldiers to the island of Santo Domingo to take it back from a bunch of ignorant black slaves who had recently rebelled there. He formed another army of the same size to move directly into New Orleans as soon as Santo Domingo was secure. While all this was happening, an envoy of President Jefferson named Robert Livingston was going to see the French foreign minister Talleyrand every day, trying to buy that little bit of land to assure passage of Ohio Valley products, and all he got for his efforts, day after day, was an offer from Talleyrand to have a sniff of good snuff.

Well. Napoleon's French army that invaded Santo Domingo ran into a fearsome black ex-slave army and an equally fearsome attack of yellow fever and was completely decimated. Having no choice, Napoleon sent his so-called Louisiana army into Santo Domingo to salvage the defeat of the first, and it was immediately decimated as well. Napoleon decided that he had already spent too much money and too many men and cannons on his cherished North American reconquest, so he turned to other things.

It is unfortunate that we have no record of facial expressions that are landmarks in the history of the world. Standing toward the top of such expressions would have to be that of Mr. Livingston on the morning he went to Talleyrand to buy that bit of real estate at the mouth of the Mississippi, and fully expecting to receive no satisfaction other than the offer of a pinch of snuff, and M. Talleyrand said to him, "My dear Livingston, what would the United States pay for *all* of Louisiana?"

It was, of course, a fire sale. The fire had occurred on the island of Santo Domingo. In Washington City, President Jefferson had a few problems convincing certain politicians that it would be money well spent—actually about twelve million dollars—or that the Constitution even allowed such a thing, but it was done anyway. And changed the course of world history.

Hence Boone Fawley, holding the hand of his eldest son and beside him Molly holding in her arms Questor, who was four years old, watched as the old Spanish flag was lowered from the staff above the governor-commandant's official statehouse and the French tricolor raised. To show that the place had been French again for a little while, and to honor the French, the tricolor was left flying overnight. The next morning everybody came back, including Boone Fawley and his family, to watch as the tricolor came down and the stars and stripes of the United States of America was raised.

You will wonder, of course, if any of the common folk who witnessed these events remarked on the fact that they had been subject to three national sovereignties in the space of only twenty-four hours. Boone Fawley did not so remark. What he said was, "Well, now we are Americans."

And Molly replied, "I have always been so!"

When Meriwether Lewis and William Clark came back down the Missouri with their brave detachment, it was a wonderful time for celebration. Late September, not soon enough for chill in the air, yet past the days of sweltering humidity. Mockingbirds in the elms and along the locust fencerows were very vocal, as though they knew it was time to sing. On the street in front of Henri Larous's tavern, in dirt-filled whiskey barrels halved, the moss roses were a riot of color, reds and yellows and pinks, the petals freshly washed from last evening's shower. On the wind blowing from the west was that scent of coming autumn unlike any other season, as though the leaves, still green but about to turn, sent out some special notice of the banquet of color just a few weeks ahead.

The dome of blue sky vibrated with the shock of cannon firing in salute, and the bell at the Catholic mission church on what was being called Main Street added its brassy counterpoint. Many trappers and rivermen shot off muskets in the air and got drunk and danced and fell into the river. There were many entertaining gouge-and-scratch and ear-biting fights, and nobody got killed. Some of those who still felt the tingle of French blood flowing in their veins used the occasion to celebrate Napoleon being crowned emperor of France—well, better put, crowning himself emperor of France—

and there were even toasts raised to the emperor's abolition of the Holy Roman Empire.

All the excited talk on the streets was about the journals and specimens of plants and sketches of animals and charts and maps and names of Indian tribes the expedition brought back. All these wonderful things would be taken quickly to the East so President Jefferson could marvel at them, and gloat a little as he displayed them to those members of Congress who had been reluctant to allow him to buy about 800,000 square miles of the earth's surface from France for something like two cents an acre. Of course, even Mr. Jefferson, optimistic and farsighted as he was, had no idea that someday a great many quarter sections of that purchase would be sold for more money than it had taken to buy the whole damned Louisiana Territory!

Well, he was certainly happy with his two pathfinding soldiers. He appointed Meriwether Lewis territorial governor of Louisiana, and he appointed William Clark superintendent of Indian tribes over that vast land. St. Louis would see a lot of those two heroes the next few years, and they would, to their dying day, be pointed out to pop-eyed urchins, as they were pointed out to John and Questor Fawley that wonderful Tuesday in 1806.

Questor, not yet six years old, tried for the rest of his life to recall what Lewis and Clark looked like, but the only image of historical magnitude his mind could draw up was the face of Sam Houston. Of course, when Questor saw Sam Houston, he was a lot older than he was the day his mother held him up in her arms and shouted, "Wave to Captain Lewis. The one with red hair!"

All Boone Fawley wanted was to be a top fur grader, maybe now and then a traveling agent for Auguste Chouteau, and live quietly and calmly and die the same way right there in St. Louis. But by 1807, the shoe was beginning to pinch.

At the heart of it was the fact that he'd always figured having a wife was a simple thing. As it had been with Old Noah and Otis. The man going about his usual business except that with a woman he didn't have to cook his own meat or wash his own shirts. And that there would be instantly available at all times release for the urges of his loins without having to spend any money on some riverfront wench. Very quickly, he discovered that a wife—Molly, anyway—created complications. It disturbed him that he had become concerned for her welfare, much more so than he had ever been in regard to Old Noah and Otis, worried about her being sick or perhaps molested in the attentions of a rutting male in a rather wild town where there were still only a few females who weren't Indians. The fact that he did not know how to express his tender concern didn't help matters any. Neither did it help that he absolutely did not understand how a woman's head worked.

Take the naming of the boys. The first one she said would be John, for her favorite of the Jesus Gospels in the King James Version and also in honor of the nation's second president, who was a good man, Molly said, even though probably a Congregationalist. And Molly didn't consult Boone about it. She didn't ask. She told him. And that was it.

It was well thought out and Boone Fawley could accept it without any fuss. But then the second baby was born, and there was no reason or rhyme about how she came to his name. Questor. A name she had apparently discovered from making odd noises with her mouth until she found a sound that pleased her. At first, Boone suspected she had slipped in another Bible name on him so he spent time secretly leafing through the Book, knowing there was a lot of it he'd missed when he read it to Old Noah and Otis. But he couldn't find Questor.

The boys were still toddlers when Molly said something that took a while for Boone to comprehend. She said, "When boys a little older, yours to teach what you can. But always, at night and on Sundays, they belong to me!"

Molly, who Boone reckoned could speak the King's English as well as any Anglican bishop, had this disconcerting habit of dropping words from her sentences, like articles and pronouns, and it made her sound like some ignorant French river voyageur.

Anyway, the boys were just old enough to sit up at the table when Boone Fawley realized what his wife meant by that "belong to me" business. Every evening, she had those boys learning to talk, read, and finally write, turning Boone into a thief as bad as Old Noah had been, only not by bringing Chouteau furs home but rather fistfuls of paper, which could be somewhat scarce. And using charcoal they wrote not just the alphabet and words, but numbers.

Maybe especially numbers. And on Sunday mornings, when they were big enough to get there and back without being carried, she took them to the Protestant congregation meeting that occurred in various places, wherever the aging Owen Prather, backsliding Methodist divine who had now double backslid into preaching again, could commandeer a hall.

Chorine Fawley was right there assisting with her nephews, too. On evenings and Sundays, Boone Fawley felt like a bull locked out of the cow barn. Oh, he could join in, but only as a silent observer. At first, he accompanied them to church, but it didn't take him long to get a bellyful of Owen Prather's brand of Welsh Methodism, which invoked the fervor of the congregation gone half-crazy testifying about their experiences with Jesus.

He could see that if he was going to have any hand at all in bringing up his sons he had to take action, so he began taking them into the town with him every day. As he worked in the warehouses they got the rest of their education, not from Boone, but from the streets and the riverfront. That might have been a mistake, too, Boone Fawley reckoned, because it was from all that St. Louis education that they started getting smarter than their pa.

That wasn't all. There was the uncomfortable awareness that Molly understood what being an American meant and Boone Fawley didn't, like a lot of St. Louis people who had never had any experience of government outside the French and Spanish system until that flag with all the stripes and stars was raised and somebody said, "Now, you are an American!" Boone Fawley's only personal contact with the American government had been that trip to Louisville he'd made for Auguste Chouteau.

Old Noah, for all his efforts at being English to the marrow of his bones, had never bothered to explain to Boone about how a system of common law worked. Because he likely didn't know. So now here Boone was subject to a system of justice that had grown directly out of English common law. Under French- or Spanish-style colonial rule, a man did a crime, he was hauled before the governor-commandant, who heard testimony and made a judgment and that was the end to it. Quick and simple. Not now. Now there was court with juries and judges and lawyers and God only knew what all, and nobody in authority who had been appointed by the supreme power decided if a man had done wrong. No sir. Now such things were decided by twelve men no different from the man in the dock.

And that wasn't all, either. Now, there was a Congress in Washington City putting rules and regulations in books as fast as they could find anybody to write them down, and in the territory there was a legislature doing the same thing. So as Boone Fawley put it, a man had to look over one shoulder to watch for President Jefferson's marshals and look over the other shoulder for the sheriffs of Governor Lewis.

"For Christ's sweet sake," he said. "It's like a man's living in two different countries at once."

"Papa's family did it Virginia," said Molly. "We all did it Kentucky."

"How can a man be loyal to two outfits at the same time? What if Mr. Jefferson's Congress gets crosswise with Captain Lewis's legislature?"

"Bring in kindling for cookstove. Let Mr. Jefferson and Captain Lewis worry about it."

You might say that Boone Fawley, without knowing it, put his finger on a little issue that would boil up pretty bad in about half a century. At the moment, all he knew was the whole thing pinched.

"For Christ's sweet sake," he said to Questor one day when he and the boy were liming the privy hole at Molly's instruction. "I ain't got two governments to worry about. I got three! Mr. Jefferson's, Captain Lewis's, and your mama's."

Then the Aaron Burr thing came up and was the talk of the town because it would have affected them all. The former vice president was arrested and tried for treason because he had made plans, it was said, to form a separate country out of much of Louisiana and a large chunk of northern Mexico. He was acquitted, but it left a sour taste, especially in Boone Fawley's mouth. Molly asked him what he could expect from a man with the same name as the one who'd caused Moses so much trouble.

It took Boone a week of surreptitious searching in the King James to find the right places in Exodus, and he felt a twinge of guilt for sympathizing with Aaron on most counts.

So maybe the pinch was the real reason Boone Fawley decided to strike out on a hunt for less settled environs. If it was, he never admitted it, not even to himself, maybe least of all to himself, because for such a venture he couldn't think of it as running *away* from something, but rather as going *to* something.

So after a frantic two months of talking to people who had had some experience in such things, buying what he thought they'd be needing, and convincing Molly and Chorine they wouldn't be captured and eaten by wild bears or Indians, it was time to depart.

Henri Larous came to say good-bye on that early dawn. Boone Fawley had said Henri could have the lot and house and whatever furniture was left, and Henri had asked Boone to sign something he'd called a quitclaim deed or some such thing. Boone had said he would if it wouldn't get him involved with any of Mr. Jefferson's or Captain Lewis's juries, and Henri said it wouldn't, so Boone signed. Henri stood in the yard before the forlorn and lonely-looking house and waved a white handkerchief as the cart creaked away, just like an old granny bidding farewell to her progeny. He had to wipe a few tears from a graying beard.

Clovis Reed, who had been there the night before helping to load the cart, was nowhere to be seen. Boone Fawley figured the son of a bitch would follow along behind in the woods. But after that first hectic day, when Boone and Questor could look back in the evening at the lights of St. Louis, there was still no sign of the Ulsterman. Boone reckoned maybe he'd decided to forget Chorine and return full-time to sucking around Manuel Lisa. It was about the only positive thing Boone Fawley could count up that first night as he crawled under a blanket with his Molly, already in an exhausted slumber, and lie there listening to the sounds of the woods around them, a rather restful noisy silence. And of course, he discovered that strange mosquitoes were a lot hungrier than the old familiar ones back in St. Louis had ever been.

5

Afterward, Boone Fawley would recall it as the fourth day out. He always thought of it like that, *out* meaning the moment of leaving St. Louis. They'd paused at noon in their passage along the river trace—although intervening foliage seldom allowed them sight of the river—for midday cornbread and to allow the women to go off into the brush for necessities. All of this done, Boone Fawley and his younger son were at the rear of the cart checking the load, which by now had settled into some semblance of stability, like flour sifting into a more compact mass after you've tapped the sides of the can a number of times with the rolling pin. All that morning, not a single thing had fallen off.

It was then that Questor said "Pa" with the same simple, quiet urgency he'd have used if he'd seen a snake in the path. Boone Fawley turned and saw them, not twenty paces behind the cart, standing in the trace. Three of them. Apparently just having slipped out of the woods, where God only knew how long they had been, unseen.

"Oh damn!" Boone Fawley whispered.

From the waist down, they were clad in buckskin leggings, loincloths, and moccasins, heavily fringed and grease stained. From the waist up, they were naked except for a tangle of fur and metal and glass necklaces and amulets hanging down over chests and bellies sweat-streaked with old paint. Their skulls were shaved, with the usual interwoven rattlesnake skins and blue-jay feathers in the long hair roaches. All wore white shell and blue glass bead decorations in their ears, across the tops, nothing in the lobes. One had a blue tattoo grid of lines across his chin.

Boone Fawley could smell a strong odor of wood smoke and meat and some musty scent, and knew that likely they were smelling his foreign sweat and tobacco and white man mustiness as well.

"No black paint, Pa," Questor whispered, and Boone Fawley knew his son was telling him to note that they were probably not hostile. It didn't help much. He felt naked and defenseless because he could see at their waists sheathed knives and a French trade hatchet with a cake-knife blade, and on their backs unstrung bows in rawhide quivers. The one in front, the biggest of them, held a flintlock musket, held it high, near the muzzle, and stamped the butt along the ground like a walking cane as he slowly advanced, the others following. All were watching with hard, unblinking eyes.

He'd seen plenty of Osage men, and women, too, in St. Louis. But seeing them there in the wilds was a very different matter. As they moved closer, Boone Fawley edged out to meet them, but there was a bone-hard knot in his throat and he didn't know exactly how to start a conversation.

He needn't have worried because the Osage with the musket started the conversation himself. It was a sputtering rendition of French, and all Boone Fawley could collect out of it was *le sucre*.

"He wants sugar, Pa," whispered Questor.

"I know that, I know . . ."

Then came the explosion. At that instant, Boone Fawley thought it was the loudest explosion he had ever heard, and he leaped up and whirled. To one side of the cart was Molly, barely visible in a great cloud of white powder smoke, holding the Pennsylvania rifle in her hands with the muzzle elevated so high that later Boone would say he didn't expect the ball hit even the top of the nearest seventy-foot hickory tree.

"Sweet Jesus Christ," Boone Fawley screamed and spun back around, vaguely aware that his young son had done the exact jumping and whirling, and now both were in a crouch like one gets into to repel an assault and were facing the back trail and the Osages.

Only there weren't any Osages. In the time it had taken Boone Fawley to leap and whirl and curse and leap and whirl back again, they had gone. Disappeared. Vanished! In the dense foliage alongside the trace near where the Osages had stood, not a leaf stirred.

"Sweet Jesus Christ," Boone Fawley yelled, and whirled again.

Now John and Chorine were on the far side of the cart from Molly, both saucer-eyed, and Chorine was holding her head with both hands as though trying to keep her scalp from being ripped off. But at least her open mouth gave out no sound of wailing or screaming. John's eyes were as big as his aunt's, but there was no terror in them, only a kind of intense inquisitiveness as he bent forward slightly in the posture of a boy, which he was, waiting to see his pet frog jump.

"For Christ's sake, Mol," Boone Fawley shouted, panting a little. She stood there, still visibly trembling and holding the rifle. A thin stream of smoke roiled up from its muzzle, and the cloud of black powder smoke, here in the trees untouched by any breeze, lazily lifted toward the sky like a little cloud trying to gain altitude. "You know the hell you done? They'll come scaldin' back in here with a lot of their friends, and they'll . . ."

He stopped. Obviously panting now. Then slowly controlled that and turned his eyes to John, who was still leaning forward, waiting for the frog to jump. Their eyes locked. When Boone spoke now, it was in a low, ominous cadence.

"Who loaded that rifle?"

Nobody said anything. Somewhere toward the river, a blue jay scolded. Then Questor said, "Pa, it wasn't no account unless it was loaded."

But Boone Fawley knew it wasn't Questor who'd loaded it.

"All right," he said. "So it was sure of good account being loaded, wasn't it?"

Then after another long pause, he said, "All right. You may as well load it again because we likely gonna need it now, and Questor, dig the Lancaster pistol out of the duffel and load her, too, if you know how."

Molly, who had stopped trembling now and seemed to hold the Pennsylvania rifle with considerable confidence, said, "Did I hit anybody?"

"Sweet Jesus!"

It didn't help Boone Fawley's disposition any to see how quickly and efficiently his two boys loaded and primed the weapons, proving to him that they knew more about firearms than he did, just like they seemed to know more about everything than he did. While this rearming went on, Chorine, still holding her hair with both hands and starting to whimper like a whipped pup, had begun to pace back and forth, and Molly was beside her, trying to calm her, stroking her cheeks.

But when Questor came up with the pistol and the extra powder horn and the extra thonged lead and flint pouch, Boone Fawley was still thinking about something besides calming his sister.

"Where'd you learn that?" he asked.

"On the river, Pa. Sometimes they let us do it."

Then Boone Fawley remembered that hardly a day passed in St. Louis without a group of trappers and hunters collected along the shore for some betting and recreational shooting, at snags and turtles and whatnot in the water, and his boys had been there with these groups almost from the time they were big enough to walk.

"Pa, I loaded the Lancaster with buckshot," said Questor.

"Good," said Boone Fawley and shoved the pistol into his belt and the flint and lead pouch into a smock pocket. "Thataway maybe I won't miss when they come back and I have to shoot the women to avoid they gettin' capture alive and cut up in little pieces to feed Osage dogs!"

Chorine stopped her pacing and glared at him and shouted, "You're tryin' to scare me, ain't you?"

Well, Boone Fawley thought, at least she's stopped holding onto her scalp.

"Let's get on along," Boone Fawley said. "We can't outrun 'em, but we can have 'em to come a little further."

It was then that John came to his father and held out the charged and primed rifle and said, speaking for the first time since any of this had started, "You want this one, too?"

"No," said Boone. "Give it to your mama. Hell, she's the marksman in this outfit, ain't she?"

Molly took the rifle and glared at Boone and said, "Yes, maybe I can get another whack at the red heathern!"

Boone stared at her in amazement and disbelief. Molly's jaw was set, her eyes hard and steady. Looking at her, Boone thought, Sweet

Jesus, with the first tremble of them Osages past, she's beginnin' to
enjoy this!

I t was spooky the rest of that day. The horse and mule could never
appreciate why the willow switches were coming down so often on
their rumps, all in the interest of speed. Molly strode along behind the
cart with the rifle. Watching their rear. Never understanding that if
they were going to be bushwhacked, it would be from the front or
alongside. Each time a hammerhead started his pounding on a hollow
oak snag or a crow flew over cawing, she assumed what she supposed
was the stance of somebody about to engage in combat. Boone was
disgusted. And spooked, too, not from fear of Osage attack but from
what he was watching happen to his wife. When something startled
her, alerting her, Boone supposed, her eyes became like an owl's.
Wide and unblinking when he first sees you, or maybe when you first
see that he sees you, with that supreme disinterest and impersonal
lifelessness, as if being inspected by glass marbles. Without one
flicker or shine of apprehension or fear.

"If you have to shoot again," Boone Fawley said to her, "take
a notion to point that thang in the direction of whatever it is you
wanta kill!"

"I'll hit one next time," she said.

Boone Fawley hoped any Osages about to waylay them would
see her before they attacked. Because she looked pretty formidable.
The women had started with hats that had hooded shades to keep
the sun off their faces—Molly said they were poke bonnets—and
now she had hers pushed back, hanging on its chin string, and it
swung just below her knot of bunned hair. She had a homespun
waist shirt and over that a tight bodice, laced to show her rather
considerable expanse of breast. But it was the woolen skirt that made
the difference. To walk more quickly, Molly had pulled the hem up
and under and tucked it into the waist of her bloomers so that she
walked with legs exposed from the knees, underpants showing and
white stockings and her little leather shoes, just like those Chorine
wore, town shoes that were already, in less than a week of wilderness wear, threatening to come apart.

"All right. Just try not to hit one of us, even if it ain't on
purpose."

"Keep apokin' at her," Chorine shouted. "You stand around and let them savages come right on to wool us around, and you talkin' about sugar and nothin' you do to stop 'em."

"You keep hollerin', Chorine," Boone said. "I'm fixin' to tie you to a stump out here and go off and leave you."

"That's right, that's right, you ain't nothin' but a damned heathen you own self," Chorine yelled, laying into the mule with her willow switch.

"Well, I'm gettin' drove in that direction, all right."

That night they didn't make a fire. Although all the cooked cornbread from the night before was gone, nobody thought too much about eating. Chorine burrowed herself into the duffel in the cart, wiggling into it backward like a badger into a sand hole to avoid a wolf pack. The rest of them slept under the cart, what little sleeping there was to it. The boys were up and down most of the night, and Boone realized they were as excited about the danger as their mother had become once the first shock of fear wore off at noon. The horse and mule snorted, and their bellies grumbled all night what with being left in harness and not much chance to crop a little grass. Boone woke in the middle of the night and found both pigs tight against his back, and he left them there.

At dawn Molly insisted on a fire, and they sliced off a few hunks of bacon from one of the two sides they'd brought. They broiled it on sticks to save time, and Boone regretted losing each drop of grease as it fell into the fire with a loud sizzling snap. They forgot that even hunger isn't supposed to dull the edge of vigilance in a dangerous time, so the man came on them quickly, from the stand of black locust scrub on the river side of the road. Luckily John saw him first and got to the rifle before Molly could. It was Clovis Reed.

"How do, Mr. Reed," Questor shouted, laughing.

He didn't look much like he'd done in St. Louis. He was woods clad, meaning buckskins head to foot, with a heavy black felt hat, one side of the wide brim pinned up to the crown with a green splinter of cedar. He had two pistols in a belt hung with pouches and a knife and a flat hammer pollax tomahawk with a long haft and in his hands, held casually across his chest, a reliable English-made musket of a caliber large enough to accommodate at least eight buckshot. And he had on a red sash with a trailing edge about two feet long, like a scarlet-painted mule tail.

"Well," said Molly, who was next after Questor to find voice. "Ain't he a sight!"

"How do, Fawleys," Clovis Reed said, and he was grinning, showing a double row of strong acorn-colored yellow teeth. "Bacon surely smells larrapin-good-lickin'."

"You tryin' to scare us to death?" Chorine yelled.

And Boone Fawley thought, but managed to keep it to himself, that he never reckoned he'd be glad to see this lickspittle son of a bitch.

So Molly sliced off more meat, and as they sat around the fire trying to avoid its smoke, it was obvious to all that not only did Clovis look different out here in the wilds, he *was* different. When Chorine gouged at him with a couple of verbal barbs, Clovis Reed acknowledged her only with a large grin.

Well, Clovis Reed said, him and some companions were rafting downriver to set up a little trading post south of the mouth of the Ohio on the opposite shore from Tennessee. He said they'd heard a considerable number of Cherokees had been crossing there into Osage country to hunt. No families yet, he said. Just men. And him and his companions were going to get a trading operation started with the Cherokees because they figured in time a lot more would be coming, even though the Osages might not be particularly happy about it, and they might, him and his companions, get some trading started with the Osages in that area, too.

Squatting there beside their morning fire, chewing on half-raw bacon, waving the gnats out of his face, and not saying a word, Boone Fawley knew exactly what was happening here. Clovis Reed and his companions were a Manuel Lisa operation and they were moving into Chouteau trading territory, and old Auguste Chouteau wasn't going to be any happier about it than the Osages were about the Cherokees who were coming across the river.

Boone remembered his daddy's stories about how the French and English had both manipulated red men to kill white men, and now here it was about to happen again, only not two countries pulling in heathen allies but two different trading interests. It occurred to Boone Fawley that things would be a lot simpler if the white men, no matter who they were, just fought each other man-to-man and let the red sticks go about their usual business of killing their own red-stick enemies like they'd been doing since before the white man came, and that way each one would stay out of the other's affairs.

At the outset of this talk, Boone Fawley felt himself being caught up in what might turn into a very nasty fur trade war, and he was ready to say good-bye and good riddance to Clovis Reed almost before he was finished being happy to see the well-armed Ulsterman appear. Small chance of that, though, because now Clovis Reed was telling the women and boys they needed to drive their rig down to the river where he, Clovis Reed, and his companions had beached their barge on a sandbar, and load up with them and float on down-river in style. They could go ashore wherever they pleased to look for a homestead, and in fact, Clovis Reed said, they had a man with them who might help in that because he knew every inch of ground between St. Genevieve and Chickasaw Bluffs. His name was Coppertop, and he was a black Africa escaped slave.

Naturally, Molly and Chorine and the boys, who didn't understand the implications of what was happening—and it wouldn't have mattered if they did—were jumping up and down with the prospect of getting off this damned river trace and onto a nice barge so they could float along peaceful and secure. So Boone Fawley knew he was trapped.

Clovis Reed also told that yesterday evening three Osages had come into his and his companions' riverside camp very upset that there were now white women in the woods who shot at people for no good reason at all, and it took a whole half-gallon jug of whiskey to calm the Osages down so they could go off and join their hunting village fifteen or so miles west of the river.

Chorine fell into a fit of giggles as Molly explained what had happened, and Boone, finally so furiously exasperated he could keep silent no longer, said it was surely a wonder his wife hadn't shot him in the back for he was standing square between her and her target—which made Chorine laugh all the harder. So Clovis Reed said as soon as they got aboard his and his companions' barge, he'd teach the women how to shoot because going out into the wilderness to make a home, one could never tell when such a talent might be useful. Though Boone said crankily that he didn't have the powder and lead to waste on such things, Clovis Reed said they could make a landing at St. Genevieve to buy more, and besides, he said, they needed to stop so Boone could buy a cow anyway, a thing he had thought to suggest back in St. Louis but had never found the right time to do so.

The only good thing about any of it, so far as Boone Fawley was concerned, was that Clovis Reed and his companions wouldn't find it necessary to charge any fee for taking the Fawley family downriver because they were going in that direction with or without passengers. Boone Fawley got the feeling that the biggest reason Clovis Reed and his companions wanted to haul along a family, cart, team, and livestock was so that any Chouteau people on shore who saw them passing would think it was just another load of immigrants and not a raid into the old Frenchman's trading domain.

In the year Boone Fawley went south with his family, a considerable migration of eastern aboriginals had already begun into that country. The Cherokees lived in northern Georgia and eastern Tennessee and the mountains of Carolina where they had established towns and farms on the white man's pattern and were generally a prosperous and respected part of their local communities. It would be another quarter century before the state governments dispossessed them and the federal government forced them to move west of what was then called the Indian Line, the approximate border between the future states of Arkansas and Oklahoma.

Before this Removal happened, the Cherokees were a growing, dynamic people and, like many whites, some of them began to explore westward. Beyond the Mississippi River and north of the Arkansas, they found an almost virgin country teeming with game. Buffalo in vast quantity were not far away, and small herds could be found in some of the wider valleys of the area. There were deer and turkey, black bear and fox, quail, squirrel, rabbit, weasel, and fresh running water and what appeared to be an endless supply of hardwood timber. So, many bands of Cherokees began to explore and hunt and trap that wilderness ground.

The only problem was that all this country was claimed by one of the most powerful tribes in North America, the Osage. And the Osages were always highly displeased when anybody came into their territory without express permission to do so. The territory the Osages considered to be theirs included not only the places where somewhat permanent towns were located, but also that vast, wild plateau that was becoming so attractive to the roaming Cherokees.

The terrain in question was a tangled puzzle of densely wooded, sharp-faced valleys and hogback ridges. There were no major rivers like the Missouri or the Arkansas marking an easily traveled highway through it. An Osage band could spend months there in splendid isolation doing nothing but subsistence hunting while they collected a certain wood that they used themselves and which was a valuable trade item between the Osages and the buffalo-hunting Plains tribes to the west.

This valuable wood was from a tree the early French traders called the *bois d'arc* because it was used for making bows. For that purpose, it was the best wood in the world. To the English speakers who came later, it was called the bodarck or Osage orange. Out of the garbled translations and hazy meanings from Osage to French to English, the tree gave this wild place its name. Indians called it Place of the Bows. Americans called it the Ozarks.

To get there, the Cherokees had to travel through the very country Boone Fawley and his family had chosen to settle.

Clovis Reed's companions were a disreputable-looking crew. From the appearance of their clothing, running heavily to buckskin, Molly said they must have been sleeping in the ashes and grease of their own campfires for the past two years. Chorine said they were undoubtedly river pirates and probably should be hanged on the docks at St. Louis with others of their kind. They were bearded and smelled bad and spoke nothing but French. However, Boone Fawley noted without comment that each had two rifles, and the rifles were spotless and well oiled. He figured this confirmed his suspicion that the party, if not actually inviting trouble, was certainly expecting some.

Once the barge was loaded, the Fawley cart and livestock amidships created a kind of separator, Clovis Reed's people staying at the rear, where one of them was always at the big fan-shaped stern sweep, and the Fawleys at the bow. The animals were tied at the Fawley end because before the loading even started there was a lot of yelling by Clovis Reed's people that they were not going to clean the shit off the barge no matter if these were Clovis Reed's friends.

Sometimes, one of the Frenchmen would be forward with a pole to push the barge away from snags, but they steered in close to the west shoreline where the current was soft so there were less frantic navigational acrobatics than there would have been in a more violent flow. Because it was spring, the river was high, but the roiling water was at midstream except on bends, where the Frenchmen moved the vessel along hand-over-hand, holding it steady by grasping over-hanging limbs of trees that at normal depth of water would have been high on the bank.

The only exception to the segregation of Clovis Reed's men and the Fawleys was the former slave, Coppertop. At first sight, it was obvious about the name. His hair was a kinky mat with a color you'd imagine a handful of Spanish pennies would make if you ran them through a fine-tooth sausage grinder. He was huge and black, a nonshining kind of black like coal smoke.

Coppertop went naked from the waist up, and Chorine after the first look refused to look again. He wore some sort of animal tooth at his chest, suspended on a string of garish orange Indian-trade beads. He spoke a completely unintelligible language made of bits and pieces of African dialects and New Orleans Creole, with some French thrown in from time to time. Clovis Reed seemed able to understand most of what the black man said, but when he spoke to Coppertop, he did so with a sign language of hands and face.

In Questor, Coppertop found some kind of soul companion, it seemed. He talked to the boy more than to all the others combined, and Boone Fawley got the impression that his son could understand more than he let on.

Good as his word, Clovis Reed began to instruct Molly and Chorine in the art of loading, priming, and shooting the Fawley rifle. The boys joined in just for the shooting part. Boone Fawley sat through these sessions puffing his clay pipe and scowling and muttering about the foolish waste of good powder.

At St. Genevieve they went ashore, Boone Fawley with the pouch of Spanish gold he'd prized off the headboard of the cart with a hatchet blade, and there they bought more powder and lead and a milk cow and another crate of chickens. Two of the Frenchmen were gone a long time and reappeared drunk and singing somewhat bawdy songs.

The whole episode worried Boone Fawley. Clovis Reed had obviously made no effort to hide the fact that he was on the Mississippi south of St. Louis in this little ragtag town that Boone knew was older than St. Louis and a Chouteau place if ever there was such a thing.

But it all seemed so calm and peaceful. As the west-bank hardwood jungle slid past, they saw no one. Here and there were old slash-and-burn fields where corn had been planted the year before and now lettuce-green sproutings of sassafras came up among the few remaining rust-colored cornstalks. A few of the older fields already had five-foot-tall black locusts growing.

They'd come into an area of white egrets, and Clovis Reed pointed out a low-flying pelican skimming just above the surface of the river and said this was as far north as he'd ever seen one. There were blue herons in all the backwater eddies and hawks on dead tree snags along their shoreline. Dawns were blue hazed and sunsets red and purple, and sometimes the sky was reflected across the water so that it looked clear as a glass mirror instead of the muddy flow it really was.

Then it started raining. The Fawleys' rigged canvas tentage lean-to did little to keep them dry. It was miserable. Maybe to raise their spirits, Clovis Reed came to them on the third night with a loin of venison from his own party's larder, and they broiled it over coals in a deck sandbox. And while they ate, Clovis Reed told them Coppertop's story.

When Coppertop was a full-grown man and upriver from the area of Napoleon Bayou near New Orleans with his master or overseer or whoever, looking for cotton land near Arkansas Post, they were set upon by a number of very hostile Chickasaws from east of the Mississippi River. In all the violent confusion, a few of the Chickasaws had their heads bashed in and so did Coppertop's master. Coppertop ran away into the swampy woods once the fight had subsided somewhat, to what purpose no one knew. None of his own party had been able to catch him, and the Chickasaws—those who remained—were interested only in getting back to the east bank of the Mississippi.

So Coppertop moved upriver, taking plenty of time about it, until finally near the mouth of the Ohio he became sick and tired of running around in the woods alone eating whatever he could catch with his hands, like snakes and lizards and slow rabbits. At Cairo, he decided to give himself to some white man.

This worked just fine, Clovis Reed said, except that none of the rivermen would claim Coppertop as their slave for whatever reason, so that when a strange white man came around, Coppertop would point out the closest riverman he could find as his master because he didn't want the strange white man to come back with dogs and a posse and chains and haul him off to the South and try him for bashing in the head of his master or maybe just hang him for the hell of it without any trial at all. Although Coppertop claimed it wasn't him who had bashed in the head of his master, Clovis Reed said, he probably had done it because he hadn't then understood how irritating it was to try and live in the woods alone on the things you could catch with your hands—like salamanders and ground squirrels and even big spiders—if you didn't have a white man to take care of you and give you at least a knife or hatchet.

Anyway, Clovis Reed said, he'd run across Coppertop in his travels as a riverman, and when the time came to assemble a few people to establish a trading post for the Cherokees, he figured Coppertop might fit in pretty well because he scared the hell out of any Indian Clovis Reed had ever seen and might be an advantage when they were trying to trade a couple of old bent tin arrowheads for a perfectly good red fox fur.

"I seen him lift a cow once," said Clovis Reed. "A cow pert near as big as that one you bought back yonder at St. Genevieve, Mr. Fawley."

In the night, after Clovis Reed had retired to his end of the barge and the Fawleys were rolled in moist blankets, Questor whispered, "Pa, do you like Mr. Coppertop?"

"He ain't the kind of man anybody in his right senses would admit dislikin' on purpose. Go to sleep."

The next morning, the rain had stopped and the moldy smell of the gray water was gone. There was a fresh breeze and the river was sunlit brown again. And that day Coppertop came to the front of the barge and he and Questor sat and fished; the young boy's line and hooks were baited with fat grubs Coppertop took from his pocket, still alive. Questor knew the big Negro had been ashore the night before, in the rain, digging that bait out of old logs or whatever. Each time Questor hooked a bullhead or a gar and flipped it onto the deck, Coppertop made a big ceremony of it, shouting unintelligible compliments.

Toward evening, with the shadows of their own shoreline trees reaching toward the far shore, Coppertop pointed to a lone king-fisher flying upstream, the pointed head like a bullet, and said something that Questor didn't understand.

Coppertop laughed and slapped both his tree-trunk thighs.

"Ha!" he shouted. Questor was aware that his aunt Chorine was staying where she had been all along, on the far side of the barge, sitting with her back to them, hands over her ears as though afraid she might hear an indecency.

Coppertop held out one massive fist and rubbed it with the fingers of his other hand.

"Noir," he said. *"Noir!"*

"Yes," said Questor and laughed. "Black."

"Ha!" Coppertop opened his fist and turned the hand over, palm up, and with a forefinger big as Questor's wrist, touched the pink-white flesh of his palm. *"Blanc. Blanc!"*

"Yes, white."

"Ha!" shouted Coppertop and gently took one of the boy's hands and opened it, palm up, and touched it as he had his own with the tip of that same gigantic finger. *"Blanc. Blanc.* Ha! *Tous le deux.* Ha? *Nous deux, blanc.* Ha?"

"Yes," shouted Questor, and he was laughing. "White, too. Both of us, white!"

He was up then, in one gigantic fluid motion, his head back, laughing, and gone around the cart and back to the stern where Questor could still hear his laughter. Boone Fawley had watched it all, and there were some of Molly's goose bumps up his own back.

That night, Questor whispered, "Pa? You reckon Mr. Coppertop really did bash that white master?"

"Go to sleep, boy."

Boone Fawley figured it was about eighty miles downstream from the mouth of the Ohio when they ran the barge ashore and tied it to a stake Coppertop drove into the sand with a ten-pound sledge. Clovis Reed said this was the place where they'd begin a trading operation and that about forty-five leagues due west was a fine homestead plot on a clear running stream the French called the St.

Francis. While Boone was still trying to convert the distance to something familiar, John said, "Fifteen miles."

They had beached on the west bank of a big eastward-looping bend of the Mississippi where there was a crescent-shaped sandbar about three miles long. It was as permanent as a sandbar could be, evidenced from the growth of willow on it, maybe a hundred paces back from the water, with a crown of lettuce-green canopy in places fifty feet high. Beyond that, there was a darker green foliage, almost blue, that rose more than fifty feet above the willows. Clovis Reed said it was bald cypress. In some of the higher, bare limbs, they could see white cranes, wings extended for balance like delicate silk handkerchiefs while they fed on the new spring cone seeds.

"Over yonder way," said Clovis Reed, pointing west to the line of cypress. "Me and Coppertop'll take you to it tomorrow. Two days, we be there, with the cart, Mr. Fawley. My boys, they'll start layin' in our camp here. Be nice, you havin' a trade post so close by."

In fact, the Frenchmen had already begun, two of them hacking into the willows with axes to make poles for shelters, two of them going back and forth from shore to the trees carrying the trade goods and all the other truck they would use to set up a post. They had flushed a family of three raccoons from the trees, and the bandit-faced animals scurried along the sandbar and out of sight, finally, looking over their shoulders with disgust at having been disturbed.

It was obvious to Boone Fawley that this might be a scruffy-looking bunch, but they knew what they were doing in the wilderness. By the time he and Clovis Reed and the boys and the women had the cart and the livestock across the sand to the tree line, there were already two weather-worthy lean-tos, a central fire pit, and the foundation outlines of a permanent structure marked out.

The only interruption to the scene's businesslike efficiency was when Chorine gave a loud, bellowing scream at sight of a long, fat snake lazily making for the river from the trees. John had the rifle almost ready to fire when Coppertop caught up to the snake and with a quick, darting movement had it just behind the ugly, turnip-shaped head. He held it up and laughed as it writhed and coiled around his arm. It was almost black, which emphasized the whiteness of its mouth as the jaws sprang open to reveal two long, needle-sharp fangs. With a quick movement of his free hand, Coppertop yanked off the snake's head and threw it in the sand, then, still laughing, the snake's body writhing about his arm, carried it back to the trees, squatted, skinned and gutted it with his fingers, and hung it on a limb to dry. It was about four feet long.

"Ole cottonmouth," Clovis Reed said, having paid little attention to any of this action that had the Fawleys staring. "Miz Chorine, you ever eat a nice old water moccasin cooked over a fine driftwood far? Miz Chorine? Where'd she go?"

Chorine was in the duffel of the cart, only her furious face showing. It took Molly a long time to coax her out from her place when the grub was ready to eat. Then, with what was maybe a show of bravado, Chorine ate as much of the snake as anybody.

Boone Fawley was more at ease than he'd been since leaving St. Louis. Full belly, the Frenchmen blowing their harmonicas, even singing a few decorous ballads, one of them up once to perform a little dance. The orange light of the fire played on Molly's face, so smooth and tranquil as she listened to the music. She looked, Boone reckoned, not a day older than she had when he'd married her in Kentucky. They could hear the "who-who-who" of at least two horned owls somewhere in the cypress, and downriver there was an occasional low whistle that Clovis Reed said was a pintail probably lost from the flock and doing what a duck seldom does, making his call at night. Just after dark, they'd heard a distant howl or bark or something, and the Frenchmen said it was a red wolf. And there was a constant chorus of bullfrogs. And the mosquitoes were not so bad, it seemed to Boone Fawley, so everything was just fine and easy and comfortable.

That began to change when Coppertop without any sound rose from the firelight, took up his rifle, and disappeared into the darkness. Then Clovis Reed sat up from his reclining position and one of his hands was on a pistol butt. And the Frenchmen stopped playing. The owl was still hooting and the frogs croaking and everything was the same. But it wasn't. And Boone Fawley started to ask why when he saw them. There were about half a dozen faces, faint in the firelight, well back from it, with eyes that gleamed like fox eyes, bright, but as though the light came not from the fire but from within. The faces moved closer, Clovis Reed stood up, and every Frenchman around the fire had his hands close to a weapon. Then all the faces stopped, still beyond good recognition, except for one, and it kept advancing into the firelight.

Clovis Reed spoke a short, abrupt greeting in French, and the man stopped. His eyes quickly went around the circle of faces at the fire, and only then did he return the salutation. In English.

"We watched you come. We didn't know you would bring women."

And from that, Boone Fawley knew these men had been expecting Clovis Reed, that some advance man for Manuel Lisa had already been along this route to say that others would follow.

"They are not with us. They come with this man and the boys to make a farm," said Clovis Reed, and his hand swept toward the west. "They are not in the trading."

"We wouldn't want to buy them, anyway," the man said. "But maybe the big black man. We might buy him."

"You cannot buy him. He is a free black man. You have free black men in your country, isn't that true?"

"Not many." The man looked around the fire again. "Where is the big black man?"

Clovis Reed shrugged elaborately, and Boone Fawley knew now that Coppertop was at that moment out there in the dark behind these men with his rifle. And the strange man knew it, too, and accepted it because he smiled slightly.

"We have some coffee," said Clovis Reed, and then a ritual began. The man and Clovis Reed squatted, across the fire from each other but going down to the haunches almost as though on the same string. One of the Frenchmen produced a tin cup, poured it full from Molly's simmering pot, and handed it to the squatting Cherokee, as Boone Fawley had now figured that's what this man and his companions were. And then the Frenchman filled another cup and took it to those still back in the shadows, who had squatted also, and they passed it among themselves until it was empty. Through all this there was no talk, only the loud sounds of the Cherokee at the fire sucking the scalding coffee between his lips from the tin cup.

Boone Fawley had never seen an Indian like this one. He was not the kind who would strike terror into Chorine as the Osages had. He wore a turban of multicolored cloth with wisps of black hair showing beneath it at his forehead and around the ears. His eyebrows were not plucked, and his ears were pierced at the lobe, where hung small copper, or perhaps even gold, rings. He had a sparse mustache, and along the line of his jaws was a trace of fine hair. His smock was of fine cured deerskin painted with decorations of vermilion, and at the open throat Boone Fawley could see a collarless gray-white shirt that looked like linen. The Cherokee wore a skirt of coarse woven English wool and leather britches and moccasins with no decoration of porcupine quill. So far as Boone Fawley could observe, he was unarmed except for a rather small knife at his waist with what appeared to be a stag handle.

"You come from Tennessee?" asked Clovis Reed, once more making that sweeping motion of his hand, this time toward the east.

"Yes," said the Cherokee. "My name is Tub. There are sometimes many of us here. We take many furs. We wish to trade. But we have guns and hatchets. We want to trade for gold."

"We can do it," Clovis Reed said, but Boone Fawley could tell from the Ulsterman's expression that the idea of trading pelts for gold with an Indian was not to his liking. "Tell your people, we will be here."

"Yes. They expected you would come."

Tub looked over his shoulder toward his party, spoke a few words in his native tongue, and then rose and extended a hand across the fire, white-man fashion, to Clovis Reed.

"We will be back here," Tub said.

"Good, I have a gift for you," Clovis Reed said. He spoke a soft string of French to one of his men, who scrambled off into the dark, quickly reappearing with a small clay jug that he handed to the Cherokee, who looked at it as though it might have been the water moccasin Coppertop had killed.

"I have a gift, too," he said, and produced a small pouch. Clovis Reed took it and smelled it and nodded.

"Good tobacco," he said, now in English again.

And it was finished. Tub turned and moved back and his men followed him, and they all vanished into the willows' darkness. After a while, Coppertop was back inside the circle of firelight, jabbering and pointing.

"Gone back to their camp, somewhere in the cypress," Reed said, not the smiling, genial man he had been before. His face was clouded with anger. "High-and-mighty red sticks. Talk about gold!

We'll have that bunch well greased with whiskey soon enough, and before geese fly south they'll sell their mamas for a crock of that vision juice!"

Boone Fawley took no serious note of what Clovis Reed said or of what it meant. He was actually flabbergasted that Chorine had not started squealing like a pinch-tail cat or that Molly had not raced for the rifle when the Cherokees first appeared. Not once in all his thinking did he remark it odd that here in the deep wilderness illiterate men had fluently expressed themselves in three languages.

TWO

SATAN'S FROLIC

Darkness which may be felt.

—Genesis 10:21

6

To Boone Fawley, a grove of big trees had always meant solid ground underfoot. But the morning they plunged off the willow-choked back side of the Mississippi sandbar, he discovered that maybe all creation was not ordered as he'd always supposed. Stretching before them was a classic cypress swamp. The water was calm and looked black. It was shin-deep to a grown man, and from it rose tree trunks like cathedral pillars swollen at the base. The mature trees lifted almost fifty feet above the water before the first limbs appeared. Root knees, like slender beehives, protruded above the water surface, and on almost every one were at least two big, transparent-winged dragonflies.

The soil beneath their feet was surprisingly firm, like a moist carpet. Even so, moving the cart through it sometimes took not only the horse and mule, Molly whipping them with rein ends, but Boone, Clovis Reed, and Coppertop hauling on towropes. It was John Fawley's task to wade near the team and slash the water surface with long willow switches any time he saw the telltale V-shaped ripples that marked the progress of a swimming snake. The cow was Questor's particular concern, not solely because she had no experience in negotiating cypress swamps but because of milk snakes. They were no sooner in the water than Clovis Reed related this

79

already timeworn myth of reptiles that attached their mouths to a cow's teat and sucked out all the milk. The Fawleys had no experience with such strange creatures and so no basis for disbelief. Clovis Reed may have believed it himself, but if not, had his private chuckle watching Questor spend a lot of attention on the cow's udders, especially after that part of her anatomy had been submerged when she stepped into a pothole in the earth floor of the swamp. Unlike the pigs, who were tied in the cart, the cow had to wade and made everyone aware of her irritation at such indignity by bawling constantly. Chorine's duty was to stay in the cart and make sure nothing fell in the water, and nobody entertained any serious thought of trying to get her out of it.

Molly had lost both her shoes but was unaware of it until they paused for breath at high noon. By that time, Coppertop had caught three more cottonmouths, killing and cleaning them with his hands as they had seen him do before, and with a wide grin at Chorine he draped the fat tube of white meat over the cart's tailgate. By this time, Chorine had lost her embarrassment about looking at the big African; maybe because his torso was covered with mud and twigs and cypress needles. Coppertop was so enthusiastic in the cart pulling and snake catching that as often as not he was on all fours in the water like a great black dog.

With the Frenchmen remaining on the sandbar to structure the trading post, Boone Fawley hadn't supposed that only two men could make such a difference in their passage of the swamp. Clovis Reed said he and his African would not only show them their homesite but help them get it started. And, he said, he'd leave the Fawleys his own musket in view of his having plenty of extra ones in his party. Boone Fawley was so grateful he forgot to worry about Manuel Lisa and Old Man Chouteau and Cherokees and Osages.

About midafternoon, the swamp began to disappear and there were little islands of sandy soil. Cypress were displaced by swamp chestnuts, and as they came onto more solid footing there were shagbark hickory, black oak, and finally pecan. At sunset, they were in a dense grove of walnut where squirrels were so numerous Coppertop and John had seventeen of them down and skinned by the time it took to start a fire and boil water for sassafras tea. Coppertop rolled these tiny pelts into a bundle and stowed it in the cart for future consideration. Even in the fading light, the skins attracted a monstrous cloud of gnats and flies.

After they ate, Coppertop cut off enough of his buckskin leggings to make Molly a pair of moccasins.

They were ready to roll into blankets—Chorine already had—when Coppertop, squatted at the fire, looked up into the foliage where the firelight made a dancing orange light on the underside of the canopy, rolled his bloodshot eyes, and made little squishing sounds with his lips.

"Tree doves," Clovis Reed said.

And they loaded everything that would shoot with small pellets. Then men and boys went into the darkness about a hundred paces, and there, as Coppertop pointed, everybody fired up into the blackness where all Boone Fawley could see was the sparkle of stars through gaps in the black foliage. Questor brought a flaming torch, and they picked up the dead passenger pigeons that had fallen like plump apples.

"Breakfast," said Clovis Reed.

Coppertop cleaned the birds with his hands, scooping the breast out free of ribs and feathers with one powerful pinch, shouting "Ha!" with each bird. The breasts were all that was kept, and they were very small. Next morning, there was enough for a few mouthfuls for everyone. It amazed Boone Fawley there was no more than that from the sixty-four birds they had killed. He kept thinking of the vast number of them that must have been in that flock roost, and he told Molly there was no worry about killing a lot of the pigeons because they were so numerous they would last forever.

The homestead site was as good as Clovis Reed had promised. Rich, alluvial soil on a flat wooded plain with the St. Francis River close enough to the east of it that you could hear the water running in its sandstone banks on a quiet night. They had found the St. Francis easily fordable, and its sparkling clear water promised sun perch and bass and blue catfish. The timber was mixed, plenty of hardwood, good for firewood and split rail fences, clusters of shortleaf pine and cedar, soft and fine to cut, good for building-logs and shingles.

It became a frenzy of work, Clovis Reed and Coppertop leading the way. Felling trees and trimming them, splitting shingles, cutting the pines into measured lengths, dragging them into the spot where Molly wanted her cabin. Clearing one patch for corn, another for pole beans and sweet potatoes, then plowing, shallow furrow, the mule working first with Clovis Reed then with Boone Fawley.

Coppertop built a hardwood-and-mud fireplace and chimney with a hearth of sandstone he'd carried from the St. Francis, smooth as glass, polished by centuries of running water. The cabin would be one room and a chicken coop abutting square against it along one side, cabin and coop both with a slab door, leather hinged.

"You have to pen them chickens inside ever' night, Miz Fawley," Clovis Reed said. "Out here, fox or coon or weasel eat ever' last one of 'em first night they left outside. You need a dog. I'll see about that when I get that cookstove you want down from St. Genevieve."

Split-rail stock pen for the horse and mule and cow, in one corner an overhang of slab pine for a roof and a pigsty.

"Them pigs can take keer of theirselves," Clovis Reed said. "None of them varmints like fox or weasel, or even snakes, will come around pigs. Let 'em forage the woods for acorns, too. Don't waste no corn on 'em. This time next year, you'll have a whole farrow from that little sow."

"Won't snakes bite little pigs?" Chorine asked.

"Why Miz Chorine, a hog'll eat a snake like it was popcorn."

And no need for digging a well. Molly said the river was so close even when she washed clothes they'd just tote pots to the bank of the St. Francis.

John Fawley had become the official hunter of their party. Each day he went into the woods and came back with meat. Always squirrel and rabbit. Once with a turkey Boone Fawley figured must have weighed twenty pounds dressed. And a white-tailed deer, a small doe that they roasted whole over a pit fire in what was quickly becoming the front yard.

At night, Coppertop cured hides. Starting with that bundle of squirrel skins left in the cart that were now becoming very ripe, indeed. He pinned them, fur down, to hewn pine planks, and leaned them against trees above red ant hills, and when Questor went and saw the sun shining on the hides and the ants swarming up to clean the meat from them down to the gray, he said, "Ha!"

On the morning of the ninth day, they finished the cabin roof. That evening Molly made her first fire in the fireplace where some of the mortar was still damp. And it started to rain. It rained all night, a gentle shower, and everybody slept under a roof except Coppertop. He slept where he always did, in the woods.

"Ha!" said Questor.

Together under their blanket, Boone and Molly agreed it was an act of Providence, raising this cabin in almost the same time it had taken the Lord to build the universe.

And the rain, just after seeds were in the ground.

"It's going to be fine, just fine," Molly said.

In the morning, Clovis Reed and the African would be returning to their trading operation, and it made Boone Fawley a little uneasy. He knew he could ask nothing more of them. He had to be grateful, even if they were Lisa men.

With dawn, they discovered that Coppertop had used most of the rest of his leggings to make them each a pair of moccasins—the curing hides in the woods not yet ready for such use—leaving him astonishingly naked. Even Chorine didn't seem to mind seeing just about all there was to see except that absolute proof of his manhood. Sitting out there in the rain, in the dark, too, because the rain doused the outside fire, he made those moccasins with his knife and strips of rawhide and those huge, wonderful hands with the white palms.

Boone Fawley would have something to remember about other things, too. That Chorine. Maybe the right bug had bit her coming through the cypress swamp. Because just before Clovis Reed and Coppertop started off in a lingering gray rain, Boone Fawley had seen Chorine standing with Clovis Reed behind the cabin, saying good-bye. And the way she was saying good-bye was allowing Clovis Reed to kiss her mouth. And his sister allowing anybody to kiss her mouth was something even more astounding to Boone Fawley than the speed with which those two men had raised this homestead.

So after no more than a moment of rest after breakfast, in the still misting rain, Boone Fawley got his family organized and out and working. Boone Fawley reckoned, maybe this wasn't going to be as bad as he'd thought. Once accustomed to gnats and biting flies and mosquitoes, maybe not so bad after all. Hands would harden up soon. Leg muscles stop aching. It didn't even bother him much that no matter what it was Clovis Reed and Coppertop tried to teach them, the boys got the hang of it quicker than he did. Hell, he'd come to expect that.

One of the great services a pioneering greenhorn's friends could perform was to show what could be eaten without fear of poisoning. Otherwise, the hungry tenderfoot might never find anything to eat except what he'd shot. But as people like Coppertop knew, there was a considerable larder in the wilds.

Pokeweed, lamb's-quarter, sour dock, sheep shower. Cattail roots ground for flour, sweet gale tea, roasted white oak acorns, chinquapin nuts, wild rice, bullhead lily roots—swamp potatoes—hackberry, papaw, chokeberry, persimmon, kudzu flour, sunflower seed oil.

And wild cherry. Not for the fruit. The birds got that. But for the leaf mold under the trees. On a cool spring or fall morning, after a gentle rain, popping up through that mold would be spongy little columns you could cook with any oil—just barely heat—a delicacy found in famous restaurants world over but eaten by few because of the expense. Yet for the Fawleys, free for the picking, growing wild.

Morel mushrooms!

7

It was a busy summer.

Boone Fawley and the boys finally got a privy pit dug and a seat with one hole and a shack around it. The shack didn't have a roof, but it boasted three walls of split-rail oak. The open side faced toward the east woods, where the St. Francis River wasn't far off. Sitting there, with the open end facing as it did, Molly and Chorine could enjoy watching the cardinals in the cedars and the downy woodpeckers in the oaks.

Clovis Reed and Coppertop returned twice together, and once Reed came alone. Boone Fawley figured these as courting trips. Each time the Scot and Chorine managed to make some excuse about hunting wild gooseberries or some such thing, but they never returned with any fruit. Boone started thinking about things more serious than mouth kissing. And he began to wonder about his possible role in forcing the issue and, if he did, how a marriage out here in the wilds could be arranged, there likely not being a preacher within one hundred miles in any direction.

Then on the Scot's last visit of the year, in October when they had just finished harvesting and shelling and hand-grinding their corn and getting bean pods into the rafters to dry, Coppertop came, too, along with a little man in a long black robe and a hat with a flat crown and a brim wide enough to shade Molly's washtub. As soon as Boone Fawley perceived what this little man was, he wondered if maybe they were about to have a wedding right there in the cabin yard.

But nobody mentioned a wedding. Brother Robert was just another of those mobile Jesuits who periodically appeared on the Mississippi from New Orleans to Canada, a kind of leftover from the time old King Louis XIV had owned the river and French military and trading enterprises wouldn't have been complete without Black Robe Society of Jesus men, who somehow had always been able to control Indians more effectively than a whole squadron of cavalry.

Brother Robert spoke passable English, and he talked about crops and about this being good land, God willing, for taking red fox and some beaver, too, in the winter. Then offered to put a little blessing on it all before he departed, which he did in Latin as everybody kneeled down, using the sign language with his hands that Jesuits and God had worked out between them to make such affairs official. The Fawleys were impressed, especially Questor.

Well, not all the Fawleys. As soon as she realized what Brother Robert was, Molly had retreated to the cabin and stayed there all day without joining in any of the talk. After the Jesuit and Clovis Reed and Coppertop had left, she grumbled and muttered about abominable papists! And told Questor and John never to let her again catch them taking their hats off for some damned Roman.

"I thought he was a Frenchman," John said.

"Don't sass me, boy!" Molly said. "I know what he was."

"Well ding bust it, Mol," said Boone Fawley. "He was just a nice little man, and hell, he carried in the stovepipe, didn't he?"

It was true. The stated purpose of this visit had been to bring the cookstove Molly had asked Clovis Reed to get her out of St. Genevieve. Which had cost Boone two Spanish gold pieces. Clovis Reed had carried two stove lids and the oven door. The monk had carried the stovepipe sections. And of course, Coppertop had carried the stove. It wasn't a big stove, but it weighed as much as John and Questor put together, being solid cast iron.

Once, Coppertop brought a small anvil and some blank mule and horse shoes and stayed two days building a forge and a bellows next to the stock pen and then showing Boone and John how to use them.

Neither became in such a short time expert blacksmiths, but both could at least shoe the animals adequately without crippling them, although the mule bit Boone so many times during this learning process that Boone said he didn't care if he did cripple that log-head son of a bitch.

Then it was late October and the visits stopped for the winter because Clovis Reed said they would make a trip back upriver and lay in more trade goods for anticipated Osage and Cherokee trappers bringing in their bags in the spring.

The woods turned to glorious color. Metallic reds and oranges and yellows so glowing they seemed to give off heat. Boone Fawley said the leaves were such loud hues he hoped they didn't keep everybody awake at night. There was a different smell to wood smoke in the fall, and on windless evenings it lay about their clearing in blue-gray wisps as though reluctant to rise and disappear against the first glint of early stars. For days and nights on end they could hear, and sometimes see, the ducks and geese winging south along the great Mississippi flyway.

For the first time since leaving St. Louis, Boone Fawley had the opportunity to rest a moment and catch his breath. And doing so, with this time to think, wondered what the hell he was doing all alone out here in the wilderness. His sense of Clovis Reed and his party being away, somewhere upriver, was very strong.

Then almost imperceptibly, another sensing caused the goose flesh to ripple along his neck. That somebody he couldn't see was out there in the timber, watching him.

The first winter was dreadful in spirit and body. In spirit because they had never seen gray windy days and ice-coated trees and heavy snowfall without knowing that a short walk away, even within sight and call, were other people, other dwellings. Now with temperatures staying below freezing for days, adding to despondency, they looked out on nothing but the bare hardwoods, limbs as metallic and inhospitable as the iron grill palisades enclosing a prison compound.

And a dreadful winter in body as well. For they would face the possibility of starvation before the redbud sprouted violet and succulent in April.

Before the end of December, Boone Fawley and the boys were out cutting firewood. They'd badly underestimated what would be needed. The pine slats they'd pinned together for window shutters and doors had cracks in them now, and the wind came through in gusts. They used what cured squirrel hides they had left to stuff the cracks, but there were not enough because Molly had been using the hides to make leggings and smocks. They tried mud chinking, but it froze and cracked and fell out and each day it had to be done all over again.

The livestock grew gaunt. Corn cob and stalk silage was gone before the new year, everyone was into the woods hacking away at summer brush or cedar boughs or anything else they might carry to the horse and mule and cow. The cow's milk had no butterfat and finally dried up completely. The two pigs had disappeared before Christmas, off into the woods, and they never expected to see them again.

Despite their precautions, a weasel or skunk or God only knew what got into the coop and killed a dozen chickens in a blood frenzy, carrying off only three of the dead birds. The Fawleys ate the others, of course. But it meant fewer eggs. And then by mid-January, the hens stopped laying completely.

Out in the timber, game seemed to have disappeared. It wasn't true, of course. But deer and bear and turkey had become accustomed to having hunters around, which meant they were wary, and with leaf cover gone, it was hard for John to see anything before it saw him first. He always took the Pennsylvania rifle now, never buckshot in the musket Clovis Reed had left, because he knew that any game he saw would require a long shot. There was only one deer all winter. Usually, they felt lucky if John came in with two rabbits. Boone Fawley began to plan how to kill and butcher a horse.

So by February, there were only a few dry beans and cattail-root flour and some salt in the larder. Well, plenty of sassafras root. Breakfast was always the same. Tea and baked white-oak acorns. That was supper, too. Boone Fawley grew more taciturn. Chorine was just as silent, and she took all day to chink shutter cracks. The boys whittled hardwood dowels for the spring's building, whatever that might be. If they lasted until spring. Molly kept up a bombardment of talk. Sometimes she read the Bible, trying to find parts that were not too mournful and tragic. One day she announced that she would cut everybody's hair with her big shears, but there was such a violent burst of opposition that she satisfied herself with combing and making a queue for Boone and each of the boys and she secured the pigtail with a twist of the red Indian trade ribbon Clovis Reed had left them.

It was during the first week of February, according to Molly's reckoning, when they got their first real snow. There had been flurries before, a number of them, but the white ground cover had melted away quickly. This was a real snow, maybe as much as four inches over two days and stopping just at evening of the second night. At first light next morning, John was out with the rifle, hoping to track a deer. There was a firm, solid footing of snow. Nothing had fallen during the night, but the sky was low and gray and there was no wind and everybody expected it to start again soon.

"You see snow falling, you get home," Molly said. "I don't want you out there lost in the woods in a snowstorm."

"I will, Mama."

He was back in less than three hours, with no game in his hand. And his face was flint hard from something besides the cold. They stared at him, everything suspended. Molly mixing a cattail-flour paste at her home-hewn pine table, Boone and Questor squatted before the fire whittling hickory pegs, and all their breathing making vapor in the cold of the cabin. Only Chorine was not looking at John's strangely stiff face. She was rolled in a blanket at one corner of the room.

"Somebody's been out yonder at the corn patch," John Fawley said, his voice breaking with almost every word because he was at that age, or maybe because of something else. "Last night, after the snow stopped!"

"Somebody?" Molly asked, her hands still in her wooden mixing bowl.

"Two of 'em. Like they was standin' there a long time."

"Watchin' the house?" Boone Fawley asked, still holding a hickory stake and a clasp knife.

"I reckon. Their toes was mostly pointed this direction. I was out west, lookin' for deer sign, and I come acrost a campsite. Fire and a lot of tramped-down snow. I don't know where they come from. They was there, I reckon, when the snow started. But I seen where they left, comin' this way, so I followed the tracks. They went plumb to the St. Francis, and they bedded down in the snow, alongside the river. Then the whole bunch went on down to the river and I reckon crossed over. But they was two of 'em come down here from that place, I seen them tracks, and right beside of em' tracks back to the main bunch."

"So you mean it looked like they was mostly bedded down and two of 'em come down here and then went back and everybody crossed the river?" Boone asked, still holding his stick and knife.

"That's what I reckon," said John.

Chorine's head had appeared above her blanket, and her eyes were large and round, as though she might be expecting to see one of those serpents from Eden.

"Them two took a long look at us," John said. "The snow out yonder at the far side of the corn patch is stomped down so they moved around some. Then went back."

"How many?" Boone Fawley asked.

"Two."

"I mean that crossed the river. The whole bunch."

"Well, maybe twenty. Their tracks went into that upper ford by the red gum snag. Looked like they was headed over to the Mississippi."

The breathing in the cabin had become very loud, louder than the huff of air up the flue from the burning logs in Molly's stove.

"All that since the snow stopped?"

"They was tracks hadn't been snowed on, so it had to be," said John. "It wouldn't have took long to cover the distance. I done it right quick. So while them others was bedded down at the ford, them other two could have been down here half the night, out yonder at the corn patch."

"You tell what kinda shoes?"

"Just moccasins. I don't know one kind from another. But they was all afoot. No horses."

Boone Fawley turned from his elder son and stared into the fireplace where a single log was burning to help Molly's stove fight off the cold. He bent and gently placed his hickory stake and pocket-knife on the dirt floor. Everyone was watching him.

"Well?" Chorine yelled, her head up above her blankets like a turtle's. "What do you aim to do about it?"

After a moment, Boone Fawley shook his head. His first impulse was to take this as an excuse to hitch the team and start back for the big river.

"We ain't gonna do nothin'," he said and then hurried on as much to reassure himself as to explain to the others. "We scald out of here now, we ain't gonna find Clovis Reed. Him and his people gone back up to Cape Girardeau or New Madrid or somewheres to lay in more goods for his spring tradin'. He told us that. Besides, in this weather, I doubt them animals could make it through that swamp. I know damned well we'd have a peck of trouble tryin' to get through it afoot. So we'll stay right here where we're at."

"Nobody goes outside," said Molly.

"Christ's sweet sake, Mol, we need more far wood right now, and we need to hunt. Without you think we can start eatin' these logs and this dirt floor."

"All right. But nobody goes outside by hisself. And Questor, no more catfish trotlines in the St. Francis, either."

"Come spring, we'll go," said Boone.

Then Molly spoke. Her two sons looked at her, a little startled maybe, because there was some kind of sharp edge to her voice they'd never heard before.

"No we won't," she said. "This here is ourn. We worked to make it. I'll live on this land, or they'll have to bury me in it!"

"Oh my God," Chorine wailed and yanked the blanket over her head.

And that night before he slept, Boone Fawley figured that he'd been wrong all along, worrying about his sons getting so smart they'd call the tune in this family. It wasn't them who were going to call the tune. It was his wife.

I t was going into March, and their short casts into the woods had produced little meat for the pot. Boone and Molly had already discussed what would be better to kill first, the cow or the horse. All the animals had been set loose to forage, but they were usually within sight of the cabin and would be no problem to find and bring in for the slaughter. They both agreed it would be the horse.

Each morning since John had made his discovery of somebody watching the cabin, Molly had risen at dawn and gone to the four sides of the cabin to peer out through the cracks. Only then would she poke life into the stove fire for boiling sassafras tea. There wasn't much more, now, and for some time they had all been going to bed at night hungry. But on this morning, a bright sunny one, Molly didn't poke up the fire after her look but took the Clovis Reed musket first and then shook her husband awake with loud whispers of considerable urgency.

There was a man standing not ten paces from the door. He was wearing a fur-side-out coat and a turban. Squatting beside him was another man, similarly dressed, who held a redbone hound pup under each arm.

"Sweet Christ, it's that man we seen at the sandbar," Boone Fawley whispered. "That man named Tub."

Boone Fawley felt naked walking out with nothing on but his deerhide smock. The Cherokees' expressions did not change when Fawley emerged. They observed him with obsidian eyes that revealed no interest in him or what he had on, and he got the feeling they would have been the same had he walked out stark naked. It was cold and Boone Fawley was shivering, as were the pups under the squatting Cherokee's arms. Boone expected there would be a lot of preliminary talking before they got to the point, which is how he'd always heard Indians did such things. But not this time. Tub came directly to the point, speaking as he had that night on the sandbar, in English.

Tub said that Clovis Reed had informed him that the Fawleys needed a dog, and it so happened Tub's band had a redbone hound bitch with them who littered during the winter—well, in the fall— and so here he was to give Clovis Reed's friends a couple of those dogs if Boone Fawley wanted them.

It all happened so fast it made Boone Fawley a little dizzy. The Cherokee had hardly stopped speaking when Questor was past his father and had the two dogs by the scruff of the neck and dragged them back into the cabin, laughing all the while. Even the squatting Cherokee grinned a little and Molly said something about paying for the dogs, but before Boone Fawley could say a word, the two Indians were walking away toward the woods below the bean patch fence. Boone Fawley stood there with his mouth open a little, watching as the Cherokees disappeared into the far trees. Still rubbing sleep from his eyes, John ran past him with the rifle, down toward the bean patch, and looked into the timber for a long time before turning and coming back.

"Well, damn," Boone Fawley said and turned into the house, realizing how cold he had become.

Everybody was excited about the dogs, and the dogs were excited, too, about to wring their butts off with tail wagging and everybody petting them and laughing, even Chorine. All except John. He stood back, watching, then leaned the rifle in one corner but still stood back, serious and unsmiling.

"Why sweet Christ," said Boone Fawley. "Them's nice men. And here we been all puckered up fer a month worryin' about somebody out there watchin' us, and it just them friendly men with that dog about to have her pups."

"Pa," John said. "Down at the woods. I seen 'em go off toward the river. I could see 'em through the trees."

"Yes siree, that's who it was, remember John in the snow, them tracks you seen. It was these good men, that's all."

"I don't reckon it was, Pa."

Everybody except the dogs stopped laughing and being excited. "Why?"

"These Cherokees was all astride horses."

By noon of the day the Cherokees came, Molly had taken the larger dog outside, cut its throat, drained the blood into a bucket, skinned it, cleaned the intestines, and brought everything back into the cabin except hide, head, and paws. She even had the skinned-out tail.

"Chorine," Molly said, paying no attention to all the others staring at her wide-eyed, "get into some heavy clothes. Take John with you. Following along toward the direction them Cherokees went, they ain't likely to be nobody there with them passin'. Go to that old marsh and see if you can't find a few bullhead lily bulbs we missed last year. Don't peel 'em there, get 'em back here. And John, take the rifle and pistol, too. And get on back here in a hurry.

"I'm fixin' to make a blood stew out of this dog!"

It wasn't a bad stew. Molly seasoned it with a handful of dried shepherd's purse pods she'd had since October, and the black pepper flavor killed the taste of liver, or most of it anyway; there was plenty of salt in the blood to make the dozen or so bullhead lily bulbs Chorine and John found taste like potatoes for anybody hungry enough not to be particular; and the pup even had considerable fat so there was a good, healthy grease feeling to it.

During preparation and the family eating, the other dog sat quietly in one corner, watching. Maybe thinking about how soon he would be in the same pot. Afterward, they threw him the bones of his brother, and he showed little reluctance in cracking them open for the marrow. So they named him Cannibal.

None of them was aware that the ancestors of these hounds were sturdy redbone hunters the Cherokees bred in the hills of eastern Tennessee. It wouldn't have mattered had they known. All they were interested in was that for the first time in many weeks they went to bed with full bellies.

Lying awake that night, Boone Fawley figured it was a fine day, but it was like a rosebush with plenty of thorns in it. The worst of which was those horses. Because if that bunch who left their tracks in the snow had not been these Cherokees, then they could only have been Osages. And Boone Fawley didn't like the thought of Osages, most especially if they were Osages who thought he might be overly friendly with a bunch of Cherokees.

Maybe it was all foolishness. The very next day, John got a big buck deer not two hundred paces from the north corn patch. Maybe the dog had changed their luck. Maybe the winter was over, and with it, their troubles. Boone Fawley started thinking about clearing land for a bigger corn crop, a much bigger corn crop.

8

Within a week of the first appearance of the redbud, Coppertop came. Even before he could hallo the house from the east woods, Questor Fawley saw him and ran, leaping and shouting, and Coppertop emerged from the timber, his laughter a great roar. Boone Fawley, plowing the newly cleared ground adjacent to the old corn patch, watched his son and the big African frolic and dance toward the cabin where Cannibal had set up a furious barking, already that deep-throated redbone voice even though he was still just a pup. Molly and Chorine rose and waved beside the boiling pot in the front yard where they had been picking the pin feathers from three plucked snow geese John had shot that morning in one of the backwaters of the cypress swamp, arresting them in their journey to Canada, shooting them while they still sat on the water, using buckshot because nothing lighter would penetrate their feathers. And just behind the boy and the former slave came Clovis Reed, shouting, waving, and grinning, astride a small bay horse still wearing long winter hair.

"Well, mule," said Boone Fawley, "I reckon that ties the knot. Spring has finally commenced."

To fix the exact time, Boone Fawley took Old Noah's stem-wind watch from a smock pocket and snapped it open and observed to the mule that it was past midafternoon, and that this was good because it meant that not too much labor time would be wasted, Boone Fawley knowing that the rest of this day, and even into evening, would be spent in the telling of experiences of the past winter.

Boone Fawley could just as well have known it was past mid-afternoon by looking at the sun. But he took every opportunity to take out Old Noah's watch, maybe because it was a link to St. Louis and civilization.

Coppertop, in his usual rush to be doing something with his hands, took Questor to the edge of the west woods and began to show the boy how to make fish traps of twigs lashed together with rawhide thongs, which he cut from the fringes of his new leggings. Boone Fawley noted the new leggings and supposed that his sister was gratified to see that the black man had finally covered his nakedness, at least from the waist down. The fish trap enterprise was of double benefit because it removed Coppertop's unintelligible and constant talk from the precinct of the cabin's front yard where everybody else gathered.

There was more than an abundance of conversation around the goose-scalding pot, with interruptions and laughter and exclamations. John Fawley squatted there wide-eyed as he observed his elders, perhaps wondering how anyone could make heads or tails of what was being said with everybody trying to talk at once. All except Chorine, whose main contribution was to reach out from time to time and tentatively touch the fringed buckskin shirt of Clovis Reed as though to reassure herself that he was really there.

Then there were Clovis Reed's spring gifts, taken from a burlap sack tied behind the saddle of the little bay. Coffee beans with a New Orleans stamp on the bag; a double hatful of already sprouting sweet potato plantings; a very large sack of seed corn; salt and sugar; a can of coal oil and a glass-globed lantern; and a blue glass bottle with a label announcing Dr. Rotar's vegetable-and-herb-oil purgative and liver sustainer, also good for the gums of teething babies and the pain of ingrown toenails. Clovis Reed, daringly Boone Fawley thought, said that in a pinch, you could drink an entire bottle of Dr. Rotar's oil and get very drunk indeed if you were willing to endure sitting in the privy for the next three days. Chorine blushed scarlet, and Molly squealed with laughter and covered her face with both hands.

There was still enough nip in the air for their breathing to make

vapor as the sun went down, but they took no notice and prepared
to cook the three geese in the yard, spitted over the hickory fire after
the pot of water was removed. As these preparations were being
made, the Fawleys gave their account of a bad winter—leaving out
the part about eating the dog, but explaining that Clovis Reed's
friends the Cherokees had brought Cannibal—and Clovis Reed said
he was expecting many more migrant savages from east of the river,
more Cherokees, that is, and he was anxious to get back to his
sandbar and help his Frenchmen set up the trading post. Boone
Fawley heard in such talk the echo of Manuel Lisa marking out a
new batch of customers for a profitable mercantile venture, albeit in
Chouteau trading territory.

By the time the geese were cooked and it was full dark, with all
the woodland frogs and bugs making their early spring chorus of
discordant racket, and with Questor and Coppertop back from their
fish trap manufacture, and Molly serving chunks of dripping goose
on their St. Louis tin plates, Clovis Reed was giving them all the
news from the "outside."

President Jimmy Madison was being inaugurated this very
month and that likely meant the end of Mr. Jefferson's embargo
against selling goods to belligerents in the usual war going on between England and France. It now looked as though the United
States of America was headed into war with Great Britain because
the British navy was always stopping American ships at sea in their
blockade against Napoleon. But more important, because the English in Canada were continuing to keep the Indians in a state of
excitement and hostiles were always attacking settlers in places like
Wisconsin, now a district of the territory of Illinois. There was now
the ominous threat that the redcoats were about to try retaking the
north side of the Ohio Valley once more and perhaps even to march
down the Mississippi to God only knew where, maybe even to New
Orleans. Which, of course, would be very bad for all of them.

None of this English, Napoleon, Canadian, Indian rigamarole
held much interest for Boone Fawley, who figured all of it was
happening so far away it would never affect anything in the wilderness. Who the hell would want this place? he kept asking himself.
So he was glad when the last grease was licked from fingers and they
retired to the cabin to sleep. At least, they tried to sleep. It wasn't
easy with Clovis Reed's snoring, which was the most impressive

snoring Boone Fawley had heard since his mother Otis had died. At least, he thought, so long as I can hear that racket, I know Clovis Reed is not out in the dark someplace with Chorine.

Their visitors left as the gray dawn broke. It was almost impossible to say any good-byes because at that time there was a flock of north-flying ducks so dense they blackened the sky, their calls a cacophony that swallowed all other sound. They were low-flying, having just risen from wet ground barely out of sight south of the homestead. John Fawley was in a dither getting the musket loaded and striking out toward the ducks' resting pools, hoping to catch a few stragglers still sitting, disappearing in the timber south of the cabin even as Clovis Reed and Coppertop disappeared into those in the east.

It would be a busy day, Boone Fawley preparing the biggest field for the seed corn Clovis Reed had brought and Molly and Chorine planting sweet potatoes in the already plowed south patch. Questor, of course, was off to the St. Francis to set his fish trap.

As Boone Fawley sweated that morning, struggling with the mule to make furrows around the stumps of just-cut trees, he wondered about the things Clovis Reed had said. Boone Fawley was one of those pioneers—and you might well wager he was one of many— who had no starry-eyed ideal of democracy, or ambition to be a part of governing. Voting and jury duty and paying taxes and such things. "Democracy" and "republic" were words he could hardly define and made no effort to understand. For him, it would be best if he were far removed from government and it from him. Independence from governors and legislatures and sheriffs and judges was indeed the only positive aspect Boone Fawley could assign to the vast wilderness.

So what he wondered about, as he and the mule and the plow turned the black earth in crooked furrows, was Clovis Reed's talk of the trading post and all those Cherokees coming across the river from Tennessee.

Boone Fawley and his kind didn't know it, but maybe there were a lot of folks other than migrating aboriginals wandering about the Mississippi Valley. There were an astonishing number of British gentlemen who decided at about this time to mount expeditions in search of butterflies, hunt game, paint pictures, and otherwise conduct themselves like tourists.

You would suppose that such a thing was reasonable considering the English curiosity about unknown places like Africa and Australia and Indochina. But the intriguing aspect of all this tourism into wild and unsettled parts of North America was that so very, very many of the intrepid travelers were either active or retired officers of the British Army or gentlemen closely associated with the London War Office. So you begin to suspect that these people were not as interested in butterflies or landscapes as they were in avenues of infantry approach and strong positions for controlling rivers and roads with cannon.

Well, beginning in 1809, there appeared in various areas of the Mississippi drainage system a number of Englishmen, many with titles, all wearing expensive clothes, armed with the finest rifles from the famous London gunsmith shops, who attached themselves as inconspicuously as possible to different sorts of enterprises so that they might have a look at rivers and roads and populations and woodlands and swamps and maybe even units of American militia if any came handy. And many of these gentlemen, within a short time, became very efficient frontiersmen themselves, and in some instances were trusted and valuable additions to whatever endeavor it was they had joined.

Americans paid them little mind. There were all kinds of Europeans wandering around. And most Americans in the great midsection knew nothing about military intelligence. How it was collected or used. And besides, these English lords or earls or whatever they were most generally moved about where population was anything but dense or sophisticated.

In the area where the Fawleys were trying to farm, almost everyone lived in a few widely scattered settlements along either the Mississippi or Arkansas rivers. The census of 1810 showed that in country that would soon become part of Missouri Territory and eventually be the territory and then the state of Arkansas, there were 1,062 inhabitants. About a third of these were black slaves. And of course, Quapaws and Osages and itinerant Cherokees were not counted at all.

It was certainly a wonderful country in which to look at butterflies and landscapes.

John Fawley had seen no further sign of passing Indians since those moccasin tracks in the snow. At least, not the same kinds of Indians. On two occasions, there had been horse tracks passing within a half mile of the clearing, but everybody reckoned these were Cherokees, and they'd already decided there was no danger from Cherokees.

So they had relaxed a little. And then a little more as the labor of getting crops cultivated took much of their thinking and at night they were too exhausted and sore backed to think of anything but sleep. Finally, they could laugh at themselves for the near panic that had seized them the day they'd discovered somebody had been watching the cabin. The weather helped. When the gray, cold, sleet-and-snow days gave way to warm spring rains and the exploding greens of the hardwoods billowed up toward emerald sky and brilliant sun, it was difficult to maintain any urgent sense of danger.

It was that kind of bright, cloudless day when the four horsemen came, riding in single file from the timber along the north edge of the big cornfield, two of them leading heavily laden pack mules. Cannibal's barking announced them only after they were in sight, as though they had deliberately come to the homestead from downwind. As soon as he saw them, Boone Fawley knew they were Chouteau men. He didn't know how. He just knew.

The women were in the south potato patch with hoes, fighting weeds that seemed to appear full-grown overnight in this place. The boys were somewhere along the St. Francis, harvesting fish traps, which had become possibly their greatest joy once Coppertop showed them the talent of tricking a bass or catfish into a wicker cage. Boone Fawley was in the yard, working with planed pine slabs to perfect window shutters that didn't have cracks so large as to allow the wind to howl through the cabin on winter nights.

The horsemen came past the cornfield and into the yard, unhurried and calm, showing no sign of hostility even though each of them carried a rifle across his thighs. Boone Fawley rose to meet them, feeling no apprehension. There was only a small knot in his stomach, which might be expected any time white visitors appeared in this uninhabited land. Only a little nervousness, trying to remember how you went about greeting strangers in a civil, hospitable manner.

"How do," Boone Fawley said, as the men reined in their horses and the two in the lead dismounted.

The obvious leader of the group said his name was Demaree, and he was the kind of Frenchman-trader Boone Fawley had seen many times in St. Louis, although this one was wearing buckskins that were almost new. There was no grease or campfire soot on his leggings. His face was dark and rather pinched, and his black beard was well trimmed, another indication that maybe he had only recently departed civilization. The other man who dismounted was a dandy who announced himself as Captain Evelyn Hadley-Moore, late of the Twenty-third Hussars of the King's Own Guard. Hadley-Moore had fought against Napoleon in Spain and was now on an extended leave of absence from the British army to convalesce from his wounds. He wore rich woolens and polished leather and a billed cap, and carried a very expensive double-barreled rifle.

As Demaree, Hadley-Moore, and Boone Fawley stood in the wood chips of the shutter work and shook hands, the remaining two men remained mounted, watching with the intensity of foxes. Demaree waved a hand toward them and said they were Fulton and Maddox, an introduction which neither of them acknowledged with the slightest nod of the head. Feeling their eyes on him, Boone Fawley had a small shiver go down his back because he had seen a few men like this in St. Louis, too. They were the breed of men Old Noah Fawley had told about in the days of Kentucky exploration, and now become the leading edge of civilization's advance into the West. They were Celtic, tawny haired, yellow eyed, faces formed by flat planes and sharp angles, clean-shaven, six feet tall, covered foot to crown in hide clothes. Boone Fawley knew them to be of that class of men who had taken to the wilderness as though born to it, as though it were a holy mission, becoming expert in it and the most successful predators in North America, with reputations up and down the Mississippi River and west of it as far as white men ventured that inspired both admiration for their resourcefulness and fear of their savagery.

Boone Fawley was finely tuned to the calm of his women. They were standing in the potato patch, leaning on their hoes, Chorine's face shaded by her poke bonnet, Molly, bareheaded, holding up one hand to shade her eyes from the sun. Had they been close enough to see these two men, Fulton and Maddox, Boone Fawley knew their complacency would have been disturbed, so he was glad they were at some distance and content for the moment to stay there. Cannibal sensed another kind of presence here, too, and was still barking at the two men who remained in their saddles, even as they slowly turned and led horses and mules back to the stock pen. They paid no more attention to the dog than they would have a casually passing gnat. When Boone Fawley threw a wood chip at Cannibal, the dog stopped his barking and, glaring back with looks of reproach, trotted to the south field and pranced around the women, still stiff legged, tail up and not wagging, looking back again to watch as Fulton and Maddox dismounted at the stock corral, tied all the lead lines to the top pole, then squatted and took out clay pipes and began to smoke. They held their rifles across their thighs, and each of them had the butts of pistols showing now under the hem of their smocks, as well as long sheath knives and double-bitted English-made hatchets, like miniature battle-axes from the days of Bosworth Field.

"Aw, yes," said Captain Hadley-Moore, smiling broadly, showing rows of tiny teeth beneath a finely clipped mustache. "Our Scots and Welsh, now turned to creatures of jungle and desert. Do not be offended if they are lacking in civility."

They sat on Boone Fawley's upturned log yard furniture, and the Frenchman produced a small jug, as Boone Fawley expected that he would. They spoke in English, though Demaree's was slightly fractured, and many of the words Captain Hadley-Moore used were beyond Boone Fawley's comprehension. Naturally, they discussed the weather. And the lateness of many of the wildfowl flying to summer nests in Canada. They passed the jug. The visitors said there was an outbreak of cholera up the Ohio and everyone hoped it didn't get this far south.

Finally, Demaree seemed to give Captain Hadley-Moore a signal, and the Englishman reached inside his military-style tailored jacket and pulled forth an oilpaper sack and handed it to Boone Fawley. Boone looked into the sack, and Demaree said it was a gift specifically for him and his family.

"For Christ's sweet sake," Boone Fawley said. "Mr. Chouteau give my mama a sack of this horehound candy the day I was born. He give my wife a sack of it when we got married."

"He said you would know where it came from," said Hadley-Moore.

"Our Old Gentleman, he hear you come down beeg river. Last year," Demaree said. "On flatboat."

Boone Fawley recalled thinking of Chouteau people all along the river watching them pass with Clovis Reed's party. Nothing much moved on that river without Auguste Chouteau knowing of it.

"Mr. Chouteau is concerned about that company you joined," said Hadley-Moore. He was still smiling, but only with his teeth, and Demaree wasn't smiling at all but watching Boone Fawley's face with his intense, black French eyes. "That company is not in his best interests."

"Well now, we never joined nobody," said Boone Fawley, well aware that he was on the defense here. "We taken a ride on that flatboat all right, we done that. It was a sight better than tryin' to get down here where we wanted comin' through the woods."

"Of course," said Hadley-Moore.

"This Clovis Reed man," said Demaree, and Boone Fawley was in no way surprised that they knew the name, "you have some plan with him?"

"Yes," said Hadley-Moore, seeing Boone Fawley's perplexed expression. "Are you connected with Mr. Reed in any business venture?"

"Why no, he's just a neighbor. We floated downriver with him, and no, he's just a neighbor is all."

"These ones, they trade with In'yuns?" asked Demaree.

"I reckon so. He traded some truck with us."

"For furs and hides?" asked Hadley-Moore.

"Hell no, I paid him gold money for anything we got from him that he didn't just outright give to us, like a neighbor does sometimes."

"Of course. But the stove, you paid for that."

Sweet Jesus, Boone Fawley thought, these men must know how long my toenails are.

"Them men, they trade with lots In'yuns?"

"I don't know. They camp a far piece from us. We only had one bunch of heathens come to the yard here, the whole time we been at this place. A few Cherokees."

"Aw. Cherokees."

"Yeah, Clovis Reed said they was a lot of Cherokees comin' into this country."

"Yes, we know," said Hadley-Moore. Well, naturally you know, Boone Fawley thought. You know everything else. He was determined to keep his mouth shut.

"You trade with the Cherokees?" asked Demaree.

"No, we never."

"Here, have another sip, Mr. Fawley," said Hadley-Moore, passing the jug. "You see, we knew from our friends that you were here, and we came to pay our respects and to tell you Mr. Chouteau wants you to know that he continues to wish you well."

"That's real nice of Mr. Chouteau," said Boone Fawley, and he knew that some of the friends Hadley-Moore mentioned were likely the people wearing those moccasins that had made tracks in the snow at the edge of his corn patch.

"Sure, Our Old Gentleman, he says tell you, we visit you maybe every year when we come here, get you some supply when you need him."

"Yeah, well, like I say, it's nice to have Mr. Chouteau worry about us down here."

But the mood had changed now. Boone Fawley knew the inquiry was finished, and he assumed he'd passed any tests they had, though he wasn't sure what the tests were.

"We got rendezvous with some of our friends who trap and hunt all winter," said Demaree. "Few miles north here, on St. Francis. Our friends come, maybe soon."

"Yes, you'll have to visit us," Hadley-Moore said. "We'll likely be in the neighborhood a fortnight or more."

"That's mighty friendly of you," Boone Fawley said. "But right now, you folks just plan to have supper with us and stay the night. My woman's got a quarter of venison hangin' in the shade side of the house, and my boys, they'll be in directly from the St. Francis and they'll have some nice blue catfish or I'm mistaken."

"We'd be delighted," said Hadley-Moore.

The Fawleys had never been in such intimate proximity to a gentleman, especially an English gentleman who had two golden rings on his fingers, a silver snuffbox, and a metal cup that collapsed into a flat disk about the size of one of those Spanish coins Boone Fawley carried around his neck. The double-barreled rifle was a wonder to the boys, and Hadley-Moore allowed them to examine it minutely. John finally whispered to Questor that it wasn't really much account for heavy duty, the bores being not much over a quarter-inch diameter while their own Pennsylvania rifle was a full half inch.

The women, after an appropriate period of flustered shyness, became completely taken with the dashing captain as he bowed and scraped and kissed their hands, then entertained them with stories of his adventures among Spanish windmills and London theaters, then in slow motion demonstrated the steps of the most recently popular cotillion, which he assured them was the favorite dance of Dolley Madison in the new White House at Washington City, and as he danced about the fire he provided his own accompaniment by softly singing "Ta de da, ta de da!"

It was warm enough to be comfortable out of doors, and they kept the fire before the cabin going in a high pinewood blaze that threw soft cascades of orange light across the bright faces and their eyes shone. They simply ignored the mosquitoes. As Captain Hadley-Moore entertained, Boone Fawley and Demaree sat on the ground, backs against the wall, and became slowly and gently drunk on the Frenchman's whiskey. Twice Boone roused himself sufficiently to throw a wood chunk at Cannibal when the dog found it necessary to look toward the smaller fire at the stock corral and go stiff legged and start a low, menacing growl.

When the food was prepared, Questor carried a large haunch of deer meat and some catfish, fried on Molly's stove, to the fire where the two frontiersmen still squatted, smoking their pipes. When he returned, this having been his first close look at Fulton and Maddox, he whispered to John that they looked like cutthroat outlaws, and the way they stared at him, Questor allowed they would as leave eat him as the venison.

Before the evening was finished, Demaree gave the Fawleys two woolen blankets and a buffalo robe and a bag of Indian seed popcorn that he said should be planted right away and then there would be a crop by October. They'd begun to tap some of the sugar maples in the area, and as soon as Demaree started talking about popcorn, Questor had visions of maple syrup popcorn balls at Christmastime.

Finally, everybody bedded down, the Chouteau people all rolled into robes at the corral. Boone Fawley lay in the dark, struggling with a whiskey haze, trying to recall what all Demaree had said. There was a great horned owl just beyond the north field making his call. Once, far to the west, Boone Fawley heard the howl of a red wolf, and for some reason it made him think of those two wilderness men sleeping out by the stock pen.

One thing stuck in his mind clearly.

"Maybe next year," Demaree had said, "we bring you many trade stuff, no? From Our Old Gentleman. Trade goods, you know? Make a good trade post right here. Our friends come, trade with you all year, no?"

And Boone Fawley, whiskey haze or no, realized that all this attention from the Chouteaus didn't spring from some concern for Fawley safety and comfort but from advancing mercantile ambition.

He tried not to think of Clovis Reed.

9

The Chouteau party's rendezvous camp was just beyond the red gum ford in a black locust grove on the west bank of the St. Francis River. On the morning Demaree took his people out of the Fawley yard and rode north, Boone waited an hour and then sent his elder son to track them with instructions to stay unseen. He explained to Molly that it was just to keep a hold on what was happening in the neighborhood.

It was a little over four miles to the camp, all of it flat ground covered with oak and sycamore and hickory. Because of the distance, John did not return home until after dark, and Molly was almost in her fury stage over Boone sending the boy out on what she called a blamed fool goose chase! But once John was safe in the cabin, she was as eager as her husband to hear his report. It took a few moments for John to catch his breath because he'd run the last three miles, being somewhat uncomfortable out in the deep timber at night. You never could tell when you might run smack into a hungry panther or God only knew what all.

The rendezvous camp had already been set up, probably before Demaree came to the Fawleys' place because there was a pole corral for the stock and five locust log shelters covered with willow branches, the lettuce-green young leaves still on. And John figured the place had likely not been set up by Demaree at all. But by the others. Everybody stared at him. John stared back, silently, and Boone Fawley could see the boy was enjoying his importance.

"All right," shouted Chorine. "*What* others?"

John said he couldn't get too close, else he might be detected. So he stayed on a low bench of ground just west of the camp, a little less than a pistol shot from the shelters. There was a tall man, rigged out frontier style with fringed buckskins and a slouch hat, and he was skinny and looked a lot like Fulton and Maddox, and John had heard Demaree yell at the man once. What Demaree had yelled was "Williams."

So, Boone Fawley thought, that means they had three of those wilderness men, which seemed a lot just for coming to the St. Francis to trade with a few Indians. In fact, as far as Boone could see, just one such man was more than anybody needed for such a chore. But he stopped worrying about it as John told the rest.

There were two Indian men, very tall, with roached hair that had turkey wattles along the crown and mussel-shell ear decorations, and one of them was wearing yellow face paint and the other had a lot of tattoos across his naked chest. Just wavy blue lines, John said. And there were three Indian women, two of them stocky and wearing long hide smocks and moccasin-leggings, and one of them had ochre on her face and the other one staggered around considerably as though she might be drunk. The third woman was slender and her hide smock was decorated with elk teeth and red-dyed porcupine quills, and she made a great fuss once about getting the robes and blankets arranged just right in one of the shelters when Demaree went there and lay down to take a nap, or something.

Whatever he went there for, he had a few sips from a jug like the one he and Boone Fawley had been sucking on beside the cabin the night before. And it was about then that John realized it was getting late, and he crawled out of there and started home.

"Is that all?" Boone asked.

And John said no, there were a couple of carcasses hung on a tree limb, one a deer and the other looked suspiciously like one of the hogs that had run away from the Fawley place last winter, only now it was a hell of a lot bigger. And that in the pole corral was a herd of four mules and seven horses, all the horses those small

Indian-type ponies except for the big gray gelding the Englishman rode. One of the shelters was for stacking trade goods, John figured, and there he saw all their truck like blankets and pots and hatchets and an extraordinary number of those half-gallon jugs and a whole stack of what appeared to be Pennsylvania-made muskets.

Boone Fawley was happy and proud. Even though he took note of Molly frowning at the mention of those women. But he was proud because his own son had slipped in there and laid doggo like a red Indian and watched those people, which was just a good example of turnabout fair play because Demaree's bunch had learned so much about the Fawleys, and had been pretty snotty and superior about letting Boone Fawley know they had, too. He was so proud, in fact, that his pride seemed to swallow everything else John had told them, so he reassured everyone there was nought to worry about.

Molly had always warned Boone that pride goeth before a fall, and the fall for this pride came two days later.

They were surprised about midmorning when Captain Evelyn Hadley-Moore rode out of the woods on the north side of their clearing, wearing his trimmed mustache smile and loudly announcing that he'd come for a visit because none of their friends had arrived for trading yet and he'd begun to yearn for the companionship of lovely ladies and honest men. It was the signal for everyone to stop work, at least for a little while, and they sat in front of the cabin and had a drink of water, and Captain Hadley-Moore passed around a small tin of candied lemon rind, which they all said was the best thing they'd ever put in their mouths.

Later, the women went back to the north field to finish planting the popcorn Demaree had brought, and the boys, grumbling, went back with axes to the west woods where they were felling dead or near-dead oak and hickory for winter firewood. For most of the afternoon, Boone Fawley and Captain Hadley-Moore sat in front of the cabin talking as first one and then the other picked ticks off the dog. Boone had taken the glass globe off the lantern and lighted the wick and placed a small metal lid from one of Molly's empty black pepper cans over the flame; as they picked the ticks, they threw them onto the hot lid where the ticks snapped and cooked and turned into grease, which was good for polishing leather. Of course, the only

leather things the Fawleys had that were not rawhide were three
belts, and it took a real load of ticks to work up any amount of
grease, but as Molly said, every little bit helped.

Come evening, the purple shadows of the trees running out into
the yard from the west woods, where they could still hear the boys'
axes working, Captain Hadley-Moore mounted the big gray gelding. Before reining away, he paused and looked down at Boone
Fawley.

"Mr. Fawley," he said. "I know young boys are a venturesome
lot. But I think it best to tell you that the other day when our party
left here, one of your sons followed us to our camp and lay in hiding
to watch us, although we would have welcomed him to come in and
visit. You are aware, I'm sure, that being secretive around another
man's camp can be dangerous, especially when there are men in that
camp such as some of those we have with us. No harm done this
time, of course, but considering the kind of tragedy that might
occur, I would suggest that you instruct your boys well on how to
behave when they are out playing in the forest."

Captain Hadley-Moore's smile was brilliant under his mustache
as he wheeled the gelding about.

"Good day to you, sir, and come to our camp for a visit."

He waved to the women and doffed his hat as he rode on toward
the north woods, and Boone Fawley swore as he saw his wife and
sister gaily waving in return.

As he went back to sharpening stakes for pole beans, he spoke
to himself, aloud, and his curses were such that had Molly heard him
she would have insisted on reading from the King James Version
after supper. Possibly the verses from Genesis dealing with the
Thou-Shalt-Nots. Or maybe the chapter describing Abraham's
preparations to sacrifice his son Isaac.

Although Boone Fawley was furious that he had been patronized
by Hadley-Moore, he found that it was impossible to maintain
any resentment. The Englishman had an air of good fellowship
about him hard to resist. Besides, it was a little intoxicating for a man
of Boone Fawley's social station to have the attention of a gentleman
with Hadley-Moore's aristocratic origins.

It seemed that Demaree's friends were taking a long time coming, and the Englishman amused himself as they waited by frequent visits to the Fawley homestead, twice staying the night. He always slept in his robe beside the pole corral, explaining that it would be unseemly for a gentleman to sleep in the same room where a maiden was taking her rest, which, of course, made Chorine blush and stammer and swell with pride at being so shamelessly flattered.

Molly began to call Hadley-Moore "our English gentleman." He treated her with great respect, as he might a lady-in-waiting to the queen, and he shared with her certain culinary talents such as how to marinate overnight a roast of venison in crushed wild onions and milk—the cow had fleshed out on spring graze and was producing again, although not in quantity and with no butterfat at all—and how to crush boiled white oak acorns into a meal for battering catfish for slow baking in the oven.

"First thang you know, she won't be able to make our grub without he tells her," said Boone Fawley petulantly.

The boys became less and less enthusiastic with Hadley-Moore's visits. He had allowed them to examine his double-barreled rifle and even shoot it, one barrel each, so to speak, but after the excitement of that experience, the boys had little to look forward to when the Englishman came. It meant their father would spend the day sitting against the cabin wall with Hadley-Moore talking and sipping whiskey, while they did the ax and hoe and plow work instead of hunting, exploring, and running the St. Francis to harvest fish traps.

As for Boone, any resistance he had quickly crumbled in the face of Hadley-Moore's stroking of Fawley pride. Once he'd learned of Boone's lineage, he asked questions about Old Noah and returned repeatedly to an emphasis on Fawley heritage, which was British and not American, so he said. Neither did it harm Boone's ego that Hadley-Moore asked him so many questions, although there were damned few answers Boone could provide. Not about Old Noah but about other things. Like the location of trails and streams to the west and south, and how long it took to go from place to place, and where there was solid ground and where there was swamp. And strangest of all, whether anybody from Cape Girardeau or New Madrid or St. Genevieve had ever approached Boone Fawley about joining a militia unit. And how many American hunters there were in the woods along the river. And whether they used muskets or rifles. And if they used French gunpowder or English.

It didn't seem to matter much that Boone Fawley couldn't provide answers to Hadley-Moore's questions. The Englishman remained cheerful and perfectly willing to talk about all sorts of things when Boone began to ask some questions of his own, and it became quickly apparent that the Englishman knew a great deal more about the wilderness frontier than did Boone Fawley. And almost everything Hadley-Moore said would be of intense, and perhaps even critical, interest to somebody starting a homestead in the woods. As with that yellow paint John Fawley had seen at the rendezvous camp.

"You need fear nothing with sight of yellow paint," said Hadley-Moore. "It is from a past day, at least three generations ago. In that time, the Osages sold captive Pawnees and others to the French for slaves in the Sugar Islands. The Osages have symbols for everything. So they began to paint their faces with yellow when they went out on slave raids against other tribes. I don't know why they chose yellow. But they did. That trade was short-lived because these aborigines could not stand the heat of the cane fields in the Sugar Islands and died quickly. So the French began using Africans. But the Osages liked the color yellow so they still wear it sometimes, only as decoration, as perhaps the king's mistress would paint her cheeks with rouge.

"So you have nothing to fear from yellow. But black, that is something else. If you see an Osage with black on his face, do not turn your back to him."

There, against his cabin wall, sipping trade whiskey with this Englishman and hearing the occasional singing of his women as they worked and the sharp whack of an ax blade in the nearby woods and the whistle of a hunting hawk along the St. Francis River, smelling the sweet honeysuckle scent of the black locust blossoms, feeling the soothing warmth of afternoon sun on his skin and the soothing warmth of whiskey in his belly, Boone Fawley got his education in the people whom he was now sure had made those tracks in the snow last winter. At least, the only education he would ever have of them.

Hadley-Moore said the French had been along all these water routes over a hundred years ago, trading with the Osages. And the Osages allowed them into their country where the Frenchmen took

Osage women and learned Osage language because the French were the first to bring them guns and because the Osages knew the Heavy Eyebrows, which is what they called the Frenchmen, were there only to trade, not to take Osage land.

With the English, whom they called the Long Knives, there was a difference. The English would trade, too, but also they wanted to push the Indians out, to destroy the game. The Long Knives had no interest in Osage women and in learning Osage ways. They brought their own women, their own families, and they did not like to be around Osages or any of the other tribesmen. They wanted the Osages to keep far away.

Then there were the Americans, whom the Osages called the Heavy Eyebrow Long Knives. They were worst of all. They wanted to take all the land, and there were so many of them. They came like stampeding buffalo, destroying the forest, killing the game. They were always in such a hurry and were utterly ruthless. And savage fighters, as savage as any enemies the Osages had ever had, and the Osages had had enemies from the Sauk and Foxes to the Kiowas. And Boone Fawley thought of those two men who had come into his yard with Demaree, Fulton and Maddox, and felt the same little chill at the base of his neck that he had felt when he first saw them.

"You do know considerable about these red heathen," Boone Fawley said, maybe wanting to change the subject, wanting to slide away from the thought of barbarous Americans.

Hadley-Moore said his father had served in the area of the Great Lakes during the Rebellion, by which he meant the War for Independence. The senior Hadley-Moore had passed on to his son all he had learned of Indians. He himself, said Hadley-Moore, had been in New Orleans and along the Mississippi at the tail end of the Spanish period, looking for native flora for transplanting on the family estate in Staffordshire where his old daddy had retired to pursue a lifelong interest in botany. But his field trip in America looking for wild lilacs and pansies had to end when his services were required with Wellington in Spain. And now, said Hadley-Moore, he was back again to study the flora, and who could avoid the fauna as well, and what better way to do it than to join an organization such as Mr. Chouteau's? It all made sense to Boone Fawley.

"Perhaps I am cursed with a wanderlust," said Hadley-Moore.

"How I envy you, Mr. Fawley. You impress me as a man who enjoys his hearth fire each evening, a settled home. Am I right?"

"I expect so," said Boone Fawley. "It sho eats on me now and again that we ever left St. Louis."

"Yes, but a fine start here in a grand new country and you at the heart of it," said the Englishman. "And you'll be safe here. If you are a known friend of Our Old Gentleman, as Mr. Demaree calls him, and even more so if you become a trader to the Osages and they know they can depend on you.

"Others have the official license to trade with them now, but the Osages do not recognize pieces of paper signed in St. Louis. They'll go on trading with Our Old Gentleman so long as they can because they have been doing it for more than fifty years, before there were any plows in this country. So long as you are a Chouteau man, they will allow you to stay without harm, for after all, you bring only one plow."

Hadley-Moore laughed but Boone Fawley could not. That official license business, to trade with the Osages. It was only now that Boone Fawley realized that Manuel Lisa was the legal trader in this area and Demaree and his people the interlopers. Why hadn't he looked into such things before he made a decision to leave the security of those riverfront warehouses in St. Louis? He'd even heard people talking about court cases and such things, concerning trade with the Indians. But he'd paid no attention to this talk because he had such little use for courts and all that legal tomfoolery of Mr. Jefferson's republic. Well, Mr. Madison's, now. From the safety of St. Louis, he might have admired the Osages ignoring official tomfoolery, and the Chouteaus ignoring it as well. But all of it wore a different face out here on the edge of civilization where picking the right friends could be a matter of life and death.

Hadley-Moore was explaining about the women in the rendezvous camp, and Boone Fawley thought maybe he'd sensed that Molly was more than a little curious about it and he took this way of reassuring her. Tell husband, and the wife will learn. Well, maybe not, Boone thought. He sure as hell wasn't going to tell her all about that Manuel Lisa and Auguste Chouteau business and how he figured Demaree and Clovis Reed fit into it.

"Two of them are wives to the Osage men Demaree has with him," Hadley-Moore was saying. "They have been in St. Louis many times. Demaree calls the four of them his tame *tigres.*

"The young one, she's Demaree's woman. This is his fourth, or perhaps his fifth, squaw. Demaree came to St. Louis as a boy, escaping the discipline of Jesuits in Canada." And Hadley-Moore laughed. "He was associated with Auguste Chouteau almost from the day that settlement was laid out. And he spent that time with the Osages. His first wife was a Pawnee, so he says, but she was so mistreated by the Osage women that he had to watch her as though she were a quail egg in a den of black snakes. So he sold her to a trader at old Henri de Tonti's Arkansas Post and since has taken only Osage women."

Boone Fawley expressed the thought that maybe it took a cruel man to live among a cruel people, and Hadley-Moore pursed his lips and tugged at his mustache and thought for a moment, frowning slightly. It was unusual enough for Boone Fawley to take note because the Englishman seldom frowned. Finally he spoke, very slowly.

"They can be cruel. And unpredictable, especially when drunk. And cruel, yes.

"But Mr. Fawley, you cannot lay a yardstick of white man's virtue alongside them. For they are not white men. They are still in an ancient way of living. And you must know, after all, that it wasn't so long ago amongst ourselves that a man in London was sometimes tied to a stake in a public place, his entrails cut out and shown to him while he still lived, and then was burned. And then his head cut off and placed over one of the Thames bridges until it rotted and fell down. At one time, there has been the capacity in all of us for what we now call cruelty."

Although perhaps Boone Fawley understood only some of the Englishman's words, they sent chills up his back.

Finally, Boone Fawley promised Hadley-Moore that he would come and visit the rendezvous camp once the friends of Demaree arrived. Once he had made the promise, he tried to convince himself that he was not taking sides but simply scouting out his options.

Trading rendezvous in Osage country was never of the magnitude it later became in the Rocky Mountain West, when hundreds, even thousands, of different tribesmen and their families would gather.

An Osage rendezvous was a miniature of this except that there would be no wide variety of red men. Only the Osages. And never any company trappers or free trappers, either, because the Osages frowned on whites of any kind trapping their domain. And the agents from St. Louis were different, too. In the Far West, they represented the big outfits like Ashley's or Astor's. In Osage land, they represented only Chouteau or only Lisa, but never the two together. The white men of western rendezvous played and danced and sang and got drunk together for two or three weeks, putting aside the rest of the year when they were trying to rob, defraud, set tribesmen on competitors, and murder one another. Between Chouteau and Lisa men, there was no such truce.

Boone Fawley, although he knew nothing of what would happen at those future Far West rendezvous, understood the local variety, partly from what he'd heard in St. Louis, partly from what Hadley-Moore had told him. It was a set routine, as decidedly ordered as the steps in the dances Hadley-Moore illustrated for Molly and Chorine.

The best goods were laid out first so the Indian men could see those things they wanted most. Like good guns. With this first layout were a few gifts to make the customers' hearts glad. Like cigars. A string of beads. A single sip of whiskey.

With the best furs and hides in the hands of the traders, swapped for guns and maybe a few gold coins, for the Osages had learned the uses of money, the second line came out. The blankets and knives and hatchets and pots and mackinaws and red silk ribbons. Soon, these, too, were gone, and in their place on the traders' wagons were the rest of the hides. But a few of the prize furs were held back by the shrewd Osage warriors. Because next, the whiskey came out. In half-gallon jugs. Grain alcohol cut fifty percent with water. Maybe cut even more. Now, the warriors traded everything they had for the whiskey. Soon all the prize fur held back for the whiskey were gone, and the warriors began to trade horses for whiskey. Then women.

And finally began to trade back the things they had got from the early furs. The blankets. Then the pots. Then the mackinaws. Then the knives and hatchets. Then the money. So that by the end of the day, the traders had everything of value the Indians brought to rendezvous plus everything they, the traders, had brought, too. Except for the guns. And the Osages had the guns but nothing more than empty jugs and vomiting sickness and unbelievable hangovers.

Thus were the aborigines taught the method of white-man business enterprise. And were among the first people of the world to understand the dictum "Buyer beware!"

B oone Fawley missed the rendezvous trading by a day. When he arrived in Demaree's camp about midmorning, he saw two Osage men and three women in the pole corral, tying packs of hides on horses and mules and looping lengths of rope around the heads to make hackamore-style halters. There were many more horses than John had reported, so Boone Fawley reckoned Demaree had traded for Osage mounts that he would run to Cape Girardeau or New Madrid or some such place and ship upriver to St. Louis along with the pelts. Tethered on the outside of the corral, wearing saddles, were three horses, and it appeared that somebody was preparing to leave shortly.

As he rode into the locust grove, the two Osage men watching him, Boone Fawley felt an uncomfortable, scrutinizing kind of cold heat, if there could be such a thing. A look that asked no questions, as most looks do, and certainly didn't give any answers. As though it was nothing if not a calculation for future reference. Both Indians had a great deal of paint on their faces, but it was smeared and streaked and their roaches drooped. Boone Fawley figured that since the paint was applied and the roaches combed, there had been a lot of sweating. The three women were mostly remarkable for their loud talking, which to most whites was a combination of guttural grunts and high-pitched shrieks, no less to Boone Fawley, who allowed that the only thing like it he had ever heard was a Welsh Methodist exhortation he'd happened to hear in Louisville when he'd gone to find Molly and people started rolling on the ground and speaking in tongues.

Molly had insisted that Boone ride the horse so he'd be back before nightfall, and even though he would have preferred walking, he'd done it to pacify her. By the time he rode past the pole stock pen and toward the camp proper, he was confirmed in his opinion. He was no horseman. Nor did he want to be.

Hadley-Moore was sprawled against a sycamore log. Before him, on the river sand, what had been a large fire was now gone down to cold ash. He was gnawing on a pork chop. At some distance across the sandbar Demaree was squatted with his three wilderness men. All of them were still as cats ready to spring on an unsuspecting mouse, and they were each of them watching Boone Fawley with a hard intensity that he could almost feel.

It was only when Boone Fawley moved to the log and sat down that Captain Hadley-Moore became aware of his presence, and the Englishman made a startled gasp of surprise. He gave his guest a most unwelcome kind of glare, so Boone Fawley thought, but controlled himself quickly and straightened his hat, which did little to conceal the fact that there had apparently been a monstrous drinking party here last night.

"You have almost missed us," Hadley-Moore said. From along the sandbar, Demaree and his three frontiersmen were still watching, still taut as tightly wound watch springs. "We are making ready to depart. We had supposed you did not wish to visit us."

Hadley-Moore looked at Boone Fawley, and Boone Fawley stammered and tried to laugh but made a bad job of it.

"Why, now, that ain't true. I been mighty busy is all."

"Good," said Hadley-Moore, and in that moment Boone Fawley was aware that across the sandbar Demaree and his men had begun to speak with one another again, their heads close together.

The Englishman offered a rib from a scattering of them lying on the ground between his feet. Boone Fawley brushed off the sand and ate, and with the first taste knew he was eating a part of his own hog, or at least suspecting it, and feeling satisfied with it because at least he'd gotten this much.

The site looked much as any campsite does that has been seriously used and is now abandoned, or in the process thereof. The shelters were already showing signs of imminent collapse, and scattered at intervals on the ground were the ashes of fires, the sandy soil around them pockmarked with the tread of feet, cast-off bones lying about as when the eating has been casual and unrestrained, empty jugs, many of them broken, tatters of cloth and fur and feather where perhaps there had been wrestle-fights or a very violent stomp dance.

Hadley-Moore's eyes were so red as to appear ready for the shedding of blood, and he was not his usual garrulous self. At least not until he produced a large bottle from behind the log where they sat. This was not trade whiskey but the New England sorghum molasses rum that had become world renowned as a result of its wide distribution in the slave trade.

Trying to do so without making any great fuss about it, Boone Fawley kept cutting his glance to Demaree and the three men. They were smoking pipes, and Demaree seemed to be talking emphatically, pointing his finger this way and that. The other three held rifles across their thighs, and Boone Fawley had the impression that these weapons were as much a part of the men as were their legs. He tried to make out the features of their faces, maybe to distinguish the two he had seen at his own cabin clearing and the one John had said was called Williams, but at this distance, they all seemed cut from the same bolt. And a very rough cloth it was indeed, from all Boone Fawley could make out.

Demaree's friends, the Osages, were not in the trade camp but they were not gone from the rendezvous. They were across the river, a sizable band of them. About twenty men, Boone Fawley calculated, and almost as many women and some children as well. As he and Hadley-Moore sat and sipped the rum and the Englishman spoke in rather injured tones of all the riotous merrymaking the night before, Boone Fawley watched the people in their camp across the St. Francis. Just seeing them there made little prickles of apprehension run along his neck. The odor of dead ashes, the heavy aroma of rum, and the greasy scent of roast pig in his hand seemed all to meld into an Indian smell, even though Boone Fawley was not sure what an Indian smell was supposed to be. Certainly he did know that those across the river were too far away for him to catch their essence, although he had heard trappers in St. Louis claim they could nose-up an In'jun as far as they could shoot.

The Osages had thrown up temporary shelters of willow in the sycamore stand along the east bank of the river. It hadn't rained for days, so not much shelter was necessary. Among these shelters, the Indian children played, the youngest of them completely naked. There were no old people that Boone Fawley could distinguish.

There were a few horses, well back in the trees. There were cooking fires, their smoke rising pencil thin and gray to the tops of the trees where a light westerly breeze dispersed it. There were no pots over the fires, only long sticks in the ground slanted over the coals where chunks of meat could be spitted for roasting, but now the sticks were empty as though nobody there was making any preparation for a meal. Which Boone Fawley took to mean that they were not planning on staying much longer. All the men were big and wore roached hair and carried a full complement of weapons, even here in camp, quivers and hatchets and knives and muskets. Boone Fawley wondered about that.

He watched a few of the men come down to the water's edge, squat, and with their palms dip up water to wash their faces and upper bodies. Then some of these moved back a few paces and squatted and took hand mirrors—a valuable trade item—from their breech pouches and began to paint their faces. Boone Fawley thought he could see black, but then supposed that in the shade of the sycamores the color was actually the deep blue the Osages seemed to enjoy.

Demaree joined Boone and the Englishman then, his eyes in even worse shape than Hadley-Moore's. As he found his own place at the end of their log, Boone Fawley noted that the three frontiersmen had gone to the corral and mounted the saddled horses and, each of them casting a look in his direction, reined away and rode into the timber, casually moving south, generally along the course of the river. He felt some strange sense of relief that they were gone.

Demaree took his sips of the Englishman's rum, smacking his lips and making comments with French words that Boone Fawley had never heard before and so assumed that maybe they were not French words at all, but Osage. But not, in either case, as an entrance to any conversation, but rather like a judgment on man's weakness for high spirits, so Boone Fawley continued his talk with the Englishman.

"Good deal of horses over yonder in your pen," he said.

"Oh yes," said Hadley-Moore. "We always trade for a few. Many Osages like being afoot anyway, from long tradition, and find horses really necessary only on the prairies to the west."

"*Oui,*" muttered Demaree.

"I expect it makes sense all right," Boone Fawley said. "Man can make right smart time afoot in the timber and hills. As when he's got a horse sometimes. But I just reckoned they got horses from you folks, druther than other way around."

"No, they obtain horses from the Plains tribes," said Hadley-Moore. "Horses came from that direction, so says Our Old Gentleman."

"*Oui.*"

"Well, I declare," said Boone Fawley. "I never knew they got thangs from way out yonder."

"Oh yes. They got horses from the Pawnees and Kiowas who got them from the Comanches who got them from the Spaniards. A long time ago. So says Our Old Gentleman."

It was a relief to Boone Fawley that this conversation seemed to be running along smoothly even though he still suspected he caught a rasp of annoyance in some of the Frenchman's words. Maybe, he figured, he was overly nervous being so close to a bunch of half-naked, painted, well-armed savages.

"Why, I see," he said. "Spanish horses."

"Not New Orleans or river Spanish," Demaree said. "Those others, you see, those Cortés Spanish. Our old man, he says Comanches called Paducahs when Mr. Jefferson send those men up the river, those Lewis and Captain Clark men, but these really Comanches."

"Our Old Gentleman says the Comanches are the horse brokers of the Plains," said Hadley-Moore, and the manner in which he said "Our Old Gentleman" gave Boone Fawley the impression that he was mocking the Frenchman a little and maybe was still a little drunk from the night before, especially with reinforcement from the slave trade rum.

"Well, I never," Boone Fawley said. "I reckoned I knowed a mite about these heathens, but I ain't never gonna do that no more."

"Guns from the East, horses from the West," said Hadley-Moore. "French and English guns. Spanish horses. So our friends, the Osages, says Our Old Gentleman, got horses from the West and scared the liver out of eastern tribesmen. Got guns from the East and scared the liver out of western tribesmen. One had never seen a horse before. One had never seen a gun before. Very clever, our friends the Osages."

Demaree cast a glance at the Englishman that Boone Fawley

could have sworn was not a look of total harmony. In fact, it was a look of some malevolence if Boone Fawley was any judge of bloodshot French eyes.

The tension, if indeed there was tension, was broken as they all turned their heads toward the river, from beyond which there was now a singing chant rising. The chant and the ripple of the water in the stream and the secret rustle of wind in the canopy of sycamore leaves made a sound that spoke of an unknown dread, something that fascinated Boone Fawley who found himself leaning forward to catch each note of it. There was no beginning or no end. It was just suddenly there in this wilderness, and if Boone Fawley hadn't known better, he'd have supposed it was just the sound of spirit talking without any single human component. And to support such a contention, Boone Fawley realized that before they'd taken any note of singing, there had been a soft drumming from across the river, where he now saw all the Osage men had disappeared, gone back into the timber. A soft drumming that was part of all the rest of these whispers that grew in intensity and persistence so gradually that one was not even aware of them until the voices began to accompany the rhyme. To heighten the impression, as he looked into the Osage camp, the children were still there, playing as before, and a few of the women, only a few now because the rest had gone back into the timber with the men and perhaps some of them were singing, too. But on sight, little had changed, except that there were no longer any of the well-armed men in sight.

Boone Fawley felt a tense attention in the two men with him on the sandbar. They were watching, looking across the river where the Osage encampment had been. Silently they watched and listened. Then Demaree's wilderness men were there, having forded the river. Osage men both mounted and afoot appeared immediately around Fulton and Maddox and Williams. Only a few words were exchanged, as though everybody knew already what was expected. Then the whole cavalcade wound slowly out of sight downstream, toward the south, toward the general direction of the Fawley homestead and the Reed trading post on the Mississippi.

The women and children in the camp appeared, in a frenzy of activity.

"They go home now," Demaree said. He waved an arm back toward the west. "Go home, across the mountains."

The women were bundling clothing, the children and dogs trying to stay out of the way, but all in complete silence, and within a few heartbeats, there was no longer a camp there. The smoke still drifted lazily upward from the fires, the makeshift shelters still stood with drooping leaves, but the Osage were gone. To the south. Swallowed in the timber.

"*Partons!*" Demaree said suddenly and rose, the Englishman following him. It was only then that Boone Fawley realized one of Demaree's tame tiger Osages had brought up two saddled horses to stand behind them, one the big gelding of Hadley-Moore. Before he turned away, the Osage who had brought the horses stared intently at Boone Fawley, and now he could see traces of yellow paint under the man's black eyes. There was no expression on the Indian's face that Boone Fawley could read, but at this close range he could see finely sculpted lips and a heavy Roman nose and ears pierced at the top and hung with mussel shell fragments. The moment lasted for less than a heartbeat, and then the Osage had turned to his own mount. Behind him at the pole corral, Boone Fawley could see the other man and the three women lining out the string of pack horses and mules, hackamore leads tied to the tail of the animal in front, making a string of beads, as it were, and snaking off toward the north and eventually east to the Mississippi.

Boone Fawley, astonished that all of it had simply disappeared before his eyes, was just rising when Hadley-Moore pulled the gelding around and looked down at him, smiling his mustache smile.

"Mr. Fawley, Yellow Head says he killed the boar in a grove of pin oak about a straight-line walk half a day from here to the west," he said. "And there was a sow with seven shoats. You might send those sons of yours to collect the pigs. Well, a good-bye to you, Mr. Fawley. We should see you again in the fall. My respects to your wife and sister."

From farther away, his moving to join the string of horses and mules, Demaree turned in his saddle and waved and shouted.

"Fawley, we come back, no? You good man. I bring more candy from Our Old Gentleman, no?"

And they were gone. All of them. All of it, the rendezvous camp. And Boone Fawley left standing beside the log. He suddenly smelled the horse droppings from the pole corral, as fresh as though there were still animals there. He turned about and looked across the

St. Francis, and there were still a few thin streamers of gray smoke to the sycamore treetops. The water in the river spoke to him. The breeze made the locust leaves whisper. There were still the bones on the ground. There was still the brown bottle that had held the slave trade rum. But everything of blood and breathing and singing was gone. Boone Fawley shivered as though he might be standing in a haunted place and went quickly to his horse, standing as any plow horse would, head down and completely unaware of the ghosts that were here.

Boone Fawley mounted with some difficulty and turned the horse's head south and kicked with his heels until the horse began to move, reluctantly.

"Get on home, horse," Boone Fawley said.

As the horse pretty much picked his own way toward the south, there was a lot for Boone Fawley to chew on and he found it tough chewing. He hadn't really expected to understand everything about this Osage trading business. But neither had he expected to come away with so much of what he'd seen providing reasonable answers. He wondered why there had been that little ill-concealed flare of temper from Demaree with the Englishman's words? And he wondered if his visit to the rendezvous meant to the Chouteau people that he was joining their ranks? He hadn't meant it to, but both Demaree and Hadley-Moore indicated they'd be back to supply him with trade goods. Sweet Jesus, he thought, I am no Indian trader and don't want to be. Yet maybe it was the only insurance he had available to keep his family safe in this land.

And he wondered why the Osage party had gone off toward the south. But he had an answer for that one less than a mile from the rendezvous camp.

It wasn't really any sound he heard. Maybe even it was a sudden silence; the woodpeckers' pounding quieted, the cardinals' territorial whistles stilled. He reined in the horse and sat listening, and then he heard the soft rustle, like wind blowing through starched cotton curtains. Then he saw them, a line of Osage women and children, and a few scrawny camp horses loaded with bulky packs, pulled along on lead ropes by teenage boys. And half a dozen camp dogs. They moved silently and quickly, heads rather bent forward as though they were going against a strong wind or else were in an inordinate hurry. He knew they must have known he was there because he'd made no move to hide himself in the timber, yet none of them, so far as he could tell, cast a single glance in his direction.

But as he watched them pass, he knew why they had moved south from the rendezvous camp. To the red gum ford, thence crossing to the west and on along this route of march deep into the wild timber country, to the plateau country, just as Demaree said they would. He watched them all pass, hurrying, oblivious to his presence. Then the last of them was gone into the hardwood jungle. But he waited, looking now back in the direction they had come, waiting to see the Osage men and the three frontiersmen of Demaree following the same path as the women and children. He waited a long time. The cardinals began to sing again, and the woodpeckers began their interrupted hammering.

With a sudden sickness, he realized the painted Osage warriors and Fulton and Maddox and Williams were not coming in this direction. They were going somewhere else, toward the south. And he had no way of knowing whether they were still on the east bank of the St. Francis or on the near bank, the side where his homestead was located. There came to him the searing and sickening image of naked, drunken savages led by three ruthless frontiersmen, descending on his homestead and only the boys there to protect the women. He'd heard enough about this wilderness to understand how kind words often preceded furious atrocity. With a great oath, he ripped off his hat and struck the horse across the ears, and the horse leaped with surprised indignation and started forward in a lurching run.

"Go on, horse, go on, horse," Boone Fawley kept repeating as he slapped his hat against the horse's head. They were driving straight south through the trees, whipped by low-hanging branches. He almost fell off twice, but both times managed to grab a double handful of mane to right himself but the second time he lost his grip on the hat and he began slapping the horse's neck with the palms of his hands and kicking the horse in the ribs with both heels. "Go on, horse!"

Horse and rider were blowing hard by the time they broke into the clearing at the north cornfield. Boone Fawley sawed up on the reins, and the horse grunted and dug in his hooves and came to a stop. Before them stretched the homestead. There was a line of smoke from the chimney. The boys were in the dooryard, cleaning fish. Chorine was coming in from the sweet potato patch with a hoe over her shoulder, and Boone Fawley could hear his sister singing. Molly was hanging wash on the rope Boone had strung for her between the cabin and the privy.

Boone Fawley let go a whoop of laughter. He knew without even thinking about it that if those Osage warriors were coming here, they would have arrived before now. Everybody in the yard heard him and stopped what they were doing and stared at him as he kicked the horse and shouted again and the horse grunted with protest and made a stumbling effort at running through the new cornstalks toward the cabin. All the other Fawleys, still wide-eyed and openmouthed, moved into a little bunch at the edge of the cabin to meet him. He dismounted, or more accurately, fell off the horse, and ran to Molly and threw his arms around her in a furious embrace, the others now really pop-eyed, then as quickly jumped back from her, embarrassed, and just stood there grinning, slapping his hands against his sides.

"What's got into you, Boone Fawley?" Molly yelled. "Are you drunk?"

"Yes. Yes, a little, I reckon."

"Where's you hat?" she said, still yelling and a little red along her neck, maybe from a blush at Boone's show of affection in broad daylight. "What happened to your face? Look at them scratches."

"Me and that horse," Boone said, grinning still. "Me and that horse run up again' a lot of tree branches is all. Sweet Jesus, Mol, I'm happy as a toad in well water."

"You're drunk is what you are; now come on in here and I'll put some coal oil on them cuts. John, get that horse in the pen and rub him some, he looks like he's half-dead."

Chorine had begun to giggle.

"What's for supper, Mol?" Boone Fawley asked, being led like a small boy into the cabin for the administration of medical attention. "I'm hungry enough eat a barrel stave."

While they ate that night, and for some time afterward, Boone Fawley told them about the rendezvous camp. Well, he told them some of it. He left out a lot that he reckoned might frighten them, and he left out some things he didn't understand. To fill in, he told a few things he made up. Like the whole camp being on the west bank of the river so he got to see all the Osages close up, close enough to smell them. But he concentrated on what Hadley-Moore had said, including the Englishman's promise to come back by fall for a long visit. That part made Molly happy, and Chorine as well, although it fell a little sour on the ears of the boys.

The euphoria at finding everything as he'd left it lasted until Boone Fawley was in bed, lying awake after making his passion known to Molly. It was his usual thinking time, when in the darkness he seemed able to make things seen in daylight come clear. And he had a tinge of the first sickness he'd felt out in the timber after he'd seen the Osage women passing and not followed by the warriors. And wondering where those warriors and those three white men had gone. And now, he suspected that he knew.

10

Well, John Fawley was just a natural woodsman and hunter, his father figured. And smart enough to have learned plenty about farming, too. But the boy preferred to be in the woods with a rifle or musket where he could display his considerable marksmanship if to nobody but himself and his victim.

Questor, now, here was a boy who was more interested in how things sprouted and took bloom and seeded, and how schools of bass collected in the cool shaded water under an overhanging outcrop of limestone along the banks of the St. Francis. Or how honeybees swarmed in springtime and a new queen went off from the old hive—usually a hollow walnut tree snag—to start a colony of her own, and how some of the drones went with her and some stayed to continue servicing the old queen.

Both boys were good at working with their hands, but Questor was better. He seemed quick to see how to make the cabin door swing without drag. Or how to build roosts in the coop and nests for the laying hens well off the ground, and how to ditch the outside wall to avoid water running in during heavy rains and drowning chicks who were too small and too dumb to climb to safety.

During leisure, of which there was small portion, John cleaned guns. Questor got out the King James and read it, sometimes aloud to his Aunt Chorine who sat leaning forward, chin on fist, elbow on knee, with a puzzled expression, watching her nephew's lips as though the words were fountains of knowledge from a well of wisdom.

Oh, John could read, maybe as well as Questor, but he sure as hell didn't make any large practice of it. In fact, Boone Fawley could never recall, outside of those early times when Molly was teaching him from the Book, seeing his elder son open the King James even to look at the pictures.

So Boone Fawley figured it that John took life as he found it. In simple terms. You eat what you grow and kill, and no great thought about it. It was how everything worked, simple as a heartbeat. You grew it or killed it and you ate it and you survived. That was John. He never enjoyed sitting and looking at brilliant red sunsets.

Questor was something different, and Boone Fawley wasn't sure just what. Questor thought about things Boone had never thought about. Like what the chuck-will's-widow was trying to say each night with his plaintive whistle. Who the hell cared? Boone Fawley said to himself. But not to Questor because when he did say such things, Questor would act as hurt as if somebody had just shot Jesus.

And in the dooryard in the evenings, when a streaking meteor slashed across the purple sky and Questor would ask where it came from and where was it going and why couldn't you see it when it got there, it being so bright? Sweet Jesus, Boone Fawley thought, who cares? Like Molly said, it was an act of God. Who could understand it? Well, that was it! Questor was always trying to understand it.

Questor, he liked being around people, and he showed it. John didn't give a damn and in fact seemed to thrive on being alone, even when he was in the middle of the family group at suppertime. Once, in a drowsy half sleep in their bed, Molly had said her baby was her morning sun lad. Yes, bright and inquisitive and ready to welcome anything new and laugh and talk and share. Maybe to be changed by whatever happened during each day.

So if that was Questor, then John, Boone Fawley reckoned, must be the bad weather steel trap, who watched everything like it was no more than the drip of rain off the cabin eaves, as hard eyed as one of those Osage men, and ready to challenge anything that didn't fit his idea of how things were supposed to be. Dependable and unchanging as metal, and maybe in the final charge, as cold.

Well, Boone Fawley said to himself, if you wanted to write a new song, Questor was your man. Well, boy. But if you had some trouble that needed deadly determination, John was the man. Yes, man. Two years' difference in age, and God only knew how much difference in temperament, could make one a boy all his life, the other a man in his boyhood.

So understanding some of the antithesis, even in his blundering way, Boone Fawley was glad it happened to be John who made the grisly discovery in the cypress swamp just beyond the east bank of the St. Francis two days after Boone Fawley returned from Demaree's rendezvous.

It was a good two hours before dinnertime, and Boone Fawley was in a dripping sweat after pulling stumps to clear a new corn patch. The gnats and blackflies were driving him crazy, and the mule was attracting some of the biggest flying critters Boone Fawley had ever seen, all around the mule's tail, and sometimes their biting produced a kicking spree with the ropes and chain thrown off and the harness gone askew and the mule braying and Boone Fawley swearing like a riverman.

"Best stay away from him today," Molly had said, and she and Chorine had gone off into the timber after various roots and herbs and maybe just to take a stroll. Questor was out of sight someplace, off to the north, Boone Fawley thought, looking for bee trees. So when John came from the direction of the St. Francis, nobody was in the clearing except Boone. From first sight of him, Boone knew something was wrong. John was walking with a stiff-backed fury, his face set in hard lines, and the Pennsylvania rifle held across his chest with both hands, not swinging easily at his side. Boone Fawley pulled in the mule and waited for his son to come up, and John walked straight to him, glancing first around the clearing to see if anybody else was there. He stopped before his father and their eyes met, and Boone Fawley knew for sure then that something was badly wrong because the boy's eyes were slate hard and his lips were puckered down and almost blue.

"Pa," John said. "I found somethin'."

"What?"

"You better come look. I don't reckon I can tell it right."

It didn't take long, Boone Fawley following his son to the river, wading it at their ford—what they had begun to call the low-water, wide-stream place where they'd first come to their homestead—and then south for a few hundred yards to a finger of the cypress swamp, where the water was only a few inches deep and the cypress fought a losing struggle with swamp oak and sycamore. Boone Fawley didn't see it at first as John stopped and looked down into a sandy pool ringed with bull lilies. Then he saw the swarm of flies and smelled it.

It was like a great black rock, partly submerged, glistening with the swamp water and crawling with the flies. But at one end of it were two legs, completely under water, and at the other, a mat of copper-colored fuzz, seeming to float on the black water.

"You want I should turn him over?" John asked.

"I reckon you best."

John bent and with one hand heaved the form over, making a splash in the water and sending up a cloud of flies. Face up it was now, and Boone Fawley saw that it was Coppertop, face already marked with the feeding of turtles. The belly was greatly extended, and as the body lay faceup on the water, Boone Fawley could hear the gases inside making obscene hisses. There were three, maybe four, puncture wounds in the chest, and Boone Fawley knew they were bullet holes.

"Jesus, sweet Jesus," he whispered. And thought, At least he got away with his hair.

"Pa?"

"Yes."

"We better bury him, you think?"

"I reckon."

There was no question of going back for a spade. On a sliver of dry land close by, in the sand, they scooped out a narrow, shallow grave with their hands. It was a hard thing, taking Coppertop's arms and dragging him to the hole.

"They ain't no rocks to cover it," said John. "Foxes and thangs like that, they'll likely dig it up."

Boone Fawley glanced to the sky, blue through the patchwork of overhanging leaves.

"There ain't even any buzzards," he said in wonder. Then shook himself, like a dog shedding water. "No matter. Best we can do. Listen."

He reached out and laid a hand on John's shoulder.

"Best we don't tell the others. Best we wait. You let me tell, when I think it's time."

And without anything more between them, Boone Fawley knew that John knew exactly what he meant. There were no more words as they walked back to the cabin, pausing in midstream of the St. Francis ford to wash their hands, scrubbing furiously. Then on home, and still no one in the clearing.

"Just like always," Boone Fawley said, touching his son's shoulder again.

"I know, Pa."

So for the rest of that day, and through the mealtime at night, Boone Fawley and his son John held this terrible secret, and before they went to their beds Boone Fawley said, as casually as he could, that he thought next morning he'd take the mule and ride over to the Mississippi and see Clovis Reed and maybe John would like to go, too, riding double. John, with his eyes hooded and not looking at anybody, not even at his father, said he thought that would be just fine.

And Molly said it would be just fine, too, so long as they left her the musket buckshot loaded in case a black bear came into the clearing after some of the honey Questor had brought in that day from an old hickory hole. Everybody laughed, Questor most especially.

"And tell everybody to come for a visit, soon," said Chorine.

And that's when Boone Fawley almost choked on his rabbit stew.

It had begun to rain by the time Boone and John Fawley and the mule came to the long crescent-shaped sandbar, nearing noon but gray and gloomy and windless, as it had been all morning. The rain fell straight and steady, making a screen so that looking to the east across the surface of the Mississippi River, they could not see the shoreline of Tennessee.

John was in rear, riding the high hump of the mule's rump,

holding the Pennsylvania rifle so the firelock was sheltered under his hide smock to avoid wetting the priming powder in the pan. Boone was well forward, almost on the mule's neck, bent toward the mule's ears, the wide, flopping brim of his hat hanging low around his head. Only yesterday, Questor in his search for bee trees had found the hat where his father had dropped it along the route back from Demaree's rendezvous camp. It was important. Hats were hard to come by in this place.

They came onto the sandbar at its far southern extension. There were no trees here. John had guided them all the way, knowing from his hunting scouts where there was the best solid footing across the swamp. Moving through the blue-black shadows of the cypress trees, they had seen no living thing, not even cottonmouth snakes, the wildlife apparently sheltering from the rain. And now, in the open, they saw nothing either, and even the movement of the river was hard to detect, as though perhaps the current had slid beneath the surface to hide. All was static except the falling rain, and that didn't seem to move but to simply be there like a widow's veil. Perpetual. Forever. The sandbar, curving north like the blade of a Turk's sword, was bounded on one side by the gray river, on the other by the somber lift of the swamp cypress canopy.

Boone Fawley reined in the mule, and they sat motionless in the rain, hearing its soft whisper on their hat brims. For a moment, a rather terrifying one, Boone Fawley had the impression that he, his son, and the mule were the only living things existing in this wet land. Then he reined the mule toward the long reach of the sandbar.

"Go on, mule," he said.

The near edge of the willows came in sight, emerging from the rain mist at first as a low, dark, shapeless hedge. But soon the individual trees were apparent and then the limbs and branches and at last, just before the mule moved in among them, the hung-down leaves heavy with water.

They were well into the trees when Boone Fawley stopped the mule and sat sniffing, turning his head from side to side. John imitated his father, but mostly watched the shadows nearby, to discover movement of any kind, from anywhere, from anything, both hands gripping the rifle so hard the knuckles were white.

"You smell that?" asked Boone Fawley.

"Yes, Pa."

It was the kind of odor you get when you douse the ashes of an old fire with water. It hung in the trees like smoke, clinging, persistent. Boone Fawley grunted and gently kicked his heels against the mule's flanks.

"Go on, mule."

The first movement they saw was sudden and almost at the mule's front hooves, and with it a wild, raucous cawing clamor. Huge black crows, shapeless in their frenzied flight, rose like shots from the ground and up through the willows, disturbed in their feeding and passing the alarm along the sandbar so that other birds rose, too, shrieking, hundreds of them, all along the willow growth of the sandspit. Great wings lifted the protesting birds like a circling cloud to hover over the sandbar.

"Sweet Jesus!" Boone Fawley shouted, feeling the thump of his heart and knowing without seeing that his son had given the same kind of startled jump and the rifle had come up, ready. But then, when they saw it was only crows, the rifle went back, the firelock protected once more from the rain.

"Just crows, Pa," said John.

Maybe it had been there before but unnoticed until this sudden jerking stop. It was the sweet, sickening scent of decaying meat. And then, without moving any farther along, the mule standing there trembling, Boone Fawley saw where the crows had been feeding.

It had once been a man. The body was face up and completely unrecognizable as human. The flesh was the color of putty, and in the many gashes and gouges blood had turned black as coal tar. The eyes had been eaten, leaving only sockets which, even as Boone Fawley watched, were filling with rainwater. The man had been stripped of all clothing, and bits and pieces of it were scattered about. One bright scarf hung on a willow branch, and Boone Fawley knew it was a turban and that this had once been a Cherokee. Nowhere about was there any sign of gun or hatchet or knife or anything else made of metal. It had all been taken. Boone Fawley could not tell if the man had been scalped.

There were no words between father and son now. There was no need for words. Besides, they were stunned to silence. Only the mule made any sound as Boone Fawley moved him gently forward, the mule grunting and snorting with obvious distaste.

Then they found the rest of it. The partly burned pole shelters. The scatter of trade goods—whatever couldn't be carried away, Boone Fawley figured—half-burned blankets and mackinaw coats and copper pots and strings of glass beads and slashed bags of brown sugar and of salt, and many, many empty and broken whiskey jugs. A musket, the stock shattered. A harmonica half-buried in the sand. A scatter of nails and tin arrowheads. A broken box spilling out spools of brightly colored thread. And all the bodies.

The bodies lay in grotesque attitudes. Two of them hung from willow limbs. One almost buried under a dead horse, the only dead horse in the willow grove. They had all been stripped. Some had been disemboweled. One had an arm hacked off. There was a headless torso. There were great patches of blood lying on the sand like discarded black scraps of paper, the earth seeming to refuse its entry. It was impossible to tell which might be white men, which Cherokees. But of one thing Boone Fawley was sure. None were Osage because the Osages always carried their dead and wounded away from a fight, even at great risk. And he doubted there had been any risk in recovering what few Osage wounded there had been because the attack had obviously come suddenly, furiously, and unexpectedly out of the swamp.

They didn't dismount. There was no reason to. They could see all they needed to see from the back of the mule. As they slowly went through the camp, above them the crows circled, cawing petulantly, impatient to get back to the task of clearing up the wilderness carrion. And Boone Fawley figured these crows were so many and so aggressive, they'd frightened away all the buzzards. At least the rain had driven off many of the flies.

Boone Fawley gave a start when his son touched his shoulder, having perhaps fallen into a trancelike shock that made it seem he was in this savage place alone. When Boone Fawley turned, he saw that John pointed toward the river.

Boone Fawley recalled that this was the exact place where the barge had pulled in the day he and his family first set foot on this land. And it was as it had been then, the willows landward along the bar and a wide stretch of sand to the river's edge. Now, where John pointed, about midway between the trees and the river, was something upright like a long fence post.

Slowly, with some reluctance, Boone Fawley turned the mule

out of the willows and down across the sandbar. As they came nearer, he could see that it was one of the big barge oars like the Frenchmen had used to navigate the flatboat downriver. There was some kind of object on top of the oar. As they drew closer, Boone Fawley could see two arrows struck into the landward side of the oar, shaft and feather vane of one painted all in red, the other all in black.

Even more reluctant now, Boone Fawley edged the mule farther down the sandbar toward the river, taking a considerable berth from the upright oar, but close enough to see clearly. And then he did see. Impaled on top of the oar with face looking toward the river and Tennessee beyond, from whence came the Cherokees, was the head of Clovis Reed.

St. Louis was as good a place as any to learn about the frontier relationship between Europeans and American Indians. The French and Spanish wilderness men knew a great deal more about the subject than most men from Britain or the United States because they—especially the French—had from the beginning taken great pains to develop a close association with the various tribes, which English speakers had never done. And Boone Fawley had been, from his boyhood, in a particularly advantageous position to hear about it at Old Noah's side and later in Chouteau's warehouses and along the riverfront.

From the start, Boone Fawley knew that Europeans coming to the New World, the very first ones, were pleasantly surprised when at initial contact with half-naked aboriginals they seemed helpful and hospitable. In fact, American Indians were largely helpful and hospitable. To their friends.

But soon Europeans began to realize that all this nonviolent confrontation did not mean that native peoples spent all their leisure time plucking wildflowers and sniffing them. Europeans discovered that American mankind was pretty much as mankind had been throughout all historical memory in Asia, Africa, and Europe. And that all that friendliness was usually an expression of joy that some-body had arrived who might help the local tribe against their ene-mies. It didn't take long for the true picture to emerge of a culture that was not a culture at all but hundreds of fragmented societies operating just like they had in the known world.

The stronger ones pushed the weaker ones around a bit. There were sometimes deadly squabbles over territory. There were those who could not resist the temptation to raid neighbors for loot and plunder, for captive women and children. It was all familiar stuff, the kind of thing that had been happening for three thousand years in Asia Minor, around the shores of the Mediterranean, and in Europe.

Seeing the opportunity to further his own ends, the white man often did help the local tribes against their enemies. Or maybe now and then it was more advantageous to help enemies against the locals. Just as they had learned to do in the Old World.

You made alliances where you could; you took advantage of old enmities; you worked for a balance of power in your favor. You enlisted others to help you do some of the killing or whatever was necessary. In return, you promised them something they wanted, like the security of firearms. Sometimes you made treaties of friendship and mutual defense with a tribe who was particularly powerful and bellicose just to keep them off your back until you were strong enough to deal with them.

All familiar stuff.

And there was nothing novel or surprising to the natives in such behavior. Obviously, they'd been doing the same things for a long time among themselves. So the newly arrived white man found various tribes bound together over many generations, for mutual defense. And they found tribes who had had implacable enemies for as long as memory served.

Obviously, these native North Americans were no more pacific than other types of humankind. In some places they were only involved in sporadic fighting because the population of red people was so sparse that enemies were hard to find. Sometimes, they went a long way just to locate somebody they could fight. When the Spanish horse came, some of them went farther still looking for trouble. After all, in most tribes, Europeans found, the young boys were taught from the first that the highest calling and honor was to be a warrior. And to be a warrior, you had to have enemies.

There were exceptions. Tribes who were peaceful farmers. And they were constantly bullied and ravaged by warlike tribes who either lived nearby or made a point of passing through periodically just to whack them and steal their pumpkins and their women. These sedentary peoples were of little interest to the white man because such Indians had little part in any balance-of-power struggle. Well, the white missionaries gave them a lot of attention because it was supposed that these docile folk were the only pagans who could be easily made into Christians.

Belligerent tribes were the kind to be made allies, although they were usually difficult to control. But these kinds of Indian allies left little to be desired in the business of how to treat enemies. The white man did not have to show them anything about hostile action. Sometimes, the white man had to restrain them.

As time went on, Europeans often saw and recorded in their journals the results of Mohawk or Seneca visits to Huron villages; or a camp of Shoshones surprised by Blackfeet; or a Lipan settlement hit by Comanches; or a Pawnee hunting party caught by Kiowas. It had to have been something like the ancestors of these white men who had come onto a battlefield where Roman legions with their vicious short swords had slashed into a formation of Gauls, or maybe like walking through the mud of Agincourt immediately after the English and Welsh archers and swordsmen had done with the French. It was no sight to be calmly endured except by those with exceptionally strong stomachs. It was, in fact, a human butcher's pen. It could be accepted as routine only by those who were a part of such barbarism themselves and hardened to it.

Boone Fawley, who had lived all his life in a large settlement and had sometimes heard of such things second, or third, or fourth hand, was not hardened to it. So during the space of one dismal, rainy afternoon, there was the shock of seeing how human slaughter looked, and that scene would appall him for the rest of his days.

Yet, in the grand scheme of things, it didn't amount to much. It had only been a tiny massacre, a few Indians and a few whites on both sides, precipitated by uninvited migrants and a small fur trade war.

II

Chorine Fawley never knew what happened to Clovis Reed and his men and his Cherokee friends and Coppertop. Nor did Molly or Questor. Their ignorance was the result of a conspiracy of deceit and silence hatched by Boone Fawley and his elder son on the ride back to the cabin on that terrible day, a ride that took them into the night, the rain still falling as though some special Providence was trying to wash away the blood and the memory. And with that intrigue between them, Boone Fawley and John became closer than they had ever been before or would ever be afterward, maybe because they undoubtedly knew that and wished to maintain the only affinity that bound them as they supposed a father and son are expected to be bound. For the rest of their lives they would hold the secret.

Mostly on the homing instinct of the mule they found their way through the cypress swamp in total darkness and into the yard, the night so complete they didn't know they were home until the startled baying of the hound almost under the mule's nose. Before Boone could reach the door and with John well on his way to penning the mule, cracks of light appeared around the shutters, and Boone knew his wife had lit the lantern and come from bed fast, surely with the musket in hand, at the first baying of the dog. No one expected them back until the next day.

That's when Boone told the lie. Well, once John came from the stock pen and Questor and Chorine were awake, peering from the blankets of their pallets, and Molly had set the musket back on its pegs above the door. Yes, they'd seen Clovis Reed, and just in time, too, because he and his Frenchmen were clearing out, the trading camp already loaded in two barges, all going back to St. Louis and leaving this area for others to haggle for Indian furs and hides. To the question in Questor's eyes, Yes, Coppertop was going with Clovis Reed, and all of them by now were well upriver and never coming back.

Molly knew from her husband's expression when he told it that there was more than he revealed, and for a time passed broad hints that she knew, but Boone Fawley maintained the lie, a lie he and his son had decided on to protect the tender sensibilities of the others, especially Chorine in regard to Clovis Reed and Questor concerning Coppertop. And for all his days, Boone Fawley would rage with doubt inside himself in Chorine's case, for he was not so sure the false witness made it any easier for his sister than the truth would have done. At least, with the facts before her, she would have known that Clovis Reed, even had he wanted to return to her as she wanted him to do, had no selection, his choice denied by an Osage hatchet.

Questor and Chorine were despondent for a time, each having lost someone they valued and reckoned didn't value them. Not enough to come and bid farewell, anyway. Questor, young and resilient, was soon past his distress. But Chorine, older and able to understand the diminishing probabilities of escape from barren spinsterhood, never recovered. She became morose and sullen and often wandered off into the woods, despite Molly's furious objections, to stay all day, appearing back at the cabin at nightfall, going silently to her pallet bed with no word to anyone, her eyes swollen, her face red and puffy. Sometimes she took the hoe and went with Molly to the field, but did little with it there. She refused to say much, or eat much, and Molly could find nothing in which Chorine developed any interest. She couldn't even bring herself to brush away the mosquitoes that hovered about her ears.

Molly was resigned to her husband's silence about that rainy trip to the Mississippi sandbar. Resigned, as well, to a different

Boone Fawley, a man now as nervous and furtive as the weasel Questor caught in the trap cage he'd devised and set beside the chicken coop door.

She was aware that John knew as much as Boone did but would not trick or trap her son into saying something it was obvious he didn't want to say. So she forced herself to ignore the whole business because she knew it was her place to do so.

Thus, in an atmosphere charged with the sandbar massacre, directly or otherwise, Boone Fawley became a Chouteau trader to the Indians. His one consolation was that Questor remained the same, untouched by the bitterness of calamity, giving Boone at least some gratification for his lie.

Demaree came in the fall that year. With him came his three wilderness men, his two couples of tame tiger Osages, and his own Osage wife. Obviously pregnant. And wearing more trade beads, porcupine quills, elk teeth, and copper bracelets than Boone Fawley had seen her wearing at last spring's rendezvous. Still slender, except for the ballooning at the middle. Boone Fawley observed to his wife that it was a wonder such a frail little thing could haul around such a lot of truck and decoration as she had hanging on herself.

Captain Evelyn Hadley-Moore was not among them. Demaree said that the Englishman had gone south to New Orleans, most likely to take soundings at the mouth of the river to discover channels where British men-of-war might make way, there being an obvious possibility of hostilities between Great Britain and America. This assessment indicated Demaree's wisdom in such things, his having been an observer of many different sovereign nations and their shenanigans along this frontier.

Boone Fawley was somewhat ill at ease. Perhaps even a little flabbergasted that his homestead was becoming one of Auguste Chouteau's trading posts, like it or not, and of course, after what he'd seen on that sandbar, he knew it might be a matter of liking it or else. But the many trade goods on Demaree's train of pack mules, of which Boone Fawley was assured he could dip into for personal use so long as he entered it on the ledger book, the spirited activity of Demaree's men to construct a shed abutting the cabin in which to store said trade goods, the promise of goodwill from Our Old Gentleman, the few stiff snorts of Jamaican rum Demaree had brought, and the extra-large sack of horehound candy for Molly induced a gentleness on Boone Fawley's mind that made acceptance of his situation almost as good as if he had ordered it.

It helped, too, that Demaree shared with Boone Fawley a kind of leisure overseer's status in all this activity, which allowed Boone Fawley to spend three days doing little but leaning against the side of his cabin with the Frenchman of Our Old Gentleman and watching while everybody, including his family, worked in the task of picking and hanging corn to dry so it could be shelled and ground. The weather was grand, with only enough nip in the evening air to make the rum go down even more beneficially than one would suspect, and before she prepared their supper meal Molly herself took a small sip on two successive days.

In fact, all this new companionship delighted Molly. And Questor, of course. Molly began to treat Demaree as though he were as much the gentleman as was Captain Evelyn Hadley-Moore, and indeed, maybe he was, and she struck up conversations with the three Osage women as opportunity permitted, conversing in rather primitive French and with sign language. From Demaree's wife, she told Boone, she had a wonderful recipe for cooking 'possum so there would not be so much grease that one choked on it.

In the evenings, at the fire in the dooryard before Molly called everyone of her family in to bed, Questor became friends to the three men Boone Fawley regarded as vicious murderers, but even that did not penetrate seriously the rum haze of good feeling, and Questor was taught how best to sharpen a large knife and how to quickly load a rifled musket and was enthralled at the stories the three men told of the great humpback cattle that lived on the far western prairie where nothing much grew except ankle-high grass.

They were a strange lot, these three wilderness men. Even in their gentle speech with the boy, so obviously enthusiastic with the chance to spin tall tales for wondering ears, there was always some glint of metal in back of their eyes and in the set of their lips.

The two Osage men stayed well clear of any social meeting. When they were near at all, they wore stolid faces and hard eyes, a little sullen and hostile. John was their counterpart, and although he worked as hard as anyone, always in his belt was the Lancaster pistol, the Pennsylvania rifle nearby, and his face wore no smile, matching the look of the Osage men. Because he was not mellowed by the Jamaica rum and he had seen that sandbar, too.

Chorine avoided them all, family and Demaree's people alike, said nothing, and ate alone in the cabin, squatting on her pallet bed, her eyes brittle and lifeless as the glass beads the Osage women wore around their necks.

Demaree said there would be no more rendezvous camps in this area. Maybe some to the west, along the White River. But maybe not there either, what with the Osages now moving farther out toward the prairie and what catch they made each winter being brought into St. Louis directly. But, he told Boone Fawley, it was his mission to provide a trading post for any Osage or other hunting party passing by, and he told Boone Fawley to make his trades saving the whiskey until last, and once the customers had the jugs in their hands, to bring the livestock into the cabin, shutter the doors and windows, and wait out the night while the men outside puked themselves sober, or at least ineffective, and then next day they would leave and the Fawleys could get back to growing corn or whatever.

Demaree also said that there were no longer such things as exclusive licenses given by the government to favored traders, but that in the United States of America there was a thing called free enterprise, which meant first come, first served. It seemed to Boone Fawley that such a system meant cutthroat competition in the literal sense, and Demaree laughed, understanding Boone Fawley's concern, and said there was nothing to worry himself about because Manuel Lisa was now directing all his energies up the Missouri toward the High Plains and the Rocky Mountains, having hired some of the people who had been with Lewis and Clark on their expedition, and therefore no longer was interested in such things as the Osage and Cherokee trade.

So it was done. With a lot of goodwill on all sides, considering that Boone Fawley, each time he looked at any of these people, could not avoid seeing in his mind the image of Clovis Reed's head on that sandbar oar.

On the last night, Demaree and his crew got very drunk, in celebration of having completed a task and returning north the next day. All the Fawleys except Boone were barricaded inside the cabin, although there was little to fear unless loud and sometimes profane language in both French and English could wound. Later, toward dawn and after Molly had unbarred the door for her husband and Boone Fawley lay sprawled and snoring before the fireplace, the Osages began a chant that sounded like a funeral dirge and went on monotonously until almost dawn, each moment of it raising goose bumps along the backs of every Fawley who was awake. Which was all of them except Boone.

With first light, John and Molly and Questor, watching through the shutter cracks, saw Demaree and his people stagger through the preparations for departure and finally, somehow, accomplish it and file out of the clearing like limp scarecrows on their horses. Except for Demaree, and he rode to the door of the cabin, lifted his hat, and shouted his good-bye.

"*Adieu, adieu, mon ami Foolie, adieu.*"

And then rode to follow his people, almost falling off his horse as he reined round the corner of the cabin. They never saw him again.

If he spent much time thinking about it, Boone Fawley came close to being sick. Was he now in league with the same people who had orchestrated the sandbar massacre? Well, he sure as hell was in business with them! And it didn't help his disposition any when Molly, after a closer inspection of that ledger-and-accounts-current book Demaree had left, explained that the Fawleys owed Our Old Gentleman in St. Louis one hundred twenty-four dollars for the trade goods now resting in the new shed abutting their cabin, so they needed to take in enough hides and furs to cover that overhead—that's what Molly called it—and maybe they'd take in some extra, which would be their profit. Boone Fawley had heard enough stories in St. Louis to know that very few independent traders made any profit if they dealt with Auguste Chouteau.

This revelation that he was now a pawn to Our Old Gentleman had a strange result that Molly thought was funny at first but then realized was no laughing matter. Boone made himself a money belt of squirrel hides; he strapped the thing on each morning when he rose from their bed and didn't take it off until he went back to that same bed at night, and in the pouches of the money belt were most of the Spanish coins left from Old Noah's horde. It was as though he expected some Chouteau agent to sneak into the cabin while he was plowing, or whatever, and steal his golden goods. Which Molly considered absurd, but she kept her mouth shut.

If the whole idea of becoming the proprietor at a wilderness crossroads trading post rather stunned Boone Fawley, the prospect was delightful for Molly. It meant she might see a few people, even though most of them would undoubtedly be pagan, infidel savages, smelling of smoke and old grease and with paint on their faces. Her initial frantic fear of such folk had turned to curiosity, and her need for the sight of some sort of human face beyond those of her family was enough to completely overpower any vestige of dread. In fact, from what she had seen of these barbarians thus far, it appeared to her that all one needed to over-awe them was a straight-in-the-eye stare and a head upheld in the glory of God. Plus a little smile now and then. Not of weakness or condescension, but rather a display of mature superiority in all things. Something like the smile you show a naughty child by way of threatening to spank hell out of him.

Nobody was ever sure how information moved through that vast, unsettled land, but it did. And so within a short time, it was known that at the Boone Fawley place, on the St. Francis, a day's ride west of the Mississippi, there was a trading post. And men came. Well, mostly men, although sometimes they had their women with them.

There were the white hunters up from as far south as the Arkansas River, a scabby bunch, with unkempt weapons and eyes as shifty as the eyes of foxes they tried to trap or kill. Some spoke French, some English. The Fawleys quickly assigned them to some notch lower than the heathen savages. Certainly they were not men like Demaree's wilderness men, sharp-eyed and dangerous. They were mostly slovenly. Mostly dirty. Mostly bad smelling. Molly wouldn't come near them, and any time they happened to be in the dooryard, she never appeared without the musket in her hands. It seemed to have a deleterious effect on any thought of an extended stay, and so they usually left quickly.

There were a few Cherokees. These always camped in the timber, well away from the house, and came as though they were making a formal visit to some government official. Sometimes, they brought their women. Molly liked the Cherokees, not least because they all spoke English, which was easier for her than French. Some of the women were very pretty, and the men sometimes had fuzzy mustaches and beards and had they not known, the Fawleys would have supposed these were just another brand of white man, like maybe Portuguese or Italians, although none of the Fawleys were expert in knowing how a Portuguese or Italian looked.

There were Osage hunting parties, sometimes as many as twenty men, usually with a few women among them. They came directly into the clearing, arrogant and proud, and almost all the men were at least six feet tall. They spoke French. At least it was the only language the Fawleys could recognize. But they were good at sign language, and their hands with long fingers were eloquent. They might have been a frightening bunch except that early on they showed a certain respect for Boone Fawley, obviously a sign of recognition that here was a representative of Auguste Chouteau, a man their fathers had traded with personally and trusted. It was reassuring.

Reassuring or no, at night, after some of the furs had been exchanged for Chouteau trade whiskey, the Fawleys followed Demaree's advice, brought all the livestock into the cabin, barred the shutters, and waited out the night as the Osages had their celebration, or whatever it was, in the dooryard, dancing and singing and raising hell. But in the morning, with the Fawleys still inside and watching through the shutter cracks, the Osages would leave, almost always many more of them walking than on horses or mules. At which time the boys began their complaining about having to clean the animal shit off the floor of the cabin to carry it out and dump on the sweet potato plants.

Molly thought she liked the Osage women even more than the Cherokee. The Osage women, after overcoming a few moments of wide-eyed reserve, seemed to have a lot more fun than the Cherokee women did. What Molly didn't know, of course, was that as they chattered and laughed among themselves, the joke that made them giggle was something said about their hostess with her freckles and bare arms muscled as a strong man's and the bulging breasts held up and out by the laced bodice that Molly still wore just as she had in St. Louis.

Nobody stayed too long. On this edge of Cherokee and Osage

land where neither was completely dominant, they were all extremely nervous about sitting too long in one place where a war party from the other faction might surprise them. Having seen the result of such a thing happening and knowing what being caught in such a meat grinder themselves would mean, Boone Fawley and his elder son were as nervous as their Indian customers. And when the Cherokees or Osages faded off quickly into the great timbered area to go about whatever business they had elsewhere, Boone and John heaved great sighs of relief.

During winter months they saw no one. It was a time for mending fence and harness and buildings and cutting trees to expand the growing ground. It was a time, too, for Molly and Boone to frown and figure over the accounts-current book, Molly doing all the addition and subtraction and Boone adding only his knowledge, learned on the St. Louis riverfront, of the value of the hides and furs they'd taken in trade. They never caught up to what they owed because each year, as winter was breaking, another party came from the north with a new load of trade goods.

The men who brought the things from Our Old Gentleman now were not Frenchmen or Spaniards. They were the new-breed Americans, always in a hurry. Once, accompanying one of these was Fulton, who said that Demaree died of cholera and his wife and little son as well, and that both Maddox and Williams, the other two of Demaree's wilderness men, were off along the upper Missouri with an outfit trying to trade with the Assiniboins and likely by now lying scalped and putrid in some Canadian bog, left there by one or the other of the tribes friendly to the English Northwest Fur Company or maybe the organization called Gentlemen Licensed to Trade Out of Hudson's Bay. And Fulton said he would not see the Fawleys again in this land, either, because after the current trip into Osage country he was going with a man named Jim Bridger who was off to the Great Shining Mountains after beaver, a man highly recommended by none less than Captain William Clark.

It was a touching thing, this hard wilderness man with a light of something in his eye other than violence as he told Questor that they would meet no more. Unless, of course, said Fulton, the lad should come to the Far West, and naturally, in his innocence, Questor said he would undoubtedly do so. And thereupon Fulton said he would teach Questor the best way to eat buffalo guts, and laughed. It was the first and only time that any of them had seen so much as a smile on the face of any of those frontiersmen Demaree had first brought onto their homestead.

The trickles of news from the outside world, like the probability of war between America and Britain and the beginning struggle for the Far West fur trade, left Boone Fawley cold. Even in St. Louis, he'd never been very cosmopolitan, and now, buried as he supposed he was in this endless hardwood wilderness, he was not inclined to pay much attention to what went forward—or backward—in the rest of the world.

Most important was the cycle of things. Clearing, planting, harvest. Laying up the tow sacks of cornmeal like a parapet against the onslaught of winter starvation as they had seen the first winter. Now, there were still a few chickens; there were the pigs growing toward butchering age in the new sty Questor had built once he'd found them running wild in the timber where Captain Hadley-Moore said they would be. The cow was healthy again, giving milk, too, although usually flavored with wild onions from her grazing along the edges of the homestead clearing. The wildlife that populated this land had already learned to avoid their cabin clearing, because of John's rifle—he had become a true expert marksman—and the dog. It meant a wider cast for meat in hunting, but it also meant that weasel and fox and panther were not too tempted to come close enough to harm domestic livestock.

With everything else as it was, Cannibal grew to be a magnificent wood country hound, unafraid of man or bear. And perhaps even aware that he was safe at last from Molly's stew pot.

As for Boone Fawley, it was the true primitive wilderness that New England poets might write about without ever having seen such a thing, and Boone Fawley wished he hadn't. For Molly, it was stunningly beautiful, maybe because it was all she reckoned was left to her now that she was living with a man still her husband but never her lover, a stranger in her own bed. For John, it was a hunter's paradise, and for Questor a theater of unfolding nature.

Maybe Chorine understood what it really was more perfectly, even though subliminally, than any of the others. Maybe in her brooding moments she felt tremors gone unnoticed by the others. Maybe she sensed this place would devour her.

Along the shores of the great river that drains so much of North America, at that point on the edge of glacier during the last Ice Age and five hundred miles north of the Gulf of Mexico, it was pristine and bountiful as any land can be that has been violated by man with little more than a few of his footprints.

The forest was razed in such minute patches that the clearings only tended to emphasize the vast timberlands all around. And the canopy of green leaves in summer and gray lace of bare twigs in winter rose up to maturity, coming down not by the ax but only with the whim of lightning or old age, and the ground below was not governed by human cultivation but by natural pollination, and the colors of spring were stunning in the sunlight of a sky without gauze of smoke from man's fires or furnaces.

The water was what the earth made it, the Mississippi often brown with the dirt of upstream erosion and just as often blue. The smaller streams flowed through the woodlands nearby crystal clear so that in rushing cascades or still pools, you could see the fish and indeed the sandstone pebbles on the bottom, at great depths, as though viewed through a wavy but completely transparent windowpane.

Throughout most of their range, deer and turkey and squirrel and rabbit and raccoon were docile and calm, well ordered in their defense against any predators they had known since time began and not yet aware of the arrival of the deadliest predator of them all. Birds that would one day be libeled as chicken hawks had lived there for eons, preying on their natural menu of mice and snakes and lizards.

Foxes and wolves and badgers and beavers and weasels and ground squirrels and woodchucks were only as furtive as they needed to be in the company of one another. It was, in short, the forest primeval. And perhaps best illustrated by the flying things that were there sometimes for only a passing moment.

There were still great clouds of passenger pigeons roosting in the pecan groves. There were still black-billed cuckoos, pairs in every oak it seemed, their rhythmic clucking heard night and day. Nuthatch, towhee, blue-winged warbler, tufted titmouse, chickadee, red-winged blackbird. And the finch migration in spring, the frantic mobs of fluttering, chirping, yellow thousands come and gone in the cedars within a single hour of daylight.

But most obvious, the waterfowl. Because of the noise they made. The mallards and pintails and teal and gadwall duck, the Canada and snow goose, in spring flying north, in fall flying south, and for endless times blocking out the sun in their millions and the moon at night, their signaling honks becoming as much a part of that place during their passage as the redbud in March and the hoarfrost in October.

For the few human animals who were there, if there was food in plenty and some expectation of safety from the hostility of others, it had to have been a paradise. A grand opera of the senses. Despite the irritants like mosquitoes and ticks and flies and gnats and spiders. Maybe such things even emphasized the wonder of the rest.

However—there is always a however, isn't there?—in this land there was a force unknown. It was inanimate and hidden and yet to announce itself. It might be described as a frontier between massive rock plates of the earth's crust, lying deep beneath the surface, rock plates that for a million years had been grinding against one another with only the smallest movement. This frontier ran generally in a line from far up the Ohio River, downstream along it to the Mississippi, and down it in turn to the mouth of the Arkansas.

One day, it would have a name. The New Madrid Fault.

12

In the late summer sky of 1811, a great comet appeared. It was seen from the Fawley dooryard for only a single night because the time immediately before and after the event was overcast. It was Questor who discovered it for he, of all the rest, seemed most curious about the night heavens and consequently was always looking up. He perceived at once that this was no normal shooting star. It moved so slowly toward the southwest horizon that you could suppose it was moving only by the short tail of yellow-white fire it left in its wake. It was much bigger than a meteorite, too, bigger even than the Evening Star which at this time of year hung over the western canopy of oaks like a cold pinhead in the velvet blackness of late evening.

Once Questor pointed it out, all the Fawleys looked at it, except for Chorine who was already in her blankets, and they looked with obvious disinterest and were soon inside the cabin once more, leaving Questor alone to watch and wonder. To him, it was like the tip of a finger tracing a line through black ashes to reveal a bed of living white flame. He was much given to such metaphor, but he had learned not to mention such things because when he did John told him he was as crazy as a drunk duck. John undoubtedly remembered that phrase from their old French tavern-keeper friend in St. Louis, who must have figured that of all crazy things, a drunk duck was craziest.

Soon, the comet was forgotten. It was the time for fall harvest and preparation for cold weather and everyone had to pitch in, even Chorine, though she did so only after a great deal of insistence from Molly that she do. For John, it was the season for intensive hunting, laying in meat to be prepared as Fulton, one of Demaree's wilderness men, had explained to them a long time before. The meat dried on racks in the sun and wind, pulverized, mixed with any fat and seasoning available, and packed tightly inside cleaned gut, tied off and cut at appropriate intervals. Left to hang in a dry place, this meat lasted all winter without spoiling and was in most ways delicious. It was, of course, the Indian pemmican that frontiersmen had known about since the time of Old Noah Fawley's sojourn in Kentucky and later elevated to a fine art on the High Plains and in the Rocky Mountains.

As winter approached, there were a few occasions when they heard thunder even though their own skies were clear blue. Sometimes it was very loud, too, and Boone Fawley said there must be a jim-dandy of a storm just beyond sight to make such a racket. During one such afternoon, Boone Fawley was in the large field plowing up cornstalks to be used as silage. After the rumble of sound from the east, he had what he supposed was a slight spell of dizziness, as though the earth had moved underfoot. But he had little time to think about it. At that moment a hornet or yellow jacket must have stung the mule because with a great snort and braying he lunged out of the field, dragging the plow behind, and disappeared into the west woods, Boone Fawley following on the run, cursing enough to bring out Molly's King James that evening after supper.

Questor found the mule almost a mile from the clearing, in a hickory grove, tangled in his lines and plow chains and walleyed and not too disposed to be brought back home. Questor used a hickory switch and some of the mule language he had heard his father use, and had she heard it, Molly would have brought out the butter paddle along with the King James, and likely well before supper.

Two days later, John came in from a hunt with thirty-two squirrels and said he could have gotten more except for running short on powder and shot. It was after dark when he returned, and

Molly since sundown had been in an agony of apprehension, but as soon as she saw that her elder son was safe this changed into a roaring rage at his having stayed out so long.

"But Ma, I seen a thang I never seen before," he said, "and had to find out."

"Find out what?" Molly bellowed.

"I don't know."

He said he had been hunting the north woods at about noon when there came a great, scrambling mass of gray squirrels, more squirrels than he had ever seen, going frantically toward the east. John had often seen the chase when an old boar squirrel was after a young male with the intent of castration, and in such circumstances knew that the young squirrel gave his attention to nothing except escape from the old boar's teeth. Now John had seen the same kind of blind rush but not of a single young male whose hope of progeny was imperiled, but of literally thousands of the little beasts, not migrating slowly from one feeding area to another as squirrels often do, but in headlong flight.

Naturally, seeing nothing pursuing them, John went to find what it was they were rushing toward. He followed the chattering, bough-shaking gray horde across the St. Francis where branches overhung the water and they could cross without getting their feet wet and on east, where John said he figured they would turn right or left at the Mississippi because squirrels, unlike raccoons, do not particularly enjoy swimming and in fact are not very good at it.

"But they never done nothin' of the kind," John said.

"They never?"

"No. They dove right into the water and swum, and it was likely a mile acrost there, and I come on downstream and seen all the drowned squirrels in the current floatin' down and a lot of them washed up on the bank."

"Into the big river?" asked Boone Fawley. "Squirrels?"

"They did. Right into the river."

"They surely gone crazy," said Molly.

There was a long silence before Questor said, "Crazy as a drunk duck, wasn't they, John?"

Well, maybe it was true, Boone Fawley reckoned. The livestock had started acting queer. The horse had taken to charging around the stock corral, whistling, and every time he passed the mule, the mule tried to bite him; the pigs had started a furious effort to root their way out of the sty; the cow was obviously going dry and stood around all day and most of the night bawling like one or the other of her stomachs were aching; and Cannibal did a lot of whining and looking off into the timber with his tail stiff as though an Osage war party was coming. And there seemed to be fewer birds. In fact, Boone Fawley, as he thought about it, couldn't recall in some days having heard crows cawing or blue jays fussing. And for a spell now, his younger son had not taken a single fish with trap or hook from the St. Francis. All Molly's chickens had stopped laying. And Chorine, from what Molly had told him, had constipation. Well, hell, you couldn't count that. Chorine always had constipation.

It was something obvious, but nobody wanted to talk about it. Boone reckoned there must be poison in the wilderness air. Molly figured it was witchcraft of some sort and started spending an inordinate amount of time reading the King James. John acted as though whatever it was would manifest itself in some form that he could shoot and thus went nowhere without the Lancaster pistol stuck in his belt and the Pennsylvania rifle in his hand, both loaded and primed, and he kept glaring around at the near woods looking for whatever it was he might be required to kill. Questor, who wanted to talk about all these strange things, restrained himself because he didn't want to be ridiculed. He was in a snit of anticipation, half fear, half joy, like a child who thinks he is about to finally see Santa Claus, eager but frightened. Chorine didn't seem to give a damn one way or the other.

So they all kept their own counsel, as it were, until finally they could no longer avoid facing it together.

Midway through December, on a crisp but not unseasonably cold night, they were in their beds. Old Noah's stem-wind watch would have shown that it was about 2:00 A.M. John was the first to sit up and throw off his blanket, but he had no chance to shout before the others were awake as well. There was a roaring crash of noise, and through the shutter cracks came brilliant flashes of red light. And the cabin was moving. Even as they scrambled into clothing, Chorine by now screaming, the wood and rock and mud-mortar fireplace was crumbling and falling into the room. The floor heaved upward and the walls squealed and buckled, the ridgepole cracked like a rifle shot and one end of the roof fell with a shower of shingles, scattering tubes of pemmican that had been hung on the rafters. Through the wild din, they could hear the insane cackle of chickens and Cannibal baying furiously, first close by and then faintly, finally gone.

"Sweet Jesus," Boone Fawley was yelling, and Questor was coming from a tangle of shingles and Molly's pots fallen from wall pegs.

"Outside, outside," Molly was screaming as the stovepipe crashed down.

They rushed, scrambled, crawled into the dooryard, still pulling on clothing, and there the ground was lifting up, then dropping like waves on a swollen stream. The landscape was bloodred with light, shot through with blinding bolts of blue-white flame. To the east, they heard the ripping splinter of trees splitting and snapping, and the thunder noise rolling on and on made Chorine clamp hands to ears. Like a wave, a roiling cloud of sulfur-smelling smoke came and was whipped along by a driving wind, and then, in calm again, settled like stirred silt in the bottom of a pool.

Then it was gone. The ground in the dooryard was firm, solid, not like one of Molly's cornmeal mush puddings. The flashes of light were gone, too, leaving everything in darkness. The sudden silence was almost as unbearable to the ears as the roar of sound had been. All that remained was the rotten egg smell. And the smog.

They squatted in the darkness, panting, close together, stunned and speechless. The only sound was Chorine sobbing. The chickens had become inexplicably quiet. The dog was gone. It made them give a violent start when the cow bawled, once, and then was silent, too. Maybe the animals, as stunned as they were, were mute in terror. They squatted there a long time, growing cold. They felt a slow wind from the east, and it was unseasonably warm and began to dissipate the foul smoke. They were still there when the dawn came, gray and dismal, no sun shining through the smoke that hung at a higher altitude.

Molly was first to speak, and her voice sounded tense and foreign, especially to her children.

"An earthquake," she said. "I heard of them."

"Earthquake?" asked Boone, and his voice even stranger than his wife's.

"I expect so," she said. "There are earthquakes in the Book."

156

"There are?"

"Yes. I don't know where just now, but there are. They must be in there somewheres."

"Sweet Jesus."

"God's will be done," Molly said, rising to her feet.

"Sweet Jesus, I'm surely obliged He made it short," said Boone Fawley. "I reckon it's all over and hope it don't commence again."

Well, it was indeed an earthquake, that initial tremor felt over an area that extended from what would be Nebraska all the way to South Carolina, from what would be Oklahoma all the way to Pennsylvania. But Boone Fawley was wrong. It wasn't over. It was only just begun.

Most affected was Boone Fawley. Except for Chorine, who didn't really count. His hands shook, and his eyes were red and shifty, like a club-beat dog. When he started to say something, he seemed to stumble over his words and could never finish what he started. It was a time requiring that somebody take command. So Molly did.

One end of the cabin was a shambles, the whole structure sagging like a spine-shot deer, and with winter coming, the cabin was first consideration. The cookstove was intact at the standing end of the cabin and serviceable, even without the stovepipe, and Molly announced her intention of kicking up a good fire and a good bait of fried squirrel so everybody would have a full belly for the considerable work at hand. And she proceeded to ration out the work details as efficiently as a color sergeant would have done in one of Captain Evelyn Hadley-Moore's British infantry regiments.

Boone Fawley went with the mule to snake in some of the logs from the north side where timber had been cut for winter wood. He went about it with a rather mechanical lethargy, still so stunned by what had happened that he was operating in a dreamworld, capable of only the most basic functions while muttering about the wickedness of the wilderness. The boys were working with axes on the yet uncut winter fuel logs, which were now measured out for repairs to the cabin. John held his weapons near, as though expecting that the monster susceptible to his gunfire was yet to appear, and Questor was in a daze of wonder at the exhilaration he had felt with the sudden rush of life-threatening danger.

Chorine was sent to gather broken branches from the west side oaks and to pile these against the stock pen where poles had fallen. A temporary measure until new poles could be installed, and the horse and mule, amazingly, were not taking advantage of the break in their fence, maybe because they had been, and were, rooted to the spot with fear. By the time Chorine was finished with this task and joined Molly in the wrecked cabin, there was a fire in the stove and a cast iron skillet of squirrel legs browning. The smell of cooking meat and the sound of the axes in the dooryard seemed to mark a return to sanity in a mad world, the only reminder now of what had happened being the chickens, still clucking furiously and hopping about across the potato patch like idiots. The pigs continued to root for escape from their sty, but they did it soundlessly. Now and again a hot breeze from the east brought the smell of sulfur. Cannibal was nowhere to be seen.

They worked with a will, glad to be doing something other than cowering in fright and helplessness. As John and Questor swung the axes in the dooryard, John's rifle leaning on a log nearby and the Lancaster pistol in his belt, Questor asked, "Did you feel the ground move?"

"How could a body keep from it?" John said.

Boone Fawley was already coming from the north woods, the mule easily pulling three locust logs at the end of the chains. Boone's hands had stopped shaking, and his confidence was building now, maybe because there was the familiar security of feeling his money belt snug about his middle just as it was supposed to be in normal times; that, along with the mule's calm, helped restore Boone's own. If only the damned rotten egg smell would go away!

Molly was at the stove, watching the squirrel cook, when she heard a faint rumble, a sound almost not a sound at all but a feeling that came up through her feet. Then what was left of the fireplace seemed to melt and gently flow out onto the floor like a bucket of small stones overturned. As Molly felt the debris of the fireplace scattering about her ankles, she saw the stove tilt backward away from her and fall against the wall, the fry pan clanking on the floor and squirrel legs scattering in the rising dust.

"Get out," she screamed and turned to grab Chorine who was at that moment half-bent to pick up a scatter of pemmican tubes. They leaped through the twisted doorframe, and Chorine's screaming was quickly lost in a tearing, furious explosion of noise that struck against their faces as they half fell into the dooryard.

The west side of the yard was lifting, tearing the stock pen apart. The earth opened there in a jagged split, spewing sand and rock and pulling trees down and into the fissure. The pigs and their sty disappeared into the crack; the cow ran free across the yard past the boys who stood transfixed, axes dropped, and almost knocked Molly to the ground, bawling and udders swinging awkwardly as she ran. And as suddenly as it had risen, the ground dropped and the fissure closed with a grinding roar, and more trees fell straight down across what was left of the corral and pinned the horse, who began a pitiful screaming.

"Shoot him, shoot him," Molly screamed. "Shoot the poor thing."

And John, galvanized to action, leaped to snatch up the rifle and ran unsteadily over trembling ground to the edge of the treefall and with one shot to the head stopped the horse's misery. Molly ran to her younger son, who fell to his knees and threw his arms tight around his mother's legs as she shouted, "Boone, Boone, Boone." Chorine was on her belly in the yard, squirming like a cut worm, screaming, hands over her ears, and John was staggering back from the once stock pen, trying to reload the rifle, looking wild-eyed for something else to shoot.

In the quivering cornfield, Boone Fawley snatched away the lines from the single tree and held the mule's bridle and pulled toward the house, shouting, "Molly, Molly, Molly." The mule now as strangely calm as he had been before except that the ears were laid back and the eyes showed mostly white. Behind Boone and the mule, beyond the edge of the north woods, there were fountains of fire and whole trees, roots and all, were thrown into the gathering black smoke like so many toothpicks tossed up with giant hand. The noise was an unending assault, and now the smell of sulfur became almost overpowering.

"Chorine," Molly screamed. Chorine had leaped up and run east toward the privy, her face a white mask of incomprehensible terror. "Chorine, come back here!"

And even as Molly watched, the ground there opened like a mouth, with a gasp, almost a sigh, and Molly saw the privy, then the cow, then Chorine disappear into the cavity. Molly started to run but Questor held her. Now there came a new sound, rushing like a huge hiss, and Molly saw the wall of water coming along the new fissure, a boiling brown slug, cutting the banks of the crack, trees on the far side undercut and falling into the flood in solid ranks. The water went slashing on to drown the old potato patch, some of it, beyond the surging torrent, running across the yard in what seemed an instant ankle-deep before the cabin that had shuddered and completely collapsed, tendrils of gray smoke coming from the wreckage where Molly's cookstove fire had set timbers ablaze.

"Molly, Molly," Boone Fawley shouted, and was now in the yard, leading the mule.

And Molly, furiously pushing Questor away from her legs, was looking west where there was less heaving of surface and where no water and no trees were being thrown into the air, but only a trembling and rumble. She started in that direction.

"Run," Molly shouted. "Run away from here."

"Chorine?" Boone wailed. "Chorine, where's she at?"

"No, no, gone," Molly shouted and with a grim determination took one of Boone's arms and pulled him toward the west. "Run, run, damn you!"

"Sweet Jesus Christ!"

They were barely to the edge of the west woods when the burning cabin's flame reached the kegs of trade powder in the storeroom and it detonated with a flashing red roar, almost a welcome sound because it was the kind of explosion they could understand, but they rushed on into the swaying timber without looking back.

"Run, run," Molly kept shouting.

And Boone Fawley, stunned, as wild-eyed as the mule, could only gasp the name of his sister.

"Help your pa with the mule, dammit, help him!"

Flashes of orange light glimmered through the increasing gloom of the rolling black sulfur smoke, and for a long time, even above the continuing crack of tearing rock at their rear, they could hear the rushing water of the St. Francis River in its new course through the once-dooryard of their homestead. In one last look behind before going deeper into the timber, Molly could see the sand and rock and water and fire and trees spewing up to fantastic heights beyond where the east wood had once been but where now every tree was lying down, one on the other like dominoes pushed over by some demented child.

"God's will be done," Molly said. "Help your pa, John, don't let him fall down. Questor, don't turn loose of that mule!"

As they staggered through that dark forest, swirling now with putrid-smelling smoke and the ground trembling beneath their feet, they had brought away with them the weapons and powder and shot, thanks to John. They had brought away some of Old Noah's Spanish gold, thanks to Boone's idiosyncrasy. And Old Noah's stem-wind watch in Boone's smock pocket. And in Questor's pocket, fishhooks and line, and in his belt a skinning knife. And the thing Molly had put in her apron as soon as she had gone back into the shattered cabin after the first tremor, the King James Bible. They had the clothes on their backs, except that John and Questor had lost their moccasins in the wash of water over the dooryard and were barefoot. And they had the mule.

13

If Molly Fawley had steered a seaman's compass course from New Madrid southwest to a point midway of the Arkansas River line in the district that would soon be Arkansas County in what would soon be Missouri Territory, she could not have been closer to taw. Of course, she knew nothing of seamen or compass, but she knew her family had to seek higher, and certainly more solid, ground. Maybe at some time in the past few seasons, one of those scruffy hunters from the south had said there were hills and even mountains in the direction she now chose. But for whatever reason, she moved correctly. And there was no mistaking that it was her, not Boone, making the decision.

At first, the ground was sometimes still, sometimes quaking. But no matter, they drove on, day and night so long as they could, and then dropped from exhaustion and slept piled close together like fox kits in a den, taking warmth from one another. And John twisting the mule's head until he lay down, apparently happy to lie awhile with the family clustered against his back.

The biggest problem initially was water. Sometimes they were wading waist-deep. Sometimes they came to streams impossible to ford and had to detour upstream to find a place to cross. All running water in the area they crossed at first was a torrent of red mud and debris, brush and trees uprooted. Always Molly pushing them southwest. Food was not a problem. There was game, and even with the pistol birdshot loaded, John and Questor kept them supplied with meat. Sometimes, when the woods were wet from rain—and this was the case many times—they ate it raw. Otherwise, they started a cook fire with flint and steel and black powder in the flash pan of the pistol.

They discovered that raw squirrel was terrible. Like eating a wet dog, so John said. Raccoon was even worse. For raw eating, fish were best, but fish could not be taken in any of the water affected by the earthquake. As they moved farther away from the New Madrid area, fishing was better and sometimes they paused a long time in places where the fishing was good and there were turtles John could shoot with the rifle. They cooked turtles in their shells, in hot coals, then stripped off the bottom plate and consumed everything they found inside the top plate bowl. It was the best eating they had, even better than a large timber rattler stomped to death and skinned as they'd seen Coppertop do it and broiled over open flames. Once, they were closely inspected by a large panther, but it ran away before they could kill it or they would have eaten that, too. John avoided killing birds because it was powder and shot used for a lot of feathers and hollow bone and damned little meat. Sometimes they found wild blackberries and persimmons the birds had somehow missed in the fall.

They'd started with only one horn of powder and began to run low and so had to ration it for the best shots at something worthwhile. It made them hungrier than they could have been.

They crossed the long hogback that would one day be called Crowley's Ridge and on into the flats beside the Black River, which was here reduced to a trickle from earthquake disturbance upstream. Then into sharp hill country, pausing more often now. They were thankful for the mild winter thus far. John and Questor were wearing moccasins of uncured squirrel skin, fur side in, and the skins smelled like hell and blistered their feet.

Sometimes, beside their evening fire, Boone Fawley would mutter the name of his sister and Molly would pat his shoulder.

"God's will be done," she would say.

After the prairie west of the Black, and then the low hills, they were into heavily wooded high ground, still moving south but more westerly now, and then down into the narrow floodplain of the White and to the colorful limestone bluffs on the north bank of the river called Calico Rock. There, Molly decided, they would lay out the winter.

By now they were as scruffy and hard-bitten as those hunters who'd come to trade with them, hunters from this same area where now they paused because there was water and game and fish and overhangs of rock to shelter them from snow flurries and rain, and where they could keep a fire going constantly, and where there were wild reeds along the river that would satisfy the mule's hunger. It was there, at Calico Rock, that they saw the first human beings since their escape from the New Madrid quake.

The two men came to their bluff-overhang camp on foot, and they were a disreputable lot, heavily bearded and hide clothes dirty and patched. Of course, Boone Fawley looked much the same as they, and the boys as well, except for lack of beards. Molly assumed a role of warm hospitality, offering rabbit and fish, and the two men accepted and asked if there was any whiskey. Boone Fawley was glad to have some sort of companionship and was almost apologetic about the lack of hard spirits. Questor was sitting at the fire, within the circle of the two hunters and his father and mother, toying with the Lancaster pistol, which he had used that same afternoon to kill the rabbit the hunters were now eating and which he had reloaded just prior to their arrival. John, at the start, had moved back against the limestone wall away from the fire and stood there now with the rifle, encouraged to stay where he was by Molly's quick glances.

These men spoke English, even though one said his name was Lejeune. They were hunting out of Arkansas Post, far south of here, and had been in the woods since fall and taken many hides, which had been carried back south by a party of their friends who were Quapaw Indians. Now, they were ranging north a ways, they said, into country they had not seen before. When Boone Fawley asked them if they might sell a little powder and lead, they said they would, and Boone made the mistake of taking off his money belt and counting out a few small Spanish gold coins. Molly could see that on sight of the money, the eyes of these two hunters took on another shine not there before, and she said later she would sooner hit her husband in the head with a cast-iron skillet than have him reveal his money before strangers again.

"Well, now, lady," said Lejeune, smiling and showing extremely brown teeth, "you appear to have some warlike whelps here with all the firearms."

"They be tolerable good hunters," said Molly, and Lejeune laughed, as did his companion and Boone Fawley.

"Well, now, lad," said Lejeune to Questor. "That there be a mighty huge pistol for such a boy. You put it to its real use now and again?"

"Now and again, he does," said Molly.

"What is it you shoot at with it?" asked Lejeune.

"Most anything," said Questor.

"You got her loaded now, I expect?" said Lejeune and laughed again.

"Yes sir," said Questor. "With buckshot."

It was an innocent statement of fact but enough to make Lejeune and the other hunter stop laughing. Lejeune glanced back into the shadows where John stood with the rifle, almost directly at Lejeune's back.

"Well, now," said Lejeune. "You got yourself some mighty stout boys, I expect, huh, lady?"

Molly laughed and reached out to rub her hand across Questor's head.

"Surely, now, but this one here is still my baby." Then she leaned forward and spoke in a low voice, Boone Fawley beside her and blinking in confusion. "That one back there, with his rifle, now he's a deadly shot but ornery, I'm afraid, and bad tempered and takes fits of commotion. It's why we ain't ask you to join us here beside our fire to sleep the night. It's hard to reckon what one so touched in his head might take and do to somebody, and even his own pa's afeared to try and take that rifle away from him."

Lejeune and his companion seemed to become more aware than ever that John and the rifle were directly at their backs. He expressed condolences that the Fawleys, such fine people, he expected, were burdened with a son of uneven disposition, and shortly rose and explained that as it was coming on dark, he and his companion would move off upstream to find their own campsite.

The two hunters were no more out of sight than Molly moved her own crew in the other direction, far along the bluff overhang to a fireless camp where anyone approaching could be observed, arranging her sons like sentries, one to sleep only with the other one awake. Both were grinning now, knowing full well what their mother had been doing all along, but Boone Fawley was as confused as perhaps he had been when the first tremors of the New Madrid earthquake had shaken his legs. And maybe would, for all his remaining years, be just as confused about things that had no more to do with that New Madrid experience than this business of the hunters did. And the maddening thing was he suspected as much.

In their dark, rocky bed that night, without even the cover of cedar branches they'd had in the old camp, he whispered to Molly.

"For Christ's sweet sake, Mol, you tell them men our older boy's touched. Make out he's dangerous."

"Yes, you fool," she whispered furiously. "Because he is, when need be. Don't you know that?"

"Touched?"

"No. Dangerous!"

The night after the hunters had visited their camp, Boone Fawley was restless in his sleep, when he slept at all. Mostly he lay awake thinking. Having known for a long time that his sons were his intellectual superiors, it was now galling to realize that Molly knew it, too. And that they could play their little games—like making those two men Molly called swamp pirates uncomfortable with Fawley company—and do it right in front of him and he not aware that any game was being played. After the two strangers had departed in some haste, Boone Fawley had seen his boys grinning at each other while he, their own daddy, was still ignorant of anything except that Molly had laid strange behavior at John's door.

Maybe what was worse, his own dumb display of their money had been what required Molly's prank in the first place. There he was, supposed to protect and defend his wife and children, and he himself created situations they had to salvage for safety's sake, at least so far as Molly saw it. He wasn't sure there was any threat from those men. He wasn't sure but what Molly dreamed up the threat in her own mind, and made him, Boone Fawley, appear an idiot in front of his own children.

He figured he didn't have anything to get a good hold on anymore. Everything had come apart, fallen down around his ears. Just when he'd almost come to terms with the wilderness, it had bitten him, taking away all his work, all his home, his sister, and now, by God, his self-esteem. And there was no doubt in his mind that the earthquake was a part of the wilderness. He couldn't conceive such a thing happening in a place like, say, St. Louis. So as much a part of the wilderness as the sandbar massacre.

And now, they see the first human face since the quake, and the first human face that Boone Fawley does not associate in some way with the massacre, and Molly gets a tic about mean and dishonest strangers willing to steal a man's goods. When all they were doing was traveling along peaceful and calm and trying to survive in this damned place, and looking pretty bad with the burden of it, but didn't everybody who had to put up with the wilderness? Everybody who was crazy enough to be here in the first place?

He was glad when the dawn came. It was a gray dawn, and beyond the protecting overhang of rock, there was snow falling. It was like chicken feathers and rather than really falling, it seemed to drift aimlessly toward the ground. It fit Boone Fawley's mood.

When he rose, Molly did not stir, and that was good because he was angry enough with her to start a row. Angry or not, he didn't want a face-off of temper with his wife because he figured he'd lose it. It was a narrow ledge where they'd slept. The mule was back against the limestone bluff wall, watching him, as was John. John was sitting some distance away, toward where their last camp had been, leaning against a huge slab of fallen rock, the rifle across his legs. Beside him, curled unto himself like a ball bug, was Questor, sleeping.

Boone Fawley pulled his hat down low, without nodding or in any way acknowledging his son because Boone Fawley was angry with him as well, and Questor, and in fact angry with all except the mule. It wasn't too cold, but he was stiff and he shook himself like a dog and started to pick a pathway down the face of the bluff toward the river. It was like a rough, uneven staircase, with fissures and clefts between the strata and a great many chunks of flat rock that had eroded away from the main wall of the bluff and lay somewhat like the fallen stones of some ancient Greek temple. Soil had collected in many of the cracks, and there stunted black willow and witch hazel grew, a regular thicket of brush high as a man's chest. The branches were all bare except for a few patches of last fall's yellow foliage that still held on stubbornly. Halfway down to the river, Boone Fawley could look back and no longer see the ledge where he had slept. He stopped once to relieve himself before going on.

At bottom, he found a large slab of limestone that had broken off the cliff—who knew how many years ago?—and slid only partly into the river, at a slant, like a roof's gable but not inclined quite so sharply that one could not move down it, with care, to the water's edge, and there squat to drink and wash. Boone Fawley did so, moving carefully so as not to slide into the river. After placing his hat on the rock beside him, with cupped hands, he dashed water onto his face and then drank. The water was cold, but it refreshed him and some of his temper began to evaporate.

Along the river, he saw a pair of kingfishers flying downstream, low over the water. Beyond them, through the softly drifting snowflakes, he could clearly see the far bank. It was flat country there, at least as far as he could tell, heavily wooded with oak and hickory and some sycamore along the low banks of the White. The only evergreen he saw were tight clusters of mistletoe in the bare branches of the hardwoods and at this distance, they appeared black.

As he watched the river and the far shore, there was a clatter of small stones marking someone's progress down the bluff, and a few of the pebbles bounced past him along his slab of limestone and into the river with the same clunking sound a bullfrog makes when he leaps into deep water. Now, he felt more well-disposed to his elder son and would at least be civil.

"Water's good and cold, John," he said.

He lifted another handful to his face and the tiny shower of rock cascading past him stopped. He rose and stretched his arms and grunted elaborately, then bent and took his hat and replaced it as he turned to his son. But it wasn't his son.

Lejeune stood grinning, his brown teeth showing in his matted beard, and he was pointing his musket at Boone Fawley's belly. In the thicket of witch hazel and willow, and some distance behind Lejeune, was Lejeune's companion, squatting in the rocks. Even at this distance, Boone Fawley was aware of his leering grin.

"Well," said Lejeune. "You aim to have a little swim in this ole river, huh?"

"No," said Boone Fawley, looking into the large bore of Lejeune's musket, the largest muzzle Boone Fawley figured he had ever seen.

"Why, sure you was, man," said Lejeune.

"No, I was just before hikin' back to camp and havin' my boys find a few young gray squirrels for breakfast, and you are surely sweet Jesus welcome to come and . . ."

Lejeune cut him off with an impatient wave of the musket and a harsh laugh.

"No you ain't. You gone take a swim in this old river, man," he said. "Only first, you take out that little ole belt you got underneath of that hide smock!"

Boone Fawley thought he heard the one back in the bluff's thicket giggling.

"Well, come on, man, I ain't aimin' to stan' all mornin', so take off that belt. Lemme see it again, man."

Boone Fawley fumbled for a moment with both hands under the smock and then had the money belt loose and pulled it out and held it and it dangled like a dead snake. Lejeune laughed again.

"Well, then, yes siree, yes siree, there it be, so drop it, man, go on, drop it on this here rock. Fore you take your swim."

Boone Fawley dropped the belt, and it made a dull thunk as it hit the limestone.

"Oh now," said Lejeune, "that's a good man, there. So you can take your swim now, and maybe you gonna be real quiet about it, ain't you?"

Boone Fawley watched entranced, like a mockingbird chick before a black snake, as Lejeune shifted the musket to his left hand, holding it by the small of the stock, and with his right pulling a pipe tomahawk hatchet with a six-inch blade from his belt. Back in the thicket, the second hunter had stood up among his witch hazel and willow. Lejeune lifted the hatchet and moved a foot forward toward Boone Fawley and Boone Fawley heard the thud of the heavy lead slug first and then the report of the rifle, and the hatchet and musket fell onto the slanting rock and slid past him and into the water, and back in the thicket Boone Fawley was aware that the second man had turned and dashed away. Lejeune's knees began to buckle as he stared with bulging eyes, not seeing really, and his grin sagged and his breath came out in a gurgling gasp and a little whine as though he was trying to speak again. Then he was down, not falling, but collapsing like a wet burlap sack, and sliding along the rock headfirst and slowly rolling onto his belly and at the last leaving behind a thin streak of crimson and then his body lodging with head and shoulders in the water of White River and Boone Fawley saw one of Lejeune's hands, still clasped as though holding the musket, and the fingers twitched once and then were still. And along the greasy deerskin jacket from under the left arm, a widening spread of brilliant red.

Then Boone Fawley heard the second shot.

"Sweet Jesus," Boone Fawley gasped, and bent to snatch up the money belt and scramble up the bluff, clutching the branches of willow and witch hazel and pausing only enough to get the belt under his smock and tied in place again. "Sweet Jesus!"

He came up to John standing on an outcrop, slamming the ramrod into the rifle, and there was still the odor of burnt black powder. John was looking downstream along the bluff, where the scrub was thickest, and he hardly glanced at his father as Boone Fawley heaved himself up to stand even with him.

"I seen the other son of a bitch," John said. "But he run like a scalded cat when I shot first, and all I got was a long one at him and he was in brush so I likely missed him, but he'll know what he's in for iffen he comes back!"

Then, finished with reloading, he glanced quickly at his father's empty hands.

"Where's his musket at?"

"It slid in the river," Boone Fawley said, and he didn't recognize his own voice.

"Well, it didn't look like it was no account anyways!"

John led back up the bluff to the ledge where Molly and Questor were waiting, stiff legged and wide-eyed, Molly with the Lancaster pistol in her hand.

"It's all right, Mol," Boone shouted.

"What was that shootin'?" Molly shouted.

"I missed a rabbit, Ma," said John. "That's all it was."

He glanced back at Boone Fawley, who figured what the hell, two people share one secret, might as well make it two.

"You missed a rabbit?" asked Questor. "Twice?"

"I reckon. If I hit him, it ain't worth lookin' for him."

"I wish you wouldn't go rabbit huntin' when I tell you to watch out for swamp pirates," Molly said and whirled and handed the pistol to Questor. "Off after some varmit, and we all might get our heads stove in, and not watchin' like I told you I wanted done."

"Yes'm," said John, and he and his father exchanged glances again. Then Molly turned back, and she had her hands on her hips.

"Well, I made up my mind," she said. "We're movin' upstream right now to find that place them men yesterday said they was somebody with a boat could get us across the river, and when the weather fairs up, we'll go."

For a moment she glared around, waiting for opposition but obviously receiving none, turned back toward the mule.

"Come on, Boone."

"All right, Mol," he said and figured at least there was one good thing. He wouldn't have to lie and wheedle around about getting them away from this place where that thing was lying at the foot of the bluff half-submerged in White River until the turtles dragged it off. And then began to wonder if maybe Molly had made up her mind to get clear of this bluff because she suspected what those shots had meant.

Left momentarily alone, Questor and John stared at each other, and Questor whispered, "You wasn't shootin' at no rabbits!"

"Hush your mouth fore you get your ass in trouble."

"Uh huh, uh huh, I'm gonna get my ass in trouble 'cept I'm the baby around here, ain't you heard?" Both boys snickered.

They began to move then, and as he swung the rifle over one crooked elbow, John could still feel a little heat in the barrel from the firing and in his mind was as calm and detached as he had been a long time ago when he'd shot and killed his first snake.

With early spring, they crossed the White, as over Jordan, Molly hoped, and maybe to a new beginning. And at least maybe now Boone would come out of his dull shock, or whatever it was that had possessed him since the earthquake, and begin acting like a husband once more in their bed at night. In fact, as she pondered on it, she realized the strangely glazed look in her husband's eye had begun after that last visit he'd made to the Mississippi sandbar trading post and discovered Clovis Reed's intention to depart.

They crossed the White River flats, then over a low range of hills that lifted higher toward the west, the easternmost extension of the Boston Mountains and the Ozark Plateau. Finally into a broad, dark-earth floodplain, heavy with timber and full of game and fish. They kept looking, kept moving, they didn't know for what yet. Unaware that this country, theirs now, was at war with Great Britain once more, at war with the land of Old Noah's birth. But at least knowing from the scouts of John and Questor that just ahead lay a great river. The Arkansas.

THREE

THE COTTON PATCH

When we sat by the fleshpots.

—Exodus 16:3

14

Twenty miles up the Arkansas River from its mouth on the
Mississippi was the district capital, a mosquito- and disease-
plagued hamlet called the Post of Arkansas, inundated by annual
floods and parboiled with steaming summers. These conditions had
persisted since the post's founding by old Henri de Tonti—a buddy
of La Salle—back in the time when this vast delta region was
claimed by the king of France and populated almost exclusively by
Quapaw Indians, a less than numerous people constantly harassed
and terrorized by Chickasaws from east of the Mississippi and Osages from the north, even though they were cousins to the Osages,
as it were, both tribes speaking a Siouan dialect and probably in the
not-too-distant past both part of a larger whole that had splintered
into smaller enclaves, as was the custom among North American
aborigines.

When he saw Arkansas Post, having come upriver with his
father in a long cypress dugout manned by a company of black
slaves, Michael Loudec was appalled. He felt betrayed by his father,
who had persuaded him to come, forsaking the delightful lace and
wine and music and gumbo of New Orleans for this obscenely
primitive place. And he was suited to a deep appreciation of lower
Louisiana's civilized enchantments, having in his veins the blood of

many peoples who had collected around the mouth of the Great River since early in the sixteenth century. A heritage of which he was not only inordinately proud but about which he was extremely arrogant, especially for a young man who was only nineteen. Maybe he owed such attitudes to his father, Mourton Loudec, who possessed those same qualities in obvious abundance. Michael's mother had died of yellow fever when he was only four, so there had been no sweet temper to soothe masculine vanity and headstrong insolence with a pinch of humility and human kindness.

Maybe pride and arrogance were necessary in a man who had become one of the well-to-do, if not wealthy, in a rapidly expanding society of cotton and rice entrepreneurs, on plantation and at the sale warehouses as well. Maybe father and son were only an expression of the time and place. Andy Jackson saved New Orleans from the British in a battle fought after the war was officially over, a very important battle nonetheless because it proved that Americans—and they needed this kind of proof after the British had burned their president's White House—could whip English regulars or anybody else, by God. And if anyone personified that conviction, it was Mourton Loudec and his son.

Maybe with this father and son, it had nothing to do with being Americans. Maybe it had to do with their French background, and of course nothing suited a Frenchman so well as whipping the British. Within a few weeks of their coming to the Post of Arkansas, in fact, they would have days of despondency upon hearing the news of what had happened in Belgium, at a place called Waterloo. But what the hell, Belgium was a long way from the cotton fields, so the despondency was decidedly temporary.

The Post of Arkansas was a scattered collection of slab-side buildings, some on stilts, and a precious few others of more substantial structure where territorial business was conducted, as directed, supposedly, out of St. Louis. There were the usual territorial officials. A district judge, a circuit clerk, a sheriff. There were a small number of white women, wives of the district judge and circuit clerk and sheriff. These were the people who took considerable civic pride in the fact that just the year before an actual ordained Presbyterian minister had preached a sermon before traveling on upriver. They were proud, too, that there was no Indian menace. In fact the only Quapaws still this far downriver had already been reduced to a gaggle of drunken beggars.

These were the people trying, with good chance of success, to make this country a territory separate and apart from the territory of Upper Louisiana. Well, more correctly, now the territory of Missouri.

Nobody was sure how many people lived there. Most of the men were itinerant hunters roaming the woodlands to the north and west and leaving behind Indian wives and half-breed children. Or equally mobile canoe and barge men on the river, also with Indian wives and half-breed children. In a real census, nobody was sure who to count. Certainly, there was not much cotton on a large scale, meaning rich planters, of course. So now it was time for men like Mourton Loudec to change all that. But there is no record that anyone recognized his coming as the advance guard of those who would start a fantastic parade of speculation in land.

There was in the town the usual allotment of taverns. In one of these, which amounted to the parlor of the district judge's home, where travelers with cash or furs might also arrange for a night's lodging upstairs, Mourton Loudec passed certain comments about the savage nature of things thereabout, much of which was taken as bruise to civic pride by his host, the circuit judge, who naturally challenged Mourton Loudec to a duel. The good His Honor said that such insult could only be exculpated with pistols, which Mourton Loudec said he understood completely and therefore would retire upstairs with his son for a good night's rest before the morrow's confrontation.

As a matter of fact, Mourton Loudec had gained some considerable renown in New Orleans for successfully competing in just such affairs, but he said nothing about this to the judge.

Next morning at dawn, Mourton Loudec and his son went to the river sandbar where such contests of honor were conducted, at least when the river wasn't in flood, and found the judge waiting with what appeared to be the entire white population of the settlement, a number of half-breeds, and at least twenty black slaves.

Mourton Loudec said that had he known his opponent was going to bring such a following, he, Mourton Loudec, would have come out the night before and built fortifications. The sally so convulsed the judge with laughter that he found it impossible to carry on and instead invited both gentlemen from New Orleans back into his home-tavern for a bracing morning toddy. Which, in the event, lasted until midafternoon, during which time Mourton Loudec and the judge became extremely drunk and Mourton Loudec ended by praising the beauty and serenity of Arkansas Post, and his son Michael was rebuffed by the Quapaw housemaid of the judge when he made an ungentlemanly suggestion about strolling in the local swamps.

Thus Michael Loudec passed through the Post of Arkansas and on upstream with his father, looking for better ground and feeling miserable until a rainstorm soaked them and cooled their fevered brows, which they exposed to the falling water by removing their wide-brim, flat-crown planters' hats and sitting in the dugout, eyes closed, faces into the rain, listening to the chant of their African oarsmen. And perhaps Michael thinking to what dreadful depths he had fallen after such a romantic family beginning in the New World three generations ago.

The first Loudec came to French North America in 1743, mostly because he was a young man unsettled in his religious convictions. In fact, he had no convictions, religious or otherwise.

He came from Brittany, which got that name from the Welsh who had come there after the Roman legions left the British Isles to the tender mercies of Saxon and Viking invaders. In about the third century. So young Loudec might have made a case for being Welsh. However, his family had long lived near Normandy, which had been populated by some of those same fierce Vikings. So he might have claimed Danish blood. But for generations, Loudecs had been subjects of the French king and spoke French as their native tongue, so he could say he was French. Which becomes rather complicated when you consider that the first Frenchmen were called Franks, who were Germans.

As a matter of fact, young Loudec at various times vehemently claimed ancestry among all those peoples. It simply depended on who he might be talking to and drinking with at the time, the drinking being important because it is usually at drinking times that young men proclaim various things vehemently, most especially their ancestry.

But the religion.

He was what you would call a Huguenot, a French Protestant. But even of that he was unsure. He was born in a time of religious squabbles, and he hated squabbles. They confused him. Most confusing of all were religious squabbles that turned into wars. They were not only confusing but terrifying. So when the War of the Austrian Succession erupted, he perceived it as a religious war, although of course it was really a contest of power. But young Loudec saw Britain and Prussia on the one hand as Protestant, which was mostly true, and Austria and France on the other as Catholic, which was also mostly true. The idea of taking sides in what was to him a holy ideological brawl was unthinkable, so he fled to Louisiana.

He took with him some financial means because, as fate would have it, only a few months previous his Uncle Emil, a bachelor in the apple country of Normandy, had died, leaving him a lifetime of profit from a process that turned applejack into a relatively respectable beverage called calvados.

New Orleans was already a city of some importance. There, Michael Loudec cut a fine figure in his beaver hat and in his various escapades met a few gentlemen who helped him invest in profitable ventures, like the slave trade and sugar plantations in the West Indies. He soon found himself with a carriage and a matched pair of bays, a house with an interior courtyard, and a beautiful mulatto woman named Cockchew, or some such pagan thing, who in 1755 gave birth to a son whom they called René.

The boy was the only issue of the union, and he became the center of his father's universe. René's mother faded into some sort of oblivion, never a part of the family record, which was not uncommon for mistresses. According to eyewitnesses, she was not present at her son's wedding when he was twenty-one to a French-Canadian lady called Paulina Guidery, or some similar Cajun name, and the affair was of such fantastic proportions that during the ball Michael Loudec had a massive stroke and was paralyzed from the neck down for the rest of his two years of remaining life. What René inherited was a large sugar brokerage firm, various business licenses issued to

Loudec from the Spaniards who were now governors of Louisiana, a large cotton plantation in Iberville Parish, and two hundred and thirty-seven African slaves.

René Loudec and Paulina had many children, but only one seemed fitted for the family enterprise. This was Mourton, their third born. Shortly after he reached his majority he married a niece of Louisiana's governor-commandant. Her name was Carlotta Maria Perez de Ortiz Gracia Mendoza, or some such thing. By that time, Mourton was at the ground floor of the rising thing in New Orleans, which was cotton, not only as a major factoring firm on the exchange and owner of the Iberville properties, which had now grown to three, but also as owner, through agents in the United States, of many acres across the river from Catahoula Parish in what would soon be the state of Mississippi.

For the family business, everything had seemed to work. The Purchase. General Jackson's defense of New Orleans. And certainly, the world demand for cheaper cloth, which meant cotton. It was therefore natural that when intelligence arrived in New Orleans that there were nice flat lands crying out for cotton seed, all along the tributaries of the Great River, Mourton Loudec would extend the empire if he could. Thus, up the Arkansas.

And with him, the son born to him and Carlotta Maria, etc., in 1797. The newest Michael, named in honor of the one who had come from Brittany. Four years after that birth, Carlotta Maria had taken yellow fever and died.

So this was the disgusted and distraught Michael that was paddled up the Arkansas by his father's slaves. He of solid stock, or so he thought. Maybe Welsh and Danish and African and French-Canadian and Spanish. But who, through some perversity of nature, or the whim of chance, or most probably because since he was twelve he'd been acting as an interpreter in his father's cotton warehouse between French and Spanish buyers and American sellers, knew English better than any of the other tongues. And he was now rather repulsed to find that he was in a land where government and private business were conducted in English, and so there was not an opportunity here to dispense with the damned Anglicans' speech and go to one of his blood.

And so he was frustrated even in the sounds he heard coming from his mouth, all of it a kind of vocal rebellion against this place.

Well, maybe he could learn Quapaw. Now after all, that maid in the judge's tavern in Arkansas Post could have been rather tasty, or at least plentiful, with perhaps a bath and some French talcum powder, after a few sips of wine!

Mourton Loudec was a man finely tuned to the happenings throughout America and Europe. He had to be if he expected to retain and expand his business enterprises. One of the things he followed most energetically was new inventions or the conditions that might produce them. Obviously, if he had prior assumptions of future differences that would assist him in his endeavors, it gave him an advantage over competitors, a situation most sacred for any good businessman.

He collected his intelligence as a matter of course, and as a matter of course as well passed on to his son what he had learned or suspected. He'd been doing this since Michael had passed his eighth birthday. As a result, the younger Loudec had a very solid grounding not only in entrepreneurial activities but in history as well.

During the first years of the nineteenth century, the United States of America was suffering a severe case of paranoia. Mourton Loudec did not use that particular word but what he said to his son meant the same thing, and Michael understood it. This national fear had considerable solid justification.

On the north were the British, always ready to contest claims of the new republic concerning land in North America. Until the Treaty of Ghent in 1816, England didn't even recognize the Louisiana Purchase! Spain was still anxious to regain old imperial splendor at the expense of the United States and was a constant threat in the Southwest and in Florida until 1819. France could always be counted on to get a toe in, if the chance came—as she proved later when French troops and a Hapsburg emperor were sent to Mexico by Napoleon III.

In Tripoli and other African nests were pirates overjoyed with the prospect of stopping ships on the high seas, taking Americans captive, and demanding ransom for them. And on every frontier edge of the nation were at least one or two tribes of people who could be counted on to be hostile. Even a pacifist like Thomas

Jefferson—whom Mourton Loudec had met in Paris—had to give much troubled thought to defense once he'd been elected president. That meant acquisition of a lot of reliable firearms. A great many common citizens were thinking about the same thing. Flintlock muskets over fireplaces from Boston to Baton Rouge were not hanging there for decoration.

No other modern nation was ever made so constantly aware of the need for weapons as the young republic. And had Michael Loudec lived into the twentieth century, he would never have wondered why America developed such a love affair with guns.

From the government's standpoint, there was a great problem. Muskets and rifles were all handmade in that time. When put to use, if a part was broken, a gunsmith had to be sought out to forge another part to fit that particular weapon. It was usually cheaper and a lot faster just to start from scratch and make a new gun.

There was a young man who was hungry because the profits from an earlier invention of his—which would change the face of history in America—had gone into the pockets of other men. So he came forward and said to the government that he could make a lot of muskets in a hurry. His name was Eli Whitney. And he started this project in 1798.

Well, it took a lot longer than he had supposed it would and there were fantastic cost overruns, naturally, but the government was so anxious to have what he offered that they continued to put money and faith into his project. All of which was justified, because he finally did it.

What he did was revolutionary. In Europe, where the people were mostly interested in textiles and steam engines, no concept such as Whitney's had surfaced. With absolutely fantastic foresight, he came up with the idea of machine tools. Now, machine tools are precisely engineered metal objects that make and adjust precisely engineered machines that make the precisely designed end product. In this case, guns.

It's very simple. You make a bin filled with hammers, a bin filled with triggers, a bin filled with sears, and a bin filled with barrels. The trick is to make each hammer like all the others. Each trigger like all the others. Each sear like all the others. Which machine tools made possible. Then, you just grabbed any old hammer and trigger and sear and put them together, and they worked. What you had were interchangeable parts! If you were in the field against a Seminole or a Spaniard or a Frenchman and you broke a part on your musket, you didn't have to throw the thing down and depend on nothing but your hatchet. You just reached in your pocket and took out one of those parts and put it on the gun, and it worked!

It was an idea so foreign in Europe that when American entrepreneurs later went to Britain to establish weaving mills, they had to send home for machine tool mechanics to service the looms because nobody in England knew how to do it. An argument could be made that it was America's greatest single contribution to the Industrial Revolution. Machine tools.

So what about that earlier invention this genius had brought? The effort that had showed so little profit for him he was reduced to perfecting a method of making firearms?

Well, the first European settlers along the southeast coast of the New World found the marshy lands near the sea ideal for long-staple cotton. Long-staple cotton is a fine grade of fiber, and what made it even better was that it could be separated from the seed by hand, using unskilled labor. Slaves. But beyond the coastal wetlands of the Carolinas and Georgia, it was impossible to grow.

There was another strain of cotton, the short-staple. The effort to separate the fiber from the seed with this plant was long and painful, so it was not considered economically feasible to develop big slave plantations to process it. Thus, for a time, it appeared that the only place where big plantations with unskilled labor could prosper was along the coastal marshes.

In Delaware and Maryland and Virginia, where big slave plantations had begun, the land had been ravaged by the crop that made plantations economically profitable, tobacco. By the turn of the nineteenth century, a lot of powerful people in those places were already thinking about phasing out slavery because it seemed to be at a dead end.

Then came Eli Whitney and that first invention, the cotton gin, for which he is best known. This gadget would separate short-staple fiber from the seed mechanically. Suddenly you could make enormous money from growing the stuff because it would grow in a lot of places and once grown, be made ready for market and no single skilled laborer's hand had ever to touch it.

Not only did the cotton gin save slavery in the United States, it enlarged it fantastically. Cotton planters were rushing across the southern country, across Georgia and Alabama and Mississippi and Louisiana and into Texas looking for flat ground where short-staple would grow.

And even while Eli Whitney was getting those machine tools set up for making guns, the miracle of his gin was sending short-staple men up the river system of the Mississippi. And they were bringing their slaves and their cotton gins with them.

Thus, Mourton Loudec into Arkansas.

Almost one hundred miles above Arkansas Post, at a place called Point of Rocks—sometimes called also the Little Rocks— Mourton Loudec found what he wanted, proceeded to mark out about six hundred and forty acres of flat land, and made a plat to identify his claim by landmarks once he went back downriver to pay whatever was required to the agent of the government handling the public domain. He needed to note those landmarks because there was no way to survey it. It would be a year yet before the United States sent a team west of the Mississippi to determine intersection of baseline and principal meridian. When they did, it would fall about one hundred miles due east of Point of Rocks and would constitute the initial benchmark from which all surveys were calculated, not only in the district of Arkansas and the rest of Missouri Territory, but also in Iowa and later Minnesota, the Dakotas, and other western lands. Until then, you had to have natural landmarks to designate your ground.

There were relatively few people in the area. A man named Hugh Evans ran a ferry across the Arkansas. Nickel for crossing, ten cents for a team and wagon. He had no license for this operation, which he was supposed to have, but he was in process of obtaining one from the authorities in St. Louis. Evans was industrious, honest, Welsh, Methodist, and prolific.

The ferry was a flatboat barge operated with a large rope and windlass that Evans had brought up from New Orleans by keelboat. It was the kind of heavy cable and machine you'd generally find only on ships and docks of a seaport city and such an oddity that locals often came to admire it.

Of course, during flood stage the ferry ceased operation, giving the opportunity for the full energy of Hugh Evans and his wife, four grown sons and their wives, and seven grandchildren, to be turned toward the major enterprise, which was a trading post and tavern located just up the bank from the southside ferry slip. This was a log and slab limestone structure that looked more like a disjointed mule barn than anything else and was grandly designated on a crudely lettered sign over the main door—it being the main door by virtue of the sign hanging above it—as the Little Rocks Hostelry and General Mercantile, Blacksmith Shop in Back. H. Evans, Prop. Whiskey Five Cents.

The Evans family alone was enough to create a settlement, but there were others in a few scattered shacks generally clustered around the Rocks Hotel, as everybody called it. There was a man named Samples who was the local representative of government, being a duly appointed and sworn deputy sheriff. He lived with a Quapaw half-breed woman whom he claimed as his wife, although nobody was aware of any ceremony attending the union. Usually, there were a couple of Quapaw women about his place, relatives of his wife no doubt. These were offered by Deputy Samples for solace to lonely travelers, for a price, the place of companionship being the lean-to room abutting the Samples' one-room residence, the price being an astonishing fifty cents, or appropriate barter, of which the woman got to keep a dime. If the transaction was for, say, a one-third interest in a red fox pelt, all she got was the goodwill of Deputy Samples.

At the north bank ferry slip there were a few squatters and a small competitor to the Rocks Hotel, an establishment operated by a man named Emil Harp who not only dealt in pop-head whiskey and bullet molds and such things but had adjoining his store a tiny mud-mortared sandstone building in which he had an altar, candlesticks, a blue cloth hanging on the wall, and certain religious relics. He called this a chapel and had personally dedicated it to the Virgin Mary. He maintained this place and held it in readiness for any chance-passing Roman cleric whom he would insist hold mass or perhaps other sacraments of the Mother Church. So far, no Catholic priest had seen, much less used, the place, most of the passing clerics in that time being fanatically dedicated to the doctrines of one or the other of the two Johns, Calvin and Wesley.

The same locals who came to see Hugh Evans's cable and winch sometimes crossed the river to see the chapel, most especially the long splinter lying on a table with candles at each end which Emil Harp claimed was a piece of the True Cross. After viewing this marvel, most locals said, "Hell, it looked like a chunk of Arkansas River driftwood to me." However, illustrating the power of suggestion, they said such things only after they were safely out of and well away from the chapel.

Certainly business enterprise at this Point of Rocks was encouraging. As when a company of soldiers from the Rifle Regiment of the United States Army keelboated upriver in 1817 on their way to establish a garrison on the Arkansas at the mouth of the Poteau, which would be called Fort Smith, and paused long enough to spend all the money they had. In fact, the river was becoming fairly well traveled and, just as important, there was a trail that crossed the Arkansas at Point of Rocks, a trail beginning in southwest Illinois that would soon become a road traveled by just about everybody from the Ohio or upper Mississippi valleys on their way to Texas.

As for actual settlers, there were only a few when the Loudecs arrived, but before long there would always seem to be a couple of land speculators boarding at the Rocks Hotel and then, as always, more and more people willing to chop out farms and try their hand at starving to death, unless, of course, they had a good sideline like a whiskey still in the nearest creek bottom or a sorghum mill hard beside the mule shed.

There were two former soldiers homesteading on the quarter sections given them as pension for service with Jackson in the War of 1812. These were not happy farmers and were more than willing to sell to Mourton Loudec. There were a few squatters, with no real legal claim to anything, and Mourton Loudec hired them all as laborers so that he could immediately begin construction of a substantial house, slave quarters, and gin shed on a knoll overlooking the river about two miles downstream from Point of Rocks.

There were two places on the edges of the land Mourton Loudec wanted where cotton was already being grown, but mostly in minute quantity. Cotton patches, he called them. But these appeared to be the community's only solid families, the Buchanans and the Campbells, good Scotch-Irish.

Well, there was one more. Upstream from the settlement, beyond the ferry slip, on ground a bit too hilly for what Mourton was interested in at present, but maybe in the future. Hugh Evans told him this was the Fawley place, some three or four years in being, a house and small barn of logs and cleared ground and put all to sorghum cane and corn and vegetable garden in summer, and run by two boys and their mother. The father, one Boone Fawley, spent most of his time at the Rocks Hotel, tavern section, with Deputy Samples, telling over and over again how they had been in the big earthquake on the Mississippi, how the family had come away from there with the boys barefoot all the way, how Boone Fawley had to fight off woodland desperadoes, and how next year, or maybe the year after that, he was pulling stakes and going back to real civilization in St. Louis where he had some very influential friends, indeed.

The Fawleys had come by their farm through a program of the United States government, in which people ravaged by the earthquake received in compensation a quarter section of land from the public domain. The agent dispensing these so-called New Madrid Certificates had long since departed, Hugh Evans said.

Shortly, Mourton Loudec had his plats, which included not only what he already called the Plantation, but a few acres immediately beside the Rocks Hotel because he had the foresight to understand that a town would grow up here and the real estate values would be something to make a New Orleans banker smile. Thus armed, Mourton Loudec went back downriver to make his arrangements for legal acquisition of the land he wanted, leaving Michael in charge of further construction, which made Michael so furious he was almost ready to murder his father.

Mourton Loudec left the work force of scruffy whites, about half his African slaves, and the promise of sending a few good saddle horses back as soon as possible. He had confidence in his young son's abilities and provided almost no advice on how to proceed but plenty of firepower to do it, a brace of .69-caliber cavalry pistols and an eight-gauge single-barreled shotgun.

Mourton Loudec's confidence was not misplaced. In a fury of activity, Michael cleared land and built buildings. And weeded out his work force. At the start, he found one of the squatter laborers a rather lazy fellow so one day escorted him, his wife, and two children to a river flatboat barge, and told them to leave and come back only on peril of being blown to bits by the gigantic shotgun, which throughout this entire process Michael Loudec had held in his hands.

Nor was he reluctant to use a blacksnake whip to keep the African slaves awake. But to prove his management ability, he discovered among the slaves one Timbou, who appeared to have leadership qualities, and who therefore was named overseer, and to make it obvious to the others, his badge of office was Michael Loudec's blacksnake whip.

"Timbou," said Michael Loudec, when conferring this honor on the African, "take the whip. Try not to kill anybody."

Thus, with a little leisure in which to find entertainment in this primitive place, Michael Loudec hunted and began a sketchbook of birds—being very talented in such things as drawing—and strolled along the river. There he met a young man of about fifteen whom he quickly perceived to be forthright and friendly and possibly the most intelligent human being he had seen since leaving New Orleans. The boy's name was Questor Fawley.

For one who had all his life been accustomed to having others bring his food to table, Michael Loudec was amazed at how some of these viands were captured. Fish and turtles and frogs—for the legs, of course—and waterfowl. Questor Fawley showed him. Michael Loudec began a sketchbook of river creatures, and most interesting was the gar, a very vicious-looking long-nosed fish with teeth like an immature barracuda, almost the same temperament, and meat that was very nearly inedible.

It was more than that, too. In the woodlands, Questor Fawley showed him the wild things that were good to eat, some delightful, in fact, like the grainy wild blackberries, or frost-burned persimmons. Michael Loudec began a sketchbook of wild plants that made good eating.

He allowed Questor to fire the large shotgun, which Questor said was the biggest gun he had even seen. By now he was large enough not to need somebody else to help him hold it, as he explained to Michael Loudec. He allowed Questor to watch Timbou work the construction crew, and to talk with Timbou. Of course, Questor Fawley told of Coppertop, but this was no Coppertop. Timbou was a big man but not much older than Questor himself.

He had been a slave initially to some Englishman in Jamaica, and he spoke English almost as well as a British army officer named Evelyn Hadley-Moore, so Questor said.

Michael Loudec was often disappointed that Questor Fawley had to hurry home to do his part on the farm there, cutting short the education in wilderness living that Michael Loudec was getting, realizing all the while that it was better to be receiving such an education from someone rather than having to learn in order not to starve.

So in the many months it took for Mourton Loudec to return with horses and more slaves and cottonseed and a gin and furniture for the plantation house, Michael Loudec formed this strange association. He and Questor Fawley. And perhaps Timbou as well, for Michael Loudec became more and more dependent on the slave. An association that would last for a long time. Michael, Questor, Timbou. A strange association indeed, which Michael Loudec realized, and maybe it was therefore even more fascinating. And maybe ill-fated. He didn't know. That fascinated him, too. He began a sketchbook of portraits. Questor Fawley. And Timbou. He never tried to draw himself. Even when he was a little drunk on some of his father's French brandy.

15

They began to call their community the Little Rocks. Like all Americans of the time, they were in a hurry, so unnecessary baggage was dropped. Hence, Little Rocks.

Americans *were* in a hurry. Toward what, few of them knew. But it was a view of themselves they liked and was somehow important. It was expected that the goal be charged, headlong, although the goal was elusive or even unknown. Even people like Silas Catchen were inspired by haste, unlikely as that might be. Silas Catchen was a hunter who spent most of winter in the wooded hills north of the river, most of summer lying drunk against the outside wall of Hugh Evans's hotel. In autumn, Silas was in a hurry to be off to the wilderness. In spring, he was in a hurry to get drunk and lie against Hugh Evans's wall.

So with the mania for "getting it done"—which often included paring down vocabulary to the shortest possible word that made any sense—the plural was dropped and the settlement thereafter honored only a single stone on the riverbank. Little Rock.

By that time, the people of the community had reached a consensus on something else as well. Boone Fawley was a pathetic drunk. Now, it was expected that somebody like Silas Catchen would spend most of his hours among them in a stupor of alcohol haze. He was a hunter and lived with a Quapaw woman in a slab-side cabin near the river's edge. Such a thing was part of the condition of being a hunter. But it was shameful that a man like Boone Fawley, with a fine white wife and two fine sons, should fall victim to the demon.

And they were a fine wife and sons, too, everybody agreed. Industrious. With a nice patch of ground. Corn and sorghum, regular as the seasons. And now, cotton as well, which they carried to the new Loudec gin, and there it was baled and shipped by barge downriver. And after gin fee and transport fee and fee for the Loudec wagon and mules that hauled the fluffy bowls to the gin in the first place, the Fawleys enjoyed about a third of what the cotton brought on the New Orleans market.

Well, there was a factor fee, and he was likely a Loudec man, too, but anyway, after all the fees, maybe the Fawleys got only about a quarter of what the cotton was worth. But it was solid cash.

So it was a shame, they said, for a man like Boone Fawley to be sitting in Hugh Evans's tavern drinking with Deputy Samples and sometimes Silas Catchen when he paused for a few drams before going outside to his usual place against the wall. Except when it was raining, when Silas took his place against Hugh Evans's inside wall.

Hugh Evans was a civic-minded man, concerned about the reputation of his town, if it could be called that. He was concerned about chickens and hogs and sometimes a goat wandering about along the street, if it could be called that, in front of his hotel. He was concerned about the quagmire all around his place when it rained too much. He was concerned about the dust. He was concerned that the only medical doctor within God knew how many miles was Clarence Biddington, the reputed bastard son of an English duke, who lived across the river in a mud-mortared sandstone house and made periodic trips downriver to replenish his stock of nostrums and drugs, whether needed or not, and who had supposedly buried somewhere behind his house a trunk filled with Portuguese gold and black peppercorns, and who made strange sounds when the moon was coming full.

Actually, Dr. Biddington was just a reclusive little man who wore Ben Franklin–style eyeglasses and kept his distance from everybody and was therefore the perfect person about whom stories could be told without much chance of contradiction. He was almost none of the things people claimed. He was an opium addict.

But Hugh Evans. He and his wife Ernestine often discussed Boone Fawley, as people always discuss those who might taint reputations, and sometimes were joined by their four sons Griffith, William, Harris, and Esten, all of whom, according to Ernestine, were named after good Welshmen who had become famous in the business of writing minor-key hymns. If the conversations were not confined to their living quarters, but rather in the store or tavern, they were joined by whoever might be handy. Provided, of course, that none of the Fawleys were about.

Like William Like, recently appointed agent to the Quapaw Indians who lived in a stone house the Evans boys had built him at proper price, not far from the hotel. And who had distinguished himself in St. Louis with his first official report in which he characterized all white people in the territory of Arkansas as bandits and his own charges as lost and innocent children, victims of the Cherokee and Osage.

Or perhaps Logan Brock, a kind of unofficial mayor of the community but really a real estate speculator. He was head, so he said, of the Trans-Mississippi Land and Cotton Company, Limited, and owned the considerable acreage around the Evans hotel that was not already owned by Mourton Loudec and the small quarter-section square beside the ferry slip that was still assigned to the Quapaw tribe, although no Indians lived on or near it. Logan Brock and his wife Lena, who appeared to be French, lived in a three-room cypress log cabin with a dogtrot, along with a man named Mercer, who was reputed to be a crack shot with pistols and maybe a bodyguard. In his front yard, if it could be called such, was the largest oak tree in the area, its trunk at the base measuring forty-two feet around.

Or maybe the conversations were joined by Idella Harp, who was not as crazy as her husband and who came across the river from time to time to visit Ernestine Evans and her platoon of daughters-in-law, she being acceptable to Methodists because she was not really a papist like her husband, or at least not crazy enough to take a chunk of river driftwood, call it a piece of the True Cross, put it on display in a chapel dedicated to the Virgin, and charge passing pilgrims a penny to see it and a whole nickel to touch it.

Poor Emil Harp. He was stigmatized by his own neighbors as a goofy religious fanatic, when in reality he was only a struggling businessman trying to attract people to his place so that maybe they would buy a single tree or a box of snuff. The folk of primitive Little Rock could hardly be expected to know that such practices were common in medieval Europe, where holy relics were collected with the obvious intent of attracting the tourist trade. In fact, if every slab of wood labeled a piece of the True Cross—excluding Emil Harp's—could be collected in one place, they would have been sufficient to build half a dozen instruments of crucifixion, each bigger than the Colossus of Rhodes.

But of Boone Fawley.

"Here he came, a good man but full of sorrow," said Hugh Evans. "Losing his all in the great earthquake. And at first, only a sip here and there, but then more than a sip."

"Leeks grow only in their own ground," his wife Ernestine said, whatever that meant.

"Aye," said Hugh.

"That poor thing, that good woman," said Ernestine, closing her eyes and shaking her head. "Know her well, me, and she said so many times, the man was no farmer and knew it and the Lord God proved it to him when He opened the earth and let it swallow his sister in it!"

"They tell me he does put on the dog, so," said Idella Harp. "About his high-and-mighty friends in St. Louis."

"Aye. A man downtrod will do it to make hisself forget."

"In his cups, too," said Ernestine, nodding, "even more will he do."

"Aye. Now most every day of the world."

"And I hear," Idella Harp said, "those boys in here to get him home when he's too bumble-headed to get there on his own two legs."

"Take him home, they do," said Ernestine, nodding and leaning closer to the others and lowering her voice. "And there the three of them take off his clothes and bathe him in Molly's kitchen." Then leaning back in her chair, still nodding but louder now. "Right in the tin tub bought here in Mr. Evans's store, it was, all the way from Cincinnati. Two dollars it cost! All the way from Cincinnati!"

"Aye, I sell what a man needs," said Hugh Evans. "And it's no sin of mine if he use it for his own sin, but each man his own responsibility. So with the whiskey."

"Sots they be in the Bible," said Ernestine. "And sots they be here as well, and no blemish on you, my dear."

"Not so my kind charges," said Agent Like. "They are the children ravaged by the vice of others."

"Ho, now, Like, I never sold a dram to any heathen, yours or any other," said Hugh Evans, his Welsh temper pricked. "So make no accusations else with proof as in a court of law."

"Nothing intended on you, Mr. Evans, and I wish there was such a thing as court of law hereabouts."

"Yeah, well, Boone Fawley still got loose change in his pockets, don't he, or have you started sellin' spirits on loan with appropriate interest?" asked Logan Brock.

"There is courts of law, there is Territorial Court at Arkansas Post," said Idella Harp. The others ignored her.

"You said he lost everything in that earthquake, but he spent a lot of Spanish gold to buy the things for that patch he's got," said Logan Brock. "And that tin tub, too."

"Well, not him, his older boy. Just a sprout."

"Mighty big sprout, I'd say," Logan Brock said. "I seen that boy close up on occasion, and I ain't many times looked so near into a mean cat's eye."

"They make a tidy sum now," said Idella Harp. "So they say."

"The boys of Boone Fawley," Hugh Evans said and laughed and slapped his legs and pointed at Logan Brock. "You know about the shining mule trade, don't you?"

"No," said Logan Brock. "I heard some stories."

"Remember that Rather?" asked Hugh Evans. "Came here, he did, bag and baggage and two black slaves and a pair of Quapaw women?"

"A reprehensible man," said Agent Like. "Two of my children not much more than slaves, as concubines even. A reprehensible man."

"I recall," said Logan Brock. "Gambler and land speculator and cad, and liked his drink, too, much as Boone Fawley does."

"More, maybe," said Idella Harp. "I heard that."

"Oh yes, and that night drinking with Boone Fawley, too, he was," said Hugh Evans, having trouble talking because of his bubbling laughter. "Yes, yes, the Dada drunk with this man when the lad came in."

"John," said Ernestine.

"Aye. John. With a tin of sorghum molasses, a Lancaster pistol, and outside a mule with carrying baskets full of cotton, maybe fifty pounds of cotton, and said he'd like to do some trading, and this Rather, his eyes got misty because he saw this chance of advantage of some poor child, and went out and there, in evening light, the most beautiful mule he'd ever seen, gleaming."

Hugh Evans had to stop momentarily to convulse with laughter, then with great effort and wiping the tears from his cheeks, continued.

"You see, sir, it was the old Fawley mule, the one brought from Missouri. But just two days before, the younger one . . ."

"Questor," said Ernestine.

"Aye, Questor, had come into this store and bought a can of the new wax shoe polish, brown, and paid his two pennies for it, and those boys," Hugh Evans paused again for laughter, then went on, "they'd shoe-polished that mule! A most beautiful mule he was, glowing in the dark and jumping around with energy while Rather inspected his one side and young Fawley . . ."

"John."

"Aye, John, punched the mule in the ribs with a black locust thorn on the other side. So Rather traded. All those things and that mule, for a younger mule, a gelding horse less than two years old, a saddle, and three hounds, thinking it was a wonderful thing because his young mule and young horse were wild as summer lightning and not knowing young Fawley . . ."

"John."

"Aye, I know, my dear. John could ride and gentle the devil himself if need be."

"Do not blaspheme, Mr. Evans," said Ernestine.

"I don't, my dear—how can you blaspheme the devil?—but this young Fawley could gentle any brute. So the trade made and the next day Rather comes sober and sees the shoe-polished mule in full light and makes many terrible sounds. And threats."

"So I heard," said Idella Harp. "Such vile language."

"Shoe polish on livestock hide," Logan Brock said. "That old trick. Everybody's heard of that."

"Not Rather."

"And he was drunk, you see?" Ernestine said. "A drunk man can see his own undoing if only he had the sense to do."

"So Rather goes out to the Fawley place, riding the shoe-polish mule," said Hugh Evans, still having trouble controlling himself. "One must suppose Boone Fawley is sleeping. And the boys are away from the house, working the farm and whatnot. So the only one Rather faces to reclaim his trade is Molly Fawley."

"God love the poor woman," said Ernestine Evans.

"When he broaches the subject, Molly Fawley, in her doorway—God love her, as you say, my dear—pulls out a musket and tells Rather that if he don't leave her property at once, she will blow a large hole in his gut. Rather was back in here quick, I tell you, panting and snorting worse than the shoe-polish mule at the rail outside, and was complaining that his own dogs had run out to bark at him when he rode into the Fawley place and again when he left."

The laughter was general now, except for Indian Agent Like, who muttered about having courts of law to settle such problems and to deal with white bandit incursions upon the rights of his Quapaw children.

"Well, now," said Logan Brock. "Boone Fawley rides that horse all over the place. Looking at the lay of the land, he says."

"Aye, but the mule, he's working that farm with . . ."

"John."

"Aye, John."

"They tell me you don't have to worry about the Fawleys starvin'," said Idella Harp.

"That you do not," said Hugh Evans. "But now, it's more than the cotton they sell to Loudec."

"That still," said Logan Brock. "They likely make more on drippin's than on fiber."

"Aye," said Hugh Evans. "And there's a secret maybe. The Loudecs had a hand in that still, too."

You would think it was John Fawley who became the whiskey dealer. It was John, after all, who had pretty much taken over all head-of-household duties as Boone Fawley's depression became too much for him to handle without those increasingly frequent trips to Hugh Evans's tavern. But it wasn't John. It was Questor.

Folk in that time and place spent considerable energy on analysis of neighbors' motives. So the whiskey still that was set up alongside a small creek in a deep and heavily wooded ravine on one corner of the Fawley New Madrid Certificate property presented enough interesting possibilities to keep conversations going when there wasn't anything better to talk about, like an Indian uprising or a duel on a sandbar of the river or a major flood or cyclone. There wasn't much question about who suggested it and who provided the initial engineering and also the promise of corn to supply the process once it was begun. Michael Loudec suggested it. It wasn't known for certain, but was suspected, that at least half the profit from the still would go into Loudec pockets. Which was a good assumption. But not because Michael Loudec wanted to realize some gain from the local thirst.

There wasn't any real risk involved. Michael Loudec could have set up a whiskey still on the front yard of his plantation house had he so desired, and nobody would have thought much about it even though making whiskey was illegal. Certainly Deputy Samples didn't give a damn who squeezed out alcoholic drippings. Indian Agent William Like could be expected to dash off protesting letters to St. Louis and Arkansas Post, but nobody paid any attention to them, either in Little Rock or at Arkansas Post or at St. Louis. Hell, nobody ever paid much attention to what Indian agents said.

Actually, although none of the locals figured it out, the whole operation was something to benefit the Fawleys over and above their small profit from cotton. Maybe it was because Michael Loudec was grateful that Questor had shown him a lot of wildflowers to draw. Or how to waste uneventful days catching snapping turtles out of the Arkansas, some of which were five feet across the top of shell and weighed four hundred pounds and if you got a finger too close to their beaked jaw it was good-bye, finger.

When they had conversations with the Fawleys, the local citizens tried to worm a little information out about what was happening, but the Fawleys were extremely closemouthed when it came to talking family things, and besides, unless Questor might have suspected, none of them knew why Michael Loudec did it. As for

Questor, he didn't care why. It was a chance he jumped at, and maybe he didn't even know his own motivation.

Ironically, Boone Fawley's capitulation to the jug and slide into alcoholism was the catalyst. The paths of everybody in the family were set off course, like the sun suddenly moving and jerking the planets into strange orbits. For the toughest of them, John, it was not much harder than a well-trained soldier changing step in the middle of his march. For Molly and her younger son, it was more difficult.

Molly watched it with what she supposed was a sad understanding of her husband's destruction, maybe even proud that she saw it so well. Better than Boone Fawley himself, she had finally realized what a wrench it had been for him to leave St. Louis and go into a wilderness, and there sleep each night with the terror of what might happen next, and finally it did happen when the earth erupted against him.

Yet, Molly only knew a part of it. She didn't know about the Mississippi sandbar massacre and Clovis Reed's head. She didn't know about John's shot that had saved Boone's money belt and his life at Calico Rock. John knew these things. And maybe because he knew them, could develop little pity for his father, as his mother did, but only disdain. After all, John had endured them as well, and maybe, just maybe, even enjoyed a lot of it in some strange secret way. Once again, like a soldier, in battle, who sometimes finds a sort of ecstasy at walking along the razor edge of danger.

So John was head of household, and Molly, surely knowing she could have done it herself, was so glad that someone was there to do it that she looked upon her elder son almost as a husband. Depending on him. Praising him. Confiding in him.

And Questor saw all this and wanted some way to make his own worth known, to put some money into his mother's apron to salve her worry about a husband who was no longer much more than a drunken caricature of what he once had been, and maybe, too, a chance to make it seem less important that his father, whom he loved and understood more than John did, could do what he pleased when he pleased and it made no difference to the family. They were still solid.

So when Michael Loudec suggested it, Questor jumped at the

chance to get some of his mother's attention, some of her praise, some of her gratitude. And maybe to put at rest some of the agony he saw in his mother's eyes each time they brought Boone Fawley home from the tavern and undressed him and bathed him and put him to bed.

Molly took the money, of course. But the pain never left her eyes. And the only one she ever patted on the shoulder for good work was John. At least she made no complaints that her younger son was distilling the very demon that ate at her man Boone perhaps because she knew that Boone, on the small coin she gave him now from time to time, could never afford to buy the high-quality whiskey that Questor made. Nobody ever told her that. She just knew.

As for Boone Fawley, there was some spark left. He never took the two Spanish gold coins from his neck to spend them for booze. And he never offered to trade for money the stem-wind watch of his father, Old Noah Fawley. And sometimes as they put him in his bed, his hand reached out and sought Questor's head, and he would feel it and smile and murmur, "Son, them's the lights at St. Louis, see 'em, and tomorrow, we'll go back home there. Look out for the damned Osage!"

Distilled spirits had been a part of the social scene for a long time. So much a part, in fact, that it was taken for granted that hard liquor should be in the daily ration of a nation's army and navy. But the republic of the United States of America had hardly been launched before many citizens began to take the view that distribution of the wicked nectar was a moral evil that should be stamped out.

Opponents of alcoholic beverages were at a decided disadvantage. Not only were they jousting with an addictive drug, not only were they sticking their noses into other peoples' personal habits, not only was most of their leadership thin-lipped fanatical, but they were trying to stop something that was easy to manufacture by anyone with only a modicum of intelligence, a few simple tools, and a supply of plant life that would rot.

In Europe, a lot of popskull was brandy, the distillation of wine or maybe overripe apples, but in North America fruit was not the prime ingredient. Grain was. Which meant corn.

It's interesting to note that American Indians, who were growing corn when Europeans didn't even know what corn was, had never figured out how to distill it.

In the early nineteenth century, there were large distilleries in centers of population. But in the hinterland, it was a cabin industry. And anybody could get involved. Everything started with a mash. Each whiskey maker developed his own formula. A favorite one was to shell corn, put half of it in a burlap bag, wet it thoroughly for a few days—until it started sprouting—and meanwhile grind the other half into meal and boil that with a minimum of water until all that was left was a moist, yellow slug.

Then the first tool of the still. A large barrel, probably oak or hickory staves. The sprouted corn and the cornmeal slug were dumped in, and the barrel was covered and allowed to sit for about ten days, with each day the lid removed and the mess inside stirred with a wooden paddle. Sometimes a little water was added, either at first or along the way. Or both. It depended on the whim of the whiskey maker.

This was the mash. After a short time, it began to take on a distinctive odor. A unique bouquet, which became more and more obvious and aggressive each time the lid was removed. When the scent was powerful enough to make the hair on the back of the neck stand up stiff, the whole mess was dumped into a large cast-iron pot. And boiled with some additional water.

Now came the critical part.

Above the steaming pot there had to be an inverted funnel to catch the rising vapor. From the spout of this inverted funnel there had to be a coil of tubing, copper, that wormed its way to one side of the fire where the drip from its open end fell into a wooden bucket. This was a large bucket. At the top of the bucket there was a sieve and on the sieve chunks of charcoal. The liquid from the copper worm fell into the charcoal, percolated through it, and dripped into the bottom of the bucket.

Now. The cast-iron pot was cleaned. First, what was left of the mash was fed to the livestock. Some said it made the horses more lively; some said it made milk cows' tails drop off. For hogs, it made no difference whatsoever. Hogs were hogs, and that's all there was to it.

The cast-iron pot was scrubbed thoroughly. Lazy whiskey makers deleted this phase. Then the liquid in the bucket was put back into the cast-iron pot, water was added, and boiling and condensation and copper worming and drip all began again. Including the charcoal filter. Now, in the bottom of the oaken bucket, there was liquid, not much compared to the amount of raw material that had gone into it, but very powerful. Whiskey. About one hundred fifty proof, maybe two hundred. Which meant alcoholic content by volume was better than fifty percent. This was now a beverage the old-timers said was powerful enough to singe the whiskers off King James I, if, indeed, King James I had whiskers—which he did, of course, and red whiskers at that.

If somebody wanted to age this beverage, they placed it in oak barrels charred on the inside. But on the American frontier, few whiskey makers involved themselves in such foolishness. They simply added some water to the final drippings and put it on the market.

Sometimes it was clear as spring water and kicked like a twenty-four-pound howitzer. Sometimes when the charcoal filter was not used, it had a yellow cast and tasted like coal oil. Sometimes, if the whiskey maker was trying to compete with rum from the Indies, paregoric was added for color, and this stuff went down like molten syrup and created a long tenure sitting in the privy. Sometimes, when rotten Irish potato peels were added to the mash, it was smoky and had the smell of a New Orleans whore's perfume.

None of this was Indian trade whiskey. For Indian trade whiskey, you used anything that would ferment in the mash like turnip tops, decaying beets, crushed acorns, corncobs, elderberries, and persimmons, seeds and all. You never scrubbed the pot. You ran the mash through the coil only once. You didn't worry with charcoal. You cut it with plenty of water.

And you never, never drank it yourself!

Michael Loudec's African Timbou, showing Questor how to set up the still and make whiskey, didn't cut any corners. And after he'd looked over Questor's shoulder as they proceeded through half a dozen batches of drippings to see it was well done and then went back to the Loudec plantation house, Questor didn't cut corners, either. As a result, his whiskey was clear as spring water and powerful as thunder. So he sold it, to Hugh Evans, of course, for one dollar a gallon, and he marketed it in clear glass jugs—provided by Michael Loudec, as was most of the corn—so everybody could see the colorless quality of what came to be called Fawley Punch.

Hugh Evans sold it for twice what he paid. Half the dollar Questor received went to Michael Loudec. Whose collection agent was Timbou. And the remaining half dollar went into Molly Fawley's apron pocket. Questor's whiskey income far exceeded anything John made from the cotton patch crop.

So he was providing. And taking a habit from his mother, Questor read a lot in the King James and found nothing there prohibiting the making of whiskey. But did find a lot about sin, and began to wonder what it was that his father had done, or maybe Old Noah had done, that would bring down such wrath on the family, like that earthquake and now his father's enchantment with the demon that prevented his doing what fathers are supposed to do. Questor began to think a lot about demons. Or maybe the number one demon himself. And began to wonder where the demon might lurk, ready to pounce.

Questor never mentioned this to John. Because he knew that if there was something John could not shoot, he didn't really believe in it. And would likely laugh at Questor and maybe even belittle him in front of their mother. The more problems he saw, the more Questor tried to find answers in the King James.

"Will you put that book down and get out there and help your brother?" Molly often said. "Sometimes I reckon it was a bad business, helpin' you learn how to read, the time you spend doin' it when there's work to get done."

Others appreciated Questor. Like Hugh Evans.

"That lad," Hugh Evans said. "Touched by divine inspiration."

"Questor," said Ernestine.

"Aye, Questor. Such a young lad and the genius for making that fine whiskey, finest whiskey on this river."

"An abomination," said Indian Agent William Like, who was not only an Indian agent but an Anglo-Saxon Congregationalist and naturally could not be expected to understand good whiskey as a Celt like Hugh Evans did.

I n the first year after Questor began to make whiskey, there was an event close to Christmastime that left a profound impression on him, even though he had no notion of what lay beneath the surface, and what lay beneath the surface was something that would affect the entire community in time.

Mourton Loudec was visiting with his son. The two of them were in Hugh Evans's tavern having a few drams, as they put it, when Mercer, the hired bully-boy of Logan Brock, made some kind of remark about dandified New Orleans autocrats' sons who spent their time enjoying the company of at least half a dozen black women who came in and out of his bedroom like mosquitoes, only Mercer, of course, called the African women niggers, and with that and other insults, Michael Loudec knocked Mercer down with his fist, not because it wasn't true but because nobody was supposed to talk about it.

Mercer, very naturally, demanded a confrontation of honor at dawn next day, which was the biggest mistake he ever made, and on the morrow, in a flurry of early snowflakes and with the faint honks of late south-flying Canada geese coming from above, the antagonists met on a sandbar of the river.

The entire community turned out to watch, standing in the cold wind on the high bank above the river, and the Fawley family was represented by Questor, who had slipped away from the cabin before anyone was awake because he knew that Molly would have forbidden his being witness to anything of the sort. So they all stood in a long line on the high bank, stamping their feet and holding their arms about their bodies against the cold, and watching as the ones active in the drama gathered below. Michael Loudec, his father acting as second, Mercer with Logan Brock his second, Dr. Clarence Biddington from the north side of the river, with a little black bag, of course, and the official referee, Emil Harp, who knew absolutely nothing about his duties but was considered a good official, being a papist and therefore as far removed from prejudice toward either side as one could be.

The opponents stepped off their ten paces each, and turning, Mercer fired first, his shot tearing a rent in Michael Loudec's trousers, whereupon Michael Loudec fired, his ball striking Mercer just above the left eyebrow. The good Dr. Clarence Biddington walked to the felled Mercer but didn't even bend down because it was obvious that there was nothing in his black bag that could bring Mercer back to life, then walked in the other direction and ministered to the bloody little scratch across Michael Loudec's left thigh.

Griffith Evans, one of Hugh's sons, then appeared with a mule and cart to take the body and carry it across the river and bury it in a small cemetery Emil Harp tended behind his Chapel of the Virgin. Griffith Evans, who by this time had become the community's undertaker by virtue of the fact that he said he was and nobody else wanted the job.

Most of the adult male population retired to Hugh Evans's tavern, the Loudecs went downriver to their plantation house, the few women who had witnessed the great event—it was the first fatal duel fought at Point of Rocks, but was certainly not the last—and Questor Fawley accompanied the remains across the river and watched as they wrapped Mercer in a bit of tarpaulin, lowered him into a shallow and rocky grave, and then covered him with mostly limestone chunks, the labor done by Griffith Evans's black slaves. Questor was back home in time for breakfast.

Meanwhile, in Hugh Evans's tavern, the men who had been witness to the killing consumed considerable of Hugh Evans's stock of whiskey—at least for that hour of the day—and Deputy Samples was heard to remark that the only way he would ever be persuaded to have a duel with either of the Loudecs was if the weapons were double-bit axes and the opponents standing in waist-deep water. Somebody else accused the deputy of having heard of such an arrangement from some traveler going upriver and that it hadn't come out of his own head, and a rather festive fistfight ensued. But no more duels. Not that day, anyway.

It soon became the common knowledge of the community, through the source of some slave probably, that this time when Mourton Loudec went back downriver, he left with his son a polished walnut box, which he had always kept near himself, and inside which, resting on blue velvet, were the two silver-mounted pistols, one of which had been the agent of Mercer's demise. And the consensus became widespread that the only way to shoot Michael Loudec was from the back, and so close as not to miss because there would be no second chance.

As for Michael Loudec—and this did not become common community knowledge—the rest of the day he killed Mercer, and after his father had departed for New Orleans, he spent the hours alone in his plantation house making sketches of Arkansas River sandbars.

16

There ain't a way in the world," John Fawley said, "that you can keep abreast of it. And it ain't nothin' to do with us, anyhow."

Thus in response to his younger brother's query about what it meant when news of James Monroe's election to the presidency came upriver.

Well, that was some time ago, Questor reckoned, and maybe John was right. Nothing had anything to do with the Fawleys. No matter all the changes, the elder Fawley boy—and he was hardly a boy any longer—constantly carped about the cotton connection with the Loudecs, constantly stared off toward the wooded high ground across the Arkansas, and talked about what he'd heard concerning the Boston Mountains where there were no towns and no plantations and where a man could breathe without neighbors and government squeezing him.

And as more and more of the plantation men from the South came along the Arkansas and brought their slave field hands and planted their fiber, John gnashed his teeth and swore, sometimes even in front of their mother.

"All we be to them people is white trash," he'd shout. "All them high-on-the-hog outlanders call little farmers white trash, you know it? Even their niggers call us white trash. We ain't no white trash! But the friends we got in this place is scarce as Adam's belly button, you know that?"

Questor didn't see things exactly the same way, but he never argued with his older brother for fear of getting knocked on his butt or at least ridiculed in front of their mother, which Molly never seemed to take as reason to scold anybody. Questor remembered the day when she would have, and sent everybody to a long reading of the King James after supper. But no more.

Questor knew. Coming out of St. Louis had been a journey from good to evil for his father but just the reverse for John. Because John had that insistent call in his soul, or whatever it was that would someday likely be called genes, that characterized mountain men and Arabian hermits and that old king of Spain who built his castle out in the wilds away from everybody and conducted his business from there in a solitude as complete as he could make it. Questor had known it all along. John liked the wilderness and all it meant, and now there was a little too much civilization creeping up the Arkansas River to suit him. John wanted to step to his front door and shoot a rifle in any direction he chose without fear of hitting somebody who just might happen to be passing by.

And there was Questor's mother, weaving a cocoon of agony and despair around herself like one of those woolly worms Questor had pointed out to Michael Loudec—who made sketches of them, of course—and shown Michael Loudec as well how the worm emerged from the cocoon as a butterfly. But there was little chance that Questor saw his mother emerging as anything at all, just slowly weaving the blanket around herself so thickly and stout there was no chance of her cutting her way out or of anybody else cutting their way in. Her only mobility of body or mind was holding the cotton patch together for her sons, and depending more and more on the elder one to take the place of her husband, who was no more a husband to her now than some passing stranger might have been. He's as addled, Questor often thought, as he'd always laughed about his own mother Otis being, that poor old, beaten, abused indentured girl who was not only Boone's mother but obviously Questor's grandmother as well, which gave him a lot of pause about the way his own mind worked sometimes.

And Boone? Well, what could you think about him? Whose only lucid moments anymore seemed to be mornings when he was struggling with a head-splitting hangover and would take the horse—nobody disputed his right to do so—and ride off saying, "I'm gonna take a look at the lay of the land." And sometimes was gone a week. And when he came home so drunk and dirty and stinking that Molly wouldn't touch him until the boys had dragged him off the horse—only God knew how he'd stayed on the horse until the horse got him home—and pulled him inside the kitchen, undressed him, and dumped him in the tin tub that had come all the way from Cincinnati, and poured hot, soapy water over him.

"I'm gettin' damned tarred of this," John would say to Questor. "One of these days, I expect he's gonna have to scrub off his own shit!"

This was one thing he never said within Molly's hearing.

So maybe John was right. Who was president didn't matter. It didn't even matter who was the new mayor of Little Rock, the man risen to that high office in the first local election ever. Cleve Buchanan, who had once been a white trash small farmer, as John would have said, and did, but who was now running ten African slaves and growing cotton on three quarter sections north of the river and bringing his short-staple across to Loudec's gin on Hugh Evans's ferry, but who still maintained residence at southside Point of Rocks and was eligible to be written onto the ballots stuffed into the box at Hugh Evans's tavern, all supervised by Deputy Samples. Nineteen people voted, too. Eighteen voted for Cleve Buchanan. One voted for Andrew Jackson.

When after the election it was determined in a victory celebration at Hugh Evans's tavern that the vote for Jackson had come from Silas Catchen, he was abused by Griffith Evans as being stupid because Andrew Jackson was not even a resident of Little Rock. Silas Catchen responded that whoever said that somebody had to be a resident of a place to make a good mayor for it was stupid, too. A small fistfight ensued, which would become a hallmark of early Arkansas elections, and Silas Catchen was beating hell out of the town's mortician until the other three Evans brothers intervened and finally subdued the old hunter, who left the place bloody but unbowed and swearing to set fire to the whole goddamned town. To maintain peace and tranquillity, Deputy Samples convinced Hugh Evans he should contribute a half-gallon jug of trade whiskey to the cause of individual liberty and freedom of speech, took the jug, pursued Silas Catchen, and took him to the banks of the Arkansas, where both men had a few sips and deplored the modern system of choosing officials. Toward morning Deputy Samples became so intoxicated that he fell into the river and drowned.

Somehow, it has escaped the written record that the first official duty of the new mayor of Little Rock was to officiate at the funeral of a man who had defended the right of a citizen to vote for Andrew Jackson.

Well, Questor knew all this, as no other Fawley did. He spent more time with the town. With its murmurings. He was with Michael Loudec on occasion, and with Timbou, who like so many of the African blacks knew more about what was happening among the whites than the whites did. When there were things to be bought in town, it was Questor who went to Hugh Evans's store, not John. Sometimes Molly went with him, but never to do more than be patted and consoled by Ernestine Evans and her clutch of daughters-in-law. Never to be a part of anything local, but rather as a museum piece that had survived the New Madrid earthquake.

Sometimes Questor sat under the chinaberry tree and read the King James and tried to find something that fit his situation. He knew the words—well, most of them—but they in combination left it all flat so often that he despaired of ever finding an answer to anything. But he read anyway, because he reckoned his mother wanted him to, but always suspecting that in these times, she didn't really care what he did.

John and Questor Fawley enjoyed a great advantage over most of their contemporaries. They had a boundless energy. Molly reckoned it was because they could read. Well, maybe that helped. But there was something else. From the moment they'd come away from the New Madrid earthquake, she had insisted they wear some kind of shoe even if it was uncured squirrel-skin moccasin. And had insisted ever since. So protected them, without either them or her knowing it, from hookworm, the debilitating parasite that entered the skin of bare feet from feces on the ground. Usually dog shit, that is, but not exclusively.

So whether they wanted to or not—well, whether John and Molly wanted to or not—they could not, being more active than hibernating bears, be insulated from the changes going on all around them. And there were changes!

The capital of the new territory of Arkansas was moving from Arkansas Post to Little Rock. There were buildings being built that looked as though they had some significance. Not only finely cut cypress log structures but even a few of native limestone and with glass windows. There was a post office, a real United States of America post office, Esten Evans postmaster, and extremely disappointed that postmasters had no badge to wear, as sheriffs did, proclaiming his importance without his having to explain it to everybody himself. The post office building was of hewn oak logs, it was true, but it had a dogtrot through the middle and a flag of the nation nailed to the front wall, personally sewn by Idella Harp. Of course, the number of stars on the field of blue was never changed often enough to keep up with new states coming into the federal Union. Only recently there had been Indiana, Mississippi, Illinois, Alabama, Missouri. It was the same flag that had been draped on Deputy Samples's coffin at his funeral, but taken off and placed on the post office wall afterward. It was the flag that had a bullet hole in the lower-left-hand corner, about a .69-caliber hole it was. The day after that hole appeared in the sacred cloth, Mayor Buchanan and his council, which consisted of whomever he could find at the spur of the moment to hold a meeting, passed an ordinance against shooting at national symbols inside the city limits, although nobody was sure where the city limits were.

Mail came as infrequently as August rain, and when it did, usually upriver by cypress dugout from Arkansas Post, the occasion was celebrated almost as much as was the time when one of Joseph Campbell's barnyard roosters defeated a fighting chicken belonging to one Mendez-Carnes, a downriver plantation owner from Baton Rouge, where he had bred a coop of colorful West Indian contestants for the cockfighting ring in New Orleans. Actually, it set back cockfighting almost two decades in Little Rock: since nobody from Louisiana wanted to risk a real fighting chicken against a homegrown fowl, the only entrants in cockfights for a long time were nothing more than aggressive amateurs from local barn lots.

There were elections now, a sport many people seemed to enjoy. Anyone who had the remote notion that they lived within the precincts of the county—nobody was sure yet where the boundaries of that were, either—could vote, and did so on selected days, when people came in to drink and talk in the street around Hugh Evans's tavern and try to decide what to do about all the goddamned Creeks and Cherokees going upriver all the time, and usually on that score deciding to let the soldiers at Fort Smith handle it. After all, that's what soldiers were for and they were in the place where the Indians were all headed, so the best thing was to sell the passing aboriginals as much as possible in the way of gunpowder and whiskey, for the growing good of the community, and let them pass on upriver unmolested.

But most of all, there was a newspaper! Not many people could read it, but many who could took great delight in standing before the log printing shop and reading it aloud to collected hunters, Quapaws, half-breeds, black slaves, children, hogs, and passing goats. The hand-levered press had been carried upriver by keelboat from Arkansas Post, where the enterprise had begun, and it was claimed to be the first newspaper west of the Mississippi, which would be challenged for two hundred years. But it had come when the territorial legislature decided to get away from the mosquitoes and floods of Arkansas Post and move to Point of Rocks because William Woodruff, the man who printed it, knew that he needed the official printing contracts of the government, that being the one sure way a newspaper could survive.

It was called the *Arkansas Gazette*. Its first issue at Point of Rocks was a single sheet, folded to make four pages, printed in four columns. When the first issue was published, Questor Fawley was there to get a copy and hurried home to read it. He exclaimed from time to time as he read it at the supper table, with John snorting in disdain but their mother showing some interest, perhaps her eyes even shining a little in the orange lamplight of the new coal oil lamp.

In that first issue there was a story of financial troubles in Kentucky, where they had suspended payment for land with gold. There were pirated stories from the *St. Louis Enquirer*. And Boone Fawley, who was at home that night and eating his turnip soup, lifted his head when Questor said the words "St. Louis." There were stories about various expeditions up the Missouri River to fur country, and John's eyes lighted. A letter to the editor pointing out a policy of the general government to move Indians like the Cherokees to new homes along the Arkansas Valley, thus visiting on local white citizens bloodthirsty carnage and pillage. Classified ads announcing jobs in tanning, tailoring, clerking. A full column on the newest mercantile store in Little Rock, Davis and Parker, as Welsh from their names as was Hugh Evans, offering dry goods, hardware, groceries, shoe brushes, chalk, nutmeg, cigars, powder, lead, queensware with a special on the blue cups and saucers, and on consignment—whatever that meant—one barrel of best proof whiskey and fifty barrels of common good whiskey.

Questor Fawley's mother made a small concession to expanding civilization, accompanying her younger son into town for a visit to the Davis-Parker emporium—in a log structure—looked at the blue chinaware but ended buying nothing more than a few yards of gingham and a package of needles. As Molly browsed in the shelves with Lena Brock, Questor conferred with William Parker and ended by agreeing to supply some of his whiskey at eighty-five cents a gallon, while Mr. Parker promised that in the next *Gazette*, Questor's drippings would be advertised as Best Quality Arkansas Distilled Corn Whiskey.

All around, it was a good day for Questor, not least of which was that his mother seemed for a while to lose her despondent Boone's-gone-bad expression and even developed some enthusiasm for the soap offered at Davis and Parker for one cent a bar, which meant that possibly she could stop making her own from wood ash.

Of course, the Davis-Parker operation had nothing of good for Hugh Evans, who complained to his wife that they were falling on hard times now that just anybody, it seemed, could come upriver and be so high-and-mighty as to sell queensware china. But Ernestine pointed out that they still had the hotel and saloon, and besides, there was the ferry, for which they now had an official license from the territorial legislature, and there were the children, Griffith with his growing business as mortician and talking about going to New Orleans for a few weeks to learn how to actually embalm somebody, Esten, the postmaster—and who knew what all that might lead to?—and William with his blacksmith shop.

"In fact," she said, "Esten has already hinted he will run for the next term of the legislature and a lawmaker be."

"Lawmaker, aye," said Hugh Evans, "and make some enemy in that legislature and called out to be killed in a duel! There is no legislator that I have seen so far that doesn't go about as well armed as some Turk."

"To guard themselves against heathen atrocities."

"Heathen atrocities, is it?" shouted Hugh Evans. "The only heathen atrocity I have seen here is the one where they lie dead drunk in the street, so that a passing citizen might trip over them and break a leg!"

It was all there. The birth pains of a city—even a capital city— one of the great marvels of nature, so Questor supposed. He'd never seen any kind of city birthing. Much less a capital city. All of it to him was more amazing than the citadels of worship that Solomon raised in the wilderness, his knowing a great deal about that from his readings in Kings and Samuel.

To Questor, it was incomprehensible that his father and elder brother could be so oblivious to the great things happening around them. Well, maybe not so incomprehensible in regard to Boone Fawley. Outside his whiskey haze, he seemed clearheaded enough, and now more and more rode off on the little sorrel horse to see whatever it was he rode off to see, coming home at greater and greater intervals.

But John! He simply went about his business of growing cotton and trading livestock as though he really liked it and as though it was all taking place far back in the wildwood away from everybody else. Questor knew John didn't like the farming part. Knew he hated it, in fact, but kept to it from some intense loyalty to something or other, Questor wasn't sure what. He did seem to enjoy the livestock business and was often gone to a place downriver that was called Elm Bluff where there was a lively stock exchange and John at great advantage because he could handle horses and mules so wild that nobody else wanted to bother with them.

There was no doubt that Little Rock was becoming an important place. Because the first lawyer had arrived!

His name was Shiring Rhett, a rather pudgy little man with eyes like a weasel about to escape the trap, a clean-shaven, pink face, tiny hands white enough to have been parboiled, and a purple beaver hat. He stayed at the Loudec plantation until his own rather impressive limestone house was completed, mostly by Loudec slave labor. His new home overlooked from some distance the south bank ferry slip. Nor was it far from the property of Logan Brock, where Logan Brock was frantically building the structures he hoped to sell to the territorial government for the conducting of official business, along with the land on which the structures stood. Close by, as well, to the cabin of the late lamented Deputy Samples. And a hunter's cabin which Shiring Rhett bought to use as an office and hung a shingle there over the door which spelled out his name, and in smaller letters beneath, these words: Austin Land Company, Ltd.

If Hugh Evans was upset with the arrival of Davis and Parker, Logan Brock was almost hysterical with the arrival of Shiring Rhett. Because Logan Brock had always considered himself to be the head boar hog in the local wallow, at least in the business of real estate. With the posting of that shingle, there was a strong suggestion that the former peaceful milieu of one king porker was about to become root hog or die!

Shiring Rhett had first heard of Texas from Old Moses Austin in Missouri. He didn't pay much attention. But then while he was in New Orleans on business, he heard a number of entrepreneurs talking about bursting into Spanish America to establish a slave-powered cotton kingdom that would make them rich beyond dreams. Shiring Rhett enjoyed the idea of becoming rich beyond dreams, and so he began to take note. He asked a lot of questions.

Returning to St. Louis, he met Stephen Austin, who answered his questions. There likely were no more than a hundred men in America who really understood the quality plum west of the Sabine waiting to be plucked. And Shiring Rhett was one of these by the time he appeared at Point of Rocks.

The most attractive aspect of his representing Stephen Austin in central Arkansas Territory was that he would enjoy part of the plucking from a safe distance, where he need have no constant worry that a Comanche war party would use his purple hat for target practice.

Shiring Rhett was a Texas expert who had never set foot on Texas soil. And he took every opportunity to expose the population of Little Rock to his vast knowledge. Why, he would say, just observe the opportunities!

It took the Spaniards—and then the Mexicans after they became independent of Madrid—two hundred years to figure out that they didn't have whatever it took to effectively colonize Texas. Not to mention New Mexico and Arizona. Hidalgos were extremely reluctant to commit family and money to the northern provinces because it was obvious that the central government in Mexico City was incapable of even the most rudimentary function of a sovereign state, to wit, defending its citizens against armed and belligerent aggressors. In this case, American bandits or marauding Comanches.

So the Spaniards called for help by inviting other folk to come and take land and establish thereby what they'd been unable to establish: a profitable economy, an educated and self-reliant society, a stable political system. As this word went out, a number of Germans responded by forming colonizing cooperatives with the intent of going to Texas. Some of them fulfilled that intention.

But the best possibility was closer at hand, and realizing this, the Spaniards and then the Mexicans began to encourage people they called Anglos to cross the Sabine and the Red to take up the creation of civilization across the northern tier of Mexico. Of course, many who came were not Anglo-Saxon at all, but Scotch-Irish Celts, North America's premier wilderness busters, and some of human history's most stubborn, bellicose, and savage pioneers.

After a time, the Mexicans took alarm at the stampede of settlement they had created. The beasts descending on their lands were not only Protestant, but many owned slaves, and slavery had been outlawed in Mexico. But worst of all, these migrating Americans had the disturbing tendency of insisting on a form of local democracy and republican form of self-government that was absolutely abhorrent to whichever aristocrat, general, or bandit who happened to be running things in Mexico City.

So the Mexican government tried to stop what they had started, which was as easy as making the Rio Grande flow uphill. And what's more, began repressive measures against the Americans already arrived. Nothing could have been more dangerous than trying to repress this particular group of people. Even the appearance of repression was dangerous. And once the seed of suspicion was planted, it was impossible for the Mexicans to retreat from such a blade-and-bullet bunch, no matter how sincere the retreat might be. Great Britain had learned that in 1776!

Best known of the American colonizers to Texas was Stephen Austin. His father, Moses, had started the whole thing but died before its fruition. There are various views of Moses Austin, ranging from inspired pioneer to businessman busted in lead-mining speculations and looking for another way to make a few bucks.

Steve Austin was no pioneer. He was a land developer and politician. He wanted to move large numbers of Americans into Texas, enough of them to control not only its economy and social milieu but the politics as well. It was a grand and honorable vision. Perhaps he really wanted to make it a viable part of the northern tier of Mexico. More likely, he wanted to make it a republic with close ties to the countries of Europe, such as Great Britain, that were the big customers for cotton. Perhaps he wanted to make it a part of the federal Union, a state of that Union, or as many as five states, so some people said.

But no matter the finished product. In coming to whatever end he envisioned, he needed certain things. People, there were plenty of, because Americans were ready to jump into almost any place where it appeared that the only obstacle to land was hostile Indians. Or some foreign government's claim to it. So there was no problem with settlers. The problem was with money and a base of operation nearby.

Thus, in observing a map, you could see that Louisiana and Arkansas were the closest organized political units to Texas and because it was always easier to operate full throttle in a sparsely settled territory rather than a state, Arkansas was the best bet. So the concentration of Texas-bound immigrants began in the territory of Arkansas. Most specifically around a small community in the southwest corner of the territory called Washington, appropriately you would suppose. And there, Austin's associates gathered and started a money-making venture in land speculation.

Now, the major overland route to Red River and Texas from Illinois and Missouri ran diagonally across Arkansas Territory from northeast to southwest, and it crossed the Arkansas River at Point of Rocks. You would obviously think that it might be a good idea to obtain some small bite of real estate at the crossing, as well as some modicum of political clout, not only to insure safe passage for Texas pilgrims but to make some cash on the side. Well, Stephen Austin thought so. Thus the consternation of Logan Brock, who knew exactly what Stephen Austin was thinking and why lawyer Shiring Rhett was in town thinking the same thing. Logan Brock, sensitive to the times, was well aware of the opportunities south of Red River. But for himself, it had seemed best to locate in a position to make money on migrations to Texas and those going up the Arkansas River to the Indian territory as well. Now, with the appearance of Shiring Rhett, there was the distinct possibility that homegrown land-speculation money in Arkansas would not stay there but migrate with all of Austin's people to the northern province of Mexico.

Maybe Boone Fawley had seen Old Moses Austin when the failed lead-mine entrepreneur passed through. Maybe he saw his son Stephen, who came later, more than once, after lawyer Shiring Rhett had arrived. Maybe he even saw Sam Houston, who was in Little Rock a number of times. Chances were good that he did, and if so, he viewed the Austins from afar, most likely, but probably shared a few sips with Sam, and a few jokes, because wherever Sam Houston went there was considerable sharing of sips and jokes. But Boone Fawley never said. Probably because he saw nothing remarkable about having seen and sipped with such illustrious gentlemen, and in fact, at the time, the gentlemen in question were not all that illustrious. Sam Houston already had a reputation for drinking and carousing, but there was nothing particularly noteworthy about that on a frontier where such men were outnumbered only by the mosquitoes.

Boone Fawley had a few sips with many gentlemen who wore beaver rather than planter's hats and some who carried canes that concealed sword blades and who were not interested in growing cotton but creating empires from those who did. In that time, a lot of Texas talk passed into Boone Fawley's ear, because there was no way to avoid it and Boone Fawley likely saw no reason to avoid it. How much such talk influenced him remained to be seen. One thing was sure. That in the proximity of these bay rum–scented gentlemen there were always a number of slab-faced, fringe-shirted riflemen of the same nature as Fulton and Maddox and Williams that Boone Fawley had seen in the Mississippi River homestead before the earth ate it.

Another thing was sure. All of these people were friends and associates with Mourton Loudec, and his son Michael, since the Loudecs were seen as the primary agents for getting Shiring Rhett into town in the first place and Shiring Rhett, by token of his shingle, was an obvious Austin man. There was a lot of discussion and speculation about the old which-came-first-the-chicken-or-the-egg. In this case, who started it, Austin or Loudec? But no matter who started it, everybody agreed, Texas was the object.

Logan Brock was panting and telling horror stories about out-landers coming in to savage the land. Aided and abetted by Stephen Austin. For example, the Austin people, headed by Shiring Rhett, of course, were going around buying up all the old New Madrid Certificates. And one such quarter section was real estate bought as public domain by Logan Brock—which he now called Government Plaza—a piece of ground set in the dominant center of what was developing as the town of Little Rock, in sight of the southside ferry slip, close to William Evans's mule pen, and just as close to Silas Catchen's place against the Rocks Hotel where he could lay drunk. When it wasn't raining.

Also sitting cheek-by-jowl with Brock's Government Plaza was the quarter section that was still Quapaw land, on it only a few black locust trees, a lot of weeds, and the cabin of Indian Agent William Like and his wife. There were no Indians there, of course. Well, from time to time a few of Like's charges came to complain about being harassed by Cherokees along the river and sometimes butch-ered by Osages north of it, and while Agent Like took what he called depositions from the leaders, the rest of the delegation got drunk and lay about the Quapaw quarter section in various stages of consciousness. To be sniffed by town dogs and occasionally pecked by roving chickens.

"It's getting to where," said Mayor Buchanan, "you can't go nowhere without havin' to step over some Gawd-damned drunk Indian, and I'm fixin' to write a letter to Governor Miller about it."

It was never exactly clear what James Miller, the appointed territorial governor, was supposed to do about the situation.

But his mansion was being completed, of native limestone on high ground well back from the hoots and hollers of Saturday nights at the ferry slip saloons. A real sheriff, Prentice Entwine, was already nosing about. A county structure was forming, most important official of which was the circuit clerk who held records of who owned what. In that capacity, this man, Galin Reed, had been three times challenged to a duel. Each time, the combat had been canceled, or at least postponed, when Sheriff Entwine publicly stated that he would hang anybody who shot at a public official, in an affair of honor or otherwise.

So the territorial legislature, meeting in Arkansas Post, made the arrangements to buy land and buildings at Point of Rocks, to establish the new seat of government on Logan Brock's plaza. And that's when lawyer Shiring Rhett, accompanied by Michael Loudec, presented to the territorial Supreme Court a suit, to wit: that Logan Brock did not own said plaza because it was New Madrid Certificate land which same had been bought by Austin's associates.

The court rendered a decision. Which was that all New Madrid Certificates south of the Arkansas were henceforth vacated. Invalid. So the Austin people had lost, and there was a furious celebration at Hugh Evans's tavern, and among those who didn't care one way or the other but were there because it was a grand excuse for another roaring drunk was Boone Fawley. Whose family home, now, was on New Madrid Certificate ground, and by decree, public domain available to sale at highest bid.

Questor Fawley knew. Because Michael Loudec had told him. Their property was in jeopardy. And John and Molly knew. Ernestine Evans had told Molly, on a special trip to the cotton patch via two-wheel mule cart, and John knew first from some sixth sense and then from William Evans at the blacksmith shop when John took in a horse to get shod, he and Questor long since abandoning their own forge.

Nobody said too much about it. But there was the sense of forting-up against attacking Indians. John Fawley had no moment of not looking grim. And twice at supper table he mentioned the terrible word. "Eviction."

"I'll kill some son of a bitch," he said.

"Don't talk ugly," said Molly, but with no conviction and no move to bring out the King James.

"We got to get outa here," John said. "Before them people come and take it all, even the new wagon I done bought, and you damned tootin', Ques, that still, too, they'll take it. Loudec's gonna eat us alive!"

"Maybe not . . ."

"We ain't got money to move nowhere," said Molly. "How we gonna move?"

"I'll kill game 'til we get somewheres."

"May have to go a far piece, then, to find game like they used to be up in the woods where we come from," said Questor. "I ain't seen hardly any rabbits lately and no deer in the corn for might near three years."

"Damn the deer in the corn," John said viciously and slammed his hand on the table. "And we can use them two gold pieces Pa keeps around his neck."

"No we can't," Molly said, and for the first time in a long while there was some of the old flint in her voice. "We don't touch them gold pieces! You hear me, John?"

"All right, Ma, all right."

Questor tried three times to see Michael Loudec, for a long walk beside the river, where they'd often talked. Questor went all the way to the gin, once, walking because he liked walking rather than riding some obstinate mule, but he didn't find Michael Loudec. He found Timbou, who looked at Questor with no expression on his face and said, "Boss busy now. Boss not thinking on talk with you."

"I surely would approve speakin' with him."

"Not now. After the big happening."

"What big happening?"
"You'll see."

It was a clear day. At least to start. There was a summer wind blowing along the Arkansas Valley from the west, hot as August sun rays, feeling dusty. Off there beyond the green lift of trees were great thunderheads, lifting like columns into a blue sky.

Something was afoot, as they would write in letters to faraway relatives. Men could be seen scampering from house to house, building to building. Nothing inhabited the streets except a few chickens and one of Harris Evans's hogs. The ferry was tied to its south bank pier. Silas Catchen had not appeared to take his place alongside the Rocks Hotel. There was no clang of hammer against anvil in William Evans's blacksmith shop. There were no ladies admiring the queensware blue china in Davis and Parker's. There were no drunk Quapaws lying about Agent Like's cabin.

And Logan Brock had gone north of the river for a picnic with his wife. A thing Logan Brock had never done before.

Something was afoot, as they would say. People peeked from windows—those who lived in places that had windows—and Questor Fawley stood on a sassafras-infested ridge not far from the town and watched, and saw a thing he would never forget. And wished he had insisted that John come and watch, too. But soon, forgot John and all the rest because of the magnificence of what he saw next.

And watching, knew not whether to laugh or cry, and as all who saw it, knew not whether it was joke or miracle.

At about noon, a surrey with a leather top, drawn by a pair of Mourton Loudec's fine bays driven by the slave Timbou, took station on some cleared high ground just south of the settlement. On the front seat with the African was Michael Loudec, bareheaded as had become his custom, the wind stirring his black hair and dropping a thick strand of it across his forehead. In the rear seat was lawyer Shiring Rhett and beside him a gentleman with a finely clipped black mustache showing streaks of gray. This man wore an expensive rabbit felt wide-brim hat and a fringed deerskin shirt that looked as though it had been tailored in the best shop in New

Orleans. On its collar was a red, white, and blue ribbon, in the nature of a military decoration. This man had a telescoping spyglass which, as activity in the town commenced, was passed back and forth among the white men in the vehicle so that they might observe what went forth below.

From various locations in the town, men began to appear. They had a striking, if not very handsome, look about them. They were naked to the waist, their faces were streaked with red and yellow paint, and they all had headbands into which chicken feathers had been thrust. All of this disguise obviously the result of what white men supposed Indians might effect, but actually seldom did. Perhaps somebody among them, or among their leaders, had read of the Boston Tea Party. For whatever reason, there they were, painted and feathered, and carrying tools and lengths of heavy log chain and hemp rope and a number of them driving teams of oxen and mules, and a couple of them with flaming firebrands in their hands.

There is but one record of this event extant, and that not by anyone close to the purpose or effect of it. Boone Fawley, who was one of the participants ingeniously disguised as an aborigine, never addressed it. Even if he remembered any of it. Nor did the observers in the surrey. Nor did Hugh Evans and Ernestine, who watched it all but apparently figured afterward that discretion was better than supplying a public record. So nobody knows who started it. But what was started did end on manuscript, for as chance would have it a certain Thomas James, en route upriver to Fort Smith, saw it and in 1847 wrote a book in which the spectacle was mentioned.

The purpose of the pseudo-Indians was to remove Logan Brock's government buildings to the Quapaw quarter section, and to this purpose applied all their skills and the strength of chains and ropes and the teams of oxen and mules. There was an occasional collapse of roof or wall. There were some buildings that refused removal, and these were promptly set afire. All of this was taken with a spirit of celebration, with singing and shouting, even though a great, black cloud was approaching from the west and there were distant mutterings of thunder.

Only Logan Brock's personal buildings were carefully spared. All those he had designed for sale to the territorial government were either displaced to Quapaw land or burned. Mr. James, when he wrote his book, seemed to recall that all the participants in this scene were "moderately drunk."

By the time the rain squall swept across Little Rock, the new seat of government had been repositioned. About one hundred yards to the west of where Logan Brock had expected it to be. And certainly not where Indian Agent William Like expected it to be. For the buildings of government were now all about his cabin home, where throughout the operation he and his wife had clung to each other in terror and expecting at any moment to be dragged out and slaughtered. In a loud voice that could be heard by the hardworking engineers outside, William Like threatened wholesale lawsuits and criminal proceedings for this assault on the public domain of the United States of America.

Well, of course, the ones who planned all this were not so stupid as to place themselves in jeopardy with the federal courts. In the month before, but thus far unpublished in Little Rock, the Quapaw land titles had been vacated for that particular spot, and the resultant real estate purchased for proper consideration by one Shiring Rhett, of the Austin Land Company, Limited, or whatever it was. In fact it had been through Shiring Rhett's activity among friends and associates that the land that Agent William Like considered Indian property had returned to the rolls of public domain in the first place. So now, as Shiring Rhett was ready to concede, the buildings belonged to Logan Brock but the land on which they stood belonged to him. And thus would the entire package be presented to the territorial legislators for purchase, and of course, the territorial legislators were anxious to complete their move from Arkansas Post and a great many of them were friends and associates—need it be said employees?—of Shiring Rhett.

Thus Logan Brock escaped with his life and enjoyed some profit, if not so much as he'd hoped for, and Shiring Rhett and the Loudecs displayed their capabilities in power games as well as providing some tax money from the territory of Arkansas for the colonization of Texas.

By the time the rain squall hit, Questor Fawley had moved and was standing with smithy William Evans at the rear of the Rocks Hotel, astonished and amazed. By that time, too, his father Boone was in one of the local taverns that now competed with the one in the Rocks Hotel—the record does not indicate which one—toasting good government and democracy. And by this time, too, the Loudec surrey had disappeared to whence it came, except that the nattily attired gentleman with the red, white, and blue ribbon on his lapel had found Boone Fawley, wherever he was, and stood beside him and gripped his shoulder and smiled and said, "Ah, Mr. Fawley, what a pleasure it is to see you again."

It was Major Evelyn Hadley-Moore, Twenty-third Hussars King's Own Guard, DSO, Retired!

17

I am surely tarred of cuttin' black locust on the west side," said John Fawley. He and Questor were sitting in spring twilight under the dooryard chinaberry tree. On log chunks exactly like those their father had placed in the dooryard of their New Madrid homestead before the earthquake. They were digesting a supper of batter-fried catfish, and from inside they could hear the clatter of pans and pots as Molly cleaned and made all ready for breakfast. And they could hear in the gum and sycamore trees in the direction of the river the songs, or whatever it is they sing, of mockingbirds.

"Ever' year I cut black locust and size 'em and haul 'em in town fer posts, but ever'body hereabouts has got their own damned black locust so I end sellin' it for farwood at two bits a rick, and then next spring I got it all to do over, the way them thangs grow. Can't you cut 'em and use 'em for that still of yours?"

"No," said Questor, and he was tossing pebbles at some of his mother's hens and their brood of chicks scratching about the yard for bugs and worms and whatever it is that hens and their brood scratch about for. "It burns too fast. I got to boil mash slow, and I can't spend my whole time just pokin' locust chunks under the pot."

"Hell, why not? All's you do is just sit there and watch."

Their eyes met and they laughed.

"I ain't studyin' no black locust," Questor said.

"No, but you're studyin' lot of that Michael Loudec."

"You aim to get on that again?" He threw a pebble hard, and one of his mother's chickens squawked.

"Well, least ways, you bein' so thick with him, maybe that's why his daddy ain't bought our land right out from under us yet."

"He knows we aim to file on it, soon as we got enough money."

"Hell," John snorted. "Old Man Loudec's friends on the Territorial Land Commission got the price on this patch so high, nobody could touch it 'cept a damned big planter. Like Loudec his own self. We ain't ever gonna have enough to file on it. So we don't own it now, and won't ever. We're some of the county's white trash, that's all."

"We ain't neither white trash," Questor said, and there were points of red in his cheeks that his brother recognized as anger beginning, and anger was rare with Questor Fawley. Or any other emotion that John could recognize as tooth-grinding passion, which was becoming more and more a puzzle to him because he spent few moments of his life without tight jaw muscles.

But now, as they sat under the chinaberry tree, something else had captured John's complete attention. He looked toward the low ridge east of the patch, jack oak covered and weeded and the trace of a road to town from wagon wheels that had cut furrows in the weeds. The hounds, like John, stood up and looked there, too, tails stiff until Questor tossed the last of his gravel at them and said, "Get on down, there," and they retreated, looking crestfallen, to the side of the cabin.

There were two horsemen coming. One of the horses was the gelding Boone Fawley always used to ride about the countryside, the best of their livestock. The star boarder in the corral where also resided a much older mare, a mule, and a milk cow, each and every one proof positive of John's ability as an animal swapper. Or maybe proof positive of his expert use of shoe polish on lusterless hides.

"It's Pa," said Questor, who didn't really recognize the rider yet but only the horse.

"Yes, and maybe sober," John said. "Least, it don't look like he's about to fall off the horse."

"Ma," Questor said, eyes still toward the approaching horsemen, but Molly was already in the doorway. "We got some company comin'."

"No need for the musket, Ma," John said, a little joke he always made about his mother's fierce instinct to protect the nest. "I reckon we know him."

"It's some dude," Questor said. "Look at that hat, I ain't seen that kinda hat since . . . Well, cat claw me, it's that English army officer!"

"Well, I do declare," Molly gasped, patting down her hair, fingering the bun at her neck to be sure none of Hugh Evans's mercantile store hairpins were showing. "I do declare!"

Former Captain, now Major, Evelyn Hadley-Moore, retired and decorated at the Battle of New Orleans and wearing the Distinguished Service Order of His Majesty, came to Molly horehound candy in hand, for he was a man who did not forget small details. And bowed and kissed her fingers, a relatively sober Boone Fawley standing to one side beaming as though it was good King George III himself doing his family such honor—well, not George III, crazy as a drunk duck now, but anyway Regent Prince of Wales doing the kissing—and Molly flustered happily and blushing like a girl and looking a full ten years younger in that moment than everybody knew she really was, and looking younger still as Hadley-Moore turned to the tall, strapping men beside him and beamed.

"Why, are these fine, big men those tads I knew along the old Mississippi?" then embraced them both as though he were a French general saluting bravery in a subaltern. "And this fine homestead." Sweeping his arms about and his teeth showing as they remembered, beneath the well-trimmed mustache.

It was the beginning of some months of joy for Molly, and Questor knew it better than any of the others, maybe even better than his mother. This Englishman's elegant dress and polished conversation, transporting Molly back to that time at New Madrid more lovely to her than anything she'd had along the Arkansas. Here she had a substantial cabin, good livestock and chickens, neighborhood women with whom to visit, two grown sons making a little money, a respectable cotton patch, and not much worry about passing white desperadoes or drunken Osages ready to dispatch everybody just for the hell of it. But in that clearing beside the St. Francis, dangerous and tentative as life was, there she had had Boone Fawley. She didn't have him now.

The Englishman had a profound effect on Boone Fawley, maybe because Hadley-Moore had been a Chouteau man once, and Boone Fawley still considered himself to be one. Now, Boone drank less, so much less that Molly and the boys didn't have to drag him into the kitchen for a bath at weekly intervals, a family ritual less frequent in winter, of course.

Hadley-Moore spent a lot of time at the Fawley cotton patch. In the shortening light of autumn days, he and Boone sat in the door-yard, under the chinaberry tree, sipping Jamaica rum and smoking pipes, watching the leaves change to yellow and scarlet. And Hadley-Moore talked, Boone Fawley leaning close to him, wide-eyed as the Englishman told of cotton kingdoms to be won in Texas, under sponsorship of Stephen Austin, and how farsighted men could become rich and influential, to make old Auguste Chouteau of St. Louis look like a timid pilgrim. And how once more the Fawley name could be linked with the country to which Boone's daddy owed his loyalty, for after all, if Stephen Austin ended by making Texas a free republic and a cotton kingdom, who bought much of the world's cotton? England did, of course!

Had Boone Fawley wanted to think about it, his memory would have served to inform that Old Noah's only loyalty was to a full belly and the safety of his hide, no matter the flag. But Hadley-Moore appealed to some hidden need for patriotism apparently, wrapping it all in the Union Jack, and Boone Fawley was buying it.

If Questor watched all of this with a kind of curious neutrality, John was openly hostile. Hadley-Moore often ate with them in the evening, and in his honor, Molly usually baked the popovers flavored with a spoonful of meat drippings—baked them in a biscuit pan Questor had bought her at Davis and Parker's—in the manner explained to her by the Englishman and which he called Yorkshire pudding. And each time, John would snort and say, "Puddin'? It ain't nothin' but biscuits!"

And once, when Davis and Parker had a barrel of oysters, shipped upriver packed in ice, Hadley-Moore brought a bucketful, and when he opened the first one, John walked out, saying loud enough for everyone to hear that he wasn't hungry enough yet to eat something that looked like he'd coughed it up after a bad cold. Even when Molly fried the oysters in cornmeal and egg batter, John wouldn't touch them.

Usually, Hadley-Moore kept his comments about the Americans and the British to those hours he spent with Boone while the boys were cleaning up the early winter fields, making them ready for spring seed. But now and then he made the mistake of bringing such topics to the table. Once, sitting back in his chair and smoking, he went into an elaborate explanation about how ragtag the American army at New Orleans was and what a mountain yokel Andy Jackson was, and how no American formation of soldiers could stand up to British regulars, and John had said, "Oh, well now, they tell us hereabouts that the British got their tail feathers cleaned at New Orleans!"

And as had happened before, Boone Fawley turned quickly to his son, as though to scold, yet when John's eyes met his straight on, Boone Fawley shut his mouth and turned his head away. And Hadley-Moore changed the subject.

It was a good winter despite John Fawley's obvious resentment of Hadley-Moore and his constant dashing of cold water onto his father's enthusiasm for everything the Englishman said. They had no snow that year and only a few days when the temperature got below freezing and stayed there long enough to kill tick eggs, which meant the following summer would be hell for the hounds.

Those hounds were becoming more and more a part of Questor's life. Often, on clear nights with everybody else long sleeping, he'd stand outside and listen to them running a gray fox, or sometimes a red, in the timbered slopes west of the patch. The sounds of their high, urgent, quavering voices made the hair along the back of Questor's hands ripple and he would shiver as though it were biting cold. The lazy, slovenly, multicolored animals that lay about the cabin or the horse shed during daylight hours seemed to be completely different creatures from the ones making those ghostly, bell-clear voices lift toward night's diamond-studded black heaven. Maybe the dogs more than anything made him come to the understanding that sometimes appearance was not the real substance of value.

Then in February, Questor came in from the still one gray afternoon threatening snow that never came, and found his mother sitting beside a cookstove gone almost completely cold. She was on a stool, hands clasped between her knees, staring without seeing at her cupboard wall. There was no indication that any meal was being prepared, although it was a time when this room usually smelled of cooking meat and bread. Questor made an elaborate show of talk and peeling off his deerskin smock and then opened the stove and fed some kindling into it. But finally had to stop and stand there before her and ask what had happened. She spoke in a gray voice, gray as the sky outside, and it was as though she spoke only to herself.

His pa had gone off with Hadley-Moore and some of the other Austin men, toward the south, they said. Toward Texas, they said. To see the lay of the land, Boone Fawley said.

"And give me no more in good-bye than a pat on the shoulder, like as he might a hound dog!"

Questor couldn't say anything. He furiously busied himself once more with the fire, trying to understand how to come to grips with a loyalty that is supposed to be rock-solid oneness now suddenly split down the middle.

Maybe he was finished with cutting black locusts. Or maybe he had some sense of what had happened. But for whatever reason, John came even as Questor was working at the fire in the cookstove. Molly didn't say anything, and Questor told his brother what had happened.

"Dammit," John gasped and rushed outside, leaving the door open, but was back almost on the sound of his own departing, running footsteps, slammed the door, and swore again. "The son of a bitch taken the best horse."

"Don't talk ugly about your own pa," Molly said, but there was no fire in her voice.

They found that Boone Fawley had taken more. Well, John discovered it because he began to look, fury etching his hard, flat face and making his eyes agate-yellow. Boone Fawley had taken not only the best horse but the only saddle, the Pennsylvania rifle, the little hard money they had—which meant mostly the two Spanish pieces around his neck—and the New Madrid Certificate, which although vacated by the Arkansas courts, was their only in-hand evidence that they now or ever had claim to this property and all the buildings on it and all the crops its field might grow. Of course, he took Old Noah's stem-wind watch as well and three gallons of Questor's whiskey.

It was a momentous springtime. First, a steamboat had appeared on the river. The *Eagle,* seventeen days out of New Orleans, with a great huffing and puffing and clanging of bell and tooting of whistle and scaring hell out of all the livestock near the banks of the Arkansas. The Fawleys, in their cotton patch field with the planting, heard the thing and went through the north wood line to the bluff above the river and saw the little vessel side-wheeling up the river, bound for Fort Smith. It wasn't a very large boat. Not much bigger than a serious keelboat. But it had a steam engine, and it belched black smoke from two spindly stacks behind a pilothouse that Molly said looked like the Fawley privy.

For weeks, it was the talk of the town, but soon steamboats would become so common that nobody paid them any mind, not even the riverside livestock.

Next was the first meeting of the territorial legislature in the buildings Logan Brock had constructed, now on the old Quapaw property Shiring Rhett had bought. (The two men had agreed to take equal shares of the money appropriated for the purpose without anybody being shot from ambush or challenged to a duel.) And now the legislators began a practice that was to become famous. There was a line of large pine trees near the edge of the government property, and each day after they had debated whatever territorial legislators debate, the lawmakers repaired to this spot and, passing around flasks and bottles, laughed and joked and relaxed from a hard day of doing government work by practicing marksmanship with pistols, tacking playing cards to the trunks of the pine trees as targets. For generations, urchins of the town would go to those old pine trees with pocketknives and dig out hunks of flattened lead. Local citizens saw it as a healthy outlet for the passions of men required to write those hateful laws and regulations.

"Hell, it's better they shoot at trees," said Galin Reed, the circuit clerk, "than shooting at each other in the chamber of the House!"

Of course, the territorial legislators had more dignity about themselves than to resort to pistols on the floor. There, it became traditional to resolve disputes with knives or canes. And it would be many years yet before one of the lawmakers was killed in such an affair. Even so, at this early date, a great many people began to suspect that to become an Arkansas legislator could be very dangerous indeed!

There was the first official hanging, on an actual gallows built directly before the door of the jail, which was appropriately enough the old residence of Deputy Samples. This was no casual hanging from the limb of an oak or sycamore. A river piracy charge it was, duly tried before a jury, the final duty with the rope performed most admirably, everyone said, by Sheriff Prentice Entwine. The culprit, named Armaund or some such thing, was sent to his just reward after a short benediction by a passing Methodist evangelist named John Wesley Bangor.

Everyone felt the site of execution long ago cleansed of sin because since Deputy Samples's demise, female companions for passing pilgrims no longer gave comfort and joy in the back room of what was now the jail. The only recognized whores were all north of the river, procured from downriver and managed by a cousin of Emil Harp who called himself Uncle Bob. Questor Fawley knew all about this den of perdition, not from personal experience but from what his brother John had told him. From personal experience, you must assume.

And finally, that spring, Mourton Loudec rode about the countryside, inspecting his various properties. He rode with a retinue of people, much as you would suppose Henry VIII had done, and in fact, if there was a king of this area, it was Mourton Loudec, although mostly an absentee one.

Mourton Loudec had grown very fat since that day he had acted as his son's second in the duel that made Logan Brock realize the kind of hazardous game in which he had involved himself and spelled the end of bodyguard Mercer. The gelding that carried Mourton Loudec obviously had some impressive bloodlines but more in the nobility of Percheron than Arabian. In short, it was a horse stout enough to carry Mourton Loudec, even had he been wearing plate armor.

Instead of armor, Mourton Loudec wore silk under linen and a gigantic straw planter's hat, brim like an umbrella against the sun. To his left, and on a horse that did look Arabian, was his son Michael, bareheaded and looking sour. Directly behind was Sheriff Prentice Entwine, who carried a short-barrel percussion rifle across the pommel of his saddle, and behind him two or three gentlemen in beaver hats and long frock coats, and behind them the African Timbou on a gray mule that was almost as big as Mourton Loudec's horse. He, unlike his master Michael, wore a hat, a narrow-brim, peaked-crown felt that was the exact color of his skin and gave the impression that his head was very tall and in the shape of a cone.

There was also a man—not much more than a boy, really—named Otis Bradford who was reading law with Shiring Rhett and who had apparently attempted to dress like the two or three gentlemen with beaver hats but only with limited funds and who carried a small valise from which protruded various ends of foolscap. He was not sure where his place was in the cavalcade, nor was his horse, and as a result he rather bounced about on the periphery like a cork in a bowl of cider trying to find secure moorings at any edge to which he might adhere.

Molly Fawley saw them as soon as they topped the wooded ridge east of the cotton patch, came to the front stoop to stand in the shade of the roof, and waited, calling just once and not too loudly, "John!"

John and Questor were both at the horse shed and they heard her, and saw the horsemen besides, so quickly joined their mother, all three of them standing back against the wall and in the shadow of the overhang. The riders came straight on, with a kind of slow purpose, all of them quickly surveying the ground around the cabin and the stock pen and shed behind and the cleared field where cotton and corn were already planted. About twelve paces from the porch, Mourton Loudec drew rein, and the others beside and behind him did so as well, and young Otis Bradley finally got his horse stopped some distance off to one flank of the main body, who were all in a clump. Mourton Loudec made a quick movement, lifting his hat and replacing it without seeming to have removed it at all, and spoke.

"Mrs. Fawley, I believe? Good day to you."

Molly Fawley, never having been confronted by so many men, each of whom was looking at her, drew a deep breath and started to speak, but before she could the initiative was taken from her by John, who stepped to the front of the porch, into the sun, and spoke, his voice perhaps a mix of many qualities, not one of which was friendly.

"What is it you want?"

All eyes among the horsemen shifted to John, rather quickly, except for Michael Loudec, who was now looking at Questor, and with the look what might have been a slight nod.

"Young man, are you the Questor Fawley I've heard of?" asked Mourton Loudec.

"No," said Michael Loudec. Very quietly, in fact so quietly that perhaps his father did not hear.

"I'm Questor," said Questor, still beside his mother in the shadows.

"I see," Mourton Loudec said. "Then you're the other one?"

"I reckon you might say I'm the other one," John said.

"I see. Well, then, I am out and about today visiting my property. Hereabouts. I have purchased this land which you are farming, and I have come to take the New Madrid Certificate you hold on it."

Maybe it was true that good horses can sense men's nervousness because with those words the animals of this posse began to shift their feet and snort gently. Except for Mourton Loudec's big gelding, who stood impassively, watching the three hounds that had finally appeared at one corner of the porch, one with a tentative little bark, but other than that standing silently for a moment before moving to sniff the droppings of Otis Bradley's mount. Which made Otis Bradley's mount snort and shift his feet some more, and wall his eyes.

Finally, John spoke again. "You can't have it."

Questor and Michael Loudec exchanged another glance, and Questor began to understand that maybe Michael Loudec didn't tell his father everything that happened around Point of Rocks because he, Questor, had recently told Michael Loudec that when Boone Fawley went to Texas, he'd taken that New Madrid Certificate with him. That had been more than a month ago, when Questor had gone to the Loudec plantation gin to make arrangements for new seed, his doing the job John normally did in that regard because at the time John was suffering from a bad case of privy spurts, as they called it, having eaten some pork not well enough cooked, or some such thing, in a visit he'd made north of the river to see Uncle Bob.

"Mr. Loudec," Sheriff Prentice Entwine said, easing his horse forward, his short rifle ready across the pommel of his saddle.

"It doesn't signify," said Otis Bradley, his voice high-pitched. "The certificates were vacated by court order and mean nothing. This is south of the river, south of the river. Certificates south of the river have been vacated!"

"Of course," said Mourton Loudec, whose expression had not changed. "We know that, Otis. I'm sure Mr. Fawley knows that as well. And you, ma'am." He touched the brim of his hat again as he looked into Molly's eyes.

"You aimin' to make us leave?" Molly shouted, and the horses all jumped at the sharp sound of her voice. Now the hounds backed off, well behind the men on horseback, and began to bark furiously, rather ineffectively, really, as fox dogs always bark when they are trying to act like protective yard dogs. But some of the horses were becoming very difficult to control.

"They come to try, Ma," said John. "Didn't you, Entwine? You'd surely enjoy pointin' that rifle at somebody, wouldn't you?"

"Now, now," said Mourton Loudec. "No need for such talk now. My son tells me we can arrange a satisfactory rent situation. And now, good day to you, Mrs. Fawley. John. Questor."

But as Mourton Loudec reined his great gelding about, Sheriff Prentice Entwine was grinning maliciously and muttered, "Not yet, anyway."

"It doesn't signify," cried Otis Bradley.

"Wait a minute here," shouted John Fawley, and his voice was harsh enough to cause the entire entourage to halt and stare at him. "Questor, you got any of that whiskey of yours about? Why don't you give these here men a little to wet their whistles while they ride off our land?"

And Questor quickly produced from inside the cabin one of those clear glass bottles—in fact, two of them—provided by Michael Loudec, and the group began to pass the bottles around as they slowly rode away, only Timbou remaining for a moment on his mule and saying to Questor, "Soon, Mister Michael talk about it."

And of course, soon, Michael Loudec did, after his father had gone back downriver. He came to the cotton patch with assurances and left with an agreement just like other tenants had, which everybody understood would put the Fawleys in debt to the Loudecs, but there was no alternative if the Fawleys wanted to stay on this land.

Molly and her younger son accepted it. Fatalistically, perhaps. But John Fawley stayed furious most of the time, thinking about the arrangement. He had only one small compensation, and even that bought him a mortal enemy. In the late fall of that same year he was north of the river, visiting Uncle Bob once more, and discovered that Prentice Entwine was there as well. John, having finished his business, remained outside the log structure where these meetings were consummated, until he was well satisfied that Sheriff Prentice Entwine was in the very middle of his purpose for coming here, then went inside again and beat the sheriff almost to death with a hickory barrel stave.

The representative of law and order at Point of Rocks never mentioned the incident, nor satisfactorily explained to anybody, not even his wife Zerelda, how he had come by a broken jaw, three teeth knocked out, both eyes blacked, and two broken fingers, having been caught as he was with his pants down—literally—nor did John Fawley ever mention it to anybody, not even to Questor. But for a month afterward, he was caught smiling a few times.

Not one of the Fawleys could have explained how old-fashioned European feudalism worked, but from the time Mourton Loudec bought the cotton patch, they became intimately acquainted with the American form of it. In feudal Europe, there had been a kind of social contract between tillers of soil and lords of manor. Tillers produced food and fiber shared with lords in return for protection against bandits and invading armies, plus dispensation of justice in local disputes.

When the feudal system dried up in Europe, because central governments, which is to say, kings, grew powerful enough to provide protection and justice to the citizenry, it had a mutation in America that was all to the disadvantage of the men, women, and children who had no talent for anything other than working the soil. Or opportunity for anything else, either. In the New World, this type of farmer would be exactly like his distant cousin in France or Saxony or Devonshire in that he would own absolutely nothing, would live on and work somebody else's land, and pay his rent by sharing what he produced with the one who did own it. So would be eventually called a sharecropper.

Unless the owner was kind and considerate—and there were a few of these—there was no obligation on his part to do anything. He might become something of a banker and shopkeeper for his tenants. Selling them things like shoes and plowshares on credit, buying for cash what pitiful little the farmer had left of his crop after giving the landlord a share and feeding his own family. And, of course, loaning money for seed for next season's crop. So the portion of his produce the tenant got into his own woman's kitchen had already been mortgaged before it was planted.

A big planter, knowing how to finance large tracts of real estate, obtained vast domains for his cotton, and around the fringes, on marginal ground—land which the owner didn't see at the time as a profitable part of his slave-operated enterprise—he laid out small plots, maybe as much as a quarter section, and rented it to tenants. Sometimes, if a big planter decided a sharecropper's plot would fit into the larger operation, he evicted the tenant for debt, burned the cabin, and plowed the dooryard.

For the landlord, the system was even more efficient than the old European feudal network had been. Without it costing him a penny, he had a supply of sorghum molasses, corn, melons, sweet potatoes, and pole beans for his own and his slaves' tables. The more delicate stuff, like cherry trees and peach orchards and strawberry patches, he grew and supervised on his own land. And herb gardens for those of French background, leeks for Welsh, white cabbage for Germans, apricots for Spaniards, barley for malt for the English.

These were the people, these landowners, who controlled—in fact, who *were*—the political power in emerging cotton places, and even though some of the tenant men might have the franchise, they voted the way their landlord told them to vote. Officeholders came from or served the landowner class. Lawyers came from or served the landowner class. Newspapers and mercantiles and land companies and mining interests and lumber barons served the landowner class.

If the system produced an aristocracy, it also produced something else. Another class as surely as black African or West Indian slaves were a class. And it was a group of people generally living without a landlord's benevolent attention, as good business practice required the landlord's attention to an investment such as black slaves. They were, of course, the tenant population, and they were poor and illiterate, unhealthy and living without hope, for those who had energy enough to think about it at all. They were looked down on by everybody, including the slaves.

The tenants were as servile as the black slaves, and as dependent on the master, and they all knew that for them and their families it was sink or swim. The master didn't much care if it was sink, because there was always another hungry, poverty-stricken family to take their place, at no expense to the landlord as replacing black slaves would be. About the only point of pride they could boast, if "pride" is the right word, was that they were white. And amazingly, much of their smoldering resentment at being held in such bondage was directed not at those who controlled the system, the landlords, but toward the one group to whom they felt superior. The blacks. Of course, neither landlord nor his slaves shared that opinion. The tenant was white trash.

There were exceptions. As there always are. Some sharecroppers, if they were smart enough and tough enough or perhaps had some small advantage in dealing with the landlord, retained their self-respect and never lost sight of the expectation of better things. Of those who kept their independence and hope, a large majority operated good whiskey stills—whiskey being almost like hard cash on the frontier—or else were shrewd and devious enough to outwit a lot of people. Or both.

18

Less than a quarter mile downstream from where Questor Fawley had his still, on the little creek that wound and gurgled through the heavy growth of sycamore and pin oak and wild cherry, there was a pool of still water where the flow paused for a moment before rushing on toward the Arkansas River just half a mile away. It was a limestone pool, clear enough to see the small sun perch swimming in it and the gray-white pebbles at the bottom full ten feet beneath the surface. Along one shore of this pool, a lovely green watercress grew. Molly went there often to collect it, for although her sons seldom touched it, she enjoyed a crisp mouthful of it from time to time during hot summer afternoons when she rested in the shade of the porch between chores. She particularly liked it with a cold slice of raw salt pork on a biscuit. Although Idella Harp had told her Doc Clarence Biddington said raw pork was very bad indeed, Molly Fawley figured that none of the people who lived north of the river at Point of Rocks—and both Idella Harp and Doc Clarence Biddington did—knew what they were talking about.

On this day in late summer, both her menfolk off with a wagon-load of short-staple cotton to the Loudec gin downriver, Molly went to the pool. She paused a moment beneath her favorite tree, an old mulberry that stood like a dowager queen among the common folk of oak and sycamore, bending its arms across the pool and making a dapple of light and shadow on the water.

Then finally pulled back the left sleeve of her blouse—one sewn from some of the yard goods Questor had bought for her at Davis and Parker's mercantile—bent to hands and knees beside the pool, and reached along a ledge of limestone toward a bunch of watercress flowing like windblown silk in a cool breeze.

When the cottonmouth moccasin struck, it was only a quick, sharp stab of pain on the inside of her arm, high up, but at once she knew what it was and scrambled back from the water, the snake still stuck to her underarm until she grasped it in her right hand and yanked it free, one fang breaking off, still embedded in the flesh. The body was long and black, glistening with moisture from the pool, writhing about her arm as she held it just behind the turnip-shaped head and smashed the head again and again against a limestone outcrop, then dropped it, shaking its coils free of her wrist, and then rising.

She stared down at the still-squirming black body, and she knew it was the largest moccasin she had ever seen, even of all those in the cypress swamp of the first homestead. And there was now a quickly growing point of fire in her arm that spread up and down into her chest, and she did the worst possible thing she could have done. She ran. Out into the hot sun and toward the cabin, screaming for Boone Fawley.

In Europe, most of the poisonous snakes had been killed off by the time the first colonies in the New World were forming. A natural condition in any area of dense human habitation for it has always been true that people will kill snakes, good snakes and bad, because there is something about snakes that people just naturally do not like. Maybe this is a reflection of the Genesis story in which a snake is the villain. But that doesn't really wash, for peoples who had never heard of the Genesis creation myth always killed snakes just as enthusiastically as Jews and Christians had done.

In the Americas, there was a lot of ground where snakes might escape clubs, slingshots, axes, hoes, shotguns, claw hammers, single trees, log chains, and the like. It would be a long time, if ever, until human feet had trod every square inch of earth in America, so it wasn't difficult for snakes to hide. In tropic areas like Florida, it might be the beautiful but deadly little coral snake. Cousin to the cobra. Everywhere else—and *everywhere* is the right word—there were the pit vipers. Easy to identify from their fat, sluggish bodies and the small neck behind a large-jawed head. Slithering demons. Rattlesnake, copperhead, and water moccasin. With needle-sharp, retractable fangs that inject a poison to the blood rather than the nerves. Hence, the bigger the snake, the deeper the bite, the more deadly the strike.

In the early years, there were all kinds of antidotes to snake-bite. Slice open the punctures, suck out the blood. Apply a tourni-quet. Soak in coal oil. Pack in baking powder. Press prechewed chewing tobacco to the bite. None of these, of course, were worth a damn. Only when injectable antidotes were discovered was there any cure for it.

But there was a treatment, and a very effective one. Which nobody really knew about. If a victim lay still and kept the heart from pounding blood at a high rate, stayed warm, and maybe had a few sips of warm liquid, chances of recovery were good. After a time of feeling like hell, of course, and swelling up like a sick hound dog pup.

Pit viper venom causes nausea, vomiting, bleeding with defeca-tion. But most serious, like wounds on battlefields, it causes shock. Nobody knows a lot about shock, except that you treat it with quiet, warmth, and liquid stimulants—not booze, either, necessarily, al-though sometimes that works. In the time of Molly Fawley at Point of Rocks, nobody even knew shock existed. At least Molly Fawley didn't. And much less the treatment for it.

Questor found his mother lying on the porch by the open door, the front of her bodice covered with vomit. Already her eyes were dilated, and she didn't know him when he lifted her and carried her inside. He was amazed at how heavy she was, a dead weight, and amazed, too, at the livid red color of her skin. By the time he'd called John in from the shed, where John was unhitching the mule from the cotton wagon, the skin color had gone, like blood running from the holes in the bottom of a bucket, leaving her skin as pasty gray as wheat flour dough. Her breath had turned to a harsh rasp, like old, brittle paper being slowly torn.

It was John who discovered the bite in her arm. Close to the shoulder, and between the two ribbons of muscle going down to the elbow, the fangs going straight and quick into the big blood vessel there. It was swollen and black and only two dots of purple blood marked the penetration, and John found the broken fang and pulled it out. It was fully three inches long.

"Jesus Christ," he whispered.

For a few moments, she tried to talk, or at least she made sounds with lips frothing bile. There were no words. Only babble. Just after sunset, she died.

Questor Fawley couldn't move. Or accept. He lay with his arms across his mother's body, trying to cry, but no tears came. John touched his back.

"All right," John said. "All right. Work now. We got to work. This hot weather. Ques? Ques?"

"I hear you, goddammit!"

"We got work to do. Me and you, Ques."

It didn't take long. Or maybe it did. Afterward, Questor could never recall it with any sense of time. John was at the shed, ripping off rough-hewn boards, pounding together a box. Questor was at the line of red gums along the north side of the cabin yard, digging, still not crying, digging frantically, his nose running, muttering words that were not words. From the west, there was thunder rumbling and a faint blue-white lightning outlined the tree-line horizon there. Questor wasn't aware of it. He was only aware of the smell of freshly turned earth.

They finished almost exactly at the same time and were back in the kitchen, Molly's body lying on her bed, face by now starkly blue-white and all the flesh collapsed like old wax against her cheekbones. Questor tried not to look at her.

"I got the grave dug," he said.

"Where at?"

"Out by them gum trees. She liked them gum trees. I'll get the preacher now."

"The *what?*"

But Questor was gone, darting out, John after him for a few

steps, then swearing, turning back to wrap his mother in their best quilt, pin it together. Hearing his younger brother riding out toward the settlement, knowing Questor had not taken time to put a bridle on the horse, and no saddle either because since Boone Fawley left for Texas, they had no saddle.

"Jesus Christ," John said.

So he did all of the rest himself, too, harnessing the mule to the cotton wagon, bringing it around to the cabin, dragging out the box into which he had placed his mother's body and nailing the lid shut, levering it up somehow into the wagon bed, driving into the dark, lighted now more often with the glow of coming thunderstorm. Swearing as he levered the box down, thumping, onto the ground, thumping again as he literally slid it into the hole, up-angled at one end until he climbed down into the grave and pulled the box in, falling, swearing, the box thumping and clods falling from the walls of the hole onto the box with hollow, ghostly sounds.

Before he climbed out of the grave and heard the horse coming back, still full gallop, he patted the top of the box.

"Ma, you never was this much trouble before!"

Alphenius Flint was a missionary sent into the wilds by the Connecticut Society of Presbyterians, whose major purpose, so it seems, was to save the souls of American aborigines from Satan and from the Catholics. It was a little strange because Alphenius Flint was not a Presbyterian. Well, at least he didn't start as a Presbyterian.

He was an educated man, having matriculated at various small centers of enlightened learning and finally at Harvard College where he determined to answer the call of divinity as a Congregationalist. However, he and the presbyters of his first church had distinctly different ideas about the message of John Calvin—different ideas about the message of John Calvin were not unique, of course. So he was ousted under a rather dark cloud and after being sent packing threw in his holy lot with an organization not too particular about the fine points of such things as predestination, and which sent him forth among lost souls. To save as many as he could.

In the great Mississippi Valley, having found a wife and sired seven children, all daughters, and having seen at first hand many of the natives whose souls he was supposed to save, Alphenius Flint determined exactly what most other missionaries had, to wit, that the savage red man was not amenable to having his soul saved until he had become civilized. In other words, until he had become a white man, which Alphenius Flint did not consider to be his job. So he began the search for whites whose souls he could save. Assuming as he did that the whites would not have another old religion to start with, as the Indians all did, which had to be torn down before Christianity could be built up.

After four more years trying to plow this vineyard, Alphenius Flint had determined that previous religion or no, the only way to save frontier white souls was to civilize them first. And that was not his job.

And so he ended at Little Rock, in the last throes of his ministry before going back to Arkansas Post, picking up his family—all of whom were suffering from malaria—taking what small money he had saved, and returning to Maine, perhaps, to buy a farm with a pond where he could harvest winter ice to sell during summer, a thing his father had done until his death. And all the while he would be nothing more than a calm, praying member of some local Presbyterian church, or even a Congregationalist one, but certainly not a Methodist or Episcopal one, trying to find husbands for his daughters, young, ambitious men who understood taking care of aging fathers-in-law and who had never thought of going to Harvard College.

He was, in fact, a bitter old man, but Questor Fawley knew he was in Little Rock and so fetched him that stormy night. Together they rode back to the cotton patch, Alphenius Flint riding behind Questor Fawley and clinging to his back more or less successfully, falling off only twice in the wild ride from town to the Fawley place.

It was, to Alphenius Flint, a ride into darkness and hell, convincing him that his decision to return to civilization was a sound one. Molly Fawley's funeral was the last religious function the old man performed in Arkansas, or anywhere throughout the Mississippi Valley, or as a matter of fact, anywhere in this world.

After the funeral oration in the dark, except for the increasing lightning, Alphenius Flint helped fill the grave. The sound of limestone chunks hitting the top of the slab-side wooden coffin was completely overpowered by the thunder. When they were finished, wet with sweat, Questor went to the stock shed and got the bridle and put it on the horse and told Alphenius Flint to ride back in and leave the animal at William Evans's stable, where it would be picked up later. John offered to pay Alphenius Flint for his services, but the good man refused, blessed them both, and awkwardly climbed onto the horse and rode away—rather uncertainly—into the night.

Back inside, John sat on his bunk and tried to console his brother with the comment that it was good they'd commenced the business of burying their mother right away so as to get shed of painful obligations and go on about their business. Questor didn't speak. He found the King James beside the tin plates in his mother's cupboard, took it in hand, and went out into the night.

"Where you goin'?" John shouted, not really expecting an answer, and grumbling, undressed, got into bed, and pondered the length and holiness of Alphenius Flint's funeral sermon, saying to himself that if this was an example of God's drummers trying to sell salvation to the world, it wasn't any wonder there were so many sinners. Then got up and blew out the coal oil lamp, and still muttering, got back in his bunk and thought that Questor looked like he'd soaked up a lot of that sin-thumping and maybe the mule and horse had, too. And finally went to sleep thinking that before the Loudecs ate up all their cash this fall, he'd go into Davis and Parker and buy himself one of those new percussion rifles.

"Ques is gonna get wet as a drown goose out yonder, wherever he's at."

And Questor Fawley did get wet, but he didn't care. He didn't even know it. He went past the new grave without pause, on through the red gum and sycamore to the outcrop that stood on the high ground above the river, without knowing why, or maybe even where he was, and sank down on his knees beside a rock as big as himself and leaned against it and held the King James tight against his chest as the rain started. The lightning was coming fast now, and the thunder close behind, and on the far bank of the Arkansas there were long blue-white bolts from the clouds all the way to the ground, each one outlining the river as though it were a silver mirror in the dark, long and sinuous as the snake that had sent his mother to glory, which was his only recognition of what was happening around him. The long and sinuous snake.

He tried to recall what the preacher had said. He couldn't connect it with his mother. He tried to remember what he'd read in the King James and couldn't connect that, either. Bits of both began to come, and he couldn't disconnect them, couldn't separate what the King James said and what the preacher had.

The crash of sound around him was deafening and the light when it came blinding. He felt buffeted, and holding the King James in one hand, with the other reached around the rock and held himself close to it.

There were no words above that dark hole with its cargo of his mother about her goodness. It came to him like the shock of the lightning bolts. Nothing about her struggle to feed her family, protect them, make them warm, cover their bodies. All there was that he could hear now in his mind was the taint of sin, no magnificent sainted mother but a mere woman inescapably losing the fight against temptation of the flesh in a world condemned by Adam's sin, that terrible disobedience to God that brought damnation to all the generations, each generation produced by Adam's sin, guilty of it, even as a babe, no escape, with only the chance—and no more than a chance—of salvation the acceptance of blood's washing the sin away. The blood of Jesus.

The names came to him. St. Paul, St. Augustine. King James or Flint's sermon? He didn't know. The repeated booming threat, like the thunder now, that desire of the flesh was punishment to all for that original disobedience. Sins of flesh! His mother? He was like a cat caught in an icehouse and trying to find some way to work the door latch. He wailed. He lifted his head, and the rain, coming hard and in huge drops, struck his face. His hat was gone, blown off somewhere, he had no idea where. He had no idea it was gone.

St. Paul said it was best not to marry. It came to him. Didn't Luke say Jesus preached the same? Didn't Luke write that Jesus said you had to forsake mother, father, son, husband, all family, to become one of his? Or was it Matthew? Better not to marry. Better not to know woman, or woman man. Better not to sin.

He shuddered against the rock and opened his eyes, and there were bolts of white fire in streaks against the far shore. And then a most explosive crash of thunder and half a dozen tongues of fire leaped across the river's water, and there were balls of green flame dancing along the surface of the water below him, crackling and popping with static and blinking as they bounded downstream, turning blue then, and white and then gone, and with their passage the hair on the back of Questor Fawley's neck stood stiff and he felt a quiver of some force passing along his body.

He was terrified. The King James had fallen from his hands. He scrambled for it in the dark, because now it seemed there was no more lightning left in the sky. And found it, soggy and dripping wet as he took it up and held it close against his chest.

"All right," he shouted. "All right. Let me make it right for her. Let me."

He didn't know what to say. He was kneeling, face up as the lightning began again, and the rain was pelting him hard against the cheeks and he squeezed the King James.

"All right. Jesus, I will. Jesus, I will."

The storm now was rolling on west along the Arkansas and after a little while, he stood up and staggered back into the trees. But not far. He found a large-bole sycamore and sank down with his back against it, in the dark. Sat panting and, slowly, his eyes grew accustomed to the darkness only occasionally penetrated by receding lightning. He began to remember. The crash of fire. The blue flame on the river.

"Oh God," he said. "What has He showed me?"

He sat there until the day came, gray under clouds that were breaking up, the rain stopped. He rose, finally, looking at the sodden book in his hand, and only then realized that somewhere he had lost his hat.

As he came to the open door of the cabin and stood there a moment, he saw his brother raise himself on an elbow and wipe his eyes and run his hand through his hair.

"Where in hell you been?"

"Just a little walk," said Questor.

"Jesus Christ," John said, swinging his long legs out from the thin cover on his bunk. "You gettin' crazy as a drunk duck, you know that?"

FOUR

THE WOMAN

And another man shall lie with her.

—Deuteronomy 28:30

19

I n Elm Bluff, there was a public stock pen. It wasn't really public, being owned as it was by the big Baton Rouge planter Mendez-Carnes, breeder of fighting cocks. It was called the Carnes Auction Barn, although the only thing resembling a barn connected with it was a line of low shelter sheds along one side of the largest corral where dice and card players as well as livestock could find protection when trading, buying, and selling of mules and horses was interrupted by rain or hail. The absentee owner had not used Mendez in the designation, recognizing the tendency in the territory of Arkansas to either change or Anglicize Spanish or French surnames. Besides, he wanted to avoid advertising the fact that a Catholic was reaping profits in a predominantly Protestant vineyard, for with each transaction in and around his establishment, a percentage went to the Carnes Auction Barn, payable to one Talmidge Biggs, majordomo.

Talmidge Biggs was a former riverman of the roughest sort who had been born again for Jesus on the occasion of his wife's dreadful death by a seizure of epilepsy at Arkansas Post in 1824. This happened to coincide with one of the frequent periods when the Arkansas River valley was inundated with Methodist itinerant evangelists, who were combing the wilds for converts to their own particular brand of Wesley's formula for salvation. As it had evolved in many frontier precincts, this formula was a mix of hybrid Anglicanism and mystic dream-reading, above all emphasizing large, outdoor gatherings of folk singing and bearing witness of revelations who were guided toward faith by a man usually clothed in garments black and severe as any worn by Jesuits; this man may or may not have matriculated in some far distant and unknown seminary where graduates were ordained. His effectiveness was measured in the ability to move the emotions of a crowd. This might be accomplished from a stump, a hogshead, a front porch, a wagon bed, or any other convenient platform high enough to raise the exhorter so the people could see him as he shouted, waved his arms, cried real tears, sang, pranced, condemned, lauded, and prayed. And, of course, attacked the Baptists.

All of which was likely making old John Wesley spin in his grave. But at least he could rest easy in that this American Satan-stomping was the preserve of the common folk and not the aristocracy. John Wesley might have been happy as well that although at first Methodist divines had been called Father, just like the Catholics called their priests, and referred to as pastors, like Lutherans referred to theirs, democracy soon triumphed and Methodists began calling their shepherds Brother and Preacher. Maybe this is as good an encapsulation of early American Methodism as you can find.

Everybody in Methodist flocks called one another Brother and Sister, and they seemed to have a roaring good time—without booze—as they heard hellfire defined and learned the joy of freewill fellowship. Perhaps, too, it was attractive to a great many backwoods folk who had a natural aversion to baths, for everybody knew that Methodists believed a soul could be saved without drowning the body by total immersion in the nearest creek. Methodists enjoyed dancing, too, an activity frowned on by most of Methodism's competitors in the race to win converts from the devil.

So in deep sorrow, as perhaps only a true reprobate who has lost his only claim to respectability can be, Talmidge Biggs came to see the light. In the presence of at least fifty whooping and hollering and joyful Methodists, his two daughters Rivina, aged eighteen, and Claudine, fourteen, and did before them fall down at the magnificent climax of a sermon by Hezekiah Howell. Not only fall down but thrash about in exact imitation of his wife's last convulsions, raise a considerable dust, foam at the mouth, and speak in tongues.

Which is to say that Talmidge Biggs made vocal noises never heard before, assumed by the gathered worshipers to be part of a dialogue between Talmidge Biggs and the Holy Ghost. The Holy Ghost's portion of the conversation being heard only by Talmidge Biggs. There was nothing unusual about all this, for it was the way conversions always occurred for those so blessed that the Spirit came to them in a language unknown.

With face beaming, Talmidge Biggs arose with great happiness, and as his daughters pounded the dust off his clothes and Brother Hezekiah Howell held a palm on his sweating head, the former river tough accepted Jesus as his Savior. Everybody in the congregation figured it was one of the best conversions they'd ever witnessed because the meaner the sinner, the greater the glory when he came to Truth.

Mendez-Carnes was not there. But he heard about it. And he figured that a man so endowed with a newfound faith and honesty— he hoped—would make a good manager for his Elm Bluff stock pen. Besides, everybody knew that Talmidge Biggs was perfectly capable of handling any fuss among stock traders, with fists or club, and would have no trouble collecting percentages.

Close by the pens, in a stand of pine trees, was the house of Talmidge Biggs, built by Mendez-Carnes slaves. It was large for that time, and imposing. Clean, slab-side cypress with pine shake shingles on the roof. A wrap-around porch, or veranda as Rivina Biggs called it. There was a two-room structure set aside but connected by a covered walkway to the main house, much like aristocratic plantation homes had detached kitchens to keep the heat away from the master. But this was no kitchen. It was what the Philadelphia Annual Conference of John Wesley Bishops called a Methodist Haven because it was seen, as were other such places on the frontier, as haven for preachers who rode wide circuits and needed a place to rest now and then.

Indeed, many wandering Methodist preachers did pause there to read and think and commune with their God in the pines. But this Methodist Haven was perhaps somewhat different from most. For from the time Talmidge Biggs had come, and from the time he had saved Talmidge Biggs, and from the time he had first set eyes on Claudine Biggs, Brother Hezekiah Howell had made more or less permanent residence there. In addition to making small casts toward Arkansas Post and Hot Springs and Point of Rocks, Hezekiah Howell conducted twice-weekly prayer meetings and exhortations beside the mule pens of the Carnes Auction Barn. One of his most ardent followers was Sister Claudine Biggs, and Brother Hezekiah Howell intended to take her to wife, even though thirty years her senior.

This entire situation was not only known but encouraged by Mendez-Carnes. The prospect of Methodist camp meetings at the Auction Barn, so-called, could be nothing but good. Many people would gather, even white women and daughters. It became, as Mendez-Carnes foresaw, a place for ladies to display their newest piecework quilts. A place where there could be horseshoe pitching tournaments, shooting contests for bulls or turkeys, and watermelon suppers. And, of course, a brisk trading and buying and selling all the while. And so he did what he could to support Brother Hezekiah Howell.

The home of Talmidge Biggs was efficiently administered by Rivina, his elder daughter. She needed no help in this save that of the rather elderly slave couple sent upriver for that purpose from Baton Rouge. Which left Claudine time to move freely about the pens when she was not kneeling in prayer before Brother Hezekiah Howell, his palm on her head. Although she was obviously reverent and could read the Bible, too, Brother Howell seemed to require many hours of praying with her.

Anyway, among all the stock traders, and their wives, she attracted attention. She was a handsome, even beautiful, young woman. And in those times, fourteen was a time of life when a woman was measured. She had hair like corn silks, a wide, red mouth early to smile, eyes so blue they were almost colorless, and she could pitch horseshoes better than anybody short of Louisville, Kentucky, people said, and knew more about livestock and how to handle a team of mules than most men who came to buy and sell these creatures.

Confidence was her hallmark. She knew she was saved for Jesus, and didn't hesitate to tell anyone so, and even to quote certain passages from the Bible. But at no point did she consider that one of the requirements of everlasting life or of enjoying the present one involved marriage to Brother Hezekiah Howell.

She was equally confident in her knowledge of horses. Mules didn't much interest her, except as beasts of burden—well, as beasts of pulling wagons and plows—but horses were much like children to her, a lot dumber than mules and needing constant guidance. Of all the people she had ever seen at the stock pens, she figured there was not one who understood horses so well as herself.

Except for one. He was a godless man, too. Quick to take the Lord's name in vain. A face nobody could call dark and romantic, as Mr. Mendez-Carnes's face was, but slab-sided as hewn hickory and with yellow eyes like a wolf's, and a thatch of hair hardly darker than her own, which she thought was surely a mark of weakness. Yet this man knew horses. It was the only thing one could admire, and that, due to all his devil-given qualities, only from afar, like Job's horse viewing war.

But it was difficult to avoid thinking about such a man. He was from Point of Rocks, hardly a promise of bright future. He was not a slave holder, hardly a sign of economic viability. He was not an Austin man, which seemed the only assurance of foresight. Worst of all, his soul had not been saved, by the Methodists or by anybody else. And maybe, just maybe, the idea of his redemption was the kind of challenge Claudine Biggs enjoyed, as with a stupid horse that at first refused to take the bit in its mouth.

He was, this man, as beautiful to Claudine Biggs as the finest Tennessee Walker, with no blemish on hide and with clear eyes and sound fetlocks.

His name was John Fawley. And he'd noticed her, too.

The old-timers will tell you—well, they would have told you before they all died off—that Comanches had a technique for keeping a horse quiet and docile in any circumstance, even a very horny four-year-old stallion within olfactory range of an entire stock pen filled with Texas mares in estrus.

Comanche horsemen carried a stick, about two feet long, on the end of which was a rawhide loop. When the time came to keep the stallions quiet, they slipped this loop into the horse's mouth so the leather band enclosed upper lip and nostrils and then twisted the stick, tightening the loop to shut off air from the nose and creating such a sensitive agony that the animal forgot mares in heat or anything else until the pain stopped.

The Comanches had not thought of this themselves. They learned it from the Spaniards, watching from hiding, maybe, but learned it nonetheless as they learned all the other things about controlling horses. From the Spaniards, who at the time Comanches first saw them knew more about horses than anybody in the world. After all, aristocratic gentlemen of the Iberian Peninsula were not called caballeros for nothing, the root of *caballero* being *caballo*. Which means *horse*.

So some of the techniques of controlling horses were passed along to those who traded with the Comanches for horses. And this included a lot of people. Like maybe some Osages. Or Frenchmen who traded with Osages. Or Pawnees. Or Kiowas. Or almost anybody. But not everybody. It was one of the finer points of horsemanship overlooked by many.

By whatever means it had come, it had not been overlooked by John Fawley. He knew as surely as he could control an ill-tempered bull with a ring in its nose that he could control an ill-tempered horse with a rawhide loop around its nostrils.

The man from Louisiana was named Burton. He'd brought a string of small Texas ponies to Elm Bluff and sold them at Carnes Auction Barn, and then spent a fortnight camping in the woods nearby in order to come back to the stock pens each day and offer a proposition to all comers that was almost irresistible to anyone who had ever sat astride a horse or mule or even an old oxen.

This Burton had a roan stud, almost carrot colored, that was not unusually large or well muscled and in fact had nothing to distinguish it other than a very large head with bulging eyes. This Burton had a sandglass timer that ran for a full minute, a tiny wasp-waisted device he'd obtained from God only knew where, and tested by Talmidge Biggs by his own home clock—which was among the furnishings Mendez-Carnes had provided from Baton Rouge—and determined that indeed, as Mr. Burton said, the sand ran in one minute flat.

Now, Mr. Burton offered any man, woman, or child—Indians excluded—a ride on his Texas roan, for one dollar, and if the rider could remain in place on the roan's back until the sand ran out in the minute glass, that rider could have the horse. He did not accept furs or meat or even whiskey, but only gold or silver. And for the full two weeks he had been there, all who paid their dollar had ended in the dust and mule shit of the corral floor within a few seconds of having climbed aboard the roan. Part of the proposition was that the ride be bareback and with no bridle other than a hackamore on the great walleyed head. Which meant there was no restraining bit in the roan's mouth.

The record indicates that on a hot July day, the sun shining through a haze of moisture and the scent of horse droppings and the honeysuckle that grew in profusion behind the shelter sheds, Mr. Burton was making his offer to a rather large group of men—there were white women there as well—for a steamboat had just passed upriver and had stopped at the dock not half a mile from this very spot, which always brought people to the place. Besides that, Brother Hezekiah Howell had announced an early afternoon meeting and was at the moment standing on the front section of Talmidge Biggs's porch smoking his clay pipe and watching all the sinners he was preparing to save.

At the rim of the pen where the roan horse stood expectantly glaring at everybody, the hackamore on his head with a trailing rein, Mr. Burton paused in his recitation when a man leaning on the top pole of the corral watching the horse from the shade of his hat brim made the comment that the barrel of this horse was a little peaked and likely wouldn't sustain long running. The man was slender, but rather tall, and was dressed as many backwoodsmen of the area were, with fringed leather shirt and rough cloth trousers and moccasins with an upper extension that reached to his calves. Beside him was a man almost as tall, but much broader, with full beard, smiling, his teeth showing through the tangle of black hair around his mouth, and with arms, and indeed an apron, of a blacksmith, which he was, William Evans come from Point of Rocks with his friend John Fawley to watch the fun.

And a few paces farther along the corral fence was Claudine Biggs, leaning on the second-from-top pole on her elbows, watching and showing delightful new-corn teeth as she smiled, looking boldly at Mr. Burton and just as boldly from time to time at John Fawley, much more boldly than John Fawley looked at her. But he did look.

"Sir," shouted the man from Louisiana, "this is the prince of horses. Never tamed, nor by you, sir. By God, one dollar a try, if you will and looking for broken bones!"

And he waved the little sandglass in its case of polished walnut wood.

"I got the dollar," said John Fawley. "But I ain't sure I want the horse."

"Go on and ride him, John," somebody in the crowd shouted.

On the porch of Talmidge Biggs, Talmidge Biggs himself had come out to join Brother Hezekiah Howell, and together they stood and watched and perhaps speculated on whether John Fawley would try to ride the Texas roan.

Of course, he did, paying his dollar, walking into the enclosure where the roan waited, taking the halter lead and wrapping it with a quick movement about the roan's muzzle before leaping up onto the withers and yanking back hard on the line so the horse's head was pulled almost against its own neck, and already making a kind of pitiful scream and then dancing around like a dog chasing its tail but not bucking a single time, only trying to free its nose from the loop.

Until William Evans, watching Mr. Burton's glass, shouted "Time!" The crowd was cheering and Claudine Biggs screaming with delight and Brother Hezekiah Howell and Talmidge Biggs nodding with approval from the porch and the Louisiana man shouting, "Foul, foul, foul!"

Once John Fawley was off him, the roan did some extraordinary bucking, all about the pen, kicking up dust, and whistling like a wild stallion is supposed to whistle. The people cheered, and Mr. Burton continued to protest. But not for long.

"It wasn't a ride," Mr. Burton said. "You bull-dogged that horse."

"You wouldn't let me ride him with no real bridle," said John Fawley.

"It's a foul, and it doesn't count!"

The crowd began to tighten around the Louisiana man and make ominous sounds, and he could see any number of reasons why perhaps he should allow the ride. Like a few rifles and a few pistols and a great many very large sheath knives among the citizens who were looking at him with what he perceived to be an eager anticipation of drawing and quartering an outlander. Even the women showed no indications of mercy.

So Mr. Burton took the logical course and produced a bill of sale for the roan, and signed it as William Evans held it across the palm of his hard hand. But John Fawley made no move to take the bill of sale. He was leaning on the corral pole again, looking at the horse, and the horse was looking at him, snorting and blowing and pawing and being in every horse-way indignant.

The crowd, sensing something else coming, quieted and waited and watched. There were some jays in the red gums beyond the pines and they were making a loud racket, and John Fawley made a great pretense of listening to them. Then finally, spoke again. But his voice was low, and even Mr. Burton and William Evans had to lean forward to hear him.

"Mister, I ain't really got much use for that horse," John Fawley said. "But I hear how he's made you some profit, and I expect you'd enjoy havin' him back. So I'll sell him to you for what you've made off him with these here little rides the past two weeks."

Mr. Burton was delighted and began counting out the seventeen dollars he claimed to have earned on the roan, at which point the crowd grew rather ugly, edging in close and muttering, and Claudine Biggs said he was breaking the commandment about making false witness because everybody knew he'd taken in at least thirty-two dollars. Some of the rougher element began to jostle Mr. Burton, and he again became acutely aware that most of the men in the crowd were armed. So he explained that he'd made a slight miscalculation and counted out the thirty-two dollars, in silver, and William Evans took it while John Fawley continued to watch the horse still snorting and kicking up dust in the pen.

Once more, the crowd grew silent and watched, expectantly.

"Mister," John Fawley finally said, "you laid heavy faith on that horse, risking him for a dollar all those times. So if you still got the same faith, I'll make you a wager I'd expect any good Louisiana man to take up. If you put a bridle on that horse, I'll ride him to a standstill without gettin' throwed. No loop on his muzzle and no time glass. And if I do get throwed, you get your thirty-two dollars back. And if I don't, I keep the thirty-two dollars and get the horse, too."

Under the circumstances, Mr. Burton could see no safe way of avoiding the bet but at least he made loud protests about bridles with Spanish or rowel or spade bits, and John Fawley said Mr. Burton could select one of his own bridles with the gentlest bit possible. This was done, and half a dozen bystanders went into the corral and after a full twenty minutes of cursing, roiling dust, flashing hooves, snapping horse teeth, and indignant squeals, got the bridle on the roan and left him standing in the center of the pen where John Fawley mounted him.

Of course, John Fawley rode the stud to a standstill, and it took less time than it had to get the bridle on him. John Fawley slid down, leaving the roan gasping and panting and head-down, and walked out of the pen and asked now for the bill of sale. Mr. Burton, in not much better condition than the roan, passed the bill of sale to John Fawley, who took it and walked along the corral fence to where Claudine Biggs was still standing, handed her the paper, and spoke.

"Missy, here's a Texas roan for you, but stay clear of him 'til I can get back down here and gentle him a little bit."

Then he and William Evans, with the thirty-two dollars, started their walk back upriver to Point of Rocks. Where, at that very moment, John Fawley's younger brother was preaching—well, saying words over the grave—at Silas Catchen's funeral, the old hunter having finally succumbed to either too much trade whiskey or too much exposure to the elements lying against the outside wall of the Rocks Hotel.

Everybody along the river marked it as the beginning of a new phase for the two bachelors at the Fawley cotton patch. Things would have to change. Even for Questor Fawley, who had over the past couple of years, since the mother died, spent most of his time making whiskey and reading a Bible and acting like a preacher. But most of all for John, because giving Claudine Biggs that Texas roan was nothing more nor less than a proposal of marriage. It was just a matter of when. And in the meantime, any other suitor she might have—John Fawley's reputation for taking no foolishness from anybody well-known—would do well to stay clear of the Carnes Auction Barn. And the interesting part was that one of the most persistent suitors might not take well to staying clear because he was a man who pretty much did as he damn well pleased. Although John Fawley could be abrasive, the other man could be deadly. For the other man was Michael Loudec.

20

It was raining. One of those October rains that made everything gray, more so, it seemed, than rain at any other time of year. It was the kind of rain you wished for in July but never got, cool and steady and coming down for two, three, four days and nights. It was the kind of rain you knew would wash off the scarlet leaves of maples, the bronze leaves of oaks, the golden leaves of sycamore. And when it was finally finished, the sun would come more gentle than it had been in six months to shine on naked limbs, and you'd know that winter was not far away.

The Fawley bachelors, as they were now often called, sat on the roofed porch of the cotton patch cabin. In midafternoon, smoking their pipes, sipping occasionally from a jug of the younger brother's recent clear whiskey drippings, and they were eating pecans. Each was strong enough to hold two of the nuts in his palm and squeeze until the hulls cracked. Then pick out the meat with the point of a pocket clasp knife. At either end of the porch, just barely beneath the shelter of the overhang, were the hounds. Two bitches, six males, all descendants and second generation of those dogs the older brother had taken in his famous shoe-polish mule trade with the land speculator a long time ago. The dogs lay motionless, the only sign of life their large, moist eyes, watching the two men who sat on stools either side of the cabin's only door.

This was what had become a typical melding of the Fawleys, the younger reviewing great and small events because the older never read the newspaper or seemed to show much interest in what was happening anywhere beyond his vision. The new president, John Quincy Adams, first Yankee in that office since his daddy held it. The death of old Tom Jefferson, lamented for months as the news spread out across the country, mourned especially by state sovereignty men and farmers and all opponents of a strong central government. The increasing ruckus over slavery, growing since the infamous Compromise that prohibited human bondage north of the Missouri-Arkansas border once Missouri was admitted as a slave state. The peculiar institution's spread and the recent call by certain firebrand aristocrats in Louisiana and Mississippi and Alabama advocating a march on Cuba and Mexico and even Central America to establish a cotton empire as great and powerful as Rome's had ever been, they said.

And through this all, the older almost always making caustic remarks that once would have brought points of red anger to the younger's cheeks but were now taken as they were meant, nothing more than deprecation of anything beyond their control to influence. So marked, maybe, one as a subdued idealist, the other as a vocal realist. But whatever, they both understood, if not in specific terms, that they were as different as steel and butter and take your pick as to which was which.

"Don't know why it is you keep talkin' and worryin' about who's the president," said John Fawley. "They ain't none of 'em ever made the cotton grow faster or help us pay our debts to Loudec."

On Jefferson's death. "By God, we owe him. He hadn't bought all this land here, we'd still been in St. Louis likely, eatin' custard pie with French garlic on it."

"Or teachin' the young uns how to talk the Spanish tongue," said Questor.

"Ain't much worry for us, is it? Teachin' young uns?"

They both laughed.

Then. "You always brang up this Missouri Compromise. Hell,

it don't signify with us. We don't own no niggers and never aim to."

"Lot of trouble brewin'," said Questor. "They's folks now sayin' we ought to break away and make a new country."

"Who? All them goddamned cotton politicians? What difference does it make? None of them people has gored my ox. Whichever bunch aims to run things, let 'em. Just leave me be. One outfit is bad as the next."

So it went that particular October afternoon in the rain. The two smoking and sipping and hulling pecans. But now there was something different, when Questor turned and looked at his older brother for a long time, which always made John uncomfortable, his brother looking at him like that.

"Well, what?" he said, throwing a handful of pecan hulls out into the rain-splattered yard.

"How soon you fixin' to brang that woman?"

"Oh, that," said John, knocking out the fire from his pipe against one leg of his stool. "Maybe in the spring. Maybe sooner. I ain't made up my mind yet."

"You know we ain't goin' to no Boston Mountains when you marry her. She ain't likely to leave from close by her pa."

"You know her, then?"

"I ain't ever laid eyes on her, but I heerd all about what she thinks."

"Who from? One of them Evans people?"

"Whoever. It's true, ain't it?"

"Yes, she ain't gonna leave her pa."

"Well, then, I reckon we ain't goin' to no Boston Mountains."

"Not just now, maybe."

"That Methodist preacher down there, he thinks he's supposed to marry with this woman. You know that?"

"Old Hezekiah? Shit, I could out-rassle him with my big toenail. And she knows it."

And John laughed again, at the prospect of Brother Hezekiah Howell marrying anybody, and Questor laughed as well. He knew Brother Hezekiah because Brother Hezekiah had often visited the Methodist church gatherings in Little Rock in his usual capacity as traveling evangelist.

"Old Hezekiah preaches the worst sermons I ever saw," said Questor. They laughed again, and the spirit of mirth was so wonderful that one of the hounds rose and slowly came over and stood between Questor's knees. He scratched the dog's ears, and the dog's big, moist eyes looked up at him worshipfully.

"We need to build me another cabin," said Questor. John looked at him, frowning.

"What for?"

Now it was Questor who shrugged, but said nothing, and John laughed. He slapped his leg.

"Well, surely, we gotta get little brother out of the room when all the rut and grunt begins, don't we?"

Those fine points of red started in Questor's cheeks, but then subsided, and he smiled and rubbed the hound's head.

"Yes. Yes, I reckon so."

But it had been a raw nerve, and John knew it, and after a while he spoke to it, without really knowing what it was exactly.

"These funerals you preach," he said. "What is it you say?"

"I don't preach, I just talk is all," said Questor. "It don't hurt nobody."

"Ques, I don't give a damn if you wanta preach, or whatever it is you do," said John, and his tone was so solicitous that one of the hounds rose and came up between John's legs but he kicked the dog away. "Get away, boy, you smell bad. But listen, Ques, I just wondered what it is you talk about."

"Well, you could come hear sometime."

"Ques!"

"All right," said Questor. "I just try to soothe the ones ast me to come do it. The family, you see? Say some good things about whoever it is. Make the family feel good, you see?"

"Good things? About old Silas Catchen? Jesus Christ, what was it you found out to say good about that son of a bitch?"

"Oh, you have to make up thangs sometimes," Questor said and smiled and rubbed the dog's head and looked out through the rain toward the line of red gum and sycamore.

"You got the call, ain't you?"

"I don't know, Jackie," which is what Questor called his older brother sometimes when something important was being said. Or maybe when it was not. But for whatever reason, and all of it remembrance of things from St. Louis as boys.

"That night we put Ma down. You been different ever since."

"Yes. It was a vision."

"Ques, I don't think I wanta hear about it."

"I can't tell nothin' much. It was a thang you can't tell about."

"I don't wanta hear. But Ques, do whatever you want. Ain't nobody gonna stop you."

Then a long time, watching the rain. Feeling somehow a closeness not felt since the first moment out of St. Louis when they stood in the woodland trace and saw three Osage warriors, painted and armed.

And then, unaccountably, Questor laughed. John and the hounds jerked to attention.

"You know, old William Like asked me to be a courier!"

"The Quapaw agent? That William Like?"

"Yes. To carry this draft for Indian annuities down to New Orleans to get the cash because nobody around here can cover it."

"Why you?"

"He said I was honest and good," Questor said, and their eyes met and they laughed so loud all the hounds began to bark.

John shouted the dogs down and then bent toward his brother and asked, again, "Honest and good? Hell, them annuity drafts has always been too much to find cash around here and old Prentice Entwine always taken 'em downriver to get cash negotiations."

"Well, Prentice Entwine now in sad repute," said Questor.

"He got bad beat two years ago for sheriff by that Campbell boy, what's his name, Malcolm? Your friend Loudec supported him. So now old Like ast *you?*"

"Honest and good." And they laughed again but only for a moment, and then John reached out and touched his brother's arm.

"How much?"

"How much what?"

"How much on the draft, for Christ sake."

"Eight thousand dollars."

"*How much?*"

"Eight thousand dollars."

"My God." John Fawley leaned back against the wall and shook his head. "Don't you never take no job like that, Ques, don't you never!"

"Old Like offered me fifty dollars to do it. Somebody got to."

"Why? If this general government wants to feed Quapaws, then let 'em send something besides a piece of paper with a number on it. And listen, Ques, don't you do no studyin' atall about goin' to New Orleans for a sack of gold or silver."

And that seemed the end of that. But if conversation ended on one subject, it seemed to encourage returning to another. With no warning or reason, John, looking through the rain toward the far line of trees, said, "That old bastard you brought out here that night never said nothin' good about our ma."

"I know it."

Questor rose and went into the cabin to stoke the fire and slice some side meat. He did the cooking now, and he did it very well, because he spent a considerable time at it. Over his own mother's stove there was a lot of time to ponder the possible design of her death, finding the serpent on the very creek where he, Questor, made the spirits, the liquid joy or destruction, for people who didn't even realize that drinking it might not be a sin but just living might be.

Well, there had to be an answer somewhere, he reckoned, and maybe tomorrow, if the rain cleared away, there'd be that revival meeting in the woods behind the line of pine trees where the territorial legislators practiced with their pistols. And the preacher was going to be the celebrated Hezekiah Howell, why celebrated, Questor did not know, but the placards nailed to places like the side of William Evans's livery barn indicated it was so. Questor had never been to Elm Bluff and the Methodist Haven there, but now he'd have a chance to hear this man again in Little Rock.

Actually, he had little hope of learning much from a mere mortal. Since that night of the blue lightning across the water, he'd about determined that revelations would come from some higher power than a strolling evangelist could muster. The only trouble with such revelations was that they came in signs and symbols, maybe, that he couldn't understand.

Had Questor Fawley been able to search through all the history of his land for a time appropriate to his personal groping for some kind of dynamic spiritualism, he couldn't have picked a better era than the one into which he came through no design of his own. He was caught up in a storm of religious fervor without the faintest notion of its extent or force. Not that he was unaware of it. But being young and only beginning his quest for life's meaning, he simply figured it was always like that. Of course, it wasn't. This was a special time.

Territorial Arkansas, like most of the early nineteenth-century midcontinent, was a religious battleground. Not a blade-and-bullet battleground as was Europe during, say, the Thirty Years' War of the seventeenth century, but a contest of words and ideas. The untouched frontier—at least untouched by any European three-hundred-year-old tradition—seemed the natural place for a wildly individualistic citizenry to develop a new kind of rough-and-tumble democracy. And that seemed to require an equally boisterous religious faith, as energetic and hard-charging as the politics.

Thus occurred one of the great Christian revivals of all history, the various denominations competing for converts with powerful, charismatic exhorters shouting their appeal to multitudes anxious to be convinced. And the areas of the South were most affected because of milder winters, and this was no indoor phenomenon. It happened outside, like a bullfight or a forest fire.

The man, or men, who had seen the light of salvation and were trying to shine it on everybody else simply advertised, found a platform, and preached. They were forceful and dedicated. There was the story of one Methodist preacher who was standing on the end of a barrel and midway through his sermon, the barrelhead under his feet gave way and he fell into the barrel—which luckily was empty—and without any pause continued his call to glory, and being a short man, only his head and his waving hands were visible to the congregation. It was said that everybody went to revival meetings in hope of seeing some preacher fall through the barrelhead. But that's not why they went. They went in search of some reason for hope that the grave was only the beginning, not the end, and it was a hope contagious as measles. Just as was the hope that a democratic republic was the antidote to all of Europe's old political ills, which most of them had not experienced but had sure as hell heard about.

So these people preached, in woodlots and corrals, in village squares and orchards, at crossroad stores and in graveyards behind log chapels. Men, women, and children crowded around, some listening intently, some crying, women hugging one another, men waving arms above heads, some falling to the ground in ecstasy, some kneeling in prayer. Farther back from the platform where the crowd was less dense, a few gentlemen engaged in low conversation, perhaps closing deals, ladies exchanged recipes for gooseberry pie, children's noses were wiped, and a spinster or two held kerchief to face and hummed an old hymn. Farther back still, the crowd thinned more, and a few young men ate apples or peaches in season, and dogs wandered about, sometimes meeting in furious fights, other times copulating until some indignant householder kicked them apart while watching children giggled or tried not to.

At greater distance were saddle horses tied to bushes, mule-drawn wagons, buggies, surreys, hacks, and boys selling apples or peaches in season, and children who had not been able to conceal giggles over the dogs being swatted on the bottom by frowning aunts. In the surrounding woods so far away from the platform that only the loudest shouts of preacher and convert could be heard, a young man and woman whispering, perhaps their hands touching, a group of boys ate watermelon, an old man picked on the strings of a banjo, a few men gathered in a tight knot, passing around a brown bottle.

And finally, at the very last distance, among the bushes, so far from the soul saving they could hardly hear any of it, a group of black children from the nearest slave quarters, wide-eyed because some mischievous white youth has told them that if they looked through the trees toward the preacher, they'd see Jesus.

The two principal antagonists in the contest for souls were Methodists and Baptists. The former a mutant from John Wesley–style Anglicanism, the latter a splinter of New England Congregationalism. The Methodists were hot revivalists, preaching brotherly love and good work on earth that God gave credit for on Accounting Day. The Baptists were hot revivalists as well, teaching that a state of grace was only possible for somebody old enough to understand what it meant. People said the Methodists didn't take their religion as seriously as the Baptists. People said the Baptists were pretty positive about what the Bible said and that the Methodists were pretty pushy about everybody learning to read. People said that sometimes a passage of Scripture could be read by the Methodists and they'd say it meant a drought, and the same passage could be read by Baptists who said it was a flood. It was almost as much fun as local elections, and it didn't involve many knife fights, either.

Some distance behind these were the Presbyterians. They weren't hot for it, but they put on some measurably good revivals, too. Most people figured Presbyterians were Calvinists who had learned to tame down the worst parts of predestination. And everybody had to admit that most big landowners, most successful politicians, and most schoolteachers were Presbyterians. The Presbyterians didn't really get into the vicious fray along with Methodists and Baptists. There wasn't much name-calling. Like the Methodists saying the Baptists were nothing more than dirt-poor Puritans, and the Baptists saying the Methodists thought you could read yourself into glory.

And then there were actually a few Episcopalians—second cousins to the Methodists. They were trusted in money and political matters. And as individuals, usually. Maybe because there was still some feeling among the rank and file of citizens about respect for lords of manor because hell, the Episcopals were richer than the Presbyterians. So even though they were regarded as English-lovers, they got along well on Arkansas's frontier maybe because they were not the same kind of gentle men and ladies that inhabited the Piedmont of Virginia.

And there were other wild splinter groups. For any man—it was not yet time for a woman to fill this role—could explode his thinking and make new waves and know that there were some who would listen to him.

And there were a few of the Old Ones. Up the river system from New Orleans, mostly, or down from St. Louis. The Catholics and Jews. Not many. Only a few. They were tolerated, usually. Most people said the Catholics were good at running hospitals. And of course, everybody knew that all Jews did was tailor men's suits. Or at least that's all they'd better do if they didn't expect a visit in the dark of night by good God-loving Christians who understood their antecedents had killed Jesus.

Sometimes, in that hell-for-leather bout between Methodist and Baptist it was hard to tell the difference. If you just happened onto one of those meadowland meetings, you'd be hard put to decide which it was. There was a lot of syncretism going on, from top to bottom, from the so-called center of each faith and the grass roots, which meant there was an effort to reconcile or maybe combine different beliefs. So just as surely as a county election in Vicksburg, Mississippi, was unlike one in Andover, Massachusetts, so a Baptist in Little Rock, Arkansas, was not necessarily like a Baptist in Providence, Rhode Island.

Usually, doctrine had less to do with conversion than proximity. Whichever evangelists were close by. So you came to grace by the means at hand and later worked out the denomination's tenets you could support or ignore. It was a wonderful proposition, the same individualism popping up in religion that had already done so in frontier politics.

All of which was not very comforting, even if it was a lot of fun, to somebody like Questor Fawley. And in fact, for him, no fun at all.

Although the fire and thunder of revival generally erupted in some open space that was large enough to accommodate the enthusiasm, the big three denominations each had a church in Little Rock by the time of the John Quincy Adams administration. Actual buildings that could be called churches, with crosses on the roof and a pulpit inside and often even a choir box. There were not any parsonages yet, except for the Presbyterians. Methodist and Baptist preachers, when they weren't out riding the revival circuit, lived with one or more of their most faithful parishioners. This was a real honor. Except for the kids in such households, who hated the whole idea because it meant so much praying and being nice and having to listen to long talks they didn't understand at the supper table.

The Presbyterian church was of limestone with real glass windows and boasted a small steeple with a brass bell. The bell having being salvaged from a steamboat wreck. Methodists and Baptists were happy with cypress log chapels. At least for the time being.

When there wasn't a meeting in the open air, attendance in these churches was usually adequate to fill the hall but not much more. The Methodist and Baptist chapels were a kind of rest area where the preacher and his flocks could catch their breath between the furious rounds of outdoor soul savings. There were Sunday services, morning and evening, and prayer meetings during the week, usually on Wednesday. Sometimes these proceedings were conducted by the lay members of the church because it was expected that any preacher in that time spend much of his energy riding about the countryside on a gentle mule, organizing what came to be called camp meetings for folk who often came from so far away that it meant camping nearby the stump-pulpit during the course of the festivities.

Questor Fawley was fully aware of all this activity. He'd been in every church along the river at Point of Rocks and attended most of the outdoor revivals. He had listened to visiting divines from as far away as Hartford, Connecticut, and Savannah, Georgia. And of course, he had heard the locals many times.

His attendance didn't go unnoted. After all, his reputation for conducting soothing funerals had become widespread. And it was well-known in the community that he was a man of integrity, of even temper, and therefore a man with few enemies, rather unusual for the time and place. And, they said, Questor Fawley could read as well as anybody and could speak French besides, and likely knew the Good Book as well or better than most clergy. Well, not so well as the Presbyterian minister and certainly not so well as the occasional Episcopal priest who passed through. But well enough.

Besides, when he talked about serious things, like the Bible, he didn't try to scare the hell out of you! Spraying the scent of brimstone was just fine, but there was also a place for a gentler ministry, wasn't there?

So the Methodists asked him to become one of their exhorters. A kind of nonordained preacher to back up the regular ones and who could do all the normal things expected of a preacher except give communion. And maybe in a pinch, even that.

Now, in the normal course of events, a Methodist bishop in St. Louis assigned ministers to the Point of Rocks area. But all local Boards of Stewards had a great deal to say about this, and the recruitment of good talkers, no matter that they were not ordained, was usually the rule rather than the exception. After all, some Methodists said, any means short of crimes against the state were completely acceptable because the goal, after all, was to beat the Baptists!

Michael Loudec heard of this offer. Michael Loudec was a Presbyterian who never went to church. But as the biggest landowner along that stretch of river, he made it his business to know what was happening not only in politics and business, but in religion as well, understanding that some disagreement over the Trinity could mean a shift in votes at the ballot box or a fluctuation in the local price of corn.

"If you want to do this," Michael Loudec told Questor Fawley, "I'll pay your way through Dartmouth College."

"Dartmouth College?"

"You know about Dartmouth College, don't you? The biggest Methodist school in the country. But if New Hampshire is too far away, then we can find some college in Missouri or Illinois where you can be ordained."

"Why?"

"Let's say because you and I have been friends a long time."

"Friends? You've got more friends than anybody I know."

Michael Loudec laughed. "Friends? Like that toad lawyer, Rhett? Like those lickspittle legislators anybody can buy at ten dollars a peck? But that's all beside the point. If you want to preach, I'll help. Do you want it?"

"I couldn't go to no big school like that! I don't even talk like people who go to school like that. I talk like what I am, a backwoods peckerwood who makes whiskey."

"For God's sake, Questor, you can read! You can write! You can think! And in a pinch, you could throw some French at those Yankee sons of bitches. You can still speak some French, can't you? You haven't forgotten that, have you?"

"Almost."

"Don't worry about how you talk. You're smarter than most of these Yankee schoolteachers."

But Questor Fawley turned it all down. The Methodists and Michael Loudec and Dartmouth College.

So then the Baptists offered to ordain him on the spot, which was also not unheard of in that time. The laity of the Baptist congregation pretty much called the tune on their clergymen. There wasn't any hierarchy of bishops among them sending preachers, one of their points of pride. The people in the pews ran their church.

Michael Loudec heard about that, too, and made no offer to pay Questor Fawley's education at Brown, the Baptist stronghold of education. Probably because he knew it was useless to do so.

So Questor Fawley turned down the Baptists. And said nothing to his brother about any of the affair, either.

But if John Fawley wasn't told the details, he knew about the tumult of mind. He had to live with it. Often, Questor would go out beyond the line of red gum and sycamore trees, where their mother was buried, and sit on a rock above the river and gaze off into space and hold the old King James tight against his chest, the old King James so water-warped and dog-eared and falling apart. Or sometimes in the middle of the night, Questor would rise from his bed and walk into the cotton patch yard and there kneel and pray, and John would rise, too, and watch for a moment from the darkness of the cabin, watch at least long enough to satisfy himself that his brother wasn't going to fall down with some kind of religious fit. And rain or good weather, Questor would take the mule each Sunday and ride into the town for worship someplace, and he seldom missed one of the revivals in woodlot or field.

And John Fawley noted that each time his younger brother came back from one of these preachings, he seemed more cranky and uncomfortable than he had been before, and so John learned to stay clear of him then.

John Fawley had always reckoned a body went to church to get some sort of spiritual satisfaction not available elsewhere. But when Questor returned from one of these events, there was small sense of satisfaction. Usually, that's when he'd go to his rock above the river and sit there all day looking like a gut-shot sheep.

Things ephemeral and fleeting, shadows of the mind, John Fawley could not understand nor did he try to do. His new percussion lock rifle, he understood. Problems of crops in drought time, he understood. Constant debt to a landlord, he understood. The physical wilderness and everything it contained, he understood. If he could see it and touch it, then it was understood.

And yet he understood as well that his brother searched in a wilderness unseen and untouchable, and even though he reckoned such a thing was like trying to turn back the flow of the river or the seasons, like trying to hold a handful of smoke, like trying to stop the coming of coolness in evening, if that's what Questor wanted, then let him have it. And although John Fawley considered the whole mash of it a bunch of foolishness, he would never deny Questor's right to do it, nor would anybody else. He might tease

Questor about it from time to time, just on the edges anyway, but nobody else had best tease about it!

Well, now, that brought up the business of old Billy Like, the Indian agent, with his proposition to Questor about that annuity draft. A thing Questor should never consider, of course, and probably never did, but old Billy Like thought it appropriate to make the offer. Why hell, John Fawley thought, Ques would get halfway back from New Orleans, go glassy-eyed from reading that Book, and the bag of money would fall into the river and Ques wouldn't even notice it.

Eight thousand dollars! That was reality. As was the fifty dollars old Billy Like offered to get that draft cashed. And the money back here to Point of Rocks agency. Hell, it would be easy. Easy as pie.

21

Nobody ever knew exactly what became of the Quapaw annuity money the year John Fawley went to New Orleans to cash the draft. Bits and pieces of it were known. The connections were mostly guesswork. In any event, it certainly provided plenty of subject matter for conversation around the store and saloon stoves and at the various ladies' quilting bees and spiced sassafras tea parties during the winter, which was an unusually harsh one. They had a snow in February that piled up at least an inch of the white fluff that didn't melt away for almost two days.

Suspension of balmy days was seen as an ill omen connected with the Quapaw money, but there was no consensus on how this was so, except that Idella Harp said the whole business was a sign of the Wrath of God—which she said in capital letters—because He was so displeased with rampant sin at Point of Rocks and elsewhere. After all, Idella said, cholera had broken out again at Arkansas Post, which proved something or other.

Idella Harp had grown in respectability in the community since her husband Emil had closed down his Chapel of the Virgin, thrown his piece of the True Cross back into the Arkansas River, and joined the Baptist revival movement. The little limestone building on the north side was now rented by Doctor Clarence Biddington, and an ailing citizen could go for treatment, providing they found the good doctor free of an opium haze, and he was indeed developing a solid reputation along the river as a surgeon who was excellent for extracting teeth and cutting ingrown toenails.

Lena Brock, on the other hand, said it was a Yankee conspiracy to embarrass the South. This had become a pretty good argument concerning almost anything unpleasant.

Lena's husband Logan said he was sorry for the Indians, all of them coming in for their annual money and not understanding why it wasn't available. But Cleve Buchanan said it was all to the good because the Quapaws only used their annuity to get drunk so maybe this would encourage the few remaining aboriginals wandering about in local woodlands to go on west where they obviously belonged.

"That's right," said Sheriff Malcolm Campbell. "Let 'em get on west of Fort Smith where no white man in his right mind would ever want to go anyway."

There didn't have to be any guessing about the first part of the drama. John Fawley had taken that eight-thousand-dollar draft downriver to get it cashed, and it was common knowledge that Agent William Like was paying him fifty dollars to do it. John Fawley, as everyone expected, didn't book passage for a cabin on one of the regular steamboats but hired on as a wood crew man, which meant that as the little boat went along he would help at the various stops to load chunks of oak onto the vessel and en route help the regular engineman to feed the wood into the fire. And sleep on the woodpile and get his food from the galley along with the rest of the boat's company.

"Penny saved is a penny earned," said Ernestine Evans. "You would expect a son of Molly Fawley, God rest her, to understand that."

Well, John Fawley got to New Orleans, all right, and found a bank willing to cash his federal draft once he had produced the letter of introduction given him by Agent William Like. He started back upriver on the steamer *Dove*. It was an ordinary steamboat that made all the ports of call along the Mississippi and the Arkansas from the Crescent City to Point of Rocks.

Later, it was learned that another man of interest had booked cabin passage on the *Dove*. He was on the passenger manifest as

Horace Jones, but a number of people on the *Dove* had seen him many times before and knew that he was not anyone named Horace Jones but former Sheriff Prentice Entwine, who had been defeated for office at Point of Rocks some two years before, defeated by Sheriff Malcolm Campbell.

Former Sheriff Entwine was in bad repute along the river. After being thrown out of office as sheriff at Point of Rocks, he had begun a new career as a river gambler and on two occasions had been marooned on a midriver sand island by steamboat captains who had found that he often played with decks of cards that had more than the standard number of aces. On this trip, former Sheriff Entwine stayed to his cabin while below on the boiler deck was John Fawley, who had no notion that the man he had beaten with a barrel stave, or whatever it was, in a north bank whorehouse was anywhere within five hundred miles.

Then, as testimony would reveal, on the first night out of Natch-ez, former Sheriff Entwine waited until about two o'clock in the morning and slipped down to the woodpile with the apparent intention of robbing John Fawley. It was also well-known that former Sheriff Entwine had on his person two pistols.

Sleeping on the woodpile, John Fawley had a small satchel, which the ship's crew observed that he kept close by at all times, but they had no idea what the bag contained. They also observed that when John Fawley was not helping stoke the steam engine firebox, he would sit at the rail and fish. He had what looked like a long leather sock and tied into the toe of this were about three pounds of lead slugs, the kinds of slugs you put on a fishing line to make the bait sink.

On the night in question, the boat's crew testified that they heard two sudden shots and then a great deal of grunting and bad language from the woodpile, and when the captain arrived with a lantern and a cocked pistol, there was John Fawley sitting on a chunk of oak with the leather sinker sock dangling in his right hand and on the deck at his feet were two pistols and former Sheriff Entwine with his face and head beaten to a bloody pulp!

Former Sheriff Entwine revived enough shortly to take a large dose of brandy, whereupon the captain put in at the next midstream sandbar island and placed former Sheriff Entwine thereon. As the steamboat pulled away upriver, he was seen sitting in the sand shouting obscenities. Meanwhile, in his pilothouse, the captain treated John Fawley's wounds. The powder burn on John Fawley's neck was doused with coal oil, and the gash in his side from a passing pistol ball was sewn tight shut with needle and silk thread and doused with coal oil. The captain then gave John Fawley a jolt from the same brandy bottle that had served to help revive former Sheriff Entwine, and then John Fawley went back down to the boiler deck and went to sleep on the woodpile. The next port of call was Vicksburg.

Now sometime before all this happened, Agent William Like was seen to take passage on a southbound steamboat, carrying a rather large carpetbag. Local folk thought it odd that the Quapaw agent would be going toward New Orleans when John Fawley was somewhere in that direction and soon to be homebound with the annuity money.

At any rate, as testimony would later reveal, when the boat docked at Vicksburg, Agent William Like disembarked and from that moment began to meet each northbound steamer coming up from New Orleans, looking, as he told various people, for his cousin whose name was Horace Jones. When *Dove* arrived, Agent William Like appeared somewhat astonished to see John Fawley, but recovered quickly and told John Fawley that urgent business had called him south but that now they'd met he might as well take the annuity money, which was fine with John Fawley who was reported to have said that he was glad to get rid of it because it attracted unpleasant insects much as did dead meat, and so the money went into Agent Like's hand. But not before John Fawley had his fifty dollars for doing the errand and a receipt signed by Agent Like, which seemed to upset Agent Like, but he really had no choice, so he signed a receipt.

Agent Like went ashore, and John Fawley continued upriver on *Dove.* When he arrived at home, he helped his brother build a second cabin on the cotton patch on a spot chosen by Questor at the edge of the line of red gum and sycamore trees east of the main cabin. Near their mother's grave. This new cabin was little more than a sleeping cell, which Questor would occupy once John Fawley went to Elm Bluff to claim his bride. Everyone knew this was preparation for a wedding, and knew it absolutely when John Fawley came into town and bought a new woolen waistcoat, a string of pink ribbon for his bride's hair, and a fairly good pair of boots that had recently been taken off a man convicted of murder and hanged by Sheriff Malcolm Campbell on order of the circuit court.

Time passed. People began to wonder what had happened to Agent William Like. The Quapaws came in for their annual dole. They began begging for food, and many good citizens gave them bacon rind and other things. Michael Loudec sent in an old cow to be killed and roasted over an open pit for them. Some of the tavern rowdies gave a few Quapaws whiskey so they could laugh when the Quapaws got sick and puked on themselves. Some of the Quapaw women prostituted themselves in the woods in order to have money to buy food for their children. Finally, the Quapaws went away.

People continued to wonder about Agent William Like. Some began to say that he had come to foul play.

Then there arrived the most impressive delegation of officials anybody had seen since 1820 when Territorial Governor Miller had come up from Arkansas Post to establish the capital at Little Rock. There was a United States deputy marshal, two gentlemen from the Indian superintendent's office at St. Louis, two field-grade army officers, and a number of hangers-on, all wearing high hats. They were there to remove the Quapaw agency upriver and install a new agent. More important, maybe, they were there to ask a lot of questions and spend some money with local room and board. And whiskey. They talked a long time to John Fawley. They talked a long time to the captain and crew of the *Dove* when that small boat docked on its monthly visit at the riverfront. They even talked with Idella Harp, who explained how God was involved in all this, and with Lena Brock, who accused them of being a part of a Yankee conspiracy.

And they talked with Agent William Like's wife Clara, who was now living with Hugh and Ernestine Evans and clerking in their store. Clara became hysterical with each interview, claiming that the Cherokees had killed her husband, or maybe the Osages, she wasn't sure which, because of his eternal love for the Quapaws.

It turned out that this investigative committee did not think that Agent William Like had met with foul play at all. For a man of Agent Like's description, and being in a great hurry, had been seen in Natchitoches, Louisiana, by one of Stephen Austin's land agents who had himself been connected with the Indian service, and who in time reported this to the United States attorney in the court at Baton Rouge, having become suspicious at the amount of money this man was willing to spend to get him quickly anyplace out of the country, like west of the Sabine.

So there it was! the folk said. Old Like had made a deal with old Entwine for the former sheriff to rob the courier, and they'd meet at Vicksburg. Not much doubt there. But after that, differing opinions.

"So Entwine would get the money, dump the courier in the river, meet Like, and they'd go to Texas," said Logan Brock. "So when Entwine didn't do his end, old Like just taken it all and cut and run."

"No," said Hugh Evans. "It was this way, be sure, they meet at Vicksburg, courier dead in the river, Entwine take his share and go to Texas, Old Like come back here and weep great tears that somebody robbed his man, and go on about his business."

"My dear," said Ernestine, "you know I told you there was a mite of trouble between Agent Like and dear Clara his wife for a long time, so I say here and now, Logan Brock is right. When Agent Like went from this place, it was because of shattered love, and the money was only a helpstone along his path away from Clara."

"Helpstone be damned," shouted Hugh Evans. "He was after the money and maybe come home and do it all again someday. Then had to flee, flee because the murderer he hired was unable to do the deed!"

"Well, I can see it now," said Otis Bradford, recent reader at law with Shiring Rhett and now in practice of his own, "Old Agent Like in Texas, passing himself as a Mexican official going about in east Texas confiscating slaves, freeing them on writ from the Mexicans, then marching them off east to the Sabine and selling them in Louisiana!"

"Why, that's a sin," said Idella Harp. "A lie, a lie, passing himself off as some Mexican official."

"Stranger things have happened, madam," said Otis Bradford. "Why, you have certainly heard of that infamous French pirate landing slaves in the Gulf marshes of Texas, and people like those Bowie brothers walking them north to appropriate places and then east into Louisiana to sell them? Because we now have a law forbidding import of slaves, but those pirates—what is it, Laffite? yes—making a great business of that."

"Jean Laffite?" asked Logan Brock. "Sir, he was a hero of the battle of New Orleans!"

"I only say what I hear from credible men."

And after he'd gone, Logan Brock saying, "Why, that Loudec pipsqueak. Why do you let him in here, Hugh?"

"A public tavern it is, man, so no me to keep somebody out who has a thirst on him."

At the cotton patch, Questor never questioned his brother. Not even about the powder burn on his neck. And when they swam naked in the deep pools of Moccasin Creek, Questor said nothing about the ugly scar across John's left side. Because Questor knew that in such matters his brother would say what he wanted to say, without any questioning. And John never said anything.

In the lower saloons at Point of Rocks, the young toughs, some of whom were real hunters and some of whom were trying to act like real hunters, talked about it and laughed. And said that it would be time for ice in hell before any of them would try to take anything from John Fawley and throw him into the river. There was much admiration among these kinds of men for John Fawley. His dark side, they said. And maybe because of that they determined that for the coming wedding they should honor the man of the cotton patch with a fine shivaree.

John Fawley was equal to his contemporaries. He had not the faintest notion of the origins of sacred social ceremonies such as shivarees. No more than he understood pagan evergreen trees as a part of Christmas. It was just there. And even had he known the genesis of this rather barbarian celebration of wedlock, it was not likely that he would have enjoyed it.

Since before anybody knew how to write about it, there were probably gatherings of interested individuals to celebrate a man and woman embarking on a project that might insure an increase in the tribe. It was a way of rejoicing over the prospect of future warriors and mothers of warriors entering the racial or ethnic or religious or tribal pool where there was the constant concern of maintaining numbers adequate to cope with cruel natural disaster and ruthless human enemies. In the parlance of latter-day crapshooters, it might have been called betting on the come. Expecting a good point to roll up if you could just perform the right incantations on the dice.

There must have been heavy overtones of supplication to the gods in these rites, where everybody by their own joy hoped to make whatever deities who created healthy children just as happy and therefore willing to do their part in bringing forth many strong offspring.

For whatever reasons, these had to have been wildly enthusiastic affairs, once the solemn vows were satisfactorily completed. In some societies, these great celebrations of wedlock have survived the centuries. Certainly a real Polish wedding is about as subtle as a Mexican revolution, and when it comes to noise, happiness, exuberance, and glass breaking, you can't beat a Jewish one.

On the other hand, a lot of things have faded away. No longer extant are those delightfully recorded weddings of, say, English kings. After the cathedral pomp, there was always a massive, drunken party, in a massive beer-sloshed hall, and in an adjoining chamber the king and his bride were practically tucked into bed by giggling and leering ladies-in-waiting and male retainers who were so involved in the thing that they sometimes almost climbed into bed themselves to illustrate, perhaps, what was supposed to take place there. Sometimes, once he'd accomplished his purpose, the king would appear again, perhaps waving his bride's nightgown and looking, you would suppose, flushed and victorious, at which time there were lusty cheers and the party really got down to serious drinking.

Well, all of this began as celebration of hoped-for offspring, result of the first night's conjugal bliss, but in many such festivities the emphasis slowly shifted from concern for a result of copulation to a rather ribald frolic focused on the copulation for its own sake. So the party often became a teasing reminder to bride and groom of what was supposed to happen and how everybody else wished it was about to happen to them.

These wedding galas must have surely been the ideas of men. It is difficult to imagine the central female character in the drama, the bride, becoming very enthusiastic about a ritual that turned one of her life's most personal and private moments into something resembling the public auction of a prize heifer.

In any event, these wedding-night riots passed down the generations and assumed many forms, maybe the most unattractive of which was when local gay blades and roughnecks alike came together in common cause to get more than moderately drunk, stagger about in the dark outside shuttered windows, and harass the young married couple inside on their wedding couch with every kind of racket and noise fertile minds could devise. On the American frontier, the rite took its most raucous form, as you would expect, and it was called a shivaree.

Shivaree comes from the French *charivari,* which in turn comes from a Latin word meaning "headache." Which is about as appropriate as a definition can get. In nineteenth-century America, it was composed of equal parts whiskey and gunpowder.

Plans were laid by the shivareers in a friendly tavern or saloon. After everyone had a sufficient lack of judgment, they went to the newlywed couple's abode. At this time, young couples who might be shivareed were of a class that expected to get back to work the morning after the honeymoon night. They did not take long trips to palm-fringed beaches or brightly lit gambling casinos. There were a few hours of thinking only of each other and then it was back to the task of survival.

Anyway, once in the vicinity of the bridal bed, the shivaree task force crept up silently, so they supposed, and then on signal began to fire weapons into the air, bang on pots and pans with iron stove pokers, shout, ring cowbells, and sing sometimes daring songs. If they could, they included a former soldier who could blow a few meaningless blasts on a bugle, for they felt this added dignity to what otherwise would have been an unseemly riot in honor of licentiousness.

Sometimes, as they staggered about in the dark over unfamiliar ground, a few of them were seriously wounded by errant gunfire. Sometimes, one or two of them would forget that his weapon had already been charged twice and charge it again so that when it was finally discharged, it blew up, tearing holes in hats, powder-burning cheeks, and mangling fingers.

It didn't matter. Everything was in the spirit of fun, and after they'd run their course in rude behavior, the celebrants staggered back toward some taproom where they could examine wounds and tell horrid jokes and have a few more drinks.

In the wedding chamber, the bride and groom, knowing their requirement could outlast the furious stamina of a shivaree mob, would get on with their business.

The shivaree they held for John and Claudine Fawley almost collapsed before it started. Everybody knew John Fawley was going to Elm Bluff and the Carnes Auction Barn and the Methodist Haven, whichever you wanted to call it, to get his woman, and they knew when he was going. He didn't make any pretense of hiding it. He rode directly through the center of Little Rock and past the territorial government buildings in early morning. Although it was the spring when the legislature was in session, at that particular hour the house had not been called to order, so probably as many as two dozen elected officials saw John Fawley ride past and knew where he was going.

Maybe a few of them said that this was the Fawley who was tenant on that nice ground to the west that belonged to the Loudecs, and that soon he would likely be ordered off it so the ground could be put in Loudec cotton without any of that share-of-crops foolishness. Those same legislators might also have said that once Michael Loudec decided to foreclose that Fawley property, nothing could stop him because he was a man intent on having his way and strong enough to get it. There was the recent story about that famous Jamaica-educated Loudec nigger Timbou, or whatever his name was, caught teaching a couple of Loudec slaves, who were exhorters in a camp meeting called the African Episcopal Methodist Assembly, how to read and how without hesitation Michael had strung this Timbou up to a post and personally whipped him until the blood ran. It was well-known that there was a law against teaching slaves to read, and it was a law to which Michael Loudec obviously subscribed because this Timbou, or whatever his name was, had always been very dear to Michael Loudec. So dear, in fact, that after the whipping, this Timbou continued to stay close to Michael Loudec just as he always had, and to serve him faithfully and was even like a bodyguard. Of all people who didn't need a bodyguard it was

Michael Loudec, who had not only introduced himself to Point of Rocks by killing a man in a duel and since then had killed another one in West Feliciana Parish in Louisiana and another in New Orleans when he had gone downriver to recreate himself among various famous high-stakes card games and equally high-quality houses where painted ladies worked.

But if local politicians thought along these lines when John Fawley passed, the rough-and-tumble sort who hung about in Hugh Evans's tavern and other grog shops near the ferry slip did not. They thought of shivaree as John Fawley rode through the streets, bareback on the Fawley horse because John Fawley had never bothered to buy another saddle after his daddy Boone had gone off to Texas with the only one they had.

The shivaree party began to form about midafternoon. They designated various people to keep a watch on the road from downriver so they'd know when John Fawley returned with his bride. By sundown, the celebration was well formed, but John Fawley had not appeared. Two of the shivareers had passed out by then. Hugh Evans had run them out of his place for being too boisterous, and they took up headquarters in another ferry slip saloon owned by Logan Brock. By moonrise, there was still no report of John Fawley having returned, and they began to suspect that he had ridden around the town and so decided to go out to the Fawley cotton patch and see for themselves. They went on foot. When they arrived at the low, wooded ridge just east of the Fawley dooryard, they paused to refresh themselves, hiding in the trees. There were no lights in the main Fawley cabin and none in the smaller one that stood at the line of red gum and sycamore in the direction of the river. They refreshed themselves again. Emil Harp got into a fistfight with one of Michael Loudec's slave overseers about the question of whether the married couple had yet returned.

At the moment when cooler heads prevailed and the combatants pulled apart, they say two dark horsemen—well, one was a woman—came into the cotton patch yard from the south. It was John Fawley and his bride, she riding the hammer-head Texas roan stud, also without a saddle. The couple went to the stock pen, dismounted, unbridled, loosed the two horses into the corral, and went to the cabin, John Fawley carrying a considerable load of duffel. There was a brief moment of orange coal-oil lamplight outlining the doorway, then the door was closed. There was considerable discussion about how long it would take the couple to get undressed and blow out the lamp and get into bed. Emil Harp, during this conversation, threw up all over himself and passed out and lay on the ground in the weeds, spread-eagle.

At last, they crept forward. Nobody was sure who was supposed to give the signal to start the celebration. It started rather haphazardly with a single musket shot, the muzzle blast brilliant yellow toward the sky. Then all the others joined in, yammering and banging and shooting and falling down and bumping against one another. After only a few wild minutes, it was finished, and they straggled back toward the ridge-line trees where Emil Harp lay.

Two of the celebrants retrieved the limp form of Emil Harp and followed the others as they went toward town. Soon, after about fifteen steps, Emil Harp became very heavy so he was dropped and left in the woods, his two benefactors hurrying to catch up to the rest.

As shivarees went, it had been a dismal display. To make it even worse, three of the participants were arrested by Sheriff Malcolm Campbell at three o'clock in the morning as they tried to break into a window of Hugh Evans's tavern. They were lodged for the night in the one-room jail that had once been the whores' crib attached to the rear of Deputy Samples's residence. God rest his soul, said Idella Harp, whose husband didn't get back north of the river until after noon the next day.

Questor Fawley knew the shivaree was coming, and when it did, lay on the corn-husk mattress bunk in his new cabin—really just a small hut—and listened, happy when it was finished in a hurry. Not that it disturbed his sleep. On that night he didn't sleep much, even after the bedlam around the main cabin. The whole day had been a little out of whack for him. From early morning when John Fawley had ridden off, grinning. John Fawley grinning!

Well, Questor reckoned there would be a lot of things different now. This thought occupied his mind all morning as he moved his meager duffel to his new nest. Not much of a nest, either, about ten feet on a side, a door with leather hinges—no window—a small potbellied stove and a stool with three legs, a wall shelf for his mother's King James and a few more books he'd collected from downriver steamboat captains with heavy doses of St. Paul's formula for salvation, a number of pegs in the unfinished log walls to hang clothing, a cigar box he'd been given by Hugh Evans to hold his comb and razor and a chunk of store-bought soap, soap that John had said smelled like Uncle Bob's whorehouse across the river, and that was all of it. No pot or pan or skillet. The cooking would remain at the main cabin and there, now, a new cook. Mrs. John Fawley.

When darkness fell that night, his ears had been keenly tuned and he knew when the two horses came into the dooryard. He figured John's new bride had come on the Texas roan. John had never mentioned the incident of the Texas roan, but it was a story well-known at Point of Rocks and Questor had it firsthand from William Evans, who had been there that day when John rode the hammer-head stud and gave him to Claudine.

Questor had a little trouble thinking of the name, Claudine. But he had even more trouble thinking of Mrs. John Fawley. And more still thinking Sister-in-Law. And that night, with all three of those designations for the new creature at the cotton patch winding around inside his head, he finally slept and dreamed of sin and redemptive blue lights flashing across black waters. When he woke, it was barely dawn, one of those cool gray dawns of spring smelling of fresh buds and sounding of wrens chirping around the overhanging eaves of the pine shingle roof of his hut, already looking for nesting areas, and the whistle of hawks soaring and watching for field mice in the still-bare fields where seeds had yet to sprout.

At the stock pen he saw the Texas roan, and they contemplated each other with mutual suspicion. Questor thought it was maybe the ugliest horse he'd ever seen. Around the cabin, he saw a couple of empty bottles, blowfly green, and knew that the spirits that came from these had not been distilled on Moccasin Creek in his still.

Then, as Questor stood not twenty paces from the porch, they were there. John barefoot and wearing his pants with suspenders and nothing more and leaning against the door frame and still grinning and smoking his pipe. And Claudine on the porch in a tight-to-the-neck gingham dress that was not fashionably bodiced and fell straight from a loose waist to her ankles. And she was barefoot, too.

Claudine came off the porch toward him, and the sun, just topping the line of trees along the east ridge, touched her hair like a yellow lamp flame. She was smiling and her eyes were shining and at their corners tiny crinkles of laughter, and Questor stared at her dumbstruck. He had never realized until that moment how beautiful a female could be.

"Now you're Questor, ain't you?" she said and stopped close enough before him that he could smell her, and reached up and took his arms in both her hands, still smiling. "You're the first brother I ever had, and I'm beholden to you for lettin' me come into your family."

Questor was stiff as a fence post, arms rigid at his sides, staring down at her, and then she quickly, darting like one of the wrens under Questor's hut eaves, threw her arms around his waist and lifted her face on the long, white column of neck, and kissed him square on the lips. Then as quickly stepped back and clapped her hands together and laughed.

"A real brother now. Questor. I never heard that name before!"

"Take your hat off, you dumb peckerwood," John called from the door, but Questor didn't move.

"Come on in now," Claudine said, reaching again with one hand to touch Questor's sleeve. "Breakfast almos' ready."

"Dumb peckerwood, Old Gal, that's what he be," said John and laughed aloud. John Fawley laughed aloud!

It was the only time he'd ever eaten a meal that he didn't taste any bite of it. All he remembered of it was John laughing at the look of consternation on Brother Hezekiah Howell's face at Elm Bluff when he'd performed the wedding ceremony for the woman he'd hoped to make his own bride. And other than that, only Claudine saying to stop saying "ma'am" and call her by her name.

The meal seemed to last forever. But at last he was out and off to the Moccasin Creek still and there furiously scrubbed the pot and funnel and coil, and without any thought of what he was doing.

That morning in the yard had been the first time since he was a very young child that he'd felt a woman's arms around him. Sometimes, Aunt Chorine and his mother had hugged him. And the kissing? There may have been a single time, maybe two, when his mother had brushed his cheek or forehead with dry lips when he'd hurt himself as a tot. But he had never, until that morning, been kissed on the lips. Never.

He tried not to think of this divine creature, and what she and his brother had been doing together in the cabin after the shivaree. But the image of it persisted, and that plus the surge of emotion he'd felt when she kissed him, unknown, frightening, overwhelming, made him sick to his stomach. He knew he'd come to Satan's fire aroused. And his own brother's wife!

Well, there was plenty in his mother's King James about brother's wives. He knew that. So in midafternoon he quit the still and walked into town and bought a wick lamp with a glass globe and a can of coal oil, on credit from Davis and Parker, because he knew from now on there were going to be long nights when he'd need to search for answers in the Book.

It made him feel a little better. But not much. All those images refused to leave his mind. And his mouth still seemed to burn from the touch of hers. And that night, after another uncomfortable meal in the main cabin, he sat in the dark and drank a great deal of his own drippings. But it only made the images come sharper!

22

It was impossible to dampen the spirit of the new mistress of the Fawley cotton patch. Bad weather and drought. Failing cotton crop as summer drug on, remorselessly blistering. John Fawley's disposition turning sour to keep pace with browning cornstalks, withering sorghum cane, drooping cotton plants. Hard times and the threat of Loudec interests swallowing them, putting them off the land, now a prospect rumored to be not only Loudec but Shiring Rhett and maybe other Austin people who held some kind of share agreement with old Mourton, still alive in New Orleans. She laughed. She sang. She danced little jigs on the porch to the music in her own soul, even in evenings still baking from the day's sun, even when only a small movement brought the sweat to darken gingham dresses.

"Lord God give us laughing, didn't he?" she asked, her eyes twinkling as though it were all a joke. "He never give it to chicken and hog, did he? Lord God give us choice to be old cluck and grunt like chickens and hogs, or laughin' like angels tastin' best of times. You just got to believe it's all best of times."

"We'll see how loud you can laugh," said John Fawley, "the day Shiring Rhett comes with a paper and Sheriff Malcolm Campbell stands behind him with a pistol."

"They ain't come yet."

Even Questor's obvious efforts to avoid her could not dent the armor of her optimism. Maybe because she understood his embarrassment with natural urges and his conviction that he was sinning just to think about them. Not in so many words she might be able to explain, but understanding just the same. And maybe, too, she was confident that soon there was a wall she could break down, with no sin involved, either.

In the first year of their marriage, Claudine convinced her husband that they should attend a dance in Little Rock, a dance sponsored by Hugh Evans to celebrate the enlargement of his mercantile store and to be held in the largest barn of his son William's livery, appropriately cleared of mules and shoveled and forked clean of manure. And with promise of a fiddle player from Vicksburg who could make the stars dance, adding his genius to the local talent of jug and banjo and washboard and spoon players.

They went, and John grinned almost as much as he had on his wedding day as his wife taught him the schottische and the two-step and confirmed what her daddy had always said. That she could dance the pins out of her hair. And the perspiration on her upper lip was like diamonds that attracted the single men and some of the married ones as well, wanting to dance with her, and John, amazingly, grinning from the sidelines, proud of his pretty wife, and Questor on the sidelines, too, but rather embarrassed and absolutely refusing to be taught any of the dancing. And along one wall, the men with high beaver hats, the Rhett and Austin men, and they wanted to dance with Claudine as much as any of the others, and Michael Loudec did. Twice.

For those two dances, John Fawley's grin disappeared and the hard, glint-eyed scowl returned, but then was gone again with the next boisterous tune and Claudine off and whirling on the hand of William Evans. And all the while her laughter sounding clear and more in tune than the Natchez fiddle.

Afterward, they walked home in the dark, John and his wife ahead, Questor trailing like one of his hounds, and Claudine teased him about being a real hard-shell, not even dancing a single time, and it embarrassed Questor almost as much as watching his sister-in-law kicking up the straw on the Evanses' livery barn floor and laughing straight into the faces of her partners, bold as any man, brassy as any of the women he'd heard about at Uncle Bob's across the river, yet with some kind of innocent sparkle in her eyes like a five-year-old eating licorice whip candy.

It was a good one, that winter. John Fawley's hard-lipped scowl seemed to have disappeared forever in the glow of his wife's smile. It would return with the drought that started in June of the year, but nobody knew about that yet. Slowly, Questor felt himself drawn closer to this strange creature, so fragile and beautiful yet with the hint that something hard as flint rock lay beneath the surface. It was like a dog reluctant to the leash but finally happy to submit because the mistress, for all her soft appearance, was made of sterner stuff than he.

Claudine seemed to understand some of Questor's confusion about his faith. She obviously had none in hers. She teased him about that, too, but in such a lighthearted, even understanding way that he found no cause to be upset. She came to his Moccasin Creek still, and they talked of many things, Questor more in love with her at each word, yet the self-knowledge of such a thing steeling his resolve to remember his vows of self-denial on the night he saw the blue lights on the water.

He showed her the quiet pool where he and John figured the snake had struck their mother. At least, he told her, that's where they'd found the giant cottonmouth, its head smashed and its blood splattered on a limestone outcrop, a snake not killed with hoe or ax or other blade from a distance, but held in the hand and smashed. And he knew Claudine appreciated his value of that image of his mother killing the snake with her hand, a signal of the grandest family virtue he could call up, the virtue of fierce, ruthless courage when the circumstances called for it.

Claudine made a habit of sweeping her dooryard each day and when she did always went to Molly Fawley's grave and cleaned it, too, and planted moss rose across it and kept them watered with buckets from spring-fed Moccasin Creek, which still had a trickle of water even at the peak of drought. She knew about Questor's special place on his rock above the river, where he'd seen the green fire, not because he told her about it—and certainly he didn't tell her about the green fire—but because she often saw him go there. She never followed until one afternoon he asked her to come and look at the fine view of the river.

She shocked him that day, for after they'd talked of a few things about their faith, like his maybe believing in predestiny and her not, like his not being sure doing good on earth helped one's chance of salvation but she was, Claudine went to her knees and prayed. Aloud. Unashamed. He sat on his rock and stared at her, having never imagined that anyone could do such a private and personal thing as pray, aloud and in company of another person. Except maybe if the other person was a preacher, or maybe if one was testifying at a revival meeting, and Questor had always been a little suspicious of such praying became it smacked very hard of the show-off, somebody trying to impress other folk and maybe even God.

But this wasn't the kind of praying he'd heard. This was not supplication. It was rather a kind of expression of joy with life and a thanksgiving that the Lord had made such a wonderful world for his children to enjoy while they practiced brotherhood and love in preparation for an even better world beyond. It was all as clear and clean and transparent as good spring water, cool with self-confidence, not hot with agony of coming hellfire.

When she was finished, she rose and laughed and went back to the main cabin to start their evening meal, everything as natural as grass, leaving Questor to sit for a while longer on his rock, looking at the river below, amazed at the variety of faith's expression.

But she never touched him. Since that first day in the yard when she'd hugged and kissed him. She seemed to sense that he thought it was a sin to even think about touching. She didn't tease about it, either. In fact, in their talk, she never uttered the word "sin," as though she understood that Questor's greatest struggle was trying to figure out what sin was. The whole business made him think she had opened a window to his soul, as nobody else had ever bothered to do, and what amazed him most of all was that he wasn't ashamed at whatever she might see there. Like everybody else, he was drawn to her. She was contagious as measles. He was helpless before her, yet somehow confident she would never hurt him.

All of which made his desire more tortuous than ever. And he was sure she felt his desire. How could anyone be around them and not see his desire? It made him uncomfortable to be alone with her and John because he was afraid to think of what John might do to anyone he suspected had such urges in her regard.

Claudine went to town often that first year, walking, of course. All the women were jealous of her, but it was impossible not to like her. There was no pretension in her, they saw, no flaunting her beauty. They even understood the men on the street doffing hats and bowing and making stumbling salutations.

"Why," said Ernestine Evans, "a pity dear Molly, God rest her, is not here to see what a shining girl her son has wed!"

"Too bad she's such a devoted Methodist," Idella Harp said, but not to Ernestine because Ernestine was a Methodist, too. Even so, Idella Harp's husband Emil, the community's most fanatical Baptist, was one of those men who could always be counted on to bow and scrape and tip his hat most elaborately when he met Claudine Fawley coming out of Davis and Parker's mercantile.

Through all of Claudine's conquest at Point of Rocks, there was Questor Fawley with those rising, violent physical urges that he had to cover by sitting down and holding his hands folded over his body, and thanking a kind Providence for the butt-length, loose, smock-type, frontier shirts he still wore because they helped hide his condition. And he knew she was aware of that, too, and when it came would move away, and maybe not aware that the sight of her retreating back was as exciting to her husband's brother as was front view of her high breasts under the constant gingham.

So she fed him and washed his clothes and drew forth his conversation. She teased him more than she did her own husband. In fact, she didn't tease John Fawley at all. Nobody teased John Fawley. She was not beneath giving tart advice on how to dress and bathe and even on table manners—"John, could you use a fork for your meat and turnips and stop taking it to your mouth with the point of that there hunting knife? You'll cut off your nose one of these days"— but she never teased her husband. Nor maybe laughed as much with him as she did with Questor.

Each night, in his sleeping hut, Questor prayed. On his knees and aloud and holding his mother's King James in clasped hands. And always closed with this: "God, be merciful. Help me be strong and pure with the sister I love."

Questor never elaborated in his prayers about all the ways he loved his brother's wife. He reckoned God had already figured that out for himself.

Maybe there was a complete turnaround by the 1820s. Maybe by then Questor Fawley was so preoccupied with religion and his forbidden love for his brother's wife that he lost interest in things happening beyond the cotton patch. While John, usually the one who didn't give a damn about politics, had become so sensitive to land tenure that he watched every move of legislator and circuit judge with the eyes of a trapped wolf.

But whatever, neither could avoid the proposition that civilization, if that's what it was, continued to creep around them like January-cold molasses crept around the edges of a buckwheat pancake. Arkansas Territory was going to be a state of the federal Union, come hell or high water, people said. If not soon, then within the immediate future for certain.

In Arkansas Territory, there was the scramble by the movers and shakers—or most of them, anyway—to get this wild, untamed frontier into shape for statehood. By the mid-1820s, the eastern and southern parts, cheek by jowl with Louisiana and Mississippi and Tennessee—had already sprouted a rich cotton economy. But in the west and north, mostly mountains heavily timbered, it was still as it had been at the turn of the century, which is to say, it was about as civilized as were the mountains of Wales when the Romans came to Britain. Only along the Arkansas River, where it cut through that area, were there any towns or settlements with any claim to being called a town or settlement, and even then, the point was usually stretched considerably.

But great strides were effected. Plans were going forward to erect a statehouse, of limestone no less, and with classic Greek pillars across the front. In fact, the whole structure would be flavored Hellenistically.

Propagandists wrote—for those who had never been closer to Point of Rocks than Hagerstown, Maryland—that the capital city was becoming a true metropolis, although in fact most of the buildings were still cypress log and pigs and chickens still roamed in the streets. And of streets, there were only about half a dozen of these, as one old hunter put it, some running lengthwise, the others running crosswise.

There was a Masonic Lodge, at least ten churches, two cotton gins in the vicinity, a brick kiln, a new jail, a horse-drawn coach to

Arkansas Post in one direction, Fort Smith in the other. Of course, the coach's schedule was subject to change without notice, and in fact operations were suspended when rain turned so-called roads to quagmires. Even in dry weather there might be bandits lurking along the wooded route, with pistols, requiring passengers to empty their pockets. Steamboat travel was best, but sometimes it seemed as many of these vessels blew up and sank as reached their destination, and the traveler along the river had to avoid gamblers, whores, and pickpockets who made the Mississippi and Arkansas their Main Street of business.

As for mail service, saying it was regular gagged even the propagandists. The Little Rock newspapers—there were two of them now, one Democrat, one Whig—complained constantly that their newspapers from New Orleans and St. Louis arrived at Point of Rocks regularly all right, but often three months old.

When you got out of sight of rivers, you could forget about the possibility of any decent road. So even august circuit judges rode their rounds on mule or horseback, having to spend their nights between small settlements in the hills with some farmer who didn't like to talk, didn't like to share his whiskey, and required the judge to sleep on a husk pallet in front of the fireplace with two or three of his half-grown sons who hadn't had a bath since the previous summer. Dispensing justice in that time and place called for an iron determination and stomach.

Well, for the Arkansas propagandists, there were other evils, not too easy to hide. Like the case of the territorial delegate to the federal Congress—nonvoting, of course—whose name was Henry Conway, and who said or did something during the course of a reelection campaign that miffed a supporter of his opponent. Naturally the supporter challenged Henry Conway to a duel, which was fought on the usual river sandbar, and Henry Conway was killed. At that early stage in the campaign, the opponent hadn't even announced for the office yet, so they had to have a special election. Mr. Conway's Whig opponent lost. But a couple of years later, the man who had killed Henry Conway won the office himself.

Well, they named a town and county in honor of Henry Conway.

"If the general government accepts Arkansas as a state," said Logan Brock, "they'll accept anybody!"

And on hearing that, Otis Bradford, whose mentor was Shiring Rhett, said that Logan Brock drank his own bathwater.

And Logan Brock, hearing that, said it was better than drinking your own piss, which he said Otis Bradford did, which naturally called for Otis Bradford to challenge Logan Brock to a duel. But shortly after that, so it was said, Otis Bradford heard that his mother was dying in Baltimore, Maryland, and he took steamboat downstream. And never returned.

"I always heard it said Otis Bradford's mama lived in Urbana, Illinois," Idella Harp said.

"Good riddance to bad rubbish," said Ernestine Evans. "Have another cookie, Idella. I wonder if Mr. Brock actually said that?"

Anyway, if the power structure was concerned with statehood and all that, the hardscrabble folk didn't give a damn one way or another. Particularly in drought years. Nothing much changed for them. Except that now the biggest threat to survival was not a painted war party disgruntled about not getting any whiskey, but a government man with a paper in his hand, backed by an officer of the law well armed to enforce it.

As John Fawley said many times, "I'd as druther get scalped with a sharp Osage knife than with a goddamned lawyer's quill pen!"

The trouble with droughts—which meant that tenants went a year deeper in debt, of course—was that subsidiary income was hit hard as well. Like making whiskey. The corn crop was so meager that year the Fawley stock had been turned out for graze. There were only a few kernels for Questor's still, until Michael Loudec bought some bushels in New Orleans and had them shipped north, all of which added to the expense of the drippings, and Hugh Evans and Davis and Parker screamed about Questor Fawley raising his price. But then nobody could buy it, so the price had to be lowered until finally he was making whiskey at a loss. It wasn't a cash loss. But it showed up on the debit to Loudec.

At a time of year when it was growing cooler and the tenant was supposed to be content and sitting in front of his cabin door almost as well fed as Loudec slaves, smoking his pipe and listening to the ducks and geese overhead in the twilight flying south for the winter, it wasn't contented time at all. It was a time of going to the woods for squirrel and to the river for catfish if there was any expectation of meat on the table. Even the cane had burned up in summer heat so there were precious few drops of sorghum molasses, and obviously, no lime-cured hominy or grits. Claudine had already found a spot to dig the lime pits to cure the corn to make the hominy, but they stood empty.

It was Timbou who brought the corn to Questor Fawley's still on Moccasin Creek. The black Jamaican never came to the house but rode on past the dooryard, in view so he might be seen, but never stopped. His figure was well-known around Point of Rocks, that cone-shaped black hat and baggy woolen pantaloons and a jacket that had no sleeves, like a vest more than a jacket, and incongruously, a pair of brightly shined high-topped shoes that Michael Loudec always ordered out of New Orleans for him. When he came to the Fawley cotton patch, he always came on his big dun mule, bareback, with burlap sacks behind, one on either side of the mule's flanks, bulging with corn. And in the top of the sacks, on the corn, some empty bottles, clear glass, and maybe a few pounds of sugar in cheesecloth bags. And maybe, for Questor to take back to the Fawley cabin, a tin of black pepper and a striped sack of horehound candy, and once even a fried 'possum from the Loudec slave quarters which none of the Fawleys would eat, not even the hounds.

On that day, the Fawleys were in the corn patch breaking up hard clods with their hoes when Timbou passed along to the woods of the creek, and soon Questor joined him. By then, the Jamaican was sitting on the upended boiling pot, smoking a long cigar, and there was a bait of corn in the covered barrel and another in a tow sack, wetted down and lying in a patch of sun that came through the trees. Even though the leaves were long past time for falling, and were dead on the branches, they seemed reluctant to drop and clung rather desperately, like dried corn husks, to the twigs, a sure sign of the past summer's drought.

"I have a seegar for you," said Timbou and handed a long, black, crooked twist of tobacco to Questor who took it and lighted it from the slave's own, then puffed and after a moment squatted, in the fashion of frontiersmen and dust farmers.

"I'm much obliged."

"Take that," said Timbou, pointing to the wetted tow sack of corn, "and put it in your house where it will be warm and sprout sooner."

"I will."

They smoked for a long time in silence, Questor Fawley looking at the slave's naked shoulders. Except for the tiny trickle of water in the stream, there was no sound in the woods, no buzz of insects or call of jays or crows, as though everything living had gone somewhere to look for a less parched land.

"I heerd Michael Loudec put a few marks on you," Questor Fawley finally said. "I see it's true."

Timbou shrugged elaborately. He watched the blue-gray smoke from his cigar lift straight up in the windless hollow.

"He oughta treat you better'n with a whip."

"It was a bad thing I did," said Timbou. "I was teaching our own Black Moses, our preacher, to read. It's against the law to teach one of us to read. Once we have it, like me, you can't take it away. But it's against the law to teach it. He might have turned me over to this sheriff, and maybe they'd hang me."

"Michael Loudec wouldn't let nobody hang you."

"Michael Loudec is white. And he treats me good enough. So I take a few stripes on my back. He sees me break the law, and he whips me, but he does not give me to this sheriff and so now I am not hanged, you see, mon? It is better to have a few stripes on the back than to be hanged."

"Well, I don't know. Seems like if I was smart as you, I'd run off. Smart as you."

For the first time, the Jamaican black's eyes met Questor Fawley's, and after a moment he laughed, a great explosive laugh.

"Run away! Where to, mon? Missouri? They catch me, ship me south to Louisiana. I been in Louisiana, I know what's there. Run away! Listen, my friend, don't you talk, white man, don't you talk run away. Don't you know there's men who come for you in the night if you talk to a nigger about run away? Don't you know they come for you and hang you before they hang the nigger, you talk about run away? You talk more dangerous things than teach Black Moses how to read. You say run away to some nigger, they come for you, mon, they burn you in fire. You hush about run away. You leave me and Michael Loudec to our own business, you mind yours, and don't ever say 'run away' to a nigger again, mon, you hear me?"

Seeing Questor Fawley's expression of astonishment at such a speech, the Jamaican laughed again.

"I tell you true, mon, I don't lie with you. I like you. You a good white mon. My old master, my English master in the Sugar Islands, I liked him, too. He be a good mon. He taught me to read when I was a very small fish. But then he sold me into Louisiana. Michael Loudec, he never teach a nigger to read, but he won't sell me. Michael Loudec, he be glad I can read and do things other niggers can't do. But he never teach me himself, see? But he glad somebody else did. He'll whip me if I break his rule, but he never sell me. He never turn me over to the rope for some night-rider white trash. So maybe Michael Loudec a good mon, too, but I don't like him much."

"I'm one of them white trash you say about," said Questor Fawley, but there was no hint of pique in his voice. "Livin' hand to mouth on this cotton patch and in debt to some plantation man."

Timbou wasn't laughing then. He sat head down, rolling the cigar in his hands, watching it smolder with the thin tendril of smoke. Never much of a smoker anyway, Questor Fawley raked out the fire from the tip of his cigar and slipped it into a smock pocket so that he could give it to his brother after supper.

"Michael Loudec still draw them pitchers?"

"Yes. All the time."

"I ain't seen him much anymore. Like to talk to him awhile."

"You and Michael Loudec, you not got much to talk about now. Things have gone off to where you can't ever be where you was before. Not your fault. Not his fault."

Far to the south, they heard a crow making a glorious racket, the first sound of birds since they'd been there in the hollow.

"Ole crow found hisself an owl, I reckon."

"Yes."

"Timbou, you ever heard Michael Loudec say anything about us? I mean, the cotton patch? He fixin' to move us off?"

"No. Not to me."

"This here Fawley place is the only one around here that's fit for cotton that him or some other cotton grower like Buchanan or some of them others hasn't took over, and I hear Old Man Loudec, down in New Orleans, wants our patch."

The Jamaican rose abruptly and went to his mule and leaped up, mounting as easily without stirrups as any Roman centurion might have, and looked into Questor Fawley's eyes, and he was no longer smiling, nor was there any touch of smile in his face.

"Old Loudec doesn't run things here now, mon," he said. "And Michael Loudec will take this patch when he wants to, but someday, not now. Listen, mon, it's something else he wants now. Stay clear away from it. It's dangerous ground, mon, to get in Michael Loudec's way, even for you."

And then he reined the mule away and was gone up from the hollow, out of the woods, and into the hazy sunlight beyond. Questor Fawley was suddenly sick in heart and soul, as he would reckon it, because now, with the Jamaican's words, he recalled what had happened only two weeks ago that then held no significance for him but now appeared with horrible clarity!

It had been on the day that John Fawley went to the Loudec gin with the last miserable load of cotton, the wagon hardly half-full. Questor, who usually left such things completely to his brother, rode along. Not to do any of the business of weighing out the cotton, figuring the Fawley share according to New Orleans price, setting what little that represented against what they owed at the Loudec commissary, settling the loan for next year's seed, getting the winter supply of salt and flour and dry beans from Claudine's list.

Questor went along in hopes of seeing Michael Loudec and talking with him about the Fawley cotton patch and the Loudec intentions there. Talking as they had in earlier days, strolling the river and watching turtles and waterfowl. Honestly and face-to-face. Of course, Questor said nothing about this to his brother but rather that he just wanted to go along for something to do. It wouldn't have mattered much, maybe, even had John Fawley known the purpose of Questor's coming, because he was so furiously grim about being in this kind of bondage that his mind could hardly compass anything else.

Michael Loudec was not at the gin so Questor casually walked up the long hill to the big house. There on the shaded veranda a black slave woman, young and attractive, told him Michael Loudec was out riding a new stallion his daddy had sent up from New

Orleans. Questor Fawley accepted that with some regret and moved along the veranda, maybe a little reluctant to leave its shade, and at a large open window with the chintz curtains pulled back, saw Michael Loudec's drawing table and on it a scatter of paper and pencils and a box of French colored chalk. On top of the other things was an almost-finished sketch—in the chalk because it was in color—of a face. A smiling, young face crowned with a cascade of golden hair. It was Claudine Biggs Fawley.

Questor Fawley's only reaction was that it was a good likeness, which didn't surprise him, knowing Michael Loudec's talent in this kind of thing and knowing, too, that Michael Loudec had seen Claudine Fawley at that dance in Little Rock and in fact, so he had been told, had seen her at Elm Bluff on various occasions when Michael Loudec had been on business at the Carnes Auction Barn before she was married.

Riding back to the patch, John Fawley silent and furious on the seat beside him, Questor figured it was a natural thing for a man who drew pictures of bugs and fishes and turtles and sandbars to draw as well the face of the prettiest woman at Point of Rocks. And thought no more about it. But didn't mention the sketch to John.

That night at the supper table, Claudine was silent and morose. She avoided his eyes and she ate in silence, and it was somewhat to Questor Fawley's relief to find her like this, for at least now he knew this fantastically happy woman could have moments of despondency just like any other human being. As for John Fawley, he was so preoccupied with his dealing that day with the Loudec gin and commissary, as he always was in those dealings, that he hardly tasted his food, much less noticed his wife's mood. In any case, it was a meal to be quickly finished, and Questor did and went out and started toward his hut.

At one end of the porch, where the well-swept yard was like the page of a book, he noticed as he stepped off toward his own quarters a litter of horse tracks. A well-shod horse that had come, stood for a while fiddle-footing, then gone off again in the direction from whence it came, toward the south cotton field. He didn't give it a second thought. Passing pilgrim pot drummers and ladies from town riding sidesaddle were not unknown at the cotton patch, so he made no closer inspection of the yard's dust to see what human footprints might be there, boot or moccasin or slipper.

Now, on the night after Timbou had talked to him at the Moccasin Creek still, he lay awake thinking about it. Trying to reconstruct from memory the pattern and shape of those prints in Claudine's yard. But couldn't. And writhed, tormented now not only with his own sin of lusting for his brother's wife but remembering the haunted look in her eyes that night he and John had returned from the gin, the night he'd seen those tracks, and with the indelible vision in his head of not only the agony in Claudine's eyes, but what it meant. And who had ridden that horse.

I t was the winter Talmidge Biggs died. It wasn't cholera or smallpox or typhoid. It wasn't the result of a knife fight or a bullet from ambush, as some of the folks who had known Talmidge in his youth would have expected. He just died.

Well, there were those who said it was the sun perch. The night before he passed the bar, they said, he'd taken on one helluva load of these little sweet sun perch fish you catch in clearwater streams well back up in the highlands away from the muddy rivers, and these fish are not only tasty but filled with tiny bones. Not like the catfish from silt-filled waters that were his usual fare when he wanted fish. So maybe, they said, ole Talmidge just swallowed all those bones, not bothering to pick them out of the flaky white meat, and they shredded his innards.

Rivina, his eldest daughter, who had fried the fish in the first place, said such talk was hogwash. She said her papa always just crunched up perch bones like he would crusty cornbread and swallowed them and had been doing so for as long as she could remember and that he'd died because the Lord called him—and who was going to argue with the Lord?

The Fawleys hitched up the mule to the cotton wagon, and all three rode the front box seat downriver to the Carnes Auction Barn, and having left in early morning arrived in time to eat a dinner that had been laid out by well-wishers on rough-planed pine lumber set on sawhorses in front of the Methodist Haven. There was fried chicken and catfish as well, and hominy with bacon and baked sweet potatoes and some pies. Nobody much minded the cold because it was a calm, river-bottom cold, not whipped against them by any sort of wind.

There were a lot of Baptists there, and Presbyterians, along with the Methodists. Maybe everybody except the Methodists claimed Talmidge Biggs had never really committed one way or the other, and so they still had a shot at converting his soul to their way of thinking, even though he lay cold as the weather in a polished oak box. The Methodists acted pretty superior, of course, saying Talmidge Biggs had witnessed in their revivals and had come to Jesus under their banner and was now well on the way to Jesus under the same flag.

Brother Hezekiah Howell preached the funeral sermon, of course, and it lasted almost two hours and Questor Fawley counted Brother Hezekiah mentioning the deceased's name only three times in all that. Most of it was about the fine qualities of Talmidge Biggs's progeny, one of which everyone knew Brother Hezekiah was going to marry as soon as sorrow for the departed had subsided. Rivina had agreed to the match even though she must have been as aware as everybody else that she was second choice, Brother Hezekiah having let Claudine escape to Point of Rocks and those barbarian Fawleys.

Well, barbarian or not, Claudine insisted that her brother, as she called him, say words over the grave, and that's the way it happened. Once Brother Hezekiah was finished, they carried the box and placed it on a wagon and two mules pulled the whole business well back into a stand of pines, maybe a quarter mile from the Carnes Auction Barn where a small graveyard had begun to develop. There, standing beside the grave, the box already lowered into the hole, and everybody standing around with their heads bowed, just as the sky had begun to cloud over, Questor Fawley said what you'd call the eulogy. He said it with his hat in hand and his eyes closed and his face turned up toward the graying skies as a flock of jays accompanied him from the nearby pines with a most irreverent racket.

"Brothers and sisters," Questor said, gripping Molly Fawley's King James against his chest, "this here was a man I never seen in his young years. Some folks will say he was wicked then. It don't matter. Because like Isaiah said, when he bore reproach of his wrongdoing and took pride in the fruit of his loins, that was beautiful and pure, the Lord will surely have mercy on him. If a son wastes his substance and then comes home, the father will love him. So be glad for this man. He's been took to the kingdom and said welcome there. Luke told us what Jesus said. That this here was a brother that was dead, and was alive again. This here was a man lost, and then was found. Lord, we don't know what this man called you when he talked with you because he done it in his heart. But you know, and now you take him to your throne with joy and gladness because he's coming home. Amen."

On the ride back upriver, John Fawley spoke once, and very quietly.

"Ques, you someday ort to run for governor."

"Yes," said Claudine, and now she and Questor were touching, had to be, sitting side by side on the wagon box seat. " 'Cause he says the good things."

"No," said John Fawley, slapping the reins against the mule's butt. " 'Cause he says it quick and gets it finished before folks goes to sleep."

The next week, news went up and down the river that Rivina Biggs had married Brother Hezekiah Howell. And now, too, Claudine's papa gone, John Fawley began to look with an almost screeching hunger toward the high country to the northwest where the green trees rose above the river.

And Questor noted that twice, again, when he and John had been away from the patch and come home, his brother's wife had been hollow eyed and laughless and unable to meet his eyes, and always there had been horse tracks in the yard. To all of which John seemed oblivious, his whole being concentrated on those far, timber-covered mountains. So each night Questor Fawley prayed fervently, but he didn't know for what.

23

It simply wouldn't register on Questor Fawley's mind. Or maybe he willed it not to do. The evidence was convincing, but he refused to accept the reality. In all his squirming prayers, in all his twisted agonizing, in all his tortured evasions, he came back to the simple rationalization that if John Fawley didn't know it was happening, then it must not be happening. Because of all the people he had ever known, John Fawley more than any other was rock-hard, common-sense, down-to-earth, see-all-the-warts. If anything went on around him, John Fawley knew about it. But obviously he didn't know this thing, or all hell would have split open. But it hadn't. So he didn't. So it wasn't!

Besides, it was a thing so vile and unpleasant that Questor Fawley didn't know how to accommodate to it. He still shuddered to think of his agony when his mother and father no longer were the mother and father he knew, the entity he had known before they'd come to the valley of the Arkansas where those two had split apart like one of the fissures in the earth along the New Madrid fault. And this thing now was ten times worse. Hell, it was a thousand times worse! It was unthinkable. It didn't happen to real people, only to King Arthur or some other character in an old tale.

So he avoided the pain. By pretending nothing was amiss. But in the second spring of John and Claudine Fawley's marriage, he could avoid the pain no longer. It sought him out.

It was April. The redbud had come and gone, its lovely violet flowering a memory. Then the wild plum and dogwoods had exploded their white blossoms among the budding green of hardwood trees. Now, the black locusts, their cream-colored flowers hanging like Chinese lanterns and smelling like honeysuckle. There were cock cardinals ready to take up nesting territory in the low cedars around the cotton patch, sending out their challenging call three times each day, warning away other males until the specific hen arrived and was ready. Swarms of yellow butterflies added to the burst of reds among the moss rose on Molly Fawley's grave, and in the gum and sycamore branches above, young squirrels jousted and chattered and charged squawking blue jays.

Claudine Fawley's sprouting lettuce garden behind the cabin was visited endlessly by pairs of cottontails, and on many mornings some of them ended in her breakfast skillet. During the north migration of ducks along the river that year, they had seen flocks of mallards almost comparable to the huge clouds of waterfowl that had darkened the moon during their first two seasons in the New Madrid area. They ate so much roast duck they were tired of it, and Questor stopped shooting them along the river well before the migration ended.

There had been February and March rain, and the earth smelled ready to grow anything where a seed was put down. There was the usual abundance of mosquitoes and ticks, but that was normal. It was a good spring with the promise of better seasons to come.

John Fawley had decided to sell or trade one of the horses, pointing out that one saddle horse was enough for their needs and if they could make some hard cash on one or the other of the horses, it might be secreted in one of Claudine's kitchen jars as the beginning of a little nest egg they would need when the time came to move to virgin land in the mountains. If not cash, then at least another mule, because having two mules made sense for their situation, and besides, the old mule was getting on in years.

Well, that nest egg jar was already begun, wasn't it? Just a couple of weeks before, Questor had taken nine new fox hound pups north of the river and sold them and come home with a total of a dollar and two dimes and a penny. Any amount from any direction was fine, John Fawley said, so long as it didn't end up in the Loudec commissary store.

So it was off downriver to the Carnes Auction Barn. Claudine would have gone for a visit with her sister, but they'd had word from Ernestine Evans that Brother Hezekiah Howell was off at this time on a big revival swing into Tennessee, stopping for almost a week of soul saving in old Chickasaw Bluffs, now called Memphis, and Rivina had gone along. Claudine said it was just as well because she'd had a bag of soft limestone from Idella Harp, to make whitewash, and was fixing to pretty up the interior of the main cabin and maybe even Questor's cell, and the best time to do it was when menfolk were not always underfoot, and she'd be safe as springhouse butter with the single-barreled ten-gauge shotgun Questor had bought the year before for goose shooting. John Fawley still carried the new percussion rifle with him wherever he went, not so much for Indians anymore but for ornery white men. Or maybe just out of old habit, which John Fawley said wasn't ready to be broke because when they went to the mountains, he'd sure as hell carry a weapon, even when he went to the outhouse. It was his kind of country, he said, where a man ought to have a weapon with him wherever he went. It was one of the things he hated about this civilization along the Arkansas, he said, where men went around with cane swords or pistols concealed under their coats instead of just outright carrying a good, old-fashioned, honest rifle in their hand where everybody could see it.

Anyway, John and Questor rode south on the two horses. They went directly through Little Rock, and even though it was very early in the morning there were a number of people on the streets who nodded to them as they passed and they nodded back. They saw Mrs. Agent William Like emptying slop jars at the back of Hugh Evans's hotel, but she didn't make any greeting to them, occupied as she was in discharging the duties of her position as chief chambermaid for the growing Evans enterprise as innkeeper. According to Ernestine Evans, she had stopped crying herself to sleep every night over her runaway thief husband and in fact had begun to say that she hoped by now some Mexican had disemboweled her former spouse with a corn knife.

"One of those big corn knifes like the Mexicans use," Ernestine Evans always said, holding up her hands three feet apart like a man explaining the length of the catfish he'd taken from a river trotline the night before.

And Hugh Evans himself, at the ferry slip preparing for his first run to the north side that day, hailed them and waved as they passed, and Shiring Rhett was just unlocking his office and saw them, too. So later Questor would remember that there was no secret about he and his brother going south and no question about where they were going, because they had both mentioned it to various people since the plan to trade up from horse to mule—or cash—had germinated almost two weeks before.

They passed along the river road in rising sun, past the Loudec gin and other outbuildings on the low slope of the hill leading up to the Loudec big house and on from that to where the timber marched in close alongside the south side of the river trace. At about that point, the dried apricots began to grumble in Questor's belly.

Luty Davis, wife of the Davis and Parker mercantile man, had brought Claudine a sack of dried Spanish apricots, but before they could be made into a pie, Questor had eaten most of them, the night before this trip to Elm Bluff. Now they were making their disturbance, creating what was called the green apple spurts, a malady of unrestrained and unrestrainable bowel movements where the discharge was very much the consistency and color of Arkansas River water during flood.

They veered off sharply into the woods, Questor leading the way on the Texas roan with considerable urgency. He did in fact make it a respectable distance back from the river trace, got off the horse— well, actually fell off—got his trousers down, and squatted before the first explosion. John Fawley, observing all this, opined that his little brother seemed unfit for further journey so better take out for the cotton patch. Questor insisted that John needed both horses for any meaningful trading venture, and besides, since he needed to stay close to some cover and concealment at all times because his gut urges would be—already were—uncontrollable and he didn't want to end up in the streets of Little Rock scrambling around for a place to dump, it would be better if he just walked home, slowly, in the timber south and then west of town, where there were plentiful trees behind which to hide as he dropped his pants.

Once John Fawley was convinced that his younger brother was not going to squirt all his intestines out onto the leaf mold, he turned again toward Elm Bluff, riding one horse and leading the Texas stud. Questor waited for a while, catching his breath, then began a slow walk back to the patch, staying well clear of town settlement and hoping he could avoid dying before he reached his little hut.

Twice on that walk Questor paused at clear-running creeks and drank. He had a few of the dried apricots in a smock pocket, the last of them, but when he took them out, he retched and threw them aside and went on hungry. By midafternoon, he came to the southeast quadrant of the Fawley cotton patch and made his way along one edge of new-planted ground, head down, aware of not much except the clods of earth that seemed to clutch at his Davis and Parker laced leather brogans. Well, he was also well aware of the stinging, burning sensation in his posterior, result of his frequent stops along the route through the woods.

But as he came abreast of the main cabin at the end of the cotton rows, he saw the horse.

It was a bay gelding, with fine saddle and bridle. Not a side-saddle, either. It was tethered by reins to a porch roof post. It was the kind of horse that any circuit-riding preacher or judge would have given part of his soul for, and the kind of horse not many people could afford to buy or even dream of ever owning. And the instant he saw it, Questor Fawley knew whose horse it was.

For a terrible moment, he stood immobile, seeing the main cabin door closed, even in this warm April weather. His breath began to be more than that, rather a harsh choking sound. And he started to run across the clearing toward the dooryard, and his hat, which he had carried in his hand for most of his interrupted walk through the woods, was dropped without his even knowing.

From one corner of his vision, there was something else. On the ridge, the wooded ridge between the patch and town where the trees were beginning to make a lacy hedge of green. He stopped, panting, and looked directly and saw the second horse— no, it was a mule—and a rider there with a cone-shaped hat frantically waving his arms, as though trying to motion Questor Fawley back into the woods, back into the cotton field, back anywhere away from the cabin.

"Son of a bitch," Questor Fawley gasped, and started his run again toward the cabin and almost there, stopped, his big leather brogans making dust rise as he did. The cabin door was opening and stepping out was Michael Loudec. The usual flowery silk cravat was loose, his ruffled linen shirt unbuttoned to his trouser belt. In one hand, a wide-brim planter's hat. Across his brow, the dark strands of hair, plastered down tight with sweat. His eyes were on Questor Fawley's face, hard and unblinking, and he began to move across the porch, sideways, like a crab.

"Don't come on," Michael Loudec said, and Questor Fawley did not recognize it as any voice he had ever heard Michael Loudec use.

"What'a you want in this . . . ?" Questor Fawley didn't recognize his own voice, either, didn't even know he had uttered a sound.

"Stand away," Michael Loudec said, moving quickly across the porch, to its end, off into the sunlight, and still his eyes never leaving Questor Fawley's, reached back with his free hand, the other still holding the hat, and brought down from the pommel of the saddle a pistol and held it muzzle down. "Stand away, don't come on."

"What . . . ?" Questor Fawley said again, but started forward, and Michael Loudec raised the pistol and cocked it.

"Stand away, Questor, I'll kill you if you don't stand away," he said, and the sound was like a new insect rasping in the April sun. "Stand away, this doesn't concern you. Let be things that be!"

Questor Fawley opened his mouth but nothing came, and Michael Loudec, without ever moving his eyes somehow from Questor Fawley's face, was up onto the bay, wheeling him, rein and hat in the same hand, pistol in the other, the muzzle still pointed. Then in a rush, looking back over his shoulder as the bay went off across the dooryard, dust rising in a flurry, hooves beating, hat and rein still in one hand, weapon still in the other pointed back at Questor Fawley standing there, openmouthed. On then to the low ridge, in a hurry, no stopping there, past the mule and the Jamaican, the slave then turning, following, and both of them gone and nothing left but the faint hint of dust and a sound of hoofbeats dwindling and quickly gone, and Questor Fawley standing, bareheaded in the dooryard, panting, sweat beginning to run down his forehead and into his eyes.

"You son of a bitch," he said aloud.

Then finally, not wanting to, turned toward the now-open cabin door.

Claudine Biggs Fawley sat on the edge of her bed, holding together at the neck her open dress. Her golden hair, usually in a neat, loose bun along the back of her neck, was stringing down on either side of her face. With the other hand, she gripped her knees close together under the dress where it was open too, showing a white petticoat falling to her ankles. Her bare feet were toed in, as though she was pushing back from something.

Her face was down turned, eyes hooded, but Questor Fawley could see the puffed cheeks and eyelids, from crying maybe, but there were no tears on her cheeks now.

"Claudine?" he whispered.

She made no sign that she heard, and he stood in the door, both hands on the doorframe, but didn't know if his hands were holding him out of the room or trying to pull him inside.

"Claudine?" he said, louder this time.

"I know you're there," she said softly, but her face was still lowered. A fly whipped across her forehead, and she lifted the hand from the collar of her dress and swiped at it.

"Claudine? What did . . . ?" He stopped, wondered what he should say. What he should ask.

"He been here before," she said, still with that low voice. "I don't know what to do."

"Claudine."

This time when she spoke, she lifted her head, and Questor Fawley had never seen her eyes so dark, a deep darkness he didn't think possible in eyes so clear blue. Her mouth was hanging open, loose, none of that shining gay smile now, and she looked into his eyes for a full ten heartbeats before she spoke again.

"He'd take the land," she whispered. "We be his slaves, too, ain't we? Like them black ones he got."

Then her head was downcast again, and she raised both hands to it, either side enmeshed with the hanging hair. He started into the room.

"Now listen, Claudine," he said.

"Don't come close to me," she said from behind her hands. "Don't you come close. Go on out now. Go on."

There was no emphasis in her words, no words muttered louder than any of the others, but there seemed some special vehemence in her voice, and needing no encouragement to be away from there, he spun crazily and dashed across the porch. He ran, across the dooryard and past his mother's grave and through the red gum and sycamore and out of that edge of timber and to the rock above the river and stood there trembling, and would have sunk down to his knees but knew from his contracting belly that he had to move back into the woods and drop his trousers once again. And did, and as he squatted, sobbed out curses against Auguste Chouteau and New Madrid and the Arkansas River Point of Rocks and the Carnes Auction Barn and Michael Loudec and his Jamaican slave and most of all cursed this debt-ridden, dismal cotton patch that was no longer blessed with bright springtime but cursed with dreadful sin.

He stayed in that strip of woods until dark. Then went out to its edge, to his own cabin, and sat throughout the night, watching and trying to think. What he watched for was some sign of life at the main cabin. Maybe some call from there to come and have his supper. But there was no sign of life there, no lamplight. The only sound was a chuck-will's-widow somewhere back toward Moccasin Creek. About midnight, his hounds wandered out to him, maybe sensing some family disaster and not out ranging for fox. He didn't scratch their ears. He didn't touch them.

The cow wasn't bawling from the stock pen, so he knew she had gone out sometime after dark and milked. He didn't know if that was good or bad. He didn't know if it was good or bad that she'd compared herself to one of the female Loudec slaves, which town gossip had it spent considerable time in Michael Loudec's bed. At least the attractive ones. After all, they said, here he was, a man well along toward thirty-five, maybe, and taken no wife.

And Questor Fawley thought more about his brother than anything else. A cold, hard knot started at the base of his neck when he thought about John Fawley. Finding out what his creditor had been doing. Finding out a reason for his still being on this land was his wife's submission to a man of aristocratic class. Finding out he had been deceived by his woman, and now that Questor knew for certain, deceived by his own brother as well. Provided Questor didn't tell John what was happening.

"Lord God," he said aloud. "John finds out, it's gonna be up for grabs who he kills first!"

Maybe even me, Questor thought, because the very most dismal part of this whole thing was that in his mind, from the very beginning, he'd wanted to do exactly what Michael Loudec was doing. And he wasn't so sure but that if he himself got involved in revealing this mess he could conceal his own secret thoughts about his brother's wife. Even though suppressed, still there.

He kicked at the dogs lying around him in the dark.

"Damn you," he said. "You let him ride right on up here, didn't you? You seen him before, hadn't you? Me and John go off, you just let anybody come in here, don't you?"

The dogs all rose and slowly moved away, heads down, sadly. Going in the dark back toward the main cabin.

As the dawn grayed the eastern sky, Questor Fawley went to his mother's grave and knelt down and prayed, suspecting maybe he was asking for assistance in the commission of a sin, but not really caring, even though it condemned him to eternal hellfire.

John Fawley was back from Carnes Auction Barn just before dusk, with no cash for Claudine's nest egg jar because specie was very scarce now in Arkansas Territory. But with a young mule, and still rode in on the Texas roan. Claudine was as she always had been, cheerful and ready with well-cooked food for the men, and Questor was astonished at her iron-willed determination to make it all as it was supposed to seem to her husband. Although throughout that evening meal, she never let her gaze touch Questor's.

But that evening, Questor Fawley knew it would never be his own doing that John understand the thing that had been happening. If it was willed by an unkind Providence that John know, then somebody else would have to be the agent. Not Questor. And in that, maybe, showed the inclination toward predestination that Claudine had teased him about in the first of their talks about the glory of truth.

He knew that he would never again look at his brother or his brother's wife as he once had. He wasn't sure about the difference, but he knew it was there. And further, that it was going to unfold without his intervention.

Except for one thing. And that was put to voice in his prayer that night, in the darkness of his hut, kneeling beside his bed, the Book in his hands, from which some of the words came. But the rest were his words.

"Lord God, remember me and strengthen me against my enemies only this once, O God, that I be avenged for my brother. And forgive me if you see fit when I do the sin of Cain, which I am fixin' to do once I find Michael Loudec at the right time, in the right place. Amen."

Then stayed on his knees for a while in the dark, holding the old King James against his breast. Then acknowledged his debt to other authors.

"From the Book of Judges, Lord. And some of it just from me."

FIVE

THE MOUNTAINS

Am I my brother's keeper?

—Genesis 4:9

24

It was supposed to have been a good year. But it wasn't. It was a disaster. There'd been cotton all right, and corn and sorghum. But the Loudec commissary people would extend no more credit, not even for seed, until some of the old debt was paid off. So all that year's fine crop disappeared without a cent of cash to show for it. The Fawleys kept the corn, half planned for livestock feed, a quarter for cornmeal, a quarter for whiskey making.

There was the cane. They hauled it to the Buchanan sorghum mill expecting the usual deal. Paying a mill fee of a quarter of the molasses to Buchanan, so if they got, say, eight gallons, there would be six to take home. But Buchanan said he was no longer doing that kind of share business. It was now cash-and-carry.

John Fawley was already losing control of his temper when he offered to sell the cane, but Buchanan didn't offer enough to buy more than a third of the syrup it would make, and that's when John Fawley lost control completely. He dumped his load of cane, grabbed a lantern from the wall of a mule shed, poured coal oil on the cane, and set fire to it. And as he whipped the mules out of the Buchanan lot, he yelled that Buchanan and his sons best not sit too close to lighted windows at night.

On the way home, the only words spoken were as bitter as gall.

"You hadn't ort to make threats like that," Questor said.

"That son of a bitch," said John Fawley, grinding his teeth so hard together that Questor, on the wagon seat beside him, could hear it. "He's just another Loudec man now, and all them big plantation bastards. They gonna scald us out, you know it? In the dead of winter, they gonna scald us out!"

"Well, it ain't our land after all."

"They'll play billy hell gettin' me offen it until I'm damned good and ready to leave."

When John said the same thing that evening at the supper table, Claudine looked at Questor, but then quickly turned her eyes away. And in his bed that night, Questor Fawley imagined John and himself going to the big house at the Loudec plantation with guns and shooting everybody, but knew it was silly even before the thought was complete. Besides, it wasn't just the Loudecs, it was the whole system. Only with them, the Fawleys, there was the added kink of Michael Loudec lusting after Claudine and her unable to figure any way out of it.

The next morning they were still at the breakfast table when Sheriff Malcolm Campbell rode up and halloed the house, and when John Fawley stepped out onto the porch, there was the Law and a couple of his deputies. And Sheriff Campbell told John Fawley that the next time he made a threat against any law-abiding citizen, he'd be put in jail and tried by the circuit judge for assault. John Fawley told the sheriff that if anybody came on Fawley property to enforce planters' idea of justice, somebody would get their badge shot off.

Sheriff Malcolm Campbell just shook his head and turned away with his people, but as they rode off, he turned back and waved a finger.

"John, don't be a fool here. They's too many again' you. Keep that temper cooled off. You ain't out in the backwoods no more."

And later, Questor would say, "He's right, Jack."

"Him and all his slave-drivin' friends can go piss up a stump!"

Well, there was nothing to do but go about their usual autumn business of clearing fields and mending harness and waiting. And for Questor to pray, and he suspected Claudine was doing plenty of that as well. Questor Fawley didn't ask God for anything specific. It was just a general "Lord help us" kind of praying. He thought about imploring the Almighty in the matter of John's bad temper but decided it would be prayers wasted. Such a plea, he reckoned, would fall on deaf ears because John was so far outside the fold that probably the Lord had no interest in reaching him until John showed some sign himself of being ready to recognize the source of grace. Questor all along had realized the futility of trying to talk John into some understanding of God's glory, and now even Claudine had stopped trying as she'd done in the early months of the marriage. The best she could do was having John accept her saying a blessing at the supper table.

John Fawley said they could butcher the two pigs when the weather got cold enough. The old cow wasn't much account anymore, giving little milk and that with no butterfat. The chicken flock had not increased. In fact, had shrunk because during one of those unexpected July gully washers all the chicks of their two best brood hens had been drowned. He started longer and deeper swings into the woods, but it was one of those seasons when game was scarce and only once did he bring back a big tom turkey that was so old and tough it wasn't any good except to make hash.

In a moment of dark humor one evening, John Fawley said they could live a couple of weeks on Questor's fox hound pack, if it came to the worst. Later, when Questor told Claudine about their mother having cooked a dog their first winter in the wilderness, she got sick to her stomach and said she never dreamed she'd married into a family of red heathen Indians.

As fall wore on, sometimes while he and his brother were working the cornstalks out of the fields, Questor Fawley got the same queer feeling they'd all had at the New Madrid homestead when John discovered somebody had been watching them. Each day he looked toward the low wooded ridge to the east, toward town, but he didn't see anybody, and once he went there and looked for footprints or the marks of shod horses but found nothing on the hard ground. He was sure if there had been a covering of snow, the tracks would have been there.

The whole business made him recall that first cold season on the St. Francis, when they'd almost starved to death, and now it seemed they were looking at the same dismal prospect, or something close to it. When he casually opened the King James, it always seemed to be at a place where there was a plague of grasshoppers or else somebody having to run from their persecutors, no matter how many goats they sacrificed. As the days wore on, his prayers became more gloomy than they'd ever been before.

It was in late October that Questor Fawley knew he'd been right about somebody watching the cotton patch. John had gone off on one of his hunting forays, riding the Texas roan, which meant he would be taking a wide swing and be gone for a few days. When John was away from the immediate vicinity, Questor always left the shotgun for Claudine so he had no particular apprehensions about her safety. John never took the scatter gun on his hunting trips, only his new percussion rifle.

On the third day of John's absence, Questor Fawley had been at the still, cooking a batch of corn William Evans had given him. This, like the last batch, he determined to keep in his cabin. Not sell it to Davis and Parker or anybody else, at least for the time being. It was just past noon when he came back into the patch dooryard and saw the big mule just topping the rise of ridgeline to the east and on the mule was a man, and even at that distance Questor could see the cone-shaped hat. It was impossible to mistake that hat.

Claudine Fawley was sitting on the edge of her bed, just as she'd been the day Questor caught Michael Loudec visiting. Only she wasn't crying this time, and instead of despair and agony on her face there was a hard anger. Questor waited in the open door, although it had turned cold overnight, and watched her without saying anything. He didn't need to say anything because for a long time there had been such a strong silent communication between them that talking sometimes seemed almost redundant. Questor Fawley reckoned maybe that was always the way of things between two people with a shared, terrible secret.

When she looked at him, her eyes were as brittle as glass, and he figured if there was any way Claudine Fawley could look ugly it was now.

"His black man," she said. "He said they knew my husband was off in the woods. And he said his boss man wants me to be down yonder at the bottom of the river bluff tonight."

"Timbou came in here, right into this house, and told you that?" Questor Fawley could feel the harsh bile rising in his throat, and later he thought maybe he'd begun to understand some of his brother's fury and raging temper.

"He don't care. John's right. We're nothin' but white trash to all them . . . bastards!" She raised her hands to the sides of her head as though she could squeeze everything of bad memory out, and her lips turned down. "I don't know what to do!"

"You don't do nothin', you hear? And you stay right here inside this house."

Questor Fawley crossed the room and took the shotgun from where it stood in a corner, and then was out, fast, almost running to his own hut, and thinking as he went, God help me, Michael Loudec is delivered into my hands.

Sitting on the edge of his bunk, Questor unloaded the gun, oiled it, tried the hammer and trigger a number of times, as though afraid he might find something wasn't working right since the last time he'd been goose shooting. He charged the barrel, tamping in the powder, then a paper wad, then about twenty corn-kernel–sized lead buckshot, then a linen patch rammed in tight on top of the shot. He pressed a percussion cap on the nipple and set the hammer at half cock.

From the doorway, his dogs were grouped closely, watching him, some sense of his tension showing in their eyes. When he rose for a moment and then knelt to pray, the dogs bolted back from the door as though he might be ready to throw a chunk at them, then paused, looking back at the open door, hearing his droning voice.

"Let me do it, Lord. Let me do it. You have delivered mine enemies into my hands, now give me the strength to do it!"

And if the Jamaican came? Then kill him, too. Somehow.

Questor Fawley knew this bluff and the crooked, switchback path down the face of it, winding through the outcrops of limestone. At the foot was a ledge of gravel and sand, underwater sometimes, but even after seasons of moderate rain, a dry strip about twenty yards wide and usually unflooded long enough for a low, bushy start of willows.

He went as quietly as possible, and on this night he wore his moccasins, which meant he moved very quietly indeed. The shotgun he carried easily at his side, careful not to let it clatter against a rocky ledge or bump against the trunk of any of the few stunted jack oak that had somehow found a purchase along the face of the cliff. His heart was pounding loud enough for him to hear it, but he expected nobody else could. He was strangely calm otherwise, almost detached.

He found a place just above the crown of brush, where leaves were still clinging even at this late season. It was a crack in the rock strata, like a cave slashed into the bluff, with its river side almost concealed by a jumble of fallen stones. The moon, coming full, was well up the eastern sky, but when he crept into the niche of rock, he was in complete shadow.

The fallen rock in front of his concealment not only hid him but provided a rest for the shotgun, and he lay it there, muzzle toward the river, and positioned himself behind it. Then settled down to wait. It did not occur to him that Michael Loudec would come to any other place along the gravel bar beneath him because he was sure that Michael Loudec—or maybe the Jamaican—had scouted this place well in advance and knew exactly where the path came down from the Fawley cotton patch.

After a while, he rolled the weapon's hammer back to full cock, not wanting even that faint metal click of hammer notch and sear once his victim arrived. Below, there was the deep, hollow croak of bullfrogs. The moon seemed to stand stationary, the earth stopped in its rotation as God had made it do for that big battle at Jericho, or wherever it was, in the King James. But it only seemed so, as Questor Fawley suspected was the case at Jericho, too. Well, anyway, it was past mosquito season, and he was thankful for that.

He knew someone was coming when the bullfrogs stopped. Now, he was aware of the same sounds, only coming faintly, from across the river. The moon was at zenith. He lowered his head to the stock of the shotgun. And almost at once, saw Michael Loudec riding along the gravel bar.

There was no question but that it was Michael Loudec. He was bareheaded, and from the very first, Questor Fawley could see the shine of moonlight on the dark hair and the pale outline of the familiar face. The thought raced across his mind that when he'd seen Michael Loudec at the cabin that day, he'd been wearing a hat. But not now. He began to hear the steel-shod horse rattling the stones of the gravel bar. Michael Loudec was coming slowly, but without hesitation, and as he neared Questor Fawley's position, he drew rein and looked up the face of the bluff. The rib of the shotgun barrel was leveled on Michael Loudec's body just above the waist. The target was about thirty yards away and this was a full-choke gun, so Questor knew when he pressed the trigger, about a dozen .32-caliber pellets would strike Michael Loudec just beneath the rib cage. His right index finger slid into the trigger guard, and he felt the cold steel of the trigger.

"Claudine?" Michael Loudec called softly, and at the sound of his voice, Questor Fawley gave a small start and was amazed that the gun had not fired. "Claudine, where are you, my dear?"

The shotgun barrel did not waver. In his mind, Questor Fawley could trace the path of the tightly grouped shot, from gun muzzle to Michael Loudec's belly.

"Claudine?"

There was a note of impatience in the voice. The kind of impatience to be expected, maybe, from a man who dealt with slaves all day and wanted instant reaction to his words. And Questor recalled what Claudine had said about their all being Loudec slaves.

"Claudine!" It was louder now, and the moonlit face was held high, searching the face of the cliff. "Where are you?"

The horse was growing nervous and began to scatter small pebbles with shifting hooves, and Michael Loudec swore softly and yanked on the reins. Questor Fawley's blood was pumping so hard in his ears it sounded like Osage war drums.

"Claudine!"

But that was all. Michael Loudec paused a long time, his mouth open to call again perhaps, but he didn't. Then slowly, still looking toward the face of the bluff, reined the horse away and started back down the gravel bar. Questor Fawley remained crouched behind the gun, his face against the stock, until the rider was out of sight. And still crouched when the bullfrogs started up again on the near side of the river.

Finally, he whispered aloud, "Forgive me, Claudine!"

He had begun to cry, the tears running along his cheeks unnoticed as he straightened, removed the percussion cap from the nipple, let down the hammer, and rose. And spoke again, louder. "Forgive me, Jack. Forgive me, Ma."

The stain on the family honor was still there, walking and breathing and talking. Still alive. The stain. Because he had been unable to pull that damned trigger. All this he thought about, in confused and even meaningless words. He leaned back against the shelf of rock and stayed there until moonset. Then wiping his nose on his sleeve, went back up the cliff path in total darkness.

L ate that day, John Fawley returned with a deer, a doe. Maybe because it was a hedge, albeit small, against hard times, or maybe because it had felt good to have been back in his real element, the wilderness, or maybe because he had some sense of changing luck, John Fawley was more cheerful than he'd been in weeks. At the stock pen, with the deer carcass hanging from a locust pole A-frame as he dressed it, he even hummed a little. It was a tuneless hum, for he had no ear and no feel for music, and in fact one of his constant astonishments was how well Claudine sang and how she sensed instinctively the movement and beat of music. When Questor walked to stand beside him to watch, John Fawley actually grinned and winked. But then looked hard at his younger brother and frowned.

"What's the matter with you? Looks like you got the dismals."

"Feel a little peaked is all. Expect it was just something I et."

"Well, by God, they's a pile of good deer steak layin' there on that hide I already sliced off this doe. Take a handful of 'em in the house and tell the Ole Gal to start fixin' supper. You'll feel better with some of that in you."

Questor Fawley took the meat to the cabin, none too happily, but there he saw the transformation that always came after Claudine's depressions and she was as bright and bouncing and beautiful as she had been the first night John had brought her here as bride. And knowing as he did the kind of agony she kept hidden behind that facade, he damned himself again for not pressing that trigger the night before at the base of the river cliff.

At the supper table, Questor finished his meal quickly and retired to his cabin, not too hungry to start with, and besides that, it was obvious that John wanted to be alone with his wife. He'd worked all day away from the main house, not wanting to face Claudine alone, and now he expected to search the King James for something, he wasn't sure just what, and then probably lie awake in his corn husk bed thinking through most of the night. He did neither. With no sleep the night before, he quickly fell into a deep slumber, without dreaming, and awoke at dawn to the day he would always remember as the one when prayers were answered. It was a Saturday, and being Saturday, as it turned out, was a part of that answer to his prayers.

All that day Questor Fawley spent at Moccasin Creek, cleaning and breaking up the still. No more cooking whiskey until spring, so he dismantled the equipment, covered it with a large tarpaulin William Evans had given him, and staked it down. It was toward evening that he came in to join his brother cutting firewood on the south side of the patch, and they walked to the cabin together.

Coming into the dooryard around a corner of the cabin, they saw two horses hitched to a porch post, and walking toward them from the line of sycamore and red gum along the river bluff was a well-dressed man, about their own age, smiling, with an air of confidence or maybe even arrogance, and whose name, as it developed, was Adam Arno, from the state of New York.

25

Questor Fawley hadn't recognized either of the horses standing at their front porch that Saturday morning. But John
had. One was a bay, intelligent head, long legs, a mare of good
breeding. About five years old. The other horse was obviously
weary. An ancient nag wearing a dusty, worn saddle. It was an
old saddle, the kind with long skirts that had flap-cover pockets
on either side. This was the gelding Boone Fawley had ridden off
the cotton patch so many years before when he went to Texas
with Evelyn Hadley-Moore. As soon as he set eyes on him, John
Fawley knew what horse it was.

As the Fawley brothers stepped up onto the porch at one end,
Mr. Adam Arno approaching from the other, Claudine appeared in
the doorway with an expression of relief on her face now that her
menfolk were here. The stranger continued his march toward them
with his head back, smiling, his calf-length boots scuffing up little
spurts of dust with each step. When he saw Claudine in the doorway, he swept off his beaver hat with a flourish, holding his arms
out as though to emphasize that he was wearing a linen ruffled shirt
under a broadcloth coat that had velvet lapels. All very fine even if
now covered with travel dust. Mr. Adam Arno had a flowing mane
of hair about both ears, but the top of his pate was completely bald.

"Ah," said Mr. Adam Arno in a booming voice, his words seeming to puff out his pink, clean-shaven cheeks with each gust. "Adam Arno here, of New York State, and I assume one of you gentlemen is Mr. John Fawley, as the lovely missus of the household has said you might be coming soon. I have been viewing the wonderful sight of river from your property."

"Where'd you get that horse?" John Fawley said, and there was little hint of hospitality in his tone. In fact, Mr. Adam Arno halted in his stride and his eyes popped and he swallowed twice before speaking, and his gaze darted up and down the tall figures of the two men before him, each dressed in what he would likely have called backwoods clothes.

"Why, I have brought that horse home," he said. "That horse, his being, as I assume, a part of the legal estate of my friend the late Mr. Boone Fawley."

"Pa?" Questor Fawley said sharply. "He's dead?"

"Why, I am sad to announce that this is true, and I have come on his recommendation, made on his deathbed no less, to bring the horse and to inquire concerning a document he placed in my hand before he died."

Mr. Adam Arno replaced the hat on his head and reached inside the broadcloth coat, produced a long, folded sheet of paper, and waved it about, smiling tentatively into the grim faces of the two men before him.

"A New Madrid Certificate, I understand it is called, made in the name of the late Mr. Boone Fawley, and deed to this property as such. The late Mr. Boone Fawley indicated to me that this document, as well as the horse, would pass to his heirs and that perhaps those heirs might indeed be interested in accommodating me in my requirements for a nice piece of land that overlooks a large river, so in addition to bringing the horse, I have come to see if we might negotiate for this instrument."

He waved the document some more, and suddenly John Fawley became a different person, jumping forward with his hand out, smiling, inviting the stranger into his home, instructing his younger brother to take care of Mr. Adam Arno's horse, and the old one, too, of course, and as he led the New Yorker inside he called happily, gaily you might say, to his wife to prepare a large bait of venison steak and cornbread.

330

And standing stunned on the front porch, Questor Fawley took a few moments to realize what was happening, hearing his brother and his brother's wife inside, laughing and talking as he had never heard them talk before, and suddenly he realized that John Fawley was about to introduce Mr. Adam Arno of New York to some Arkansas frontier horse trading and Claudine already had figured that out and was throwing her own talents into the drama as well.

"Lord have mercy," he muttered as he stepped off the porch toward the horses.

There was nothing unusual about a French surname appearing in early nineteenth-century Arkansas Territory. In fact, a long time before it was Arkansas, as we have seen, the only names you were likely to encounter there—discounting Indians, of course—would have been French. Over time, most of these were pronounced and spelled in English ways so that the French flavor became so obscure as to be almost nonexistent.

These people came from a lot of different directions. First, obviously, were those initial waves of Gallic explorers who seeped down the Mississippi during all the decades before the Seven Years' War brought the area under Spanish control. There were those who came upriver from New Orleans, French Canadians who had come to the mouth of the Mississippi from Arcadia, and a smattering of mother-country French who had come to colonize the Sugar Islands, and some, particularly after Napoleon took Louisiana back from Spain, who came directly from Europe.

There was yet another breed of French speaker, rare in midcontinent, but there as elsewhere accustomed to making their mark. They were the Walloons, later southern Belgian Protestants who came to the New World in some numbers during the various wars of independence in the Spanish Netherlands, one of the motivations for immigration being religious persecution in areas where Hapsburg armies were in control.

The prime area of settlement for these people was New Amsterdam. The Dutch had first colonized it in about 1614. One of the nasty little Netherlands wars was in full career in 1620, so at that time a good many Calvinist Walloons were looking for someplace to go. New Amsterdam was ideal. In their own country, the Walloons had long been neighbors of the Dutch and shared not only many business interests with one another but were both a part of the Protestant Reformation.

What was most important was that the Dutch in New Amsterdam didn't care one whit what a person's religious views were, critical at the time because the various Protestant denominations had already begun serious persecutions against one another. And really, really important was the fact that the Dutch were perhaps the best businessmen in the world during the seventeenth century, so it was a place where a lot of influential men understood making a buck.

The fact that in 1674 New Amsterdam was ceded to the English and renamed New York didn't change any of this.

Cornelis Arneau was an early Walloon arrival in New York. He did not come destitute but was well-heeled, with funds provided mostly by a Dutch bank that had commissioned him to indulge his love of large hardwood trees by finding as many of them as he could so he might cut them down and sell the timbers to the Dutch navy. And the English as well, so long as the English continued their support of the wars against the Spaniards in the Netherlands.

It was a thriving enterprise because if there was a single thing upstate New York had in abundance, it was hardwood trees. Cornelis Arneau became well-to-do. Not as well-to-do as the great Dutch families like the Reggenfelders and Vanderbilts and Roosevelts who had beautiful estates the size of small countries and overlooking the Hudson River. But well-to-do enough. Cornelis Arneau's progeny, all of whom loved trees as much as he did, prospered. All the way down to the late eighteenth century when the most recent of the line, Adam Arno—whose papa had changed the surname—was operating the mills with a mix of wage laborers and black slaves.

But Adam Arno was more ambitious than his predecessors. He also had a certain yearning for adventure. So when an opportunity arose that offered the chance of going to a new land and there finding trees to love and founding a great estate above a magnificent river, just as the ancestors of his Dutch neighbors had done two hundred years earlier in New York, he jumped at it. The direction he jumped was southwest, toward Texas.

Now, Adam Arno was a very shrewd businessman. But he left a lot to be desired when it came to geography. He visualized the rivers of the Southwest being Hudson-like, with majestic stands of tall, ship-mast–sized trees on bluffs overlooking the wide water. In fact, of course, natives of Texas had seldom in their lives seen a single tree tall enough and straight enough to make a ship's mast, much less stands of such timber covering square miles.

Anyway, Adam Arno rid himself of the lumber business in New York, as well as the slaves he used in its operation, making a great profit on both. This was possible due to what had gone before in New York state, events that seemed designed to ensure profits for Adam Arno.

The legislature in the state of New York passed an Ordinance of Manumission in 1799. It specified that no more African slaves could be brought into the state. Those already there—and the census of 1800 indicated this amounted to almost twenty thousand people—would be unaffected, although the spirit of the law was that as black slaves grew older, their owners would free them voluntarily. For children born to resident slaves after 1799, females would be freed at age twenty-four and males at twenty-eight.

There was a strong flavor of Jeffersonian thinking here. The idea of eliminating slavery through a slow, peaceful process over a period of time. The New York legislators who passed this bill figured that by 1840 perhaps, slavery would be completely abolished in their state. It was a measure similar to those in other northeastern states, and its passage was not universally hailed as a good thing, most especially by slave owners who would not be appropriately compensated for their property.

But many of them, being as they were enterprising business-men alert to opportunity for profit, found a way to make the law more attractive than it at first appeared to be. Most of them did, indeed, free slaves held in 1799 as these people grew too old to work effectively. And they rid themselves of those born after 1799. As the men and women of this group approached the age at which they would be automatically freed under New York law, say, twenty-three for women, twenty-seven for men, they were placed on ships bound for South Carolina or Georgia. And there, at Charleston or Savannah, they were taken to the slave markets and placed on the auction block.

This was against the law, of course. But it was a law never enforced too terribly well, and besides, by the nineteenth century, Americans had learned all the tricks of smuggling. As the British discovered a quarter century before.

Besides, the Ordinance of Manumission clearly stated that a slave could be sold out of state if the slave agreed!

Well!

Hence came into the lexicon of slave history in the United States of America the term "Sold South."

It was wonderful. A lot of people made some money. There were more Africans to pick cotton in Dixie. And there were more people in Yankee country with a clear conscience.

So leaving his wife and three children in New York to wait while he searched for trees and a Hudson River–Dutch-estate-type setting for a new home, Adam Arno set off, hoping to satisfy his urge for adventure and to eventually sell a lot of timber to somebody's navy. Thus, in due time, arrived at the Fawley cotton patch.

The lengths to which John Fawley was willing to go were illustrated early when he asked Claudine to say grace over the venison and cornbread and baked sweet potato and dried apple pie. All of this except the meat thanks to Hugh Evans, who was the only man in Little Rock still extending credit to the Fawleys.

Claudine, in her clear, musical voice, said a wonderful prayer of thanksgiving which favorably impressed Mr. Adam Arno, who said that he and his wife and family were devout Christians. But perhaps showing his diplomatic bent, did not mention the denomination of their church. In fact, Claudine in all ways favorably impressed Mr. Adam Arno, keeping his plate full and smiling and touching his arm now and again and listening with rapt attention to his recitation of adventure, fluttering her eyelashes and at appropriate times allowing little gasps and ah's and oh's to escape her parted lips.

John Fawley was just as attentive to Mr. Adam Arno's cup, keeping it filled from a clear glass jug of Questor's latest whiskey and telling Mr. Adam Arno that this was part of the batch they had cooked specifically for the territorial governor of Arkansas. Questor almost choked on that one because he wasn't sure that his brother even knew the territorial governor's name.

Questor figured he ought to join in this soft-soaping of the visitor, but hardly knew how to improve on his brother and Claudine's performance. Besides, he was much too intent on hearing about his father to bother his mind with any strategy of faked hospitality.

As the level of liquid in the glass jug slipped lower and lower, Mr. Adam Arno's words became more and more slurred, but between exclamations about this being the best liquor he'd had since leaving the environs of good upstate New York apple brandy, his tale was clear enough.

First, he made a great deal of the fact that he had enjoyed a considerable profit from selling all his slaves south before they could be freed by New York law, which caused Questor some furious discomfort, then told of his dreams for a mansion in tall trees, overlooking river water, and that on their property he had found just the thing in case the Fawleys might be interested in making a little money themselves. Then he went into a long monologue of his Texas endeavor, John refilling his cup as required and Claudine fluttering her eyelashes.

Yes, he had seen Texas, all he wanted of it. He had even met Stephen Austin and had been in San Antonio and made plans to become a Mexican citizen until he learned that he and his family, once they arrived, would have to convert to the Catholic faith. So he had left Texas, ending in southwest Arkansas Territory at a small community called Washington. Where he found a whole pack of Austin people—families as well as individual men—waiting to leave when called for and meantime doing what they could to raise money on land speculation, money to help the colonizing effort.

He spent considerable time scouting the countryside and indeed found many tall trees, but these were soft pine trees and Mr. Adam Arno had his heart set on hardwoods. Then he went into the various kinds of materials necessary in shipbuilding, all this told around mouthfuls of meat and cornbread and between gulps of Questor's whiskey.

Yet, John Fawley was patient. So patient and kind and calm and understanding that Questor could hardly believe this was his brother, and he knew the great effort John must be making to soften the normally hard lines of his face. It was no surprise to see Claudine exuding charm. It was just a matter of moving up a notch on her usual vivaciousness. But John's act was very nearly incomprehensible. What was almost as amazing, without a word between them, John Fawley and his wife both knew exactly what they were going to do as soon as Mr. Adam Arno mentioned that New Madrid Certificate. And even this far along in the charade, Questor still wasn't sure about the direction in which they were heading. So he kept quiet and listened.

In Washington, said Mr. Adam Arno, there were many strange men. One was named Bowie, who, with his brother and other rather hard cases, went off into Texas and Louisiana from time to time on various errands, which Mr. Adam Arno said he had heard were connected with smuggling slaves. At this point, he rose—rather unsteadily—and went to the porch where Questor had placed his duffel, and returned with a bundle which he unwrapped, placing on the table a magnificently brutal knife. This was a design by Mr. Bowie, he said, and Mr. Arno had commissioned the same blacksmith to make one for him, although Mr. Bowie's knife had a walnut wood handle and the one lying before them on the table obviously had a polished cow-horn grip.

John Fawley held the knife in his hands with admiration shining in his eyes, and Questor knew it was a genuine admiration and not part of the playacting.

This was no hunting knife, although the blade was shaped like most hunting knife blades. It was a combat knife. The blade was fully fifteen inches long, almost a Roman short sword, said Mr. Adam Arno, with the point sharpened on both edges and sharpened all along the curved concave length of metal to the brass cross-guard. On the straight edge of the blade, the metal was almost a half-inch thick. In the lamplight, steel and brass and greenish cow horn gleamed wickedly.

"What a pig sticker," John Fawley said, almost to himself.

Anyway, continued Mr. Adam Arno, it was in Washington that he had met and befriended Boone Fawley. Mr. Fawley, said the visitor, had been there for some time, having arrived in company with a British gentleman—"Evelyn Hadley-Moore," said Questor—and these two had made a number of trips into Texas and back again, on errands for Stephen Austin. On the last of these journeys, the British gentleman had not returned, having in San Felipe joined a local lawyer named William Travis, so Mr. Adam Arno understood. Travis was also undoubtedly into land speculation, and was very intent on Texas independence from Mexico, and had persuaded the British gentleman to remain there and help him organize the militia. It was Travis, said Mr. Adam Arno, who said he would defend nearby San Antonio from any Mexican punitive expedition sent to chastise the unruly Anglo Texans, although, he said, there wasn't any fort there that could be easily defended and that about all he had seen that would fill such a purpose was an old mission and former Mexican army barracks called the Alamo.

But somewhere in their journeying, Boone Fawley had come onto adequate funds to allow him to take his ease in Washington, among all the lively residents there, and observe the varied humanity.

"You mean he stayed drunk all the time," said John Fawley.

"Well, we did have a few sips together."

As Mr. Adam Arno spoke of Boone Fawley, Questor felt some tight knot in his throat, and he remembered his father long ago, in St. Louis and then at the St. Francis River homestead and the talks he'd always wished they'd had but never did. And he was acutely aware that no such images of their father were clouding John Fawley's thinking.

So Mr. Adam Arno and Boone Fawley had spent many leisure moments together, sucking lemons and watching cockfights and listening to tales of how cruel and brutal the president of Mexico had become, an army officer named Santa Anna who had said he would punish to death all these Anglos who had such crazy ideas about self-government.

Then Boone Fawley became involved in a duel.

"A duel?" Questor cried. "Pa? In a duel?"

"Well, no," said Mr. Adam Arno. "He wasn't one of the duelists. He was only watching and stood too close, the contestants using sawed-off shotguns. One of the pellets struck my friend, the late Mr. Fawley, and lodged in his liver, it seemed."

They carried Boone Fawley to the surgeon, who was also the town barber, and lay him back in a barber chair, and it was there, his knowing he was about to die, that he gave Mr. Adam Arno the certificate and asked him to deliver his horse to his sons, knowing from what Mr. Adam Arno had already said about getting back toward the north that he was likely headed in the direction of Little Rock anyway. It was then, too, that Boone Fawley said his sons and wife—never having heard that Molly was dead—might consider signing over the certificate in the space provided for such things on the back of the document, the signatures notarized of course, and all for appropriate consideration.

By this time, the meat and cornbread and apple pie were finished, and Claudine cleared the table of all the tin plates and pans, touching Mr. Adam Arno a few times in the process and fluttering her eyelashes and smiling. John Fawley poured Mr. Adam Arno another drink and asked to see the New Madrid Certificate, which was taken out and spread on the table before the host.

"Yes, Mr. Arno," John Fawley said. "The Lord in his mercy has sent you at a good time. I been called to Fort Smith by the Indian commissioner in St. Louis, to take up duties in the agency up yonder. We'll have to leave right off. Now, there's lotsa people who would like to get their hands on this here certificate, but none of them has ever showed us all the good Christian fellowship you done here by bringin' our pa's things all the way up here. So we'd a lot rather you'd get 'er than any of them, ain't that right?"

"Of course, Mr. Arno," said Claudine, fluttering.

"That's right," said Questor and thinking, Indian commissioner? Agency in Fort Smith? My God!

"Oh, fine, fine, that's fine," shouted Mr. Adam Arno, and he threw down the rest of the whiskey in his cup, and John immediately refilled it.

"Now then, here we be, ready to make it all right and correct, so we may as well get 'er settled. It's a quarter section and good buildings on it. I'll throw in our milk cow and that horse you brought and give you a bill of sale for them on a blank page tore right out of the family Good Book that our old pa held so dear. You pay us cash now, and I'll let you keep the certificate, and tomorrow you can go in town and rest on the Lord's day and come Monday, me'n Questor here'll come in and have 'er notarized and made legal, and why don't you throw in that knife for your part of the bargain? We'll do the whole thang for one hundred twenty dollars, gold or silver, whichever suits you."

Mr. Adam Arno sat blinking, his mouth hanging open like a

small black cave in the center of his cherry red, fat cheeks. His eyes darted looks at the three of them, and his breath wheezed in his throat.

"A hundred twenty dollars? Why. Why, I expected it would be . . ."

But then stopped and began to unfasten his coat and shirt and after considerable struggle brought forth a money belt and began to count out gold coins. Claudine helped him count it. Then, with the little stack of gleaming coins on the table alongside the knife and the New Madrid Certificate, he finally got the belt back under his shirt but left the shirt and the coat unbuttoned.

"It's a deal," he said.

"That's fine, Mr. Arno," said John Fawley and picked up the certificate and handed it to Mr. Adam Arno. "Now, we'll leave the cow and the horse here in our pen because if you take the horse in town tomorrow, one of them people who wanted this paper might recognize him and ast where you got him at, and Mr. Adams . . ."

"Arno. Adam Arno."

"Mr. Arno, you just find a room at Hugh Evans's place, he's a good man, but don't say nothin' to him or anybody else, so we can come in Monday after we've all rested on the Lord's day, and get us a notary public and sign this paper for you and that's all they is to it."

"I have never had dealings with anybody so accommodating," blurted Mr. Adam Arno and then lowered his head to the table and fell into a deep but noisy sleep. They quickly lifted him from his chair and dragged him to one corner where Claudine, giggling, covered him with a quilt.

"Ques," said John Fawley. "Hitch the mules and bring around the wagon. We pack ever'thang but the cookstove so in the mornin' we can make him some breakfast before he goes in for his Sunday rest."

"He won't be able to eat none of it," snickered Claudine.

"We could just light out now," said Questor.

"Hell no, boy. Think! By mornin', he smell it out and go foggin' for the law. We give him a Christian send-off to town, soon's he's out of sight, *then* we light out. He sleeps most of the day, then come Monday waits for us and probably finds a notary like maybe that damned Buchanan boy Cecil, and by noon he gets suspicious and comes back out here. The horse and the cow will be here, but we won't. So then he's got to ride back into town again to find some-body to help him. So instead of a few hours, we'll get a full night and most of a two-day head start."

"You got 'er figured out, ain't you?" Questor said, and he wasn't so sure he enjoyed the idea, but the prospect of clearing out of here, and away from Michael Loudec, made it worthwhile no matter what. "Yeah, you sure got 'er figured out!"

"They ain't no purpose in suckin' on the hind tit all the time," said John Fawley.

I t was a busy night. They cleaned out the main cabin except for stove, table, and a few stools. And enough utensils to cook and feed their guest a fried egg and hominy. All the while the visitor sleeping noisily in his corner. They cleaned out Questor's hut. They rigged a willow crate and put the chickens in it, the hens indignant at being roused from sleep. They drove the wagon to Moccasin Creek, Ques-tor leading on foot with a lantern, Claudine driving the mule team, loaded the still equipment, even the oak stave barrel which they would use to pack clothes—despite the fact that their underwear might come out with a faint scent of corn mash.

There were no bows for the wagon so they fashioned loops of willow limbs and set aside the tarpaulin William Evans had given Questor to be used for a storage cover. Tools and plow and harness, powder and lead and rope, buckets and cured deer hides, all were loaded, but they left room at the rear of the wagon for last-minute items like the stove.

"Just a mite of far in there tomorrow, Ole Gal, then soon as he goes over the ridge to town, we'll dump the hot ashes in the door-yard and try not to burn our fingers off on the hot son of a bitch when we load 'er in the wagon."

They'd leave the table. Too big. But take all the stools. And the leather vanity case Claudine had brought with her on her wedding day, for ribbon and a broach and needles and spools of thread. Luckily, the two pigs were only yearlings so they could carry them tied in the wagon.

"Pigs in the wagon for a spell, anyway," said John. "Soon's we get well off from the scent of their old home wallow, likely they'll be willing to just tag along."

The cornmeal and dried venison. Into the mash barrel in their own parfleches of deerskin, right on top of the clothes. Dry beans, from Hugh Evans's store, and salt as well.

"For Christ's sake, don't forget the salt."

"I ain't gonna forget nothin'," Claudine said, still unable to talk without laughing, even though at one point during the night her excitement was so great it upset her stomach and she had to pause and vomit, leaning against the outside cabin wall, but even that with laughter.

"Gotta hide the wagon and team in the locust grove by mornin'. Don't want ole Apple Brandy to think we so anxious to fog outa here."

And twice during their furious activity, Claudine grasped Questor's arms and squeezed hard and smiled, her eyes shining with triumph in the lantern light. No matter what had to be done, it was worth it for Questor just to see her with that expression of joy on her face. It gave him a tug on the heart to think of what it meant to her, just to be free of this place and what it had come to entail.

"Praise the Lord," Claudine kept panting, a little breathlessly.

But the whole business still troubled him. Maybe it was bravado that prompted him once to say, "Like to see the look on that Adam Arno's face when somebody tells him what that New Madrid Certificate's worth."

Finally, they had it finished. Even the Texas roan was bridled and wearing Boone Fawley's worn saddle, and he and the mules and wagon concealed in the trees behind the stock pen. John Fawley decided they should saddle Arno's horse and bring her to the cabin and hitch her there so when he came out to ride into town there'd be no reason for him to go to the corral and see that everything was gone except Boone Fawley's horse and the cow.

There was a faint graying of dawn in the sky as they walked back toward the house, Questor leading the horse. Somewhere toward the east they could hear a single blue jay fussing with himself or with the coming sun or with whatever it is blue jays fuss at so early in the morning. And Questor couldn't help but think that this was the last dawning he'd ever hear anything on this place where he had come to full manhood, where he had seen the blue fire over the water. Where his mother was buried.

"What if he don't do like we thank he will?" Questor asked.

"He'll do ever'thang just right," said John.

Then a few steps more and Questor again.

"I don't much enjoy studyin' on runnin' from the law for Lord knows how long."

John Fawley stopped, so suddenly that Claudine went two paces farther before stopping, turning. Questor stopped, too, and the mare nudged his back with her nose.

"What in billy hell is wrong with you, Ques?"

"Well, we did sell land that don't belong to us."

"Land? Land?" John Fawley said, his jaw thrust out. "You never heerd me say a thang about no land. Not the whole time. He wanted that piece of paper, I fixed it so's he'd get it."

"He thought it was about land."

"I can't help what he thought," said John. "Anybody takes a old piece of paper from some drunk and thanks it's still title to land somewheres is askin' to be hornswaggled for his greed."

"He give us money."

"Listen. Listen, Ques. Didn't you watch what I writ on that page we tore outa your book? A bill of sale. I writ on there we sold Mr. Adam Arno a milk cow and a horse in consideration of one hundred twenty dollars. And he put his name on 'er right beside mine."

"He was drunk."

"It's still his signature by his own hand, and they ain't any law nowhere, especially around here, gonna say we sold him anything we didn't own. It was our horse and cow, wasn't it?"

"Them folks in town," Claudine said, "they find out how we outswapped that Yankee outlander, good gold money for an old cow, a broke-down horse, and a New Madrid Certificate ain't been worth nothin' for years, they laugh their heads off!"

As the other two went on toward the cabin, well defined now in the fading darkness of predawn, Questor Fawley stood there with Mr. Adam Arno's mare, watching them, and thinking maybe this wasn't as wicked as he'd figured. Maybe it was retribution on Mr. Adam Arno for his sins of pomposity and greed and arrogant pride and maybe even a little lusting after his host's wife. And maybe the worst sin of all, Mr. Adam Arno's obvious expectation of taking any advantage that he could among members of a family grieving for the death of a father.

Grieving? John grieving for their father?

Suddenly, Questor Fawley realized the same cold, hard fact his brother had known from the instant Adam Arno had begun to wave that New Madrid Certificate around. That Boone Fawley in dying had done more to sustain this family than ever he had done in living.

And Questor Fawley liked to believe that his father had sent that defunct New Madrid Certificate back knowing it was worthless, but knowing as well that his elder son would know how to take advantage of it if so inclined. A last legacy.

And with that, Questor began to suspect that Boone Fawley had known a lot more than Questor ever realized he did about how savagely ruthless John Fawley could be.

26

They moved upstream alongside the south bank of the Arkansas because that's where the road was, even though John Fawley was anxious to get north of the river.

"I sure'n hell ain't goin' back downstream to town and Hugh Evans's ferry to do it," he said. "So we light out for Conway County. I hear they put in a steam ferry up there."

From that ferry all the way to Van Buren, the best road was on the north bank, connecting the hamlets where settlers had located near clear streams running out of the high Ozark Plateau, being, as are all settlers, partial to clear water rather than a source such as the Arkansas River, which some said was three quarts mud to the gallon.

It was a forty-mile run away from Little Rock, and that's what they made it. A run. They only stopped to rest and graze the animals once for a couple of hours in midafternoon and again after dark, pausing then about four hours. It was long enough for Questor Fawley to drop lines in the Arkansas and come up with half a dozen catches, a couple of them eight- to ten-pound catfish. They didn't eat the fish at that stop but carried them along, Questor driving the team while Claudine sat beside him and cleaned fish in the darkness, by touch alone, throwing entrails and heads into the back of the wagon bed where the two pigs were tied. At a little past sunup, they stopped long enough to fry the fish. The rest of the time, they subsisted on venison jerky, throwing shards of it off the back of the wagon to the dogs who followed along in their constant little many-colored cavalcade strung out behind.

They made the Conway County ferry on its last crossing before nightfall on Monday, passed through the scatter of buildings on the north bank of the river, and hurried along the road to the northwest, John Fawley pushing the mules almost to exhaustion. By dawn on Tuesday, they were ready for real rest and pulled off the road into a dense stand of black oak and found a spring in a sandstone pocket of the limestone bluff.

Questor walked back to the river with line and hooks. John took the shotgun up the ridge above them, where old walnut trees stood in dark, leafless ranks and invited squirrels, of course, and on the top of the bluff he could look northwest and see the gray lift of timber-covered ground that he knew was the beginning of the Boston Mountains.

While her men were gone—and that's how she always considered the brothers, *her men*—Claudine unhitched the team and hobbled them along with the Texas stud in good high grass for graze, lifted a few cook pots off the wagon, started a fire with the plentiful fallen dead limbs, and put water on the fire for sassafras tea. When he returned, Questor was astonished at her energy, knowing that probably she hadn't had two uninterrupted hours of sleep since Friday night and it was now Tuesday afternoon, but still bouncing and laughing and bright as a twelve-year-old who'd just risen from bed after a long night's rest.

And now, once away from Loudec land—away from Loudec—there wasn't that little kink of reserve, that little twitch of eyelid, as there had been when they were alone together back at the cotton patch. As if traveling a little over sixty miles had removed the memory of evil secrets. As if the secrets not only no longer existed but never had. And it was not the first time Questor Fawley thought about Claudine as he'd come to know her, devout, born again for Jesus, loving her Savior, hating sin. And yet with an irrepressible physical vitality that had its appeal to any man who came near, and a vivaciousness she not only was aware she had but was aware of how it affected men around her, yet stoked it as she did her kitchen stove fire.

And maybe, he finally figured, that was her greatest appeal, the innocence of accepting her own attraction as so natural that to have tried to suppress it would be like violating God's will. Like trying to stop moss rose blooming.

With that revelation in his slow and deliberate thinking, he suspected that on this first moment of real rest they had since watching Mr. Adam Arno disappear toward Little Rock with aching head early Sunday morning, he loved her beyond all reckoning. Beyond any earthly desire of flesh, as he might love an angel of the Lord, who, of course, was to be adored but never touched, nor even the thought of it. It almost drove him crazy!

But exhaustion drove him instead to a bed of deer hides under the wagon, and there, warm and protected from autumn's sharp temperature, he slept.

In firelight, after fish and squirrel—John Fawley had brought enough squirrel from the walnut ridge for them and a dozen more for the dogs—they discovered that the skirt pockets in Boone Fawley's saddle were not empty. Apparently, Mr. Adam Arno had never bothered to look inside the pockets, or if he had, found nothing he wanted or else considered the contents a part of the horse to be returned to Boone Fawley's heirs.

There was a very dirty flannel shirt, which Claudine immediately consigned to a boiling pot of water, a half-eaten plug of chewing tobacco, a handful of tenpenny nails, a printed six-page pamphlet extolling the virtues of Texas. And Old Noah Fawley's stem-wind watch. When John wound it, the thing began to tick as loudly and as surely as it must have done so long ago when the old man bought it in St. Louis. So long ago that his own children had been born as citizens of Spain.

John Fawley was so delighted that he laughed aloud. When Questor explained the origins of the watch, Claudine clapped her hands and said it was a sign from God, a portent of wonderful things to come for this family, and she fell to her knees and with eyes tear-shining, offered up a prayer of thanksgiving.

Well, if to her the watch was a symbol from God, to Questor Fawley it just seemed to confirm what he'd suspected. Or hoped, anyway. That his father was thinking of his family at the last and wanted to be sure that what was maybe his most prized possession continue among the Fawleys for another generation. And he knew what John reckoned, too. That Boone had put the watch in the saddle pocket and forgotten it, else would have long since swapped it for a gallon of whiskey.

In any event, her menfolk listened respectfully to her prayer, maybe because they both knew that one sure way to rouse Claudine's temper was to interrupt her personal communications with her God, even if she did it publicly. But when she was finished, John got in his little tease.

"Ole Gal, while you was at it, you ort to have ast Him if maybe we got some ill-disposed people followin' us, He could see fit to have 'em drown when they cross the river!"

But she laughed at that, too, because John had said it with a laugh.

The high mood lasted. The next morning, John Fawley suggested that Ques take the mules and ride to a river settlement and lay in a few provisions, making some pretty broad hints that it was time he and his wife had a little time alone together. By the time Questor returned late in the day, he figured John had taken full advantage of his day alone with Claudine. John was rolled in deer hides and sound asleep in the wagon. Claudine was sitting at the fire, looking pensive, but when Questor started unloading his pack mule she came and helped, once more with the verve returned and bubbling. He'd brought a sack of shucked corn, another of meal, a side of bacon, and a tin of coffee beans. While they were working, she told him John had said they'd be off again in the morning.

"I wonder where he's goin'?" Questor said.

"He doesn't know," she said and laughed. "Just high wild country."

The road to the northwest ran between the river on the left, sharp bluffs and hills to the right, everything densely timbered with hardwoods that had lost much of their foliage. John Fawley and Questor alternated riding the Texas roan and on the wagon seat with Claudine, who drove the mule team. Once that morning she had to rein in, climb down, and vomit, bent over with both hands on the front wagon wheel. John, riding ahead, didn't even notice the pause in the wagon's progress.

Back on the seat, Claudine wiped her mouth with the hem of a half-apron she was wearing and said, "My old sour stomach won't stop actin' up."

"You want me to take the lines?"

"No, it's better if my hands is busy."

When they came to the mouth of a wide creek that would someday be called Illinois Bayou, they turned along its bank, traveling now a flat-floored valley where steep walls narrowed as they moved north. The stream line was choked with black willow and river birch, and on higher ground were cottonwoods and shagbark hickory, and up the higher slopes were hop hornbeam and white oak. In the sheltered valley, many dead leaves still clung to branches, but ahead they could see where the valley became little more than a gully cut into rising ground, a kind of shelved escarpment with bare-limb oaks everywhere.

"Best camp before this valley peters out. Let the team rest before we tie into that," John Fawley said, inclining his head toward the high ground without looking at it, but knowing it was there and with the yellow glint of exhilaration in his eyes because now at last—well, tomorrow morning—they'd be going into country where he'd wanted to go for years.

"He's got the scent of it," Claudine giggled. "He's a regular pig in clover, ain't he?"

So come dawn, they assaulted the southern face of the Boston Mountains. Along Illinois Bayou valley, they'd been able to pick a route between trees. But now it was a matter of finding ground not too steep to negotiate with the wagon, cutting down anything in the way. The axes came out and sometimes, with small trees and brush, John Fawley used the cow-horn knife, slashing with it as though it were a machete. Or, as Mr. Adam Arno had said, a Roman short sword.

Sometimes they had to rig rope harness for the Texas roan to pull on the wagon alongside the mules, and sometimes they pulled themselves, ropes tied to the front axle, and sometimes they pushed from the tailgate. Once, a whiskey still bucket fell out of the wagon and bounded downhill for a hundred yards before hanging in a tangle of wild blackberry briers and persimmon trees. The hounds followed the bucket, in full voice, as though they might think it was a gray fox.

"If your damned dogs had any sense," John shouted, "they'd a done more'n chase it. They'd brought it back."

When Questor went for the bucket, he found a porcupine in the briers, hissing at the dogs, who were still barking but staying well clear of the quills.

"They treed a pincushion hog," Questor yelled, and everybody thought it was fun except the dogs, who were quivering to attack but eventually had better sense than to try.

During all this excitement, the two pigs, only that morning allowed to do their own walking behind the wagon, ran off up the rocky slope, and Claudine spent a half hour driving them back. It reminded Questor of that first trip they'd made into the woods out of St. Louis, and once they were started again he told Claudine about his mother shooting the old flintlock rifle the time the three Osages appeared on their backtrail. Claudine laughed so hard she had to stagger over to the trunk of a large white oak and throw up again.

"What the hell's ailin' her?" John Fawley asked.

"Sour stomach," Questor said. "Need to get an ole hen outa that chicken coop and have her eat some of that tonight at supper."

Even now with winter coming, they saw many birds, some kinds they'd never seen before, and Questor Fawley said maybe they were the first white people a lot of these birds had seen. Assuming that birds made such a distinction. Once, in broad daylight, they saw two red wolves watching them from a rocky ridgeline above their trace, and when the hounds caught scent of these wild cousins they roared off into the timber, but didn't stay long before returning to the wagon and spending the rest of that day stiff tailed and sniffing the wind suspiciously.

"Well," said John Fawley, "your dogs got enough sense to know a wolf from one of them foxes they always yowlin' after."

There were all sorts of deer sign that John pointed out to Claudine, and once they moved close beside a wild plum tree where a black bear had torn down lower limbs trying to reach the fruit above.

It was growing colder. Which was fine so long as they didn't get snow or one of those fierce Ozark Plateau ice storms. Temperatures were low enough to put a thin lid of ice on standing buckets of water overnight. But doing the kind of work it took to move the wagon upward in midsummer would have been unbearable. It felt good at night, John and Claudine in the wagon under quilting, Questor under the wagon in deer hides and his pack of dogs tight around him. It was good on the cold, sharp mornings, too, when John and Questor shaved, breathing the hard, clear air and smelling the bacon cooking over Claudine's fire.

And no matter what, they shaved each day, as they always had. It was a Fawley trait, staying clean-shaven. Maybe they all figured whiskers and mustache did nothing for their appearance. But from Old Noah forward, one of a male Fawley's first possessions was a straight razor and a hunk of soap, hidden always in some pocket. It started when the first peach fuzz appeared on cheeks and continued all their lives. Now, John had begun shaving with the cow-horn knife, and he took a little teasing from Claudine about that from the first moment she watched him slide that gigantic, gleaming blade along his jaws.

So they went. Heaving the wagon up near perpendicular slopes sometimes, terrific work for them and their animals. Holding the wagon back as they guided it down the other side was almost as mean. It was about forty miles from the mouth of Illinois Bayou at the Arkansas to the high ridge overlooking the bluff spring that was its headwater, and it took them two weeks to get that far, and good time at that.

In a small lightning burn scar among the white oak along a hogback ridge, they stopped, preparing to camp a few days and rest. From there, they could see they had topped out onto the plateau and to the north were the sharp folds and slashes of wooded ridge and deep canyon all the way to the horizon. At least, they wouldn't have any more climbing to do, except when they had to leave ridgelines and dip through the stream-cut valleys.

"I expect Missouri's up yonder," John Fawley mused, looking at the endless ranks of virgin timber stretching to the north.

"How far?" asked Questor.

"It don't signify," said John. "We ain't goin' that far no ways. Missouri's a state now, so that means all type of rules and laws a man's supposed to live by, and plenty of sheriffs and judges to see he does. So plague take 'em all. We'll pull up short of that kinda foolishness. Get the stock hobbled. I'm gonna see if they's a spring of water around here somewheres."

They woke to their first morning in this camp to find rain. It was a slow, cold November rain, and the clouds were dense and seemed low enough to touch. And in fact, at this altitude, they almost were. It took all the good-natured banter and laughter out of them, that gaiety they'd felt since they'd left the valley of the Arkansas because it made them feel so good to be on their own, with nobody ordering their lives for them. And, Claudine felt too sick to leave the wagon. And one of the pigs had run off into the woods during the night.

Questor Fawley had a hard time finding dry wood and an even harder time keeping it burning. Finally, he and his brother quickly structured a dead-limb lean-to protection for the fire, and Questor managed to cook the last of the cured bacon they'd bought on the Arkansas. John took some of it to the wagon, along with a bottle of drinking water, and when he came back to the fire and Questor asked what was wrong with Claudine, John gave a slight little shrug. His face had gone back to that chiseled-hardness look he'd worn for months at the cotton patch.

They decided to slaughter the remaining pig, the sow, because she wouldn't be much good for breeding a new farrow with the boar off into the woods someplace and probably eaten by red wolves by now. John left the cow-horn knife for Questor to use, and he went off to the mules and the Texas roan and fussed around them, then went to the wagon again, then back to the mules and the horse and moved them to another place where they could reach some under-growth graze.

Questor caught the little sow, tied her rear legs with one end of a long rope, tossed the rope over a sturdy limb of an oak tree, hoisted the squealing hog until her nose was just above ground, and cut her throat. While she bled, he built up his fire and improved the lean-to that sheltered it. Well, almost sheltered it. He saw his brother go back to the wagon a number of times and stick his head under the tarpaulin.

While he worked on the fire and the lean-to, his pack of dogs edged in close to the draining pig and began to sniff and take tentative licks of the blood-splattered leaf mold just under her snout. But they made no attempt to take a bite out of the hog. Finally, Questor got a cast-iron pot of water on the fire but then decided he wouldn't scald the hog but just cut out the meat beneath the skin and feed the hide, hair and all, to the hounds and let them worry about bristles. John wouldn't be interested in curing a hog's hide right now anyway.

About midmorning, John was at the fire, squatting and smoking his pipe, not helping with butchering because with only one small sow, Questor was perfectly capable of doing it all himself. There was a sharp little cry from the wagon, and John jumped as though he'd been shot and ran to the wagon and then ran back and grabbed a bucket and took some hot water and ran back to the wagon and disappeared under the canvas. Questor stood, the cowhorn knife in one hand, a bloody slab of side meat in the other, immobile, uncertain.

"Lord, have mercy," he said aloud and then concentrated on thinking about butchering this hog and not what was happening in that wagon, whatever it was, and twice he thought he heard Claudine cry out again and the second time he almost cut off a finger.

Time inched along as slowly as the rain seemed to fall, and Questor got his pig cut up and Claudine's large Dutch oven on the edge of his fire, where he started baking the hams and shoulders. The chops and bacon he sliced properly and laid on a patch of hide he'd cut off for that specific purpose. He cut down what was left of the carcass, dragged it well back from the campsite, and let the dogs have it. Then squatted beside the fire, smelling the pork bake and trying not to look at the wagon.

The rain was making little whispers on the wide brim of his hat, and the crown was so soaked the water was running down around his ears and along his queue of hair at the back and coursing down his spine, and it was uncomfortably cold. He figured he'd go over to the wagon and see what was happening but then almost at once changed his mind. He had never before felt the sharp distinction between his and his brother's relationship to Claudine. She might still call him her brother, but no matter what she called anybody, John was her husband.

He thought he might go to the wagon and dig the King James

out of the duffel under the wagon seat, but changed his mind about that, too. Then was amazed to realize that on that tortuous journey from the Arkansas to this high plateau, he had not once taken out the Book. Had, in fact, seldom thought about it. And had the agonizing thought that his faith was weak, maybe even nonexistent, when he was happy. Strongest when he needed support. Can a man need his God only in adversity of soul and ignore him the rest of the time? It made him dizzy.

From the corner of his eye, Questor caught movement at the wagon and rose even as he looked, expecting to go over and see about Claudine's condition, but one look at John made him stay where he was because there was some stiffness, some rigidity about his brother's posture and movements that made Questor believe this wasn't a good time for conversation. And even from this distance, he could see under the shadow of John's wide-brim hat the grim frown.

John Fawley had a bundle in his hand, a bundle that appeared to be what was left of Boone Fawley's old flannel shirt. He walked around the wagon and took a long-handle shovel from under the seat, and walked off into the timber, Questor watching and not moving, not moving for about ten minutes in fact, when John appeared again carrying only the shovel. He placed that under the wagon seat and took out the bridle and went to the place where he'd hobbled the livestock.

The Texas roan was of evil disposition, standing tied in the rain, and Questor saw the stud's eyes roll as John approached him. Usually, if the roan fought the bit, John would talk him into it, but not this time. This time when the horse pulled his mouth away, John began to slash him across the face with the bridle, and not cursing as he always did when in a fit of temper, but silently, furiously. And the horse began to plunge and squeal. Normally, Questor would have run to help, but now he felt that had he suddenly come to his brother's side, John might well use the bridle on him, so he stayed where he was, watching.

Finally, John Fawley had the roan under control, the bridle and bit in place. He went up on the horse bareback and reined him back to the front of the wagon, reached in and took out rifle, powder horn, and bullet-and-cap pouch. Then pulled away, and Questor watched still as John and the roan disappeared into the deep timber and the rain. He watched that spot in the trees for a long time after horse and rider were gone. Then he looked at the wagon.

"My God," he breathed aloud, "she's died!"

He moved then, ran, but at the tailgate stopped and heard her crying under the tarpaulin cover. When he'd run, his hounds had paused in their gorging on pig parts and ran after him and now stood looking up at him, questioningly, as uncertain as was he. But Questor wouldn't intrude on this, whatever it was, so turned back to his smoldering fire and the dogs returned to their banquet.

All afternoon, he kept hearing things from the woods that he had been unaware of hearing before. That and the cold water seeping down the back of his shirt made him shiver and he began to think of their St. Francis homestead, and of Osages. On all the trip into these high hills, he had not once thought of hostile Indians. But now he did and so went to the front of the wagon for the shotgun and the second powder horn and bullets and caps and back at his fire drew the load and reloaded. And for the rest of the time, kept the weapon at hand.

Dusk came early. The rain had stopped, but it seemed that it hadn't. He decided he'd waited long enough and with the cow-horn knife sliced some meat off one of the baking pork roasts, put it on a tin plate, and, carrying the shotgun, too, went to the wagon.

"Claudine?" The crying had stopped.

Under the bowed canvas they had made a cleared space on the wagonbed for a pallet. She was lying there in the dim, almost-darkness gloom, but he could see her eyes shining as she watched him move under the flap. He placed the tin of meat beside her.

"Here's grub," he said. She didn't look at it. It was a long time before she spoke, and then her voice was little more than whispering.

"I lost the little baby," she said. "Hit wasn't hardly nothing much yet, just a . . ."

Questor Fawley squatted there, feeling the wetness of his shirt against his back, and it took a moment for the message to sink in. When it did, it was almost as though some detached voice inside his head said, That's what John buried in Pa's flannel shirt. And then, trying not to think about whose baby it might have been.

"You orta eat," he managed.

"I ain't hungry. I feel so peaked. But I ain't bleedin' no more. He seen I wasn't bleedin' before he left. He left, didn't he?"

"He rode off to hunt, I expect."

"No, he never. He left. He looked real mad. I heard the horse takin' on. He just left."

With the rain finished, a harsh little wind had sprung up from the west, and it cut across the ridgeline and billowed and flapped the wagon cover. It was the only sound for a long time. She'd closed her eyes.

"I told him," she whispered. "About that other, back yonder at the patch. I couldn't hold it a secret no more. I never told him you knew."

That vicious anger with the roan, and now Questor knew why. "So he left."

"Now, don't take on about it, he'll be back."

"No."

"Why, sho, now, he will. You told him about why, didn't you? I mean back yonder at the patch, you told him why, didn't you?"

"Yes. I don't expect it matters to him. And I reckon now I'll go to hell anyway."

"Good Lord," he said, and becoming a little exasperated with her and then remembering what he'd said at her own father's funeral. "You ain't neither. You know the story about the prodigal from the Scriptures. You know that good as me."

She opened her eyes again, but she stared up at the billowing canvas and not at him.

"You go on now, Ques. Leave me alone now. Go on."

He wasn't ready to retreat. His own temper was up. Well, maybe not his temper, but some kind of indignation.

"You know Abraham's wife, Sarah, and this kind of thing wasn't no sin on her."

"No, but John never offered me up to nobody like Abraham done to Sarah."

"It don't matter. Listen—"

"No," she cut in, still whispering, but urgent. "Go on, now, Ques. Leave me alone."

I t was a miserable night. Questor Fawley couldn't bring himself to sleep in his usual place, under the wagon. Just beneath the place where somebody's child had been miscarried. So he enlarged his lean-to and made a branch bed and stayed by his fire. But he didn't sleep much. He went back to the wagon a number of times, and Claudine was always asleep. Or at least pretended to be.

He almost wished some howling Osages would come. Well, maybe a small band. Maybe two or three of them. It would stop his thinking, anyway. And there was much to think about. He didn't pray. Not once. At the moment, prayer seemed to have forsaken him.

First there was Claudine, all this time laughing and joyful on the surface, but that turmoil underneath that had to come out. That sin that had to be confessed. And he couldn't see that confession had been particularly good for her soul. He kept thinking of Claudine's bright smile, right up to the time of revealing the secret. It was like one of those Roman candles he'd seen them shoot in Little Rock on Independence Day. The fireballs brighter and brighter, and the brightest just before everything went silent and dark, and with the odor of dank Hades about it. And he didn't have to wonder much about why Claudine had revealed the adultery. She'd thought she was dying, most likely, and didn't want to start her journey to glory with such a thing hidden on her conscience.

Worst were his thoughts of John Fawley. In a blind rage, a kind of brutal mindlessness with the roan. He'd thought he knew his brother, thought he'd seen the worst of his fits of anger, but there had never been anything approaching this silent, savage rage where it seemed John Fawley was capable of destroying anything that came within reach.

By morning, their ridgeline campsite was smothered in low cloud. The white, moist fog was so dense that Questor could barely see the outline of the wagon from his fire. It muffled sound like a cloak of wet cotton, like a heavy snowfall. He figured a large Osage war party could get within twenty paces of him before being detected. He was so despondent he didn't much care.

He enlarged his lean-to again, improved his bed under it. He took more of the pork to the wagon, and he crushed some of the coffee beans and took steaming cups, too, and although Claudine always seemed asleep, the meat and coffee disappeared. All day, she did not speak when he came, although he was sure she was not really asleep. But he had no way of being sure. He didn't know how women acted when such things as miscarriage happened to them.

The fog was still there at nightfall. By now he'd collected a large pile of firewood, all wet, but he kept the flames so high that it dried the wood when he threw it on. It was warm, the heat reflecting off the inside slant of his lean-to, and the dogs came and lay around the orange glow of the fire, alternating sleeping or watching Questor with their large eyes.

Now, at last, he had the King James out again and read a few verses. But his mind wouldn't focus on it.

And John Fawley did not come.

27

When the clouds passed off to the east, the sun came out and so did Claudine. She wasn't bouncing and laughing, but neither was her face any longer puffy and her eyes lead-dull as Questor Fawley had noted each time he'd taken her food and water. He knew she must have left her bed for necessaries, but she'd apparently taken care of such calls of nature while he slept because he hadn't seen her out of the wagon during the four days since John Fawley rode away.

Seeing her in that crisp but not bone-chill-cold November morning, walking toward his fire with a woolen shawl over her shoulders and wearing one of those little linen caps women had worn as far back as the Revolution to keep their hair up, Questor had a surge of pride that she didn't look at all defeated now. Maybe there was no bubbling delight with the mere fact of being alive, but there was no despondent shadow on her face either. Instead, there was a rather serene calm, delicate maybe, but surely not fragile. Questor reckoned it might be a female quality, seeing Claudine now and remembering his mother, this ability to grow confident as adversity piled up.

She came to their problem head-on. With the unspoken assumption that John Fawley was gone for good, what would they do now?

There was a solid commonsense understanding between them, also unspoken, that talk about anything gone before was a waste of time. So what now?

They sat before the fire on a log, what was left of a small tree Questor had cut down and dragged to the camp for fuel, and once trimmed, good as a bench. The bright sunlight through the overhang of branches cast a lacy shadow across their faces. The trees here in the old lightning scar were locusts, maybe three years old, and with foliage shed, their branches were as dainty as etchings in steel. They could hear the hammering of a number of big pileated woodpeckers, and not far distant a rook of crows were in raucous argument. These were all sounds with which they were familiar, and it made this wild, unknown place less ominous. They drank coffee, with sugar, too, brought in Claudine's duffel from the cotton patch. Altogether, and under other circumstances, it would have been delightful.

Well, they couldn't stay where they were all winter because on this ridge there was no protection from wind and they'd not found any spring nearby. Water would have to come from rain and snow caught in bucket or barrel or cook pot or whatnot, or carried a long way. So they had to move.

"With only you and me and two mules," said Questor, "we'd have a peck of trouble gettin' the wagon back down the way we come."

"If we done that, if we went back, we'd have to leave most of our thangs behind. Besides, I won't go back down there anyway."

That was as close as either of them came to mentioning unpleasant experiences along the Arkansas.

So if not back, then forward.

She said, "We can at least commence with the wagon. Maybe we won't find a way to get it very far. But just go and see how far we can get."

"At least find better ground for winterin' in," Questor said. "I ain't keen on just strikin' out without knowin' where we're goin'. But it seems like we ain't got too much selection."

"I know it. Just strike out, best way we can," she said.

So they'd start tomorrow. Meanwhile, take this sunshine day to get everything in readiness. Claudine allowed she didn't feel like moving too fast. That's all she said about her condition, and Questor didn't try to draw her out on it. Hell, he wouldn't have known what to ask anyway. There may have been something about such things in the King James, but if there was, he'd missed it, and expected the details would have been pretty slender anyway. He'd heard old Brother Hezekiah Howell say that everything a man needed to know was in the Bible, but Questor was beginning to think maybe there'd been a few things left out.

They ate some of the baked pork. As they did, Claudine smiled her first smile, and Questor wished it had stayed longer than it did.

"Poor little ole boar hog," she said. "Runnin' off in these wild woods. What do you reckon gonna happen to him?"

"Same as this poor little ole sow hog," Questor said. "Get et. By wolves, I expect."

"I reckon gettin' et is all a hog's good for anyway."

"I can't think of nothin' else."

It was late afternoon. Claudine was at the fire, frying pork chops, all of them, because cooked meat would keep longer than raw. Not much longer, but somewhat. Questor Fawley had the wagon chocked up with rocks, one of the wheels off, and was packing axle grease in the hub. All day he had refused to think of the possibilities opened up now for some kind of new relationship between him and his brother's wife. Not for the first time he remembered references to brothers' wives in the King James, which hurt more than it helped because so many of them were contradictory. He struggled to keep the whole situation from his thoughts, because it scared the hell out of him, but like the purple cow, it insisted on retaining a primary position in his brain. He wondered if Claudine was having the same kind of trouble.

To his vast relief, it didn't long remain a problem.

First hint of something unusual was the alarm sounded by the dogs. For no apparent cause, they were up with a mad scramble from their sleeping places about the fire and then dashed off into the woods along the ridge toward the west—the wind was coming from that quarter—baying with the kind of excitement you'd expect if the grandfather of all foxes had run past and nipped their noses. As the discordant racket—fox hounds seem capable of sounding notes on chord only when after a fox—diminished with distance, Questor

Fawley moved quickly from the wagon to the fire because that's where the shotgun lay against the log. By the time he arrived at Claudine's side, her staring after the dogs, too, the sound of barking stopped, and the only thing they could hear was the sizzle of cooking meat in the cast-iron skillet at their feet. Neither of them spoke, and they, like everything else, seemed suspended, motionless.

It was Claudine who saw first and caught her breath with a sharp little gasp. Then Questor saw, too. It was the Texas roan and John Fawley, and as they came toward the campsite the hounds trotted along like an escort on either side, tongues lolling from smiling mouths, tails lifted like buggy whips that quivered with each bouncing step.

"Lord have mercy," whispered Questor. And the word that bounded about in his head was "Resurrection."

Wide-eyed and openmouthed, the two of them stood immobile and watched John Fawley ride directly to where the mules were tethered, his recording acknowledgment of their presence with a single glance from beneath the shadow of his drooping hat brim. He dismounted and tied the stallion to a low bush and walked toward them, hounds still on either side, and the rifle swinging loosely in his hand. His eyes moved back and forth quickly, as though he might be assuring himself that everything was as he'd left it. They could see that the expression on his face was no different than it might have been had he just returned from a casual morning ride.

Once more, John Fawley looked into their faces, first Claudine's, then Questor's, a glance not furtive, square and calm and eyes unclouded with rage or ill-temper or even much curiosity. Coming closer, he spoke, they still standing rigid as stone, stunned not so much maybe with John Fawley's return as with his nonchalance.

"Ain't much good for game now. Rain has drove ever'thang to cover, I reckon. Seen one buck, too far off to make a shot."

He leaned the rifle across the log, beside the shotgun, and squatted close to the fire and fingered out a chop, passing it quickly back and forth from one hand to the other, swearing softly with the bite of hot grease on his fingers, and began blowing on it.

"You're about to burn this meat, woman," he said and began to tear at the chop with his big front teeth, lips peeled back to avoid the heat. Claudine squatted beside him, still without a word, and with the fork she'd had in her hand all along, turned the chops in the skillet.

"Found us a pretty good way north, mostly ridgeline. Some of it been traveled. Likely an ole Osage trail, partways." He spoke around a mouthful of meat. "Ole trail, though. I ain't cut much sign of recent Osage around here. Or anybody else, neither."

He tossed the pork chop bone in the general direction of the dogs and fingered out another one from the skillet, going through the same ritual of blowing on it before taking the first bite.

"See you're gettin' the wheels greased, Ques. Good. We orta get on from here, in the mornin', if all agrees."

"Yes," Claudine said, but she didn't look at him.

"We figured it was best to get ready to start up again," Questor said, watching his brother start on the second chop. "Soon's you got back."

"That roan needs a rubdown. I'll see to that. I need to cut these damned whiskers, too." For the first time, Questor was aware of a stiff blond stubble on John's cheeks. "You go on with them wheels, and woman, you get all the wagon truck packed in."

And he looked at her, chewing, and she nodded but didn't speak. She forked the last of the chops onto a tin plate, then with John still squatted at the fire and Questor still standing across from him, she rose and walked quickly to the wagon and they watched her kneel down and clasp her hands at her breast and bow her head.

"Well," John said, watching his wife pray. "I reckon she got somethin' to say to her Lord she don't want us to hear."

"I expect so," said Questor.

And that was all. Nothing seemed to have changed. As though John Fawley had simply come back into this camp and by his power of will forced it not to change, to remain as it had been. Questor was a little breathless as he hurried back to his axle grease, pleasantly so, but he could not reconcile the idea of his brother calmly squatted by the fire eating pork chops with the image of John beating the roan in silent, savage fury.

There was one difference Questor noted throughout the remainder of that day. John Fawley didn't once call Claudine "Ole Gal," which had been his custom until now. When he found it necessary to identify his wife to Questor, he said "she" and to Claudine's face, he addressed her only as "woman."

That night, John Fawley slept in the wagon with his wife, and on the ground beneath, with his dogs banked around him, Questor listened to see if there was any conversation between them. But he heard nothing except the hoot of a great horned owl that had come to one of the tall white oak trees at the edge of the lightning scar.

28

Calvin Lacy was one of those Ulstermen commonly called Scotch-Irish whose father had come to the mountains of western Virginia before the Revolution. As a young man, Calvin Lacy had set out for new terrain before the War of Independence was well under way. By 1820, he had finally settled for good in the valley of the Buffalo River in Arkansas Territory, some fifty miles south of the Missouri border, having over the intervening years left the graves of four wives in the mountains of Kentucky and eastern Tennessee. Now, with wife number five—she was half his age, an Ulster Scot, and his first cousin—he was in his own person and family and a few friends the only real civilization between the White and Arkansas rivers along a general north-south line of the Ninety-third Meridian.

This tiny community of English-speaking pioneers was in the very wildest part of the Ozarks, just north of the Boston Mountains, so far out in the sticks, people would later say, that even after Arkansas acquired statehood no circuit judge or tax collector came near the place, everyone elsewhere being convinced that the only inhabitants were black bears and occasional wandering bands of Osage hunters. No one even cared to whom it belonged until 1842, when the area was finally organized as a county and by then Calvin Lacy was long dead, having survived until his ninety-third birthday.

Of course, much of that area had been ceded to the Cherokees—the early arrivals in the Jacksonian Removal Policy—but nobody except mapmakers in the federal capital and maybe a land speculator or two in Little Rock or St. Louis knew exactly where the boundary lines were. Besides, by then everybody understood something like a cession of land to Indians would pretty quickly be extinguished and the land turned to white settlement.

Calvin Lacy knew nothing about any of this and wouldn't have cared even had he known. Virgin land was there to be taken by the strong, and to Calvin Lacy and his kind any place inhabited or claimed by red-stick aborigines was virgin land. Someday—and Calvin Lacy knew this—the organization inherent in territorial status would overtake the interior Ozarks.

Well, in the early 1830s, all of that apparatus of government was far in the future, so far that the Buffalo River Lacys couldn't imagine it, much less worry about it. Had they done so, their natural inclination would have been to pull stakes and head west looking for more mountains, less densely populated. Of course, thus far they had gone from high ground to high ground in rather short leaps and jumps, but had they followed their usual pattern of migration, the closest mountains were over seven hundred miles away, most of that across flat and treeless plains, and if there was anything the Lacys hated worse than government it was flat and treeless plains. So regardless of what they suspected of the future, you'd expect the Ozarks to be their last stand. And it was.

Calvin Lacy had scattered progeny all along his route and was never sure how many there were, even legitimate ones, having sired them in bunches, like litters of hound puppies, one litter for each wife, until finally, now in the old Louisiana Purchase, he had around him seven sons and as many daughters, all of whom had made the trek with him from Tennessee into Missouri and then Arkansas, and were themselves married and had children, a few of which were older than Calvin Lacy's present wife. The first itinerant Baptist evangelist to find the settlement later claimed that if you stood in front of old Calvin's front door and yelled "Osages!" Lacys would come running out of the woods for thirty minutes. It was the kind of mild exaggeration hill evangelists were partial to, but it made a valid point.

As for Osages, the Lacys never had any real trouble with them or with Cherokees, either. The few Cherokees they saw seemed docile in the presence of white men and were taken as no threat. Osages might have been a lot different simply because they were, to the Lacys and other whites, less civilized Indians. Now and then a mule or horse was stolen. Other than that, all social intercourse between Lacys and Osages was cordial and peaceful. Mainly because the Osages never came to the area in great force, and the hunting parties who did come were smart enough to avoid controversy with a large group of people—the women as well as the men—who were as woods-wise as the Osages themselves, expert riflemen, numerous as seed ticks in summer, and vicious as a pack of hungry wolves when their feelings were hurt.

Old Calvin had brought his entourage from Missouri, an entire ox train of them, and established the settlement alongside the clear rushing water of the Buffalo where the wide valley by which they'd come offered ground for cultivation. They grew corn and sweet potatoes and melons. And on some of the sharp slopes they had slash-and-burn patches for hill sorghum cane and pole beans and pumpkins. Of course, most of the terrain was rugged and tree covered. Hunting country. And that's what the Lacys were primarily, hunters.

This was no claptrap arrangement of bark-and-twig shanties. On one of his trips back to Missouri, Old Calvin had traded enough red fox pelts—plus a number of hours of skilled labor by three of his sons—to buy a small steam-powered sawmill. It took a month to ox-cart the thing back into the mountains and the rest of the year to figure out how to set it up and make it work. But work it did.

They'd brought a sorghum mill to begin with, mule powered, of course. And they built a race on the Buffalo and there ground their own meal, the entire contraption made of hand-crafted hardwood except for the millstones. Two of Calvin's sons could have made a living in any town across the country as carpenters. They knew everything about dowel and joist and rive and clapboard and mortise and treenail. They built gabled cabins with garrets and cocklofts.

Two other sons were blacksmiths. Two others were expert

on masonry and could make limestone cement and dig wells and root cellars. The grandsons specialized in furniture making. Usually walnut.

And they could all shoot running squirrels with a rifle. And within two years of the Hawken brothers of St. Louis making their famous percussion cap rifle, Old Calvin had two of them hanging over his fireplace, calibers .44 and .53. Which he said was more than big enough, either one of them, for anything that might happen to come through his front door.

Every year, two or three of the boys went back to Missouri, with a bundle of fox fur and some wolf and bear, maybe, and they brought back anything they figured the family might need, always sure to include coal oil and black pepper and coffee and salt because those were things even Old Calvin couldn't teach one of his sons or grandsons how to make.

Nor were they an illiterate band of scaly-necked peckerwoods. The women saw to that. Everybody bathed at least twice a year, and they all learned their alphabet and reading. In fact, there was an ancient linen tapestry that hung on the wall of Old Calvin's main room—near the Hawken rifles—faded but still showing colors in the illustrations that accompanied each Bible-related verse, and every Lacy child spent hours sitting before it, reciting aloud. It went from

> A   In *A*dam's fall   *A*dam
> We sinned all.

> to

> Z   *Z*accheus did climb the tree   *Z*accheus
> Our Lord to flee.

Like most Ulster Scots, they were Presbyterians. Well, in name anyway. There was no church and no minister. From time to time, Old Calvin called a prayer meeting in the elm grove beside the millrace, and his young wife would read from the Bible. She had a soft contralto voice which pleased Calvin very much indeed, and anything that pleased the patriarch pleased everybody else. Anybody not pleased had a lot of embarrassing explaining to do.

Like most New World Protestants, these people had moved far

enough away from Paul and Augustine and John Calvin himself to believe that life could be enjoyed, that it was not simply a burden to be borne on the way to glory beyond the grave. In other words, to them, heaven began on earth.

In addition to having no minister of the gospel, there was something else lacking. Good whiskey. They had all the hardware and supposed they had the knowledge, but every adult male in the settlement had at one time or another tried to distill corn with a resultant liquid that tasted like some of that Missouri coal oil and on ingestion gave you stomach cramps and a day of furious diarrhea. And in that winter of the 1830s—nobody ever seemed to recall the exact year—they suddenly, tragically needed both a preacher and bracing spirits when Calvin Lacy's wife of the lovely contralto voice took appendicitis and died.

Olen Lacy, Old Calvin's eldest grandson, was out hunting bear with some of the family's black-and-white-spotted hounds. He was out hunting because he had stood all the tears and grief at the Buffalo River settlement he could stand, tears of grief over the demise of his own step-grandmother. She had been a woman he had never liked much anyway. Bossy as hell she was, and him a good four years older than she.

It was a gray day, a cold December wind whistling through the mountain timber, with a spit of snow now and then. He hadn't come far. Straight-line, it wasn't much over two miles to the cabin where his grandpappy Old Calvin Lacy was bent over the walnut coffin bearing the remains, holding his face in his hands. But it was five miles by way of the upstream ford he had had to use to cross to the south side of the river and into the high bluff country, where he saw the wagon.

Afterward, the old-timers would laugh and marvel at this first meeting between Lacy and Fawley. Laugh because even with a lot of furious and enraged barking, the two packs of dogs never did tie into one another but maintained a safe distance and showed off their bravery by voice alone. And learning the temperament of John Fawley and knowing Olen Lacy's already, marveled that these two hadn't started shooting as soon as they saw each other. Well, they said, the Lord did work in mysterious ways.

Olen Lacy was riding a mule. John Fawley was beside the wagon and up on a roan stud. Both had rifles across the saddle pommel. On the wagon seat was John Fawley's wife and brother, although Olen Lacy didn't know the kinship yet. He did know that the man on the wagon seat had a shotgun in his lap and his face wasn't any friendlier than the face of the man on the roan. There was the briefest nod between the two mounted men. Olen Lacy began to circle the wagon and John Fawley's eyes followed. But almost at once, Olen Lacy saw something under the tattered tarpaulin wagon cover that made his eyes widen. He licked his lips.

"Is that air a still I see?" he asked. None of the Fawleys said anything but continued to glare at him. Olen began to grin. "You fellas make whiskey?"

"We made a right smart of it in our time," said John.

"Can you drink it? I mean, without givin' you sour stomach?"

"It'll fetch you a lot of thangs but they ain't a sour stomach in a barrelful."

Well! Barriers to amiable conversation in the hills were never more quickly destroyed than by mention of good whiskey, once all parties involved had assured themselves that the other principals were not deputy sheriffs or federal marshals. This meeting had no possibility of anything but a happy end after Olen Lacy offered to lead them to his grandpappy's settlement, forewarning them that the place was sunk in despondency due to a death in the family and nobody to say words over the grave. At which point Claudine Fawley said that her husband's brother was as good a preacher as anybody could expect when it came to burying folks, his having done so with admirable effect when they'd interred her own daddy. The sight and sound of Claudine Fawley could have left nothing but hospitality in Olen Lacy's heart. As he said later, when he first clapped eyes on Claudine he could see that she wasn't anything to brag about for stout but she sure was hell for pretty!

Everything fell into place as though ordered by Divine Providence, which both Calvin Lacy and Claudine Fawley said it obviously was, and the first order of business was to get the deceased underground for even though it was cold weather, none of the Lacy tribe's talents included embalming.

Questor Fawley's graveside address satisfied everyone, especially Old Calvin, who his younger grandchildren and great-grandchildren observed carried on better than anybody, crying so many great tears that they wet his waist-length gray beard right down to the last and lowest hair. It was pretty much the same speech Questor had made over Claudine's daddy's body, only he didn't hit the prodigal son part at all and concentrated on the dearly departed's coming home to grace, lost in the world of wicked men but now found in the company of Jesus. It was a useful theme that Questor would use all his life because it fit anybody whose remains happened to be lying in the coffin.

No sooner had the last clod of earth been patted firmly on the grave mound than Calvin Lacy dried off his beard and asked about that whiskey still.

Once more, as had happened so much recently, John Fawley surprised his brother by becoming as garrulous as he had been when he sold that dry cow, wind-broken horse, and useless land title to Mr. Adam Arno, and Questor understood. John realized that here in this valley of the Buffalo head-of-household was Law, and he was taking advantage of circumstance. Questor was beginning to appreciate that his brother, taciturn and ill-tempered as he most usually was, could adjust to the flow. Without compunction. Without remorse. Without guilt. And Questor admitted at the same time that he vaguely disapproved on the basis of some morality he could no more define than he could touch the moon.

Well, you betcha, John Fawley told the Lacy patriarch, his brother made the finest whiskey ever cooked, which gave Calvin Lacy a jolt of joy because, he said, any man so blessed by God Almighty to speak such words as he heard spoken over his recent wife's grave must also surely be blessed in the business of making good whiskey! But, said John Fawley, neither his brother nor anybody else could make good whiskey right out in front of everybody where a bunch of snot-nosed kids would always be poking into barrels and coils and buckets and mash and tipping things over on the ground. Good whiskey making needed seclusion as well as clear water.

Why, hell, Calvin Lacy understood that!

And, said John Fawley, mash needed warm climate, so it would necessarily have to ferment in some sheltered place because now, in December, you couldn't just lay it out and expect the sun to do the job.

Why, hell, Calvin Lacy understood that!

There was just the place. He'd been half expecting one of his own to go there and make his homestead. Only about five miles distant. And there the Fawleys, if they approved, could set up housekeeping, and all of the many Lacy men would help. Building structures. Clearing fields for spring. And about the time they had a nice, snug cabin ready, maybe the mash would be ready too, because Calvin Lacy would keep it in his kitchen, which was always warm. In his very own kitchen.

And yes, a site for the still just a rifle shot away from the cabin, and yes, there they could build another cabin for Brother Questor, with real Lacy shingles and fireplace as good as the main cabin, and about the time all this was finished—after all, there would be about twenty Lacy men working on it—maybe the drippings would be ready. Yes?

"Well, likely, but then it takes a day or two more."

"I see, I see."

"Now this land. Where do I lay claim to it?"

Indignantly, Calvin Lacy explained that once the Fawleys had squatted on it, the land was theirs. Who would say no? Of course, if John Fawley was accustomed to filing a claim with some jake-leg government outfit, then he, Calvin Lacy, would help draw a plat showing all the distinguishing topographical features—it would be many years before this area was surveyed—and the next time somebody happened to be going along the White River to an Arkansas circuit clerk or land office, they could take it and register it. Maybe in the next five or six years. After all, said Old Calvin, his brood only went normally into Missouri, because those towns were easier to get to, and nobody in Missouri gave a good goddamn about who lived along the Buffalo.

If you were looking for a place to live in the second quarter of the nineteenth century and a top priority was relief from government officials saying what you could and could not do—and collecting taxes—and if you weren't enthusiastic about going to far western places where you might have neighbors—like Blackfeet or Sioux or Apaches or Comanches—whose language and religion were incomprehensible and who were sullen and sometimes outright hostile, then the ideal spot for you would have been the interior Ozark Plateau. More specifically, the upper valley of the Buffalo River.

The families of Calvin Lacy and John Fawley were looking for just such a locality, so it was not completely by chance that they came together. They did not think specifically of any plan to drop out of sight. To disappear from the census. To become noncitizens in the very middle of a geographic entity where citizenship and high praise of democracy were almost like a sacrament. They did not have the normal national pride of a revolution that had worked, particularly sweet after another one in France had produced a dictator and almost two decades of war and grand theft—art, gold, and cavalry horse fodder, to mention only a fraction of the indictment. Whether or not they specifically planned it, that's how it worked out. They became, by location, a black hole in the constellation of America.

Somebody who has a mania for making everything neat and quickly understood has said that when counties in new territory were organized, areas were mapped out so that all citizens could go to their local seat of government in the daylight hours of a single day. On horseback. Eventually, this was usually how it ended. But it didn't start that way.

The year the Lacys and the Fawleys came together, the county seat nearest them was Russellville, some seventy miles to the south, on the Arkansas River. The intervening terrain was the wildest, roughest, most impassable ground in all the Ozarks, and there was no road that traversed it. Equidistant to the west was Fayetteville, another county seat that had until recently been called Washington Court House but when a post office was established there, the name was changed to honor the Marquis de Lafayette. Well, the ground between there and the Buffalo was less harsh than that to the south, but still roadless and brutal to all but horseback riders.

Travel at that time was still mostly by navigable rivers. And some roads that always followed the line of least resistance. And population followed. Where the Lacys and Fawleys settled was a vacuum of people. The northern and eastern boundary was White River. On the south was the Arkansas. On the west was a wagon trace that followed the new line between Arkansas Territory and Indian country. No rivers or roads traversed it. This meant that on the Buffalo, at the heart of the wild country, was a pristine wilderness. It meant that the few white people who were there had no notion what county they were in or where their seat of government was located. In fact, most of them considered that they had no seat of government. That's why they'd settled there.

From the moment the Lacys and Fawleys met, it would be more than a decade before enough people interested in organizing local government would settle in that section and initiate actions to form a county in what would be by then a state of the federal Union.

Until that day, the only law was what the Lacys and Fawleys said it was, enforceable by the strength of their hands and their will.

The Fawleys, Questor figured, were surely some of God's chosen people. How else could anybody explain that twice within his own lifetime the Fawleys had marched into the wilderness and there been helped by other competent men to establish their homestead? First, on the St. Francis, it had been Clovis Reed and Coppertop. Now, in the Ozarks, it was the Lacys.

And he began to suspect that brother John had been right all along in his yearning for the mountains. Instinctively. Feeling in his gut that the Fawleys belonged in wooded high country. Where a man and his family could develop some dignity and independence. And having come at last, assistance there in the form of a whole platoon of men eager for the taste of good whiskey.

He and John and Claudine could have done it all themselves. It would have been hard. But they were capable of it. Now, the help of sudden friends was apparently preordained.

Claudine thought so. Before they started for this new plot of ground, she had gone to her knees beside their wagon and sent up one of those fine Methodist prayers of thanksgiving, in a loud voice, as usual. Loud enough for Old Calvin Lacy to hear and be impressed.

"Why that air handsome woman is as sho a preacher as this Questor fella, and Mr. John Fawley is a man smiled on by God his havin' at his side two such pious folk."

Then blinking and stroking his beard and looking around at some of his gathered tribe, continued in a low voice.

"Appears like maybe Mr. John Fawley is no such a godly man and may need whatever help the Almighty can send him. Now listen well, you will know henceforth that John Fawley be a good neighbor, but never do you get him crosswise with you, or hell's to pay!"

Two miles downstream from the Lacy settlement, a creek flowed into the Buffalo from the north. It came from a narrow valley that wound up sharply to limestone bluffs where it began with a number of springs about midway to the crest of the hardwood-covered ridges. There was a wagon trace along one slope of this valley because the Lacys had snaked walnut and cedar down from the stands of that timber just short of the bluffs. There was still a quarter acre of ground where this clearing had been done. The Lacys called it their furniture-and-shingle patch, which was the use they made of the walnut and cedar.

Here, the Fawley homestead was raised, close beside a lower-level spring and only a rifle shot from the main creek below. Farther back in the timber, and higher, along another spring-fed brook, they built Questor Fawley's still and cabin. This time, Questor would have a fireplace of his own, and the cabin was large enough for him to have all his dogs inside if he wanted. It was only a short walk to the main Fawley house, and it was expected that Questor would continue to take his meals with his brother and Claudine.

Questor Fawley's first batch of Buffalo River whiskey wasn't up to his usual standard, which would come with summer's sun to help with fermentation, but the Lacys thought it was just fine and so good, in fact, that Calvin was indignant when John Fawley tried to pay him for a supply of sugar and coal oil and cornmeal.

It was the best of winters. Maybe three days of snow and the three of them so busy the cold days passed quickly. They planned patches of corn and sweet potatoes and hill sorghum cane and peas. Enough ground downslope from the cabin and across the wagon trace had been cleared for this, the cut timber used to raise their buildings. There was a livestock shed and a chicken coop.

Questor Fawley saw the harsh lines on his brother's face soften. There was good hunting enough to satisfy anyone, even John Fawley. In fact, until the herds became wary of them, almost every morning deer would parade through the dooryard on their way to the lower slopes for graze and ice-free water, and once Claudine killed one with the shotgun when it stalked up onto the porch. Claudine was jealous of that porch. It overlooked the deep valley below, and sitting there when the weather permitted, she could look out across mile after mile of blue-gray ridges.

When they skinned out venison, they had to hang it high in an oak tree to keep the red wolves from getting it. At dawn, it had to be taken down and hung under the porch roof because if they left it in the tree, crows were attracted by the hundred.

Questor Fawley went down into the main valley and found the good fishing holes. There was plenty of blue mountain catfish and bass and sun perch.

What was left of the flatland chicken flock disappeared completely by the third night they were there. Weasels. But John Fawley consoled Claudine, telling her that come spring he'd buy her a new flock and a milk cow besides from the Lacys. And a pair of breeding pigs, too.

Questor's hounds were as happy as John Fawley about this new place. Within a week, they had become acquainted with the local fox population, which was considerable and very crafty. Listening to the dogs run in the high mountain terrain created more chills in a minute than a whole night's race in the flatlands. With leaves off the trees, sound traveled far, and as the fox led the pack into deep valleys, their chorus would be faint, like echoes in a crystal cave, and with astonishing suddenness burst forth as the chase came across a ridge, full throated and clear, as though they were running near enough to reach out and touch. Questor began to appreciate why mountain people took their fox racing as a majestic celebration of life—and death—simple and sharp and always in a movement of sound, pulsing like a heartbeat pumping blood so clear and deep it was black, and binding the timbered hills to the void of star-spiked sky. A sound fiery hot as life's great passions yet threaded through a world frigid enough to shatter like ice under a hammer's blow any time the dogs actually caught the fox.

Questor realized that not the least of his brother's satisfaction in this new place was that once they'd helped build the Fawley homestead, the Lacys had gone back to their own settlement and returned only when asked. Well, now and then one of the sons or grandsons of Old Calvin might ride by on a hunt and pause long enough to talk a spell, but even then, they'd never dismount from their mule unless asked. Yet the Lacys were close enough so with a day's ride, the Fawleys could go there and get home before dark. It was not only a place to use as a store for needed supplies, but a place where Claudine could visit and exchange recipes and quilt patterns with the Lacy women.

Questor saw another thing that made him happiest of all. Claudine was again the bouncing, laughing girl he'd seen that first day his brother brought her to the cotton patch as bride. He saw no shadow in her eyes, no hint of sorrow or dismay. As though she was finally, really, actually born again, as she had always claimed to be anyway. But now, really.

Well, John never called her "Ole Gal," but his gaze often went to her with a tenderness and affection Questor had never thought possible in those yellow eyes.

So through that busy winter and even busier spring and summer, there seemed no single cloud on Fawley horizons. The soil was good and there were gentle rains and seed sprang forth, and Questor got a Jew's harp from Olen Lacy and played it while Claudine danced on the porch, raising a sweet-smelling dust while John sat nearby smiling. Well, at least not frowning.

By the time crops were near to harvest, it had been many months since Questor Fawley had thought of Michael Loudec.

29

Each year during the fall, the Lacy tribe went to their fields along the north-reaching valley where corn had been harvested to cut the stalks while there was still some green in them, to be hauled back to the settlement for silage. It was a final outing of temperate months before settling in for winter, and they'd established it as a kind of summer's end celebration, usually staying a couple of days, clearing fields for spring planting, foraging the hills for wild blackberries and persimmons, and roasting a pig over an open pit.

Once it was a ewe that one of the grandsons brought back from a trading trip to Missouri. For what reason nobody ever knew. After that particular feast, Old Calvin had called a prayer meeting on the spot and everybody sang Welsh hymns. Then the patriarch thanked God Almighty for creating him and his in a time when a body could take on nourishment from venison or pork and not have to depend on mutton as the holy men of old apparently had had to do, and closed his prayer with the fervent plea that all his sons and grandsons be endowed with the wisdom that would preclude any of them ever again bringing a sheep into the Ozarks from Missouri.

It was at this exact time of year that Questor Fawley came down from the mountain on one of the mules, his pack of hounds trailing along behind, to deliver the last batch of warm-weather whiskey. It was carried in so many clay jugs, not glass bottles as had been the fashion along the Arkansas River. Questor carried the family rifle, too, a little unusual, but there had been stories of a mean-spirited bitch red wolf in the neighborhood, and in case he saw her the rifle would likely be the only chance of killing her because she'd never come close enough for shotgun shooting.

It was one of those hill country autumn days when the ridges were crowned with gold and scarlet, the hardwood leaves that would fall with the first hard rain of October, leaving limbs bare and stark. But on this day, with the sun bright, the colors were like wave on wave of jewels going away to every horizon, so intense they seemed to excite all the senses. People such as the Lacys had been in those hills long enough to take such things for granted, ignoring them, but for Questor Fawley the sight was still sharply soul-stirring.

He was perhaps as happy as he'd ever been. He was reconciled to spiritual love for his brother's wife and in fact a little proud of himself for a victory over the tyranny of flesh of a kind denied to Adam. He didn't dwell on it because he could recall everything his mother had said about pride and the fall, but it was difficult not to feel just a tad of self-satisfaction now and again. And self-pity, too, maybe.

Questor figured that his reconciliation to things as they were had something to do with the high, primitive country, where he and his dogs made sport of midnight hunts that were not hunts at all but musical carnivals where each side admired the capabilities of the other and then after it was finished, man, dog, and fox content and tired and nobody hurt, each go to rest and sleep the sleep of purity. Those fox races and his own situation were so bound up together that when the dogs caught and killed a fox—which sometimes happened—he spent days of anguish because he thought it might portend his violating his brother's wife. But then after a few more races when the fox got away, the old confidence was restored.

Well, that's how Questor Fawley worked it out in his mind anyway.

On this fall day, what Questor found at the Buffalo River was a settlement deserted except for a few of the old Lacy women. And Olen Lacy, as luck would have it.

Olen Lacy had returned from the picnic to fetch a homemade

banjo. Old Calvin had put the thing together during the past winter and aimed to try playing it this year as he sat under a chinquapin oak—where he always sat—hulled the delicious nuts from their spiny burrs, watched his tribe bring in the blackberries and persimmons and roast a hog, and enjoy, as spectator only, the annual game of blind-man-find-me. Well, the younger kids played blind-man-find-me.

This was perhaps the old man's favorite moment of the entire year, sitting there and eating chinquapin nuts and watching grandchildren and great-grandchildren playing blind-man-find-me and trying to figure out who the hell all of them were.

And this year, he would master the banjo as well, as he took his ease, but had gone off from the settlement without it. So now Olen Lacy was back looking for it—no easy task because Old Calvin had forgotten where he'd put it.

Perceiving what Questor Fawley had brought on the mule, Olen Lacy forgot about the banjo. He suggested that he help unload the jugs and place them in the pantry of Old Calvin's kitchen, where such things were usually kept. It wasn't much of a job and didn't take any time at all. Olen then invited Questor Fawley to sit awhile and visit, and Questor agreed because he always enjoyed sitting in one of the Lacy walnut chairs and leaning his elbows on a Lacy walnut table. Outside, the Fawley hounds and the few Lacy hounds that hadn't gone on the picnic were having a dog visit as well, by this time the two packs being familiar with one another. As evening came on, Olen Lacy wondered if any of the whiskey Questor had brought down from the mountain might have gone bad on the way, and Questor said he'd never heard of such a thing, but maybe they should check one of the jugs just to make sure.

As they sat checking the whiskey, one of the old Lacy women came in from a nearby cabin with a plate of fried quail and a chunk of cornbread and some buttermilk. She was Olen Lacy's great-aunt or cousin or half-sister, Questor didn't know which and doubted that Olen Lacy knew either. During the course of their meal, and more testing of the whiskey, Questor said maybe they should try to find that banjo, but Olen said Old Calvin had taken a good supply of Brother Questor's Nectar, as he called it, up the valley and by now had probably forgotten the banjo himself, so why didn't they just visit some more? He invited Questor to spend the night right there in Old Calvin's kitchen, and Questor accepted.

Olen Lacy tried to convince Questor Fawley that he should train a few of his hounds to coon hunt, but Questor demurred, saying that fox dogs should never be tainted with any other kind of varmint contest, pointing out that any fox dog that took to chasing rabbits should naturally be shot. Whereupon Olen Lacy told a long story about two of Old Calvin's dogs who had gotten into the hen coop and discovered the wonderful taste of raw eggs, and naturally, a bullet in the head from a good rifle was the only way you could deal with a suck-egg hound because there was nothing a man might do otherwise to break that habit once begun.

It was likely well toward midnight when Olen Lacy said, "I reckon your friend from the flatlands found you all right."

All taste and sensation from the whiskey evaporated instantly for Questor Fawley, or at least seemed to, and he stared at his friend in the orange glare of the coal oil lantern they had been using to light their testing of Fawley whiskey.

"What flatland friend?"

"Why, that flatland fella come in yesterday, said you and him and your family was old friends, Brother John and Claudine, too, and him and some others was up here huntin' and thought they'd pass by and say howdy, so I told 'em where your place was at. I reckoned they'd come by and say howdy today, maybe. Didn't look like much of a huntin' man, mostly cloth clothes that'd wear out in a week, out in the woods, but he said—"

Questor broke in, furiously. "Did he say his name?"

Olen Lacy sat back, eyes wide. "What's the matter with you? You act like you was yellow jacket stung."

"Did he say his name?" Questor asked. So urgently his voice broke.

"Why no, I don't recall he done that. Said he used to be a sheriff or some such thing in the flatlands. But he never mentioned . . ."

"A toad-looking man? Pop eyes?"

"Now you mention it."

Questor Fawley told Olen Lacy this was no friend. He reckoned it was Prentice Entwine, and he told Olen that once John had pert near killed him and he wasn't any friend to any Fawley. And did he say where he was camped?

"Approximate. I reckon I could find it, if he's still there."

"Come! We gotta find that camp," and Questor jumped up from the table.

"Now?"

"Right now! You hear me!"

The dogs, by now thinking that it would be a night of rest around the Lacy main house porch, were collapsed at various distances from Old Calvin's back door, but when the two men burst from the door, one with a rifle, the other with a lighted lantern, they were all up quickly and off around the cabin toward the woods, thinking it was the start of a hunt, and running silently now, as good fox dogs do until one in his cast discovers a scent and yelps and the whole pack converges to begin the race.

"I'll saddle one of our mules," yelled Olen.

"No, no time, I'm in a hurry, come on up, double on this one."

So on the mule, Questor with the rifle, Olen with the lantern, Olen directing them as the mule broke into a lumbering trot out from the cabin and downstream along the Buffalo.

To find your way with a lantern in pitch darkness over densely wooded, uneven ground riding double on a mule is impossible. Every tree trunk reflects what little light there is back to the source, and between the trees the night goes on endlessly like a bottomless pit of black water. But Olen Lacy knew this ground well. And the lantern did serve one purpose. It attracted attention.

Questor Fawley sensed they'd gone about two miles along the Buffalo and were in a valley ridged on one slope by high ground that extended north to lift in bluffs behind the Fawley homestead. His first indication that someone was before them in the trees was the mule coming to a dead stop and pointing her ears forward like a fox listening to approaching hounds. And maybe in some mysterious order of things, at that exact moment, from the opposite direction, there was the distant peal of the dogs finding a trail and bursting into full pack chorus along it.

"Somebody out yonder," Olen Lacy whispered, and he and Questor slid down off the mule, one holding the lantern high above their heads, the other trying to keep a grip on the reins and hold the rifle in a ready position. When Questor made his shout, he did it softly.

"Hallo? Hallo? Who's there?"

From between the lantern-lit tree trunks, a dark figure emerged, a man with gleaming eyes and a narrow-brim hat with a cone-shaped crown, and an open-front, sleeveless coat.

"Lord have mercy," Questor whispered. "It's the Jamaican."

"Blow out light, mon," Timbou said harshly. "Quick, mon, blow him out!"

"Do it," Questor said, and Olen Lacy lifted the lantern globe and blew out the lighted wick, and total blackness captured everything with breathtaking finality. They felt, rather than heard, the slave move close to them, and Questor had trouble holding the mule as she shied away.

"I saw light, mon, from camp. Others asleep."

In the dark, Questor Fawley pushed the rifle against Olen Lacy's belly and Olen Lacy took it, and Questor reached out, fumbling, and found Timbou's shoulder in the night and lay his hand there, as if to be sure this was real and not some apparition.

"What are you doin' up here in the hills, so far from home?"

"Boss come, I come. Boss sleeping now, mon. Speak low, you don't want to wake up Boss now."

"Michael Loudec?"

"Boss, mon. Sure."

"Who is this nigger?" Olen Lacy whispered.

"Hush. I know him. He's . . . he's a friend. Timbou, what for?"

Under his hand, Questor felt Timbou shrug.

"The woman, mon. Boss come to get the woman."

"What woman?" Questor asked and knew the answer before he asked the question.

"Brother John's woman, mon. For Boss, what other woman is there?"

The whole idea was preposterous, of course, a raid on a family homestead to steal a woman, like pirates Questor Fawley had heard of, taking wenches off a ship they'd overhauled on the high seas, or like abducting women from a defeated city in the Old

Testament of the King James and selling them into slavery for some Egyptian harem. It was outlandish, laughable. This was America, for God's sake, and well into the nineteenth century.

But it was also Michael Loudec and big planter power and raw, still primitive country where there were few important territorial officials who didn't owe men like Michael Loudec more favors than they could ever repay.

So there was no joke here. And Questor discovered just how little there was to laugh about as the three of them squatted in the darkness, faces close together, the mule now calm beside them, the burnt coal oil smell of the extinguished lantern thick in the air, the faint sound far back in the mountains of hounds in full voice coursing a fox.

With Timbou spinning out the details, Questor Fawley was alternately astonished and angry. The first revelation was perhaps most stunning because it seemed to put a legal seal on something that was really nothing more than simple kidnapping.

Michael Loudec had come with bench warrants, issued by one of his accommodating judges, for the arrest of Mr. and Mrs. John Fawley, charging land fraud for selling real estate they didn't own, flight from debt incurred by them as tenants on Loudec land, destruction of Loudec property in the matter of burning a crop of sorghum cane, and threat to do bodily harm and murder against one Cleve Buchanan and family.

"That there's crazy," Questor whispered frantically. "You take me in to that camp and let me tell him. We never sold no land. We sold a cow and horse is all."

"No, mon, it's all fixed on them court papers. And you go in there, they put iron on you legs and chain you to a tree and then take you south with Brother John and woman. They got a warrant for you, too."

"This here is crazy, crazy! And how'd you find us anyway?"

"Boss, he got all friends along that big river, like money just as much as them two friends he got with him now like it. And up through mountains, you left broke-down brush and trees and marked ground enough for a blind beggar to follow, even a year later."

"You're crazy, crazy. All of you!"

"No, mon. I ain't free enough to be crazy. Me, just a dumb nigger, do what he's told. Boss, maybe he's crazy."

The Jamaican told Questor to go back to his homestead now, fast, and warn everybody so the lot of them could escape, run off into deeper mountains.

"They ain't no deeper mountains. Besides, he found us here, he could find us somewheres else."

"Tried to slip off, warn you folks," said Timbou. "Couldn't do. Boss watch close these days. Boss ready with whip these days. I get plenty of that whip since Boss gets crazy when Brother John leave with his woman. That woman drive Boss crazy maybe. But I couldn't do no good anyway. I didn't know where to find you even if I get shed of Boss watching me."

Questor reached out in the dark and touched Timbou's shoulder again.

"I'm beholden for it, anyway."

"You messin' with mountain people here," said Olen Lacy. That statement, repeated a number of times, was his only contribution to the conversation.

So just who had Michael Loudec brought to help him with all this craziness? Well, Cleve Buchanan, Jr. A Loudec lickspittle and by implication one of the people Brother John had threatened. And Michael Loudec had had Junior Buchanan made a deputy sheriff to serve those warrants.

Then there was Prentice Entwine. The last heard from him, he was sitting marooned on a Mississippi River sandbar island, but he'd surfaced again in Natchez where he found a position fitting his disposition and abilities. He was majordomo and backstairs ramrod at the Estelle LaRue River Haven Hostelry, which was supposed to be the fanciest bordello in a town famous for fancy bordellos. And the Estelle LaRue River Haven Hostelry had been owned by old man Loudec, which Michael Loudec didn't know until the old man died (at about the time the Fawleys quit the cotton patch) and left the brothel to Michael Loudec as part of the estate. So now Michael Loudec owned it and Prentice Entwine was his employee, and besides, everybody could imagine that Prentice Entwine would be willing to sell his share of hell for another whack at John Fawley, the man who had very nearly killed him with a sack loaded with lead sinkers.

Michael Loudec didn't make his plans public knowledge. But Timbou was too close to him not to see every detail as it developed.

Once John Fawley was taken care of—Questor was just an incidental irritation—Claudine would be established as a permanent resident of the River Haven, not for any whore's work, but in her separate apartments, mistress of Michael Loudec who could visit when he pleased. There wasn't a big planter anywhere along the river who didn't have such an arrangement, or couldn't have if he wanted it. She'd be watched over by Prentice Entwine and treated like a queen, with linen and taffeta dresses and French perfume and gold and emeralds on her fingers and a surrey with red wheels and a matched team of bay geldings waiting on her call when she wanted to take a ride through the countryside. She would live in the kind of luxury her sort of women had never dreamed possible.

It had taken almost a year to put all this together, not because the germ of it hadn't been taking form as soon as Michael Loudec learned about the River Haven property, but because after the old man died it had taken a long time in New Orleans for Michael to get the estate settled.

"And just how does Michael reckon my brother's gonna stand still for all this foolishness?"

"You messin' with mountain people here."

"Two ways, mon. Boss don't care which it is, either."

Claudine had once gone a good distance to keep Michael Loudec from throwing John Fawley off the land he considered his own, Timbou said. So Michael Loudec figured maybe she'd be willing to go a little farther to save John Fawley again, hoping for something better down the line. But most important, if John Fawley was told how she'd given her favors to Michael Loudec before, he might be happy to be shed of her, especially if Michael Loudec threw in some boot, say, a thousand dollars. After all, everybody knew John Fawley was a fine-tuned horse trader, and this would be a mighty good trade. In which case those warrants would be torn up and forgotten, and Claudine could ride back south on the extra horse they'd brought—with a sidesaddle, of course—and everything would work out pretty as you please.

Now Questor was faced with the decision of telling or not telling Michael Loudec's slave that John Fawley already knew about those so-called favors, and that both he and his wife, and Questor, too, considered them not as favors but as rapes. He started to blurt that out, but something made him stop. He wasn't sure why. Maybe he didn't completely trust Timbou. Or maybe he just had the notion that there were some items of family business that should remain family.

"And what if my brother don't do this?"

Then, said Timbou, they'd all be arrested and they'd start back south to the flatlands, the Fawley men in chains. Only, he said, John and Questor Fawley would never make it out of the mountains. That was part of the job Prentice Entwine was already licking his chops about, Timbou said.

Questor Fawley and Olen Lacy caught their breath on that one. You couldn't make it any plainer. And for the first time, really, Questor Fawley realized the ruthless determination of Michael Loudec. It was hard to think of such a man sitting at his desk in the Loudec big house above the river, smelling the honeysuckle, admiring the magnolia trees across the lawn, and making color sketches of woodland jack-in-pulpits or sandbar yellow butterflies. And Questor couldn't help but recall in that moment that this same man had offered to send him, Questor Fawley, away to an expensive school to get an education and ordination in some church denomination; now, with a sick feeling in his stomach, Questor had to believe that it wasn't for him that the offer had been made but to get him out of the way. And it followed in Questor's thinking that maybe it was possible that Michael Loudec had suspected all along that John's wife was as precious to Questor as she was to John, and hence better to have him off in Vermont or Rhode Island or some such remote place so John could be dealt with alone.

"It's near daylight," Timbou whispered. "Need to get back, mon."

Questor touched the Jamaican again, holding him in place for a moment longer, and after a long silence spoke in a voice he knew trembled.

"I thought he was my friend."

Now it was Timbou who waited to speak, but finally did, lifting his own hand to Questor's, still on his shoulder, and touching it briefly with his fingertips.

"No, Questor Fawley. You was always just accommodation. You was always white trash to Boss, just like all your people. I thought you knew that, mon."

It wasn't a serious proposal but only to show support when Olen Lacy, once the black slave had slipped away, suggested they follow him into the Michael Loudec camp, kill him with the rifle and the rest with sticks of wood. Even had he supposed such a thing could work, and him willing to try, he had to have known that Brother Questor Fawley, speaker at gravesides and more familiar with the Good Book than Old Calvin himself, could never agree to such a course.

Here in the deep valley, it was still night, but looking up, they could see through the scattered foliage still on the branches a sky turning lead-gray. And with urgency, now, Questor Fawley told his plan.

"Olen, they's bound to be hell openin' up at our place," he said. "We need help."

"You got mine and ours!"

"Take this here mule and ride fast as she'll take you back to your grandpappy and brang him on to us. Tell him to come in a hurry."

"What you aim to do? Ambush 'em?"

"No. I aim to get to John, tell him," Questor said. "The flat-landers'll go along the Buffalo to our valley and up the trace to John's place, 'cause you told them where it was at and that's the easy way to go, even on horseback."

"Questor, I'm tore up about that. I never knowed . . ."

"It's all right. Just go fast on this mule."

"But what about you?"

"I aim to go up over this ridge and warn John."

"Goddammit, Brother Questor, hit's might near five miles to yore place and mostly uphill and heavy timber all the way."

"I can run it. I'll get there before 'em. Now go on."

So Olen Lacy leaped onto the startled mule and wheeled her about and started back along the track they'd come the night before, and Questor Fawley, trying to carry the rifle easily in one swinging hand, started up the timbered slope, running.

30

It was one of those sparkling fall mornings that made Claudine Fawley want to dance, if to no other music than that in her soul. The sun, in a brass-blue sky, had come from behind the far misty hills to the east like a great chariot of light, she thought, a blaze of God's glory. She loved those far hills to the east. Beyond them somewhere was the place where her John had been a boy and lived to see the great New Madrid earthquake.

Brother Questor had told her about that experience, and now, recently, John had talked of it as well, and of many other things as they lay in bed before sleep, his voice softer than she would ever have imagined it could be, he lying close beside her with his hand in her loosened hair. There were these special moments she treasured because it seemed then that her husband, usually so taciturn and hard, was trying to show without saying it in so many words his understanding of her agony and despair in the cotton patch homestead.

God shows his light unto me, she thought. She knew it. She felt it as she worked in the still unfinished house but a house being built slowly and solidly, inch by inch. Even now, her John in back of the cabin splitting cedar shingles for the new rear room behind the kitchen he and Questor had already walled. And with a window.

Well, it would have real glass, too, as soon as the Lacys brought it from Missouri as they had promised to do next spring. There was a window in the east room now—still without glass—one of two rooms already completed and used for sleeping but would become the parlor, John said, as soon as that addition at the back was finished and their walnut bedstead moved into it. Well before December, he said, so they would have room for a tree in the front room at Christmastime.

It had been a quiet morning, her and John eating breakfast alone, as they usually did. Questor took his morning meal in his own house at the whiskey still normally, but on this day he was still in the valley. They'd heard Questor's dogs running in the night and the predawn. They had been stilled only when the fox denned at day-break in the hills to the west. None of the hounds had come home yet, and were not expected until well into the day when they would come straggling in, bone tired from the race. Some of them would likely sleep in the woods all day.

A gentle silence hung over the hills. No crows were cawing. Even blue jays were giving not their harsh calls but only the froglike gurgle that made their feathers fluff out like a store-bought duster. Yesterday, Claudine had heard a cuckoo, which was always a sign of good luck. So maybe this was the day she should tell her husband that she knew there was a new life growing inside her own body.

At midmorning, she left John to go inside and prepare their noon meal. She left him reluctantly. She took unashamed delight in watching him work, naked to the waist and his fair skin gleaming with sweat. He was splitting cedar with the cow-horn knife, using it like a meat cleaver, bringing down the great blade along the grain of wood crosscut to shingle length.

In her kitchen, she opened the oven door on the little stove they had so laboriously hauled up from the flatlands and took out a pan of cold baked rabbit. As she sat the pan on their split oak table, she thought she heard a voice calling from high on the ridge, from the edge of the woods there that marked a long, cleared slope to the door-yard. She was still humming as she went to the window of the front room and then she heard the flat report of a shot from up the slope and almost at once another shot from just in front of the house.

Running to the open front door, Claudine saw the horsemen. Three of them and a black man trailing on a mule leading another mule and a riderless horse. The leading man was almost at the foot of the porch steps, close enough for their eyes to meet, and she recognized Michael Loudec and called John's name even as the second man began to shout.

"You all's under arrest in there, you all's under arrest, come out and throw up yore hands!"

Questor Fawley's breath came in harsh gasps and his legs felt like water-soaked deadwood. He was drenched with sweat as though he'd been running in an April driving downpour of rain. He'd lost his hat somewhere along the long slope up from the valley of the Buffalo and the ribbon had come loose from the pigtail at the nape of his neck, so all his hair lay plastered against his forehead and the sides of his face.

When he reached the crest of the ridge behind his brother's house, he found that running downhill was as painful as running up had been and twice he fell, but staggered up and on until finally he came out of the line of trees and saw at once the flatlanders who had moved so much faster than he'd thought they could. And recognized them all, even at this distance. Michael Loudec leading, almost to the front porch, immediately behind him, Junior Buchanan, rifle up. Then a short interval and Prentice Entwine, and at a greater interval Timbou and the extra mule and sidesaddle horse.

"Wait, wait," Questor Fawley shouted, and his voice was a rasping croak. He ran on, lifting the rifle and firing it into the air. "Wait!"

With his shot, the cavalcade jerked to a halt and all their faces turned toward him. At once Prentice Entwine's rifle came up, and he fired, first the balloon of white smoke, the smack of the slug into the rocks a few feet in front of Questor Fawley, then the report. And already the two leading men, Loudec and Buchanan, were dismounting, running up the steps, and now Michael Loudec had a pistol in each hand and Junior Buchanan was shouting something Questor couldn't make out.

"Oh God, please wait!"

He ran, dropping the rifle. Prentice Entwine was still mounted, reloading, and Timbou seemed to be backing off the mules and the sidesaddle horse, and Questor in that sickening instant realized his shot to catch their attention had been taken as hostile, sealing all hope of any options for John Fawley.

His lungs were ready to burst, his legs turn to rag, and sweat was running into his eyes, but he saw it all as it unfolded, like a scene out of the King James. From his angle, he couldn't see the front door to the house, but he could see the top of the steps and the first few feet of porch. As Michael Loudec came to this point, there was a sudden, billowing white cloud directly in his face and the explosive clap of a shotgun, and Michael Loudec jerked back, the pistols swinging wide at the ends of his flailing arms and firing into the porch flooring.

Michael Loudec spun backward and crashed into Junior Buchanan, and both tumbled down the steps and Junior Buchanan's rifle fired. Even as Junior Buchanan struggled to get out from beneath Michael Loudec's spread-eagle form, Questor Fawley saw his brother leap down the steps, through the muzzle-blast smoke of the shotgun, and as Junior Buchanan rose, screaming, was on him, slapping at him, forcing him back to earth, and then Questor saw the flash of sunlight on metal and realized John Fawley had the cow-horn knife in his right hand.

The two horses nearest the house reared and turned and ran, stirrups flapping, to the road and into the edge of the cornfield beyond, and Prentice Entwine's horse was rearing, too, and squealing and trying to turn and Prentice Entwine threw the rifle aside, the ramrod still in the barrel, and yanked a pistol from beneath his smock as John Fawley, leaving Junior Buchanan lying with one leg twitching on Michael Loudec's face, ran toward Prentice Entwine, and now Timbou had backed his mule farther away and dismounted, and his mules and the sidesaddle horse rushed off to join the other horses below the road, milling there walleyed. And now John Fawley running at Prentice Entwine, crouched low like a running cat.

Questor Fawley made for the Jamaican, choking for air, trying to shout but no longer able to bring any sounds from his throat that were words. He saw Prentice Entwine's horse turn, Prentice Entwine desperately trying to hold him, trying to align his pistol, but the horse was squealing with fright and turning its rump uphill toward the house and John Fawley went up over the horse's tail and clasped Prentice Entwine close against his own body even as Prentice Entwine's pistol discharged into the air and Questor saw his brother stroke with the right hand and the blade going in again and again, and then slashing again and again, and the two of them, welded together, John Fawley and Prentice Entwine, going off the side of the horse and the horse running for the lower field as the two men struck the ground in a roil of dust, the right arm of John Fawley still working, and then leaving a lump beneath him. Rising, John Fawley looked toward Timbou and then started toward the Jamaican, bent forward, but slowly now, the knife swinging just a little, low to his side, like the flick of a snake's tongue, and his front— buckskin trousers and naked belly and chest—glistening with blood.

Timbou obviously knew what was about to happen, and he began to back away, his arms up, his palms out. John Fawley was stalking him with the terrible, savage blade, and Questor Fawley knew he had to get there first, and after a last, wrenching effort, did. But couldn't raise his own arms. And saw his brother's face, completely expressionless except for the eyes, like yellow flames, furious, mindless, raging. And tried again to raise his arms, but couldn't, and knew that John Fawley would attack anything in his path unless the rage burned out. Even his own brother.

"Please, Jack," Questor Fawley gasped. "Please. He helped us. He tried to warn us."

John Fawley gave no indication that he heard, and came on. The blade weaving back and forth.

"John Fawley!" It was a small cry, yet sharp and piercing. Coming from the house. And when it came, Questor watched his brother pause, his lips parting then, and a long sigh and intake of air. He began to straighten, and Questor could see the flat, inhuman flame in the eyes dim until they were hooded as John looked down at himself and at the knife, now held loosely at his side. For a long time he stood like that, and then in a voice as casual and clear and steady as if he'd been doing nothing more than grinding corn, spoke.

"Ques. I'm pert near done with them shingles."

Then turned and walked toward the house, and Questor, still unable to stand straight, stared after him and then for the first time looked at the front door, which he could see now, and realized how incredibly fast this entire passion had begun and ended, for there was the tendril of smoke still trailing upward from the muzzle of the shotgun held in Claudine Fawley's hands.

There was no connection, but some of the fox dogs and Calvin Lacy's posse began arriving at the Fawley place almost before the breeze had blown away the last scent of black powder. Of course, there was considerable interest shown by both the dogs and Calvin Lacy's people in the bodies, two at the foot of the steps, face up. And one by the road, face down. Most especially the one by the road, for there a great vertical gash in the abdomen had allowed a considerable length of intestine to spill out into the dust.

"I don't reckon I ever seen nothin' like that," said one Lacy grandson.

"Looks like, iffen he had the time, Brother John would have hung this fella to a limb and gutted him like you do a hog at butcherin' time," said another.

"Well, he done a right smart job of that as it was," said a third.

The Lacys found Questor Fawley in the exact spot where he'd stood when John Fawley's fury burned out. Only now Questor was sitting there, head down, either crying or trying to catch his breath or both, with the black man kneeling beside him and occasionally reaching out to pat his shoulder.

Old Calvin, from all his long life in various mountains, was not a stranger to scenes of carnage, although they usually involved Indians in one way or another. And he knew the best thing to do was organize everything as quickly as possible so folks could get on with their business until the next catastrophe came along. So it didn't surprise any of his clan that he took immediate charge.

Brother Questor was obviously all right, or would be once he'd finished with crying or catching his breath or whatever it was he was doing. So Old Calvin went to the house to see about Brother John and his woman and returned to report rather proudly that Brother John was buck naked and sitting out back in a barrel of rainwater and his woman was helping him wash all that gore off his front, none of which was Brother John's by the way. He instructed all his tribe to stay clear of the house and let things there take their natural course.

The first problem was the bodies. They were beginning to attract autumn flies, and it was only a matter of time before one of the dogs would take a notion to have himself a big bite from one of them, so Old Calvin detached a half-dozen grandsons to haul the whole mess off and bury it.

"Grandpappy, whyn't we just drag 'em off in the woods somewheres and leave 'em for the varmints and buzzards," somebody suggested.

"Hell no!" shouted Old Calvin. "You put 'em in the ground and then you take off your hats and you say the Lord's Prayer over 'em. We ain't no damned barbarians up here in the hills, you know!"

The next problem was the black slave and what to do with him. Calvin Lacy assumed they'd just hang him and be done with it. After all, he'd come up here from the flatlands with the marauders. But Olen Lacy finally convinced his grandfather otherwise, explaining that without Timbou, the Lacys would never have known to come here.

By this time, Questor Fawley was back to his normal self, Old Calvin allowed, so they discussed various things as they sat on the edge of the front porch and contemplated the view, which was just the way it had always been what with the dead having been removed by now for Christian burial.

There was disposition of property to be made. There were four good horses, two mules, and the gear that went with them. There were two rifles and four pistols and a lot of personal truck in mule pack and saddlebag.

Questor said the Fawleys didn't want any of it but Timbou ought to have his pick of the livestock and the camp truck, a proposition to which Old Calvin raised considerable fuss but finally agreed, giving in to the judgment of whom he considered a man of God.

"Let him take whatever," Questor said. "I'll write out a bill of sale for any of the livestock he wants so some jake-leg law don't think he stole it; then I'll write out a freedom paper for him so's he won't be a slave no more and can go up to Missouri."

"I had a notion he'd want to go back down yonder to the flatlands where he come from," Calvin said.

"No. The only thang he had that kept him down there was shot half in two on this porch a while ago."

"Well, that's fine, but Missouri ain't so good for a nigger nowadays, even iffen you write him a paper," said Old Calvin. "But he can go west and maybe join one of them new Indian bunches they're bringin' in from Georgia or somewheres."

"He don't know the way."

"Hell, I'll have a couple of my boys take him to White River, then it's just goin' upstream until it peters out and then strikin' out due west for a week or so. He's smart enough to do that, ain't he?"

"Yes. He's smart enough to do that."

So Timbou decided to take the two mules and a rifle in case he had to hunt along the way, and all the camp truck, and Questor gave him two jugs of whiskey for trade, which didn't please Old Calvin too much, and before the discussion of it was hardly finished, the Jamaican was on the way, not unaware of Old Calvin remarking a number of times, "We don't want that African son of a bitch in these hills!"

He came to Questor Fawley, still sitting on the edge of the porch, and Questor would have shook his hand but Timbou didn't offer.

"Stay away from them flatlands, mon," Timbou said, and that was all, and he was gone, him and the two mules and a pair of Old Calvin's grandsons.

They found leg irons in the saddlebags, and Old Calvin was fascinated. He said he'd always wanted some of those in case one of his grandsons might get contrary about doing what he was told. Such a thing had never happened, but you never could tell, he said.

The Lacy tribe stayed at the Fawley place only a short time, though it seemed longer. John never appeared. Olen Lacy peeked around the corner of the house once and saw the elder Fawley still sitting in the barrel of rainwater, staring off toward the wooded slopes behind the house and smoking a clay pipe. Claudine came to the door once and offered everybody a cup of sassafras tea, but Old Calvin declined. When the burial party returned, the Lacys rode back toward the valley, some of them looking back and shouting invitations for the Fawleys to come for a visit soon.

Questor Fawley had kept one thing from the miscellaneous truck in the saddlebags. One of Michael Loudec's sketch pads. Finally alone on the porch, he leafed through it. There were the drawings of wood violets and a mockingbird and a big snapping turtle. And the portrait of Claudine, looking as fresh as she had looked when she first came to Point of Rocks. Looking, in fact, as she still did today. After a long time, Questor rolled the pad into a compact cylinder, rose, and went into the house, on into the kitchen. He could hear Claudine and John in back, talking in low tones, maybe, he thought, as people talk after the tornado has passed on by with no damage except the terror of it. He yanked open the stove's firebox door, but before he could push the sketch pad inside to the flames, Claudine was back in the room.

"What's that?" she asked.

"Satan's dream," he said, and shoved the cylinder of drawings into the stove and slammed the firebox door. He straightened and looked at her, and for a long moment they stared into each other's eyes. Then she made an impatient movement with her hands and spoke.

"Go on out back and talk to your brother awhile," she said. "It's time I got supper."

EPILOGUE

Our days on the earth are as a shadow.

—Kings 29:15

So they prospered. Even after the wilderness became not-so-wild and the Buffalo River settlement became a county seat with a two-story, limestone courthouse. And Questor Fawley became renowned all the way into Missouri for the fine whiskey he made, and John Fawley never again had need for mindless, savage rage.

The Fawley farm massacre, as it became known, was legend, each passing generation knowing less and less of fact and creating more and more of myth to surround it, for Old Calvin Lacy imposed a code of silence on his own tribe, it being none of their business, he said, and the Fawleys never mentioned it to others or to themselves.

Where the victims were buried in the woods was never common knowledge. But the story went that one of the Lacy grandsons who helped with that work told Questor where Michael Loudec lay, and each October, so they said, Questor went there alone and stood among the oak and walnut and hickory trees and read aloud from the Bible. Likely from Kings, they said. Probably about Sampson, they said. Then left a garland of late-summer bull thistle on the sunken place, the delicate violet blooms marking a last rest, and in spring, they said, morel mushrooms grew there in the deep leaf mold.

But nobody ever actually saw Questor Fawley do such a thing. And each time someone gathered morels in the forest, they said that likely under these very mushrooms lay the earthly remains of that mad, lowland aristocrat who dared come into the mountains to steal a mistress.

Nor was anybody in the hills ever concerned with the many wrangles and court cases disposing of the Loudec properties. Nor did they even know that along the Arkansas everybody assumed that Michael Loudec had gone bear hunting in the Boston Mountains and there was bludgeoned to death by a slave, Timbou, who had been whipped many times in full sight of other citizens, and everybody knew a slave thus treated would take first opportunity to murder his master.

Nor did they know that among the litigants in the disposition of the Loudec estate, most prominent was a lady named Estelle LaRue of Natchez, Mississippi, who appeared with so many letters and other documents that her attorney said gave her claim to properties from New Orleans to Point of Rocks.

As for the slave, convicted by public opinion of murder, he was indeed shown the White River along the northern border of Arkansas and told to travel with his two mules along its course and then west, which he apparently did, and there maybe joined with some Indian tribe. Or maybe not. Maybe, regardless of the paper he carried, taken back into bondage and sold by a white man to a Creek or a Seminole or maybe the other way around. Or maybe en route took cholera or heart failure and died. And if anyone supposed such a thing, they did not make legends about morel mushrooms growing on his grave.

The mountain people all recognized the voices of Questor Fawley's hounds in the night. They agreed that next to whiskey making, Questor Fawley was best at breeding fox dogs. And nobody was ever heard to call him or his brother or his brother's wife white trash. In fact, it was a widespread belief that if one did not contract for Questor Fawley to speak over the grave of a dear departed, that dear departed was getting the short end of the stick in the matter of having a quality recommendation for God to consider in deciding heaven or hell.

The young ladies collected around him at watermelon suppers and cabin raisings and banjo dances and revival meetings when some Baptist or Methodist preacher came through saving souls. But he resisted them all, remaining as pure as John the Baptist, they said.

And as the years ran down, John and Claudine Fawley became known as Pa and Ma Fawley in that Buffalo River valley, he saying little but always watching, she making the best sweet potato pie in the hills, and what was wonderful, a woman who could dance the pins right out of her hair. But the men, all of whom admired her, touched only her fingers in the dance, never even thought of touching her elsewhere because her husband was watching and everybody in those mountains knew a man best not go crosswise with John Fawley.

In fact part of the legend was that. An outlander once asked a Lacy urchin to show him the Fawley place and whiskey still, and on being offered gold money the urchin agreed, and insisted on having his coin before showing the location. When he was told he'd be paid after the outlander saw the still and came back, the urchin replied, "Mister, when you go up there, you ain't comin' back."

But called Pa and Ma Fawley because that's what they were, without any legend. The next generation came to them. Five sons and a daughter, all of whom married Lacys, of course. Well, the ones who married at all. Some never did, not because they didn't want to, maybe, but because other things intervened.

Because of the time, you see? The earthquakes were past for them, and their lives were gentle and calm. As gentle and calm as a mountain life can be, anyway. But things beyond their control were in motion. For the children, 1861 was just ahead. And a war that none of them understood or cared about but that would destroy them all. Except for the dogs. Maybe now, on a dry October night, crisp and moonlit, you can still hear their progeny running in those same mountains where the oak and walnut and chinquapin and bull thistle and morels and legends grow.

But maybe not. Maybe it's gone. All of it.